D0237355

Alexander Fullerton has been a submarine officer, Russian interpreter, shipping agent, salesman and publisher. Through nearly all those periods, he has also been a writer – he has lived solely on his writing since 1967 and now has several bestsellers to his credit.

Praise for the novels of Alexander Fullerton:

'The research is unimpeachable and the scent of battle quite overpowering'
Sunday Times

'Has the ring of truth and the integrity proper to a work of art'
Daily Telegraph

'The accuracy and flair of Forester at his best . . . carefully crafted, exciting and full of patiently assembled technical detail that never intrudes on a good narrative line'
Irish Times

'The most meticulously researched war novels that I have ever read'
Len Deighton

'You don't read a novel by Alexander Fullerton.
You *live* it'
South Wales Echo

THE BLOODING OF THE GUNS

Alexander Fullerton

WARNER BOOKS

A *Warner* Book

First published in Great Britain in 1976 by Michael Joseph Ltd
Published in 1993 by Little, Brown and Company
This edition published in 1998 by Warner Books

A CIP catalogue record for this book is
available from the British Library.

ISBN 0 7515 1620 1

Typeset in Times by Solidus (Bristol) Limited
Printed and bound in Great Britain by
Clays Ltd, St Ives plc

Warner Books
A Division of
Little, Brown and Company (UK)
Brettenham House
Lancaster Place
London WC2E 7EN

Iron Duke
18th June 1916

The Secretary
of the ADMIRALTY,

SIR,

Be pleased to inform the Lords Commissioners of the Admiralty that the German High Sea Fleet was brought to action on 31st May 1916, to the westward of the Jutland Bank, off the coast of Denmark.

(Opening paragraph of Sir John Jellicoe's despatch)

Author's Note

To provide homes for fictional characters, three fictional ships – HMS *Nile* (battleship), *Bantry* (cruiser) and *Lanyard* (destroyer) have been added to those which actually fought at Jutland.

All other ships and their movements are as recorded in despatches, narratives, personal reminiscences et cetera, and are described as the fictional characters would have seen them from their own areas of the battle.

For readers who may find it useful or of interest, a 'cast' of the Grand Fleet's ships, squadrons and flotillas may be found overleaf.

Finally, two technical assurances to readers whose own more recent naval experience may suggest that – as the instructors used to say – 'error has crep' in'. (1) It is a fact that at the time of the 1914–18 war a port helm order was needed in order to produce a turn to starboard; (2) it is also a fact that at this time four-inch and even smaller calibre ammunition was separate, not 'fixed'.

THE GRAND FLEET
Squadrons and flotillas as on 30th May 1916

(A) AT SCAPA AND CROMARTY

BATTLE FLEET (Fleet flagship *Iron Duke*)
2ND BATTLE SQUADRON (at Cromarty)
1st Div: *King George V – Ajax – Centurion – Erin*
2nd Div: *Orion – Monarch – Conqueror – Thunderer*

4TH BATTLE SQUADRON
3rd Div: *Iron Duke – Royal Oak – Superb – Canada*
4th Div: *Benbow – Bellerophon – Temeraire – Vanguard*

1ST BATTLE SQUADRON
5th Div: *Colossus – Collingwood – Neptune – St Vincent*
6th Div: *Marlborough – Revenge – Hercules – Agincourt*

BATTLE CRUISERS (Temporarily attached, ex Rosyth force)
Invincible – Inflexible – Indomitable

CRUISERS
1ST CRUISER SQUADRON (at Cromarty)
Defence – Warrior – Duke of Edinburgh – Black Prince

2ND CRUISER SQUADRON
Minotaur – Hampshire – Cochrane – Shannon – Bantry*

LIGHT CRUISERS
4TH LIGHT CRUISER SQUADRON: 5 ships, plus 6
temporarily attached

DESTROYERS
4TH FLOTILLA: 19 ships   11TH FLOTILLA: 16 ships
12TH FLOTILLA: 16 ships

(B) AT ROSYTH

BATTLE CRUISER FLEET (Fleet flagship *Lion*)
1ST BATTLE CRUISER SQUADRON
Lion – Princess Royal – Queen Mary – Tiger

2ND BATTLE CRUISER SQUADRON
New Zealand – Indefatigable

5TH BATTLE SQUADRON (*Queen Elizabeth* class battleships)
Barham – Valiant – Warspite – Malaya – Nile*

LIGHT CRUISERS
1ST LIGHT CRUISER SQUADRON: *Galatea* plus 3

2ND LIGHT CRUISER SQUADRON: *Southampton* plus 3

3RD LIGHT CRUISER SQUADRON: *Falmouth* plus 3

DESTROYERS
1ST FLOTILLA: 10 ships

9TH FLOTILLA: 8 ships

13TH FLOTILLA: 12 ships including *Lanyard**

*fictional ships

Chapter 1

'Sub!'

Nick took his eyes off the wilderness of black, grey-flecked sea. It was still dark, but greyer eastward as dawn approached. The glow from the binnacle lit the bony sharpness of his captain's face.

'Sir ?'

'What's the date?'

'May thirtieth, 1916, sir.'

All destroyer captains were mad. One knew that; everyone did.

'Sure it's not the thirty-first?'

'Certain, sir.'

'What's the displacement of this ship?'

'Eight hundred and seven tons, sir.'

'How d'ye know that?'

'Looked it up, sir.'

'Devil you did . . . Where were we built?'

'Yarrow, sir.'

'What's our horsepower, d'ye look that up?'

Sub-Lieutenant Nick Everard, Royal Navy, with salt water streaming down his face, neck and inside his shirt, nodded as he grabbed at a stanchion for support. 'Twenty-four thousand,

1

sir.' *Lanyard* lurched, staggered, her stubby bow seeming to catch in a trough of sea like a boot-toe in a furrow; spray rattled against splinter-mattresses lashed to the bridge rail. Nick had forgotten, until now, that the bridge of an eight-hundred-ton torpedo-boat destroyer, when she was steaming head-on into even as moderate a sea as a Force Four wind kicked up, was like the back of a frisky horse only wetter. Mortimer, her captain, spat a lungful of salt water down-wind; he'd appeared on the bridge a few minutes ago, wearing a long striped nightgown and a red woollen hat with a bobble on it; he'd looked like something out of a slapstick comedy even before the nightgown had been soaked through, plastered against his tall, angular frame like a long wet bathing-suit. He spat again, and laughed.

'You're wrong, Sub! Twenty-four thousand five hundred!'

The innacuracy seemed to have elated him. Nick stared back, not yet sure of him, wary that what looked like a friendly grin might turn out to be a grimace of fury. One couldn't be sure of any of these people yet. Nick had joined *Lanyard* only forty-eight hours ago – he'd been ordered to her suddenly, without any sort of warning, transferred at a moment's notice from the dreadnought battleship that had housed him for the last two years. It had seemed so unbelievable that there'd had to be some snag in it. In spite of the sensation of relief and escape, he was still ready to find the snag, and meanwhile all his experience of officers senior to himself warned him to be cautious, to look every gift horse in the mouth.

'Everard.'

'Sir?'

'My first lieutenant informs me that you have the reputation of being lazy, ignorant and insubordinate. Would you dispute that?'

Nick stared straight ahead at the empty, foam-washed sea. Johnson, *Lanyard*'s first lieutenant, was a contemporary and friend of Nick's elder brother David. He was standing behind, and holding on to the binnacle, beside Mortimer and within about three feet of Nick's own position. You couldn't be very much farther from each other than that, on a bridge about as large and which seemed just about as solid as a chicken-house roof. Johnson was officer of the watch, and Nick, who lacked as yet a watchkeeping certificate, was acting as his dogsbody. In the last few minutes the first lieutenant had been listening to Nick's exchanges with Mortimer while pretending either not to hear or to have no interest in them.

Nick said stiffly, 'No, sir.'

'You don't dispute it?'

'I'd rather not contradict the first lieutenant, sir.'

'Hear that, Number One?' Johnson nodded, poker-faced. He had a thin, pale face, dark-jowled, needing two shaves a day by the looks of it. Rather a David-type face, Nick thought gloomily. *Lanyard* had her bow up, scooting along like a duck landing on a pond; Mortimer asked Nick, 'What's cordite, when it's at home?'

'Blend of nitro-glycerine and nitrocellulose gelatinised with five per cent vaseline, sir.'

'Vaseline ?'

'Petroleum jelly, sir, to lubricate the bore of the gun.'

'What's the average speed of a twenty-one inch White-head torpedo when it's set for seven thousand yards?'

'Forty-five knots, sir.'

He was wondering when the difficult questions were going to start. But Mortimer was apparently satisfied, for the time being.

'Number One!'

Johnson turned to him. 'Sir.'

'I suspect you may have been partially misinformed. This officer is neither wholly ignorant nor pathologically insubordinate. Only time will tell us whether or not he's lazy. Give him plenty to do, and if he shirks it kick his arse.'

'Aye aye, sir . . .' Johnson pointed out over the starboard bow. 'Everard. Fishing vessel there, steering east, bearing steady. What action if any would you take ?'

'Alter course to starboard, sir, until past and clear.'

'Right. Come here.'

Nick stepped closer.

'Our course is south fifteen west, two hundred and sixty revolutions. Take over the ship.'

'Aye aye, sir.'

'I'll be in the chartroom.' He tapped the starboard voice-pipe's copper rim. '*This* pipe. Let me know the minute we raise May Island.'

Nick watched Johnson and Mortimer leave the bridge together. Things really did seem, so far, to have changed quite strikingly for the better!

Not that one could count on it. Johnson, until he proved otherwise, was an enemy. He'd obey Mortimer's orders to the letter, but whether or not a man was 'lazy' was a matter for individual interpretation, and 'kicks' came in different shapes and sizes. Most disconcerting of all was the fact that this Johnson was a friend of brother David's who was up in Scapa as navigating officer of the cruiser *Bantry*. Bright, successful, correct brother David, whom one tried not to let into one's thoughts too often. Johnson's decision to leave one up here alone in charge of the watch wasn't any sign of trust or encouragement. An officer in a destroyer who couldn't keep a watch was a semi-passenger, leaving a lesser number of watchkeepers on the roster, and since the only way to get a watchkeeping certificate was to acquire experience it was in Johnson's interests to make sure he got some.

It was in Nick's too, though – for present convenience, not career reasons. He'd decided long ago that he'd quit the Service when he could. There'd been no point in mentioning it to any one, not even to Sarah, his stepmother, to whom he confided most things. As long as the war lasted, one was stuck; one could only think of it as something that mercifully wouldn't last for ever. Like a prisoner sitting out a gaol sentence. And in those terms, the events of the past two days had left him feeling like a long-term convict unexpectedly offered parole.

He'd been in his battleship's gunroom, writing a letter to Sarah, at Mullbergh. She was the only person he ever did write to. He wrote about once a month, and never mentioned the Navy or the war. What would there have been to say about it? There was no action – only pomposity and boredom. Somewhere distant, other men were fighting and being killed.

He wrote a lot about the Magnussons – he'd never told another soul about these Orcadian friends of his – and fishing, and the landscape of the Orkneys, that kind of thing. The Magnusson family and fishing provided the escape which as a midshipman and then junior sub-lieutenant in a battleship in the Grand Fleet he'd so badly needed; escape from boredom drills, bugle-calls, and from such horrors, too, as 'gunroom evolutions'.

Being well able to look after himself physically, he hadn't suffered much from the bullying rituals which were justified by the word 'tradition'; but he'd had to witness them, and pretend to take part in them. And they'd be in full swing again now, in the gunroom he'd just left. When he'd been promoted sub-lieutenant and become mess president, he'd stopped it all; but he knew the man who'd taken his place, and there was no doubt the 'evolutions' would have been re-established; evolutions such as 'Angostura Trail'. A midshipman would be blindfolded, forced to his hands and knees and made to follow with his nose a winding trail of Angostura bitters; if he lost the scent, all the others would lay into him. Or 'Running Torpedoes', which involved a boy being launched off the gunroom table as hard and fast as his messmates could manage it; if he tried to shield his head or break his fall, he'd be thrashed.

Nick thrashed a sub-lieutenant, once. The evolution had been 'scuttle drill'. The victim had to haul himself out of one scuttle and swing along the outside of the ship to the next, and pull himself back into the gunroom through it, and only a well-grown midshipman had the length of body or arm-reach for it. The reigning sub-lieutenant was insisting on a particularly small lad – barely fifteen, and undersized – attempting to perform the impossible. The boy was shaking with fright, close to tears, and what broke Nick's self-control was that in the faces of the other midshipmen, this small one's friends, he could see the same sadistic excitement as in the sub-lieutenant's. He grabbed the sub-lieutenant by an arm, swung him round and hit him; within a minute the mess president had been knocked down three times and lost several front teeth.

Midshipman Everard was awarded twelve cuts with a cane, and a dozen more unofficially with a rope's end, and three months' stoppage of shore leave. He was also given extra duties which meant that during those three months he had only short periods of sleep and never time to finish a meal. And with that, it was pointed out, he'd been let off lightly; for an attack on a superior officer he could have been courtmartialled and dismissed the Service.

There'd been two possible reasons for the leniency. One was that Nick's uncle, Hugh Everard, had just returned from the Falklands battle, the destruction of Admiral Graf von Spee's squadron. Only a week before he hit the sub-lieutenant Midshipman Everard had been summoned to pace the quarterdeck beside his godlike captain, and to listen to a summary of the battle and its results. What it had boiled down to had been that the name of Everard was in favour at that higher level; Nick, the captain told him, had 'a great deal to live up to'. The other point was that the investigation into what had provoked the assault had established that the little midshipman could not have reached from one scuttle to the other, would therefore have fallen into the Flow, and quite likely might have drowned.

Killed on active service, would his family have been told? So many shams, right from one's earliest memories. Mullbergh: being woken in that freezing mausoleum of a house with his father's bellows of anger echoing through its corridors ... Sir John Everard was a man of power and influence; Master of his own hounds, magistrate, Deputy Lieutenant of the county. He was a brigadier now, and doubtless he'd come back from France a major-general, covered in medals, even more of a respected figure. With his young wife – Sarah was twenty-eight, closer to his sons' ages than to his own – at his side. So beautiful and so loved!

Poor, lovely, Sarah ...

To whom he'd been starting a letter, two days ago. He'd sat down at the gunroom table which was no longer used as a launching ramp for human torpedoes and he'd got as far as putting the date, *28 May 1916*, at the head of the first sheet of paper, when a messenger had arrived to summon him to the ship's commander. He'd hurried up two decks, to the senior officers' cabin flat, and knocked on the wood surround of the commander's doorway.

'Sir !'

The commander was three parts bald; his face was dark red and he had ginger hair curling on his cheekbones.

'You're leaving us, Everard. Or did you know it already?'

'Sir ?'

The commander growled, 'The destroyer *Lanyard* sails for Rosyth tomorrow. You will join her this afternoon. *Now*.'

Nick failed to understand.

'Sir, d'you mean I'm taking passage to—'

'Who the blazes said anything about taking passage?'

'I'm sorry, sir, I—'

'You are joining *Lanyard*. You are to report aboard her forthwith. Pack your gear, then present my compliments to the officer of the watch and ask him kindly to provide a boat.'

'Aye aye, sir!'

This was actually happening . . .

When those three months of stopped shore leave were over, he didn't give the Magnussons any reason for his not having seen them recently. It would have been difficult to explain, something so foreign to them that it wouldn't have made sense.

They'd probably thought he'd been away at sea and couldn't speak of it. Ships came, ships went; there were so many of them, and why should the crofters know their names, or care?

Greta almost referred to his long absence. She'd told him, 'The spring run were grand, Nick. Ye'd no've believed the fish we took!'

'Very glad to hear it.' He'd hesitated. 'I wish I'd—'

'Och, ye'll get your chance.' Her father had put an end to the need to talk about it. Nick could read the thought in the old man's eyes; if you had something to say, you'd say it, and if on the other hand you preferred to hold your tongue . . .

'I've missed you all.'

Greta had laughed; 'So I should hope!'

'Come intae the hoose, lad.' The old man stooped, leading the way into his gloomy little cottage. Greta stood back, smiling, making Nick go next.

He'd met the old man fishing. Over a period of months they'd encountered each other from time to time, at first with no more than a wave, a grunt. Then they'd begun to exchange a word or two – the weather, or the fish, or how the sheep were doing. Finally one afternoon Magnusson had invited him to the croft for 'a dram tae keep the cold oot', and he'd met Greta and her mother.

Escape and a lack of any kind of sham. The Magnussons had

made Scapa bearable. They'd be wondering in a day or two where he'd got to; there'd been no way to send a message.

Peering into the binnacle, he saw suddenly that *Lanyard* had swung nearly ten degrees off course.

'Watch your steering, quartermaster!'

'Aye aye, sir!'

Searching the horizon again, he checked suddenly: on the beam, that dark smear was the low protuberance of Fife. 'Sub-Lieutenant, sir!' The signalman was pointing ahead. 'May Island, sir!'

Everything came in sight at once, as if a curtain had been rung up suddenly on the day. May Island's lighthouse was a white pimple poking out of a grey corrugated horizon. Nick put his face down to the other voicepipe.

'Chartroom!'

Johnson's voice floated out of the copper funnel: 'Chartroom.'

'Fife Ness is in sight to starboard, sir, and May Island's fine on the port bow.'

There was silence, for about three seconds. Then Johnson told him, 'I'm coming up.'

He was chewing, when he reached the bridge, and his lips were wet. He crossed to the starboard side of the bridge and studied the land; glanced ahead, frowning, at the clearing shape of May Island.

'How long have you had land in sight?'

'I suppose a minute, or—'

'Look.' Johnson pointed. 'The Ness is well abaft the beam. It was no further from us ten minutes ago than the nearer land is now.

Nick agreed. 'Visibility's improved a lot in the last few minutes.'

'Hardly that much.' Pale eyes flickered at him, and away again. Judged – condemned. Nick, smarting, held his tongue.

The destroyer's motion eased rapidly as she closed May Island; there was shelter from the gradually engulfing land and at the same time the wind was dying. Johnson turned to him again.

'Go down and get some breakfast. Back up here in thirty minutes.'

'Aye aye, sir.'

And the hell with you, too!

But he was still a damn sight better off, he told himself, than he'd been two days ago. He moved to the back of the bridge, over the lower level that served as signal-bridge and was dominated by the searchlight above it and, a few feet abaft the searchlight mounting, the slanting tube of the foremast. He nodded to the port-side lookout – a man of about his own age, with a freckled face, a missing tooth, a gingerish tinge of beard. The sailor asked him, 'Yon'd be the Forth we're enterin', would it, sir?'

'It would, yes. What's your name?'

'MacIver, sir.'

MacIver. Ginger, freckles, tooth missing. There were a lot of names to learn; he'd start a list, add a dozen a day until he knew the whole ship's company. He let himself down the ladder from the destroyer's salt-wet, black-painted bridge, down to the upper deck. Turning aft, he passed the ship's boats lashed and gripped in their turned-in davits, with the galley between them. Now the foremost of the pair of funnels: *Lanyard* was one of a small number of her class that had only two instead of three. Walking aft, he scanned the deck layout as he went, passing the midship four-inch gun and then the second funnel, and aft of that the first pair of twenty-one inch torpedo tubes, now the after searchlight platform, and the other pair of tubes. Mainmast: and an inch-wide brass strip marked the start of the quarterdeck. There was superstructure amidships here, a sort of deckhouse with a door in it, and inside the door a ladder led down to the wardroom and the officers' cabin flat. Abaft it was the stern four-inch.

Nick paused and leant beside the door. The land was easy to see now, even from this lower level. *Lanyard* was only about five miles offshore, and the sun rising in the east was floodlighting that coast for her at the same time as it would be blinding anyone ashore: the light-gauge, Uncle Hugh had called it, explaining how an admiral would try to deploy his ships so as to have the advantage of it. It was strange how thinking back to Uncle Hugh's talk about the Navy still gave one a whiff of excitement and enthusiasm; it was as if Hugh Everard's own attitudes were infectious, strong enough to break through one's own more recent disillusionment and renew the longing for things which one now suspected to be myths. Daydreams; rose-coloured, like this sunrise flush that was turning the sea milky while a pink glow seeped through slats of cloud low on the diffuse horizon. But how could one explain Uncle Hugh's attitude to a Service that had treated him so shabbily?

In any case, thanks to the boost which the Falklands success had given to his resumed career, he was back now almost to where he would have been if they hadn't forced him out. Hugh Everard was captain of the brand-new battleship *Nile*, one of the crack Queen Elizabeth class super-dreadnoughts. *Nile*, with the others of the fifth Battle Squadron, had left Scapa for Rosyth only a day ahead of *Lanyard*; and might Uncle Hugh, Nick wondered, have had something to do with this move of his? Might he have pulled a string with the admirals before he sailed?

There was no reason why he should have. Nick hadn't asked for anything, or complained; he hadn't said a single word to anyone, not even to Sarah – from whom, if he had told her anything about his feelings of dead-end hope-lessness, it might have got back to his uncle.

He shrugged. It had happened, that was all. All he had to do was take advantage of it, make a go of things here in *Lanyard* – if they'd let him. And meanwhile – breakfast. Nick shot down the ladder, almost colliding with the surgeon lieutenant, Samuels, who'd been starting up it.

'Sorry—'

'If you break your neck, don't ask me to mend it.'

They seemed a friendly bunch. Reynolds, whose quiet voice and high forehead made him seem more like an academic than a naval officer, was eating breakfast. Hastings, a Reserve sub-lieutenant who was *Lanyard*'s navigator, had just finished. Tall, fair, with the skin of his cheeks pitted, presumably by smallpox; he'd pushed his chair back and he was stuffing a pipe with tobacco.

Nick sat down. 'Good morning.' He nodded to the steward: 'Morning, Blewitt.'

'Morning, sir. Bacon and egg, sir?'

'Please.' Nick told Hastings, 'We're almost up to May Island.'

'I know. I looked.'

'You'd imagine—' Reynolds addressed Nick – 'that a pilot worth his salt would be up there looking after this vessel's safety. Eh?' Nick didn't commit himself. Reynolds shook his head. 'Not this one. He sits here eating hearty meals while we officers of the watch do his job for him. What truly aggravates him is to have to use his sextant – should stars happen to become visible at night, or a sun at noon, or—'

'Don't worry.' Hastings raised a hand in greeting as the gunner, Mr Pilkington, joined them. Wizened, wiry, like a jockey. 'I'll con the old hooker in for you, by and by.'

'My dear fellow, how kind you are!'

Nick told them, 'I'll be up there too.'

'Haven't you just come down?'

'I gather I'm on permanent watch until I'm considered safe to do it on my own.'

'Well, that's reasonable.'

Hastings asked him, 'Haven't you done any destroyer time before this?'

'A few months earlier on. Most of that in the Flow and Lough Swilly.'

'Ah.' The navigator winked at Reynolds. 'Reckon he'll be getting some destroyer *sea-time* soon enough.'

Reynolds frowned. 'Even if there was anything to it, Hastings—'

'To what?'

Hastings answered Nick, 'I had to go with the CO to a briefing before we sailed. Carry the chart for him, you know? Anyway, it seems there's the makings of a flap. Or there may not be, but—'

'Flap?'

'It's no more than the weekly buzz, Sub.' Reynolds was testy. 'Meaningless, like all the others.'

'The Hun sailed sixteen U-boats on May seventeenth. Thirteen days ago. And none of 'em's showed up anywhere. Not so much as the tip of a periscope. Well, a fortnight at sea's about their limit; so if it's some fleet operation they're out to cover, it must be about due. Right?'

'Unless—' Reynolds sighed – 'they've sailed right back again, and our clever cipher boys only *think* they're still out. Or they're out and looking for targets and haven't found any yet. Or—'

'The other titbit, Everard—' Hastings raised his voice, to drown out Reynolds's attempts to cut him off 'the other meaningless item of intelligence is that there's been the devil of a lot of wireless signalling going on over there. As one knows, our wireless interception's quite hot stuff these days.'

'Your breakfast, sir.' Blewitt put a plate in front of Nick. 'Take my advice, sir, eat it while it's 'ot. Cold, it's 'orrible.'

'I'm sure you're right.' Hastings, with the steward present, had stopped talking. Reynolds muttered, getting to his feet, 'I'll see you lads up there, by and by.' He looked at Nick. 'Here's advice for you, Sub. Before you come up topsides, treat yourself to a shave.' He lowered his voice. 'Our captain may adopt a somewhat bizarre appearance when at sea, but informality is not encouraged in his officers.'

'Right. Thank you.'

'Good day.' Worsfold, the commissioned engineer, slid into a chair at the end of the table. Dark, small-boned, with deepset eyes. The others nodded to him: 'Morning, Chief.' Reynolds had gone. Nick, chewing bacon, stared at Hastings, thinking *U-boats, wireless activity: we do hear it once a week.*

Chapter 2

The Firth of Forth was misty, shiny-grey; the snake-humps of the bridge two miles seaward looked from here as if it was mist they floated on, banks of haze they linked. The mist would rise soon, as the day warmed up; there might even be blue skies later, and one of those days when grey old Edinburgh perked up, grass and granite sparkling. . . It was good, Hugh Everard thought, to see Edinburgh again.

He turned at the stern end of his battleship's quarterdeck and paced briskly for'ard again, with his hands clasped behind his back. It was going to be good – more than good, thrilling, to see Sarah again, too; after – what, a year? He gazed out over *Nile*'s starboard side, to Queensferry and beyond – way beyond, where the Pentland Hills' blueish shapes rose dimly above land-haze. Edinburgh itself lay between him and those distant ridges, while here, close to his own ship, were moored the others of the Fifth Battle Squadron: *Malaya*, *Warspite*, *Valiant*, and at the head of the line Admiral Evan-Thomas's flagship *Barham*. Each of them displacing about thirty thousand tons, with fifteen-inch guns and an armour belt thirteen inches thick, they were the most powerful ships in Jellicoe's Grand Fleet, all as yet untested in battle. One wondered, sometimes, whether they'd ever be more than the crack squadron of a 'fleet in being'.

The name-ship of the squadron, *Queen Elizabeth*, was in dock for a refit, here at Rosyth. She, at least, had fired her guns in anger: she'd done a stint in the Dardanelles, as a bombardment ship in support of the Gallipoli landings – until Jacky Fisher had insisted on withdrawing her, and had a blazing row with Lord Kitchener in consequence.

Seaward, close to the bridge, Hugh could see Beatty's six battle cruisers: the flagship *Lion*, with *Princess Royal*, *Queen Mary*, *Tiger*, *New Zealand* and *Indefatigable*. The battle cruisers were faster, sacrificing armour and fire-power for a few extra knots. The 'strategic cavalry of the fleet', Churchill had called them; and it had been Churchill, not Jellicoe or Fisher, who'd put Sir David Beatty in command of them.

One had such faith in Jellicoe; as a seaman, a leader, a professional. One was less sure of Beatty's suitability for high command. You couldn't help thinking, for instance, of the Dogger Bank action, last year, when Beatty with his 'cavalry' had managed to sink one German armoured cruiser, the *Bluecher*, while the more powerful units of the German raiding squadron steamed away to safety. It was all very well to blame Rear-Admiral Moore for it; the simple truth was that Beatty's ambiguous and unnecessary flag-hoists had muddled his subordinate commanders. The public, ignorant as ever, had applauded a great victory; but the frightening thing, to Hugh Everard's mind, was that Beatty had seemed to regard it in the same light. His flagship *Lion* had been badly mauled; he'd claimed innumerable hits on the German ships, whereas Intelligence reports had now indicated that the British shooting had been extremely poor. Beatty remained arrogant, confident, the public's sailor-hero, with his cap at a slant and his uniform cut to his own design. Hugh Everard frowned, questioning his own feelings – whether there might be envy, jealousy sharpening them.

Beatty, after all, was exactly his own age . . . *Cavalry of the fleet?* Confidence was fine – so long as there was some basis, some reason for it. But mere dash, panache, an assumption of Nelsonian superiority: that, in terms of what was needed in a modern fleet commander, was more dangerous than beneficial. No, one's view was not distorted by personal feelings. Sir David Beatty's ambitions and his view of himself were his own business, but the effectiveness of a vitally important section of the fleet was a matter in which others were entitled to be concerned.

Commander Tom Crick came stooping under 'Y' turret's massive barrels. Straightening his long, ungainly frame, he saluted.

'Boat's alongside, sir.'

Crick was tall – several inches taller than his captain, who was himself only a hair's breadth under six foot and pink-faced, with ears that stuck out like wings, seeming to support his cap. He'd served with Hugh Everard in the Falklands expedition, and when Hugh had been offered command of *Nile* Crick had come with him as second-in-command.

He fell in beside his captain, pacing aft, picking up the step. Hugh asked him, 'Any problems?'

'None worth bothering you with, sir.'

'Defaulters?'

Crick pulled at one of his outsize ears. 'We seem to have made some inroads into the crime rate, sir.'

Hugh's glance rested on Lady Beatty's yacht *Sheelah* which, fitted out now as a hospital tender, was anchored half a mile off Hawes Pier.

'I'll be out at Aberdour. Until about the middle of the afternoon, probably. If you need to, you can reach me by telephone at this number.'

The deep-water moorings had shore telephone connections at their buoys. Crick's long fingers pushed the folded sheet of signal-pad into a pocket of his reefer jacket. He asked diffidently, 'Are you visiting the Admiral, sir?'

The Beattys had a house at Aberdour.

'No. It's a – a personal – er—' he hesitated: then he finished gruffly, annoyed with himself for being self-conscious about it, 'A private visit, Tom.'

His own words echoed in his head as he tested them, wondering how they'd sounded, and at the same time aware of a distinctly pleasant feeling of excitement and expectation. He'd written from Scapa, when he'd been told of the squadron's forthcoming move south, to suggest to Sarah that she might find it a good time to visit her father, who was living in retirement near Aberdour. It might do her good, he'd suggested, to get away for a while from that great, gloomy house down in Yorkshire.

It was more than a year since he'd seen her. Writing that letter, he'd rejected the thought that his motives for proposing what amounted to a clandestine meeting might be open to misunderstanding. What was wrong with seeing his brother's wife in her own father's house, her father's presence, probably? He'd hinted, rather than put the proposal bluntly; but she'd replied by telegram. He'd thought, reading her wire and immediately crumpling it in his fist, *She feels it too, then* … And then at once, angry with himself, he'd questioned, *feels what*? He liked her, cared for her, his feelings for her might be avuncular or paternal or big-brotherly, there could be no question of any sort of – well, there *was* no such question. Neither he nor Sarah felt anything except friendship, affection, empathy.

He was concerned for her. With John away in France she must be feeling very much alone now.

Although – to be truthful about it – with John at home, he'd have had even more sympathy for her.

He told Crick, 'It's my brother's wife's family. I'm sure you'd be more than welcome, Tom, if you'd care to test your land-legs one day?'

'Most kind, sir.' Crick beamed. Genial, lobster-pink Crick was a torpedo specialist, and a great deal cleverer than he looked. They'd halted now: Hugh Everard had, and then his commander had followed suit: they stood side by side, looking towards the light cruiser squadrons' anchorage. Three squadrons, twelve cruisers; those were the scouts, the eyes of the fleet. Hugh looked to his right, at the new destroyer pens and inshore moorings crowded with the low, black hulls of the first, ninth, tenth, and thirteenth flotillas. There were about thirty destroyers altogether, with two more light cruisers as their leaders.

'Well, I'll be on my way.' As he turned towards the gangway he was aware of Crick's signal to the officer of the watch, Lieutenant Mowbray. Mowbray snapped, 'Man the side!' There was a swift surge of movement round the gangway's head: the side-boys mustering, the Marine corporal of the watch hurrying to join them, the bosun's mate wetting his lips and thumbing the mouthpiece of his silver call as he took his place there. Hugh murmured to Crick, 'Telephone me if you should need to. Otherwise grant shore leave as usual. I'll let you know when I want the gig inshore again.'

'Aye aye, sir.'

The commander nodded, understanding perfectly what had *not* been said. His captain had carefully not mentioned the talk of a 'flap', the rumours that were circulating about activity on the German side. There'd been so many alarms and so much disappointment; one didn't want to add credence to fleet gossip. Mowbray, a big, slow-moving man who looked too old for his lieutenant's stripes, ordered quietly, 'Pipe!' His hand jerked up to the salute as the bosun's call shrilled; a low note that swelled higher, hovered, fell away again. Crick was saluting too. Hugh put a hand to his cap as he stepped on to the platform at the head of the ladder and saw his gig waiting at its foot, bowman and stroke oar holding her there with boathooks whose brass fittings gleamed like pale gold. The other four crewmen had their oars turned fore-and-aft and sat to attention as Able

Seaman Bates, Hugh's coxswain, saluted him.

He stepped into the boat and sat down, picking up the yokelines of the tiller. He nodded to Bates, who sat down in the sternsheets a few feet further for'ard.

The role of captain's coxswain made George Bates much more than just the man who looked after this gig and steered it when Hugh wasn't actually in it. He was also butler, valet, messenger and general factotum. Domestically, he organised Hugh's life for him. He was a short, wiry man, with grizzled curly hair and a monkeyish face. His eyes seemed particularly like a monkey's, brown, watchful, crafty. Toughness made up for lack of bulk. It was said that during a bar-room brawl in Durban before the war Bates had driven his fist clean through a solid oak door – an opponent having had the sense to duck.

He'd done more than his share of bar brawling – which was why he'd never made petty officer or even leading seaman. But at least he had all three good conduct badges back now, and since he'd had the job with Hugh he'd stayed out of trouble. He'd been with him at the Falklands battle, too.

Hugh ordered, 'Shove off for'ard and aft!'

Sunlight glittered on the boathooks as they were shipped.

'Oars forward! Give way together!'

They rowed with the slow, sweeping, ceremonial stroke exclusive to a captain's personal crew. They were a privileged bunch of men, and proud of their jobs. If Hugh had had a house of his own ashore he could have used them to mow grass, fell trees, groom horses, drive motors. The gig was his private conveyance, and its crew his personal staff. But apart from manning the boat and looking after it, either at the boom or inboard, and cleaning Hugh's cabins under Bates's supervision, he hadn't much work to offer them. At sea, of course, they kept watches and had their various action stations, like any other members of the ship's company.

Hugh took a quick glance astern, to check the straightness

of the course that he was steering; his eyes rested for a few seconds on *Nile*'s warlike bulk. He was proud of her, of his command of her. But it struck him suddenly that while aboard that ship he was God, here and now in this small boat heading for North Queensferry he felt more like a schoolboy playing truant. And with a rather schoolboyish sense of defiance. He could quite easily have had himself put ashore in, say, the steam pinnace. This gig, even without his pendant flying in its bows – as it would be on a more formal occasion – was patently his, Hugh Everard's boat. Or at least, *Nile*'s captain's boat. He was clearly in view here at its tiller; and this was the forenoon, when nobody went ashore except on duty, and when Vice-Admiral Sir David Beatty might quite likely be on *Lion*'s quarterdeck with a telescope at his eye.

Beatty could put it to his eye, Hugh thought coarsely, or wherever else he pleased. And if he wanted to see how a ship should be run efficiently and happily, he could take some time off himself and pay *Nile* a visit . . .

He must have grunted, or made some sound. Bates's eyes were on him, questioningly. Hugh shook his head.

He liked Bates. Tom Crick didn't. Crick, who'd read Bates's Service documents, the record of his past crimes, regarded him with wary suspicion. But Hugh was satisfied that a new leaf had been turned in that interesting – if not immaculate – career. He'd noticed the trouble Bates was taking to keep it turned – by, for instance, the simple though somewhat drastic expedient of hardly ever going ashore, unless Hugh actually sent him on some errand. Bates obviously knew his limitations, one of which was that in shoreside bars he tended to become provoked.

All up and down the Firth, warships lay as still as rocks in the glassy, shimmering tide. The mist was lifting rapidly, except down near the bridge where it still hung about in patches. A collier was casting-off from a destroyer depot-ship; picket-boats traced lines across the polished surface. A tug puffed up-stream with barges placid as ducks astern of her, but leaving a great roll of wash to rock ammunition-lighters moored in trots in St Margaret's Bay. A string of multi-coloured bunting broke at a cruiser's yardarm, hung limply in the windless air; within seconds a red-and-white answering pendant slid up above another ship in the same squadron. A shore signal-station sprang to life, sputtering a message to seaward in blinding flashes. Out of habit, Hugh watched it, piecing words together: *Berth on oiler at number* . . . Turning, he saw the narrow, almost bow-on shape of a destroyer coming up from the direction of the bridge at about five or six knots, with her signal letters flying and her searchlight above the stubby bridge acknowledging in quick stabs of brilliance each word as it reached her from the shore.

Hugh called, 'Oars!'

His men took one more slow stroke, then sat stiff, motionless, holding their oars horizontal, blades flat to the river's surface. But the destroyer had appeared suddenly out of the seaward mists and the gig still had way on which would take her too quickly into the wash.

'Hold water!'

As upright in the stern as the crew were on their thwarts, he used rudder to compensate for the boat's tendency to slew, until the way came off her.

'Oars!' He sat still and waited for the destroyer to pass ahead.

Lieutenant-Commander Mortimer, immaculate now in what was probably his best uniform – a destroyer captain, who with various special allowances was paid more than three hundred pounds a year, could afford to pay his Gieves bills – glared at *Lanyard*'s navigator, Sub-Lieutenant Hastings.

'Well? Which *is* number eleven buoy?'

Hastings had been comparing the marked chart in his hands with the actual scene into which *Lanyard* had been steaming at what had felt, in the last couple of minutes, like breakneck speed. But he'd sorted it out now; he pointed, trying to look as if the matter had never really been in doubt.

'There sir. That's our oiler.'

Mortimer raised his glasses. He muttered, 'And that's a destroyer alongside her. If they'd meant us to double up, they'd have said so.' Lowering the glasses, he looked round at Hastings. 'Are you certain that's the oiler?'

Hastings nodded. 'Perhaps we're supposed to berth on her other side?'

'Who took that signal?'

'I did, sir.'

Mortimer looked round, and asked the man who'd spoken, 'Garret, are you certain the number was eleven, not twelve?'

'Number eleven they said, sir.' Garret was bony, haggard-looking, with pale blue eyes burning in a narrow, sea-tanned face and dark hair greying at the temples. A leading signalman, he was the senior signal rating in the ship.

'We'll take a chance on her inshore side, then. Pilot, come round a point to starboard. Number One, we'll be berthing port side to the oiler.'

'Aye aye, sir . . . Everard!'

'Sir?' Hastings was calling down to the quartermaster for a change of course; now Mortimer was pushing him aside and taking over. It all seemed haphazard – a pleasant contrast to the battleship rituals one was used to.

'Yes, sir?'

'Go aft, tell Lieutenant Reynolds port side to, and stay there and assist him.'

'Aye aye, sir.' Heading for the ladder, he heard Mortimer call for slow speed, then the clang of telegraphs from the steering-position, the lower bridge. Nick dropped down to the upper deck and hurried aft . . . A gig lay on its oars, bow-on; he'd only glimpsed it out of the corner of his eye, and by the time he'd stopped and turned to look at her more closely she'd been left astern. But a six-oared gig, with a tallish senior officer at her tiller – Nick had been left with a snapshot-like impression of a broad-shouldered man and a gold-peaked cap.

Might it have been his uncle? It could be: that was the Fifth Battle Squadron over there. But he'd been thinking about Hugh Everard, and he might have imagined it: the boat had appeared and then dropped astern so fast. He could see her again now, a long way back, see the slow sweep of her oars as she pitched across *Lanyard*'s wake.

He saluted Reynolds, whose berthing party of a dozen sailors was lined up 'at ease' on the quarterdeck. 'First lieutenant says port side to, sir, and I'm to stay and help you.'

'You're entirely welcome.' Reynolds glanced to his left. 'Hear that, Petty Officer Shaw?'

'Yessir.' Shaw took a pace forward and turned about. 'Port side to, then. Thomson, 'Arris, Wills – jump to it!'

Reynolds asked Nick, 'What's Morty doing? Singing hymns, this morning?' Nick looked surprised. Reynolds added, 'He does quite often, entering harbour. He's quite cracked, you know.'

Cracked or not, Mortimer handled *Lanyard* as if she were a skiff. Within minutes, she was secured alongside the oiler, and if there'd been a crate of eggs floating at the waterline they'd all have remained intact. One had heard often enough that destroyer captains tended to be both marvellous ship-handlers and personally insane. He was coming aft now, followed by his first lieutenant, to whom Nick was waiting to report.

The oil pipes were already being dragged over and screwed to *Lanyard*'s fuel intakes up for'ard, under Mr Worsfold's sharp-eyed supervision. Mortimer glanced at Nick.

'What are you giving Everard to do this forenoon, Number One?'

'I'll be instructing him in his duties as assistant GCO, sir. After that he can lend a hand with storing ship.'

'Good. Now look here – I need someone to go into Edinburgh for me. God knows whether we'll be granting shore leave, but at least we're safe until we've fuelled and stored and I have to go and pay my respects to Captain (D.) Who can you spare?'

'Garret, sir?'

'Why him?'

'Well, sir, as you know, he got spliced, two days before we left here. I understand he's – well, anxious to – er—'

Mortimer shook his head. 'The possibility that Leading Signalman Garret may be in a state of – er – suspended animation, shall we say, is hardly relevant. I'm not offering someone a run ashore, I simply want a package delivered to my bank.'

'Garret would still be a suitable messenger, sir.' Johnson glanced over his shoulder. 'Wouldn't you say so, Cox'n?'

Chief Petty Officer Cuthbertson nodded. He was a heavy man; thick-necked, bulky round the middle. If he let himself get out of condition, he'd be fat.

''Ighly suitable, sir. Very responsible 'and, is Garret.'

Mortimer gave in. 'All right. Send him along, right away.'

'Aye aye, sir.' The captain went below. Johnson cocked an eye at Cuthbertson: 'All right, Cox'n?'

'Garret's messmates 'll bless you, sir. They say its bin like livin' with a mad stallion on 'ot bricks.'

'Tell him to report to the Captain. And warn him not to let us down. If he spends half an hour with his wife, we shan't know about it; but if he stays there an hour or more . . .'

The coxswain's eyebrows twitched. 'What I'm told, sir, five an' a 'alf minutes is about what 'e'll need.'

On the bridge, Johnson showed Nick how to operate the Bar and Stroud fire-control transmitter.

'Three dials, which are manually set according to my

orders. The guns are laid and trained individually by their crews, and the gunlayers apply ranges and deflection as they read them off their receivers – which of course show the same as I put on here. D'you follow that?'

Nick was relieved that the system was so simple.

'Third dial here shows the orders: load, fire, rapid independent, cease fire . . . Clear enough?'

'Yes sir.'

'I order settings and corrections and our wardroom steward, Blewitt, puts them on the transmitter. It's easy for me to control the for'ard gun, since it's just down there, I can actually look down on it and talk to the layer by voicepipe. But you'll take charge as officer of the quarters aft – of both the other guns. If I'm knocked out, you take my place here. Same if the captain's hit – I take his job, you take mine.' He stared at Nick as if he was trying to see inside his skull. 'Is that all clear, Everard?'

Nick asked a few questions and Johnson answered them without impatience or criticism. Talking directly to the point like this, he seemed far less of a David-type character; his professional interest in the subject under discussion seemed to clear away the personal prejudices or reservations. It was possible, Nick began to think, that things might not turn out too badly.

'We'll go aft now, and take a look at the guns themselves. And one other vitally important aspect, namely—' He checked, and asked Nick, 'Namely *what*?'

'Ammunition supply.'

'Good.' The man actually looked pleased. 'I've made some changes in the after supply parties. They seem to know what they're doing, but you'll need to keep an eye on 'em while they settle down. And you must see to it they learn each others' jobs, so they can switch around and no hang-ups in the routine if we get casualties.'

Casualties . . . Walking aft, half listening to Johnson, glancing round at the quiet although busy harbour scene, the idea of deaths or woundings seemed remote. Obviously it was not, and one had to realise it and be prepared; this was a warship, designed and built for battle. But to imagine damage, shell-bursts, here where a group of bluejackets were chipping away old paint, others polishing brass, another neatly flemishing a boat's fall; Nick closed his eyes, trying to imagine what it would feel like to be under fire.

'What the *blazes* are you doing, Everard?'

Opening his eyes, he found Johnson staring at him; with that Davidish expression . . .

'Sarah – I couldn't begin to tell you how much I've been looking forward—'

'Ah, Everard!'

He turned, with his sister-in-law's hands still clasped in his, as her father came slowly through the door of the morning room. 'Well, sir! Splendid to see you again!'

'A great pleasure to see *you*, sir.' White-haired, lame from gout, Sir Robert Buchanan extended a limp hand towards his guest. Then he gestured towards the bell-cord: 'Pull that, will ye, gel?' Hugh glanced round the stuffy, high-ceilinged room; a long-dead salmon topped a book-case, and stags' heads stared down glassily, resentfully even, from the brownish-papered walls. He told Buchanan, 'You're looking well, sir.' Like an old, tired sheep, he thought. 'But Sarah's rather pale, would you agree?'

'Which is more than anyone could say of *you*, Hugh dear.' She smiled as she returned to them. 'You're as brown as a sailor ought to be. Is it all sunshine in the Orkneys?'

'How long shall we have you with us, Everard?'

'Ah.' Glancing back at her father. 'It's hard to tell. Not very long, I fancy. But more to the point, how long is Sarah to be here with you?'

'I think I should *like*—' Sarah paused, as a servant appeared and her father sent him to fetch biscuits and madeira – 'I think I should like to come and live here permanently – I mean, while John's at the front. You can't imagine how dreary Mullbergh's become, Hugh and since Father's on his own here—'

'First-class idea. Wouldn't you say so, sir?' Looking back at Sarah, he said, 'You'd leave a few people to keep Mullbergh warm, I suppose?'

'Warm? *Mullbergh*?'

'I needn't tell you, my dear, you'd be more than welcome here.' The white head nodded. 'Sit down, Everard . . . Entirely welcome, whenever you like and for as long as you like. Longer the better, in fact. But don't you think your husband might rather you kept his home fires burning?'

Hugh coughed. 'My brother's first thought would surely be for Sarah's comfort.' But he thought, *last thought, more likely*. He was studying Sarah, her hazel eyes and soft brown hair and that tender, vulnerable mouth. She was paler than she should have been; but even if she'd turned bright blue, he thought, she'd still have been beautiful.

'Since Mullbergh's lonely for you, and it was always a damp, cold, place why not tell John you propose to come up here?'

Buchanan, Sarah's father, was a widower, and rich. He'd been a shipowner twenty years ago. Now they'd found coal under land which he owned here in Scotland, and he was piling up yet another fortune from the royalties.

'I'd like to – I'd *adore* to. But it's quite impossible.' Sarah was telling Hugh, more than her father. 'Mullbergh has to be looked after. It's my—' she made a face – 'war-work, I'm afraid.'

They talked about Hugh's brother, and what he'd said in recent letters. He'd spent a leave at Mullbergh several months ago; Sarah had no idea when she'd see him next. The fighting was still fierce around Verdun, where French losses were hideous in the face of a German onslaught which hadn't slackened since it began three months ago, and there was talk of a new British offensive being mounted to make the Hun relax that pressure. It would be on the Somme, people said.

War-talk with madeira and the old man crunching biscuits. Small, rapid jaw movements; like a rat's, Hugh thought.

'A pity you don't expect to be here long, Everard. It must be grand to come under the orders of Sir David Beatty, after your stuffed-shirt Jellicoe up there!'

'Jellicoe's the best we could have, sir!' Hugh spoke sharply. 'Certainly no stuffed shirt. He's brilliant – and the whole fleet loves him. Believe me, he is the one man we trust.'

'But Beatty, surely—'

'Beatty holds his command *under* Admiral Jellicoe, our Commander-in-Chief.'

'Would you not say that Beatty was – was an exceptionally able and inspiring leader?'

Hugh hesitated. One could hardly express one's views on such a matter to an outsider like Buchanan, or to anyone, in fact, except close friends in the Navy. Beatty was – well, as a young lieutenant he'd commanded a gunboat on the Nile during Kitchener's campaign against the Mahdi, and out of that he'd won a DSO and promotion to commander years ahead of his contemporaries. Then he was on the China station when the Boxer Rebellion started, and he was landed with a party of sailors and marines to break through to the relief of the Pekin legations. Another display of dash and courage – he was wounded, decorated and promoted to post captain at the age of twenty-nine.

Hugh said carefully, 'His early achievements were certainly spectacular.'

'And isn't he the sort of leader our Navy needs? Not just the Navy – the *country*?'

'Well . . .' Hugh rubbed his jaw. 'There's always room for leadership, certainly.'

But did a young, hot-blooded, self-opinionated Irishman

who was useful with a cutlass in a rough-house necessarily grow into a modern fleet commander?

Buchanan said stuffily, 'Sir David and Lady Beatty reside now, as you're perhaps aware, at Aberdour House here. Lady Beatty is the most charming, delightful person. A major asset, I may say, to our small community.'

'I'm sure she must be.'

She was American. Back from China with wounds newly healed, the glamorous young Captain Beatty had married the daughter of a Chicago millionaire, Marshall Field. London's society lay open to him. In 1910 he'd become the youngest admiral since – Nelson and Nelson had only completed the course in one year less. But that comparison, in Hugh Everard's view, was ludicrous.

Buchanan was like a dog with a bone . . .

'Was it not Winston Churchill who appointed him to command the battle cruisers?'

Churchill had made Beatty his naval secretary in 1911. Despite that meteoric rise, Beatty had seemed to have reached his ceiling; he was on half-pay and close to being compulsorily retired. He'd refused an appointment in the Atlantic Fleet, considering it beneath him, and Their Lordships were not thinking of offering him alternatives. They'd warned Churchill that the young admiral had already been over-promoted; but Churchill took to him, liked the vigour of his personality, which he'd felt matched his own.

Beatty, Hugh Everard felt, had had a run of stupendous luck. For the Navy's sake one had to hope that it had not run out.

Leading Signalman Garret of HMS *Lanyard* was so sick of jokes and innuendo about his marital condition that he'd considered, just for a moment, asking to be excused the privilege of carrying the captain's package to the bank.

He'd hesitated, seeing in the corners of his imagination the winks and nudges, hearing his messmates' guffaws . . .

But the hell with them! He wasn't passing-up a chance to see Margaret.

'Aye aye, Cox'n.'

'Don't look so sad about it, lad. It's a favour we're doin' you!'

The destroyer berthed on the oiler's other side had had a boat actually alongside and about to cross to Hawes Pier; Sub-Lieutenant Hastings, acting as officer of the day, had arranged for Garret to steal a ride in it. From Hawes Pier it was only a stone's throw to Dalmeny Station, and from there a short train journey to the Caledonian Station.

From Princes Street he turned into Hanover Street and found the bank, where an elderly asssistant manager in striped trousers took the package and gave him a signature for it on the captain's chit.

Duty done. Now to surprise Margaret. He'd get a tram and then cut through the back streets. He hoped to God he'd find her at home. She'd been about to start finding out what jobs might be going; until now she'd helped her mother in the shop, but they were determined to start saving, so she wanted to earn money now, not just pocket-money. There was no certainty he'd find her, only hope. Fearing disappointment, he warned himself as he hurried up Hanover Street and turned right into Queen Street, crossing it diagonally then towards the tram stop, don't count your chickens, lad!

They'd known before the wedding that *Lanyard* and the rest of her flotilla would be sailing in a day or two for Scapa. What they had not known was that having arrived there she'd develop trouble with an A-bracket and have to dock to fix it; worse still, have to wait more than a week until the one and only floating dock was able to receive her.

He was burning to see Margaret, see she was all right; see her, speak with her; to establish contact, that was the urgent need. At first he'd put up easily with the shipboard humour; then he'd begun to hate it, and his increasingly short temper with his messmates' teasing had only made things worse. They were decent lads, but in the last few days he'd come close to loathing them.

He was smiling at his own thoughts . . . They were all right. He'd let it get him down, but from now on everything would be back to normal. He was rattling north-eastwards . . .This wasn't his town, it was Margaret's – and she called it a 'toon'! He smiled again as he dropped off the tram at a corner which he recognised by its horse-trough with angels over it.

He broke into a trot. The thought that he might just miss her by minutes or even seconds tormented him. He was in a bit of a jumpy state, he knew that; but he knew also that taking Margaret's hands in his, looking into her eyes and talking to her, hearing her voice, was the only medicine likely to do him good. Rounding a corner, he had to slam on starboard rudder to avoid collision with a hawker's cart, a load of vegetables; his cap went skidding, he stumbled, scooped it up, ran on, an old man's cracked laughter floating after him. At the end of this cobbled part he'd come into the wider, newer street, and just a short way up it was the shop.

The skipper had been as fair as he could have been. 'Back aboard by noon, Garret. That'll allow you – oh, an hour or more, for your own purposes.'

Say half an hour. There'd be other days, and shore leave granted. Sundays would be the best, if he could swap watches with unmarried men – which wouldn't be difficult, since three-quarters of *Lanyard*'s ship's company were bachelors – because whatever job she found herself, on Sundays Margaret wouldn't have to work. And since all shore leave expired at sunset . . . Well, they'd known, both of them, they'd faced quite clearly what sort of half-life they'd be leading in terms of marriage; it was the war, the way things had to be in wartime. What they were investing their lives in was a long-term future, the time when there'd be no war.

The bell on the shop door clanged dully as Garret burst in, breathless.

'Mrs McKie, it's me! Where's—'

'Wha's that ? Wha's that ye—'

Margaret's mother had swung round, as cumbersome as a turret in a battleship. Now she was goggling at him across the counter. There was practically nothing in the shop; Lord only knew how they made a living.

'Och, *you* back, wi' us, Geoffrey!'

He nodded, anxious, and already edging towards the back, the stairs door. 'Is Margaret in? Upstairs, is she?'

'Aye, but – I'd thought tae let her sleep, she's been sae—'

'She's not ill?'

'I'd not say ill, no, I couldn'a say *ill*, Geoffrey; but she's no been hersel', she's—'

He realised that she'd shifted her broad-based bulk so that it was now blanking-off the doorway. And was Margaret ill, or wasn't she? He thought he saw confusion – hesitance, a sort of fear, even – in the woman's face. He stared at her. She was uneasy, caught off-guard, it was as evident as the black hairs curling on her chin.

Pushing past her, Garret hurled himself up the stairs; narrow, curving, hollow-sounding under his heavy boots. Before he was halfway up he heard Margaret's voice call sharply 'Who's there? Who's that?' He wrenched the door open.

'Geoff! *Geoff!* Och, I canna *believe* it!'

He could hardly believe his eyes, either. She wasn't dressed nor quite undressed either. Just enough on for decoration, to make her look like something wicked – something that stunned him, winded him. He kicked the door shut with his heel.

It was necessary, he realised, to speak.

'What's she on about, you being ill ?'

Margaret laughed, put a finger to her lips. She was kneeling on the bed. He'd forgotten how she thrilled him: or *had* she, had she ever, quite like this? He could hardly get his breath in or out.

'She doesn'ae want me lookin' for work, that's a'!' Laughing: he laughed with her. He'd forgotten what suspicions had been in his mind when he'd come rushing up the stairs. She asked him softly, 'Lock the door?'

He'd only come to see her, talk to her.

They'd lunched late and very slowly, and then Buchanan had wanted to smoke a cigar with his guest before he'd hauled his old bones away to rest them. It was nearly five before Hugh had Sarah to himself, and by that time he was uncomfortably divided in his impulses. He'd had no real chance to talk to her, but he felt he should soon be starting back; on the other hand it had been his idea that she should come up from Yorkshire. He could hardly spend so short a time and just rush away.

The chance of the fleet being ordered to sea was nothing new. The ships were always at short notice, and there were always 'buzzes'. Besides, there'd be no time wasted in getting back, since the old man had placed his motor and chauffeur at his disposal.

Still, the feeling of being an absentee persisted. There was a tension in him which refused to be dispelled.

Sarah had asked him a question about Nick.

'Hasn't he written to you lately?'

She nodded. 'He writes quite often. But about everything except the Navy.' She touched her brown hair; a filtered ray of sun from the window gave golden tints to it. 'I worry for him. He's so – so *wholehearted*, and responsive to friendship. One might almost imagine he'd never had any! He admires *you*, enormously, but you're—' she gestured upwards – 'out of his reach. The Navy seems to – isolate people, somehow?'

Hugh cleared his throat.

'What Nick had to learn is that one has to fit into one's

surroundings as one finds them. We – the Navy – have our
faults, there's no body or organisation that doesn't. But we
know the faults, and we work to remove them. It's no good
just—' he turned back from the window – 'Nick's too ready
to stand at bay, so to speak, and tell everyone to go to the
devil. Perhaps that's how he's learned to cope with – oh—'

'With his father?'

'In the Navy, it won't do.' Hugh frowned. 'One thing that
might help him, probably, would be some action. That's my
fault, I dare say – when he was younger I rather fed him the
glamour of the Service; battles, victories, the great days . . .
And as you say, he's – a forthright lad, at heart. All he's seen
has been Scapa Flow and a lot of drills and no fighting – and
this in time of war, too. I suppose that is a lot of his trouble.'
He raised his eyebrows and spread his hands. 'But for
heaven's sake, it's the same for all the rest of us – and
nobody can whistle up the German fleet just to please one
discontented little sub-lieutenant!'

Sarah smiled. He went on, 'Strictly between us, though –
I've done what I can towards getting him a second chance.'

'Has he lost some first chance?'

'He's in danger of going "under report", as it's called. It'd
mean he'd be kept more or less for ever in a capital ship and
have reports on his conduct submitted to the Admiralty. It's
a system I'd like to see abolished, frankly – it does no good,
and often makes matters much worse. Very few sub-
lieutenants who get to that stage ever get promoted to
lieutenant, I can tell you.' He sat down. 'As you can
imagine, I'd like to avoid it happening to Nick.'

'And you think it's just that he's bored – disappointed at
not to have been in any fighting?'

'I don't know . . . except he's got to pull himself together.
Did you know that when he was still a midshipman he
physically assaulted a sub-lieutenant?'

She shook her head.

'I'm sure he must have had good reason.'

'During an evening of what's called "gunroom evolutions". It's a sort of traditional horseplay they indulge in. I think Nick was largely in the right, but you can't have people striking their superior officers, you see. These "evolutions" are harmless enough if they aren't overdone; but up at Scapa, cooped up in gunrooms with no real outlets for their adolescent energies . . .' He shook his head. 'It can get, well – it can degenerate into plain bullying. I've put a stop to it in my own ship – had the doors taken off the gunroom, so the young savages have less privacy than they'd like.'

Beatty, he'd been told, encouraged 'evolutions', even insisted on them for his own after-dinner entertainment.

Sarah asked him, 'What sort of second chance?'

'I don't know if anything's been done. I sent a note – a letter – to Doveton Sturdee.'

'The Admiral?' Hugh nodded. She asked him, 'Now, how is it I know of him ?'

'You'll have heard of him because he commanded the Falklands operation. It was through him that I went out there. He's an extremely capable and forthright man, and a good friend. He also happens to be flag officer of the Fourth Division of the battle fleet, and the Fourth Division includes Nick's ship. I asked him whether he'd forestall the inevitable by having Nick moved to a destroyer or a light cruiser. If it's at all possible, I think he'll do it for me.'

'I'll pray for it.'

'Then between us we'll have a double-barrelled prayer.'

Sarah laughed. 'You are simply *not* the ironclad you're supposed to be!'

'Me? Ironclad?'

'Oh, what's said, here and there. Perhaps you don't hear it. The brilliant Captain Everard, who should never have been allowed to leave the Navy and who's bound now to become an admiral ?'

'More power to their sooth-saying!'

'It truly does matter to you, doesn't it. More than – anything?'

'Perhaps.' The window, with the bright colours of the garden, drew his eyes. 'Yes, I suppose so.'

'What are you really after, Hugh? To square accounts?'

'Good Lord, who with? Fisher's gone. In any case, he had his reasons. No.'

'You want to prove you can do it.' He nodded. She asked him, 'Prove it to whom ?'

'Perhaps to men of my own vintage who saw me forced out. Or younger ones who've shot up the ladder since. Look here, it's said I've done well since I've been back – and perhaps I have – but there's a man named Dreyer who's captain of *Iron Duke*, Jellicoe's flagship. I'm forty-five, and he's only thirty-eight and he's where I would've been, d'you see?'

'And this is *your* second chance. It's vitally important to you, isn't it. Before any other consideration.'

Her hands moved expressively. She was inviting comment, and he'd none to make. She said more quietly, 'I'm sorry. It's none of my business. I've no right to pry or criticise.'

'It would be the most glorious thing imaginable if you did have such a right.'

He'd heard himself say it. He could still hear the words. And see Sarah's eyes on him, wide and startled.

Was this how lives were changed, re-directed ? By words that spoke themselves? There'd been no forethought, he'd not had the least intention . . .

They were staring at each other as if each was trying to test the solidity, the safety of new ground. And there was no safety in it whatsoever, he realised. It would be as reckless as it would be – marvellous. As damaging as the idea of it was thrilling. How long had it been in his mind – without his knowing it?

It must have been there. I've just put it into words . . .

To act on it would be suicide. His brother's wife: the war, and his brother at the front. How much more of a destructive scandal could one invite?

'You mustn't—' Sarah looked away – 'we mustn't allow ourselves even to think of—'

'I know.'

Two words, as final as 'full stop'. As if a door had been open a crack and suddenly slammed shut. If he'd answered in some quite different way . . .

Well, he hadn't. He'd made the opening: or it had made itself: and he'd looked through it into a new world, a whole new future. And then – shut the door. For the sake of – safety? But what did one want most?

Looking at her, he thought he knew the answer.

'Sarah, Sarah, listen . . .'

Her eyes rested on his face. He'd paused: he was lost, he needed time to test the words before he uttered them. She shook her head just slightly, almost imperceptibly, as if it was some idea of her own she was rejecting. She asked him, rather stiffly, 'If they let Nick move as you've asked, would it make so much difference to him?'

'It could.'

His mind was still on her, not Nick.

'What if he's just not interested? I know how you feel about the Navy, but does that mean *he* has to?'

The change of subject was a tide one went with, unwillingly. He said, 'There've been Everards in the Navy List for two hundred years.'

'But the Navy List has you in it, and it has David. Isn't that good enough reading for you?'

It wouldn't have been easy to explain, even if his mind had been fully on it. He thought Nick was right for the Navy, but he was less sure about David. Some lack of stamina or leadership, that one sensed? Hard to say why, in the light of Nick's performance so far, one should have such feelings: and a feeling was all it was, an *instinct*. He explained,

'Nick's *in* the Navy. It's what he always wanted to do. It's up to him to make a go of it.' He set himself to play devil's advocate. 'As David has. David's won first-class passes in all subjects, he's well thought of in his present appointment, he's—'

'He's the most selfish—'

She'd glanced round, at the door. Hugh heard it too: the telephone bell. He thought immediately of *Nile*, and that it might well be Tom Crick calling him back aboard. There was a clink out there in the hall as the old butler, McEwan, lifted the receiver. Hugh checked the time and saw that it was five forty-five, later than he'd thought . . .

'Indeed he is, sir. If ye'd hold the line a wee moment?'

'Sarah, excuse me?'

He was out of the room, dodging the heavyweight McEwan as he crossed the hall. The receiver was hanging on its cord; he scooped it up, put it to his ear, stooped to reach the mouthpiece. Buchanan was a small man and he'd had the thing mounted too low on the wall for comfort. 'Everard here.'

'Crick here, sir. We've orders to raise steam. May I send your boat in?'

'Yes. At once please, Tom.'

Hanging up, turning, he saw the butler hovering and Sarah in the doorway of the drawing-room.

'I'm sorry, Sarah. I've no time even to thank your father for his hospitality.'

Sarah spoke to McEwan. 'Would you tell Alec to bring the motor to the front, please?'

'Certainly, m'lady.'

The old man lumbered away. Hugh took Sarah's hand.

'We've had so little time to talk. And – what I began to say earlier—'

'You should not have.' She smiled. It was kind and friendly, nothing else. She laughed. 'And now your country needs you!'

'Sarah—'

'Are you off to sea again – off to fight the foe?'

McEwan came shuffling ponderously back into the hall. Hugh shook his head. 'No such luck.'

'Shall I be seeing you again soon, then?'

'I can't tell.' He saw her frown and added, 'But stay a while? I'll telephone when I can.' He heard the car arriving, and as he let go of her hand his thoughts left her too, settled five, six miles away where a fleet was raising steam, recalling libertymen, would soon be hoisting-in boats, shortening-in anchor cables or passing slip-wires at the buoys. There'd be bunting fluttering from the yardarms, searchlights winking out their messages, boat traffic heavy for a while and then decreasing, dwindling until the capstans turned and bugle-calls floated across a darkening Firth which, when daylight came tomorrow, the citizens of Edinburgh would find empty.

Just this Rosyth force, he wondered? Or the whole Grand Fleet, the squadrons and flotillas from Scapa and Invergordon too ?

Chapter 3

'By May 28th it became clear that some considerable
movement was on foot, and at noon on 30th May a message
was sent to the Commander-in-Chief, Grand Fleet, that there
were indications of the German fleet coming out. The
position still remained obscure . . . At 5.16 pm a message
went off to the Commander-in-Chief, and Senior Officer,
Battle Cruiser Force, to raise steam, followed by a further
wire at 5.40 pm ordering the fleet to concentrate to eastward of Long Forties ready for eventualities. The operations
had begun.'

Narrative of the Battle of Jutland
(H.M. Stationery Officer, 1924)

Another North Sea sweep; one was used to them by
now. David Everard peered into the dimly-lit binnacle as *Bantry*, port screw going slow astern and the other
slow ahead, swung her stern to starboard so that her bow
would point south-east towards Hoxa Sound. She and the
other cruisers and after them Hood's battle cruisers and then
the dreadnought squadrons, would be parading southwards
through that two-mile gap during the next ninety minutes. It
was nine forty pm. Ten minutes ago the destroyer flotillas

had left their moorings and, invisible in the gathering night, streamed southwards through the destroyer exit, Switha Sound, while at the same time the light cruiser squadrons had weighed and started south. Boom vessels would at this moment be dragging back the great steel-mesh nets which guarded the fleet's base against torpedo and submarine attack; beyond them, minesweepers had been busy for the last two hours, ensuring clear water as far down as Swona Island.

'Light cruisers passing ahead, sir.'

Commander Clark, hunched in a wing of the bridge with binoculars at his eyes, made the quiet report. Wilmott, *Bantry*'s captain, raised his own glasses to watch the low, grey ships slide past. He was close on David's right; his light-brown, neatly trimmed beard shone like gold in the binnacle's soft radiance.

'Pilot, how's her head ?'

David called down the voicepipe to the helmsman, 'Stop port.' He told Wilmott, 'A point to go, sir.' He'd been watching the slowly circling lubber's line as it crept round the compass card. He called down again now, after a fifteen-second pause, 'Stop starboard.' None of the ships showed any lights. The routine for leaving the Flow in darkness, established in great detail in the commander-in-chief's standing orders, could be initiated and conducted with few signals and no wasted time. Jellicoe had made his first signal at five forty pm, 'All ships prepare for sea'. At that point, a thousand different preparations had automatically been put in hand. At eight seven the second signal had come, 'Fleet will leave harbour at nine thirty pm by the DT3 method'. No further instruction had been necessary; with nine thirty established as zero-hour, all ships and squadrons knew the order of departure, the intervals at which they'd point ship, weigh anchor and move out. There'd be a gap of four thousand yards between the rear ship of each squadron of big ships and the leading ship of the next squadron following, and successive squadrons would pass alternately north or south of the Pentland Skerries, the last small, jagged bits of rock they'd see as they steamed east.

There'd been no wireless signals to alert the enemy to Grand Fleet movements. Even the Admiralty's orders to Jellicoe and Beatty had been sent by land-line.

'Cable's up-and-down, sir !'

'Vast heaving.' Wilmott stooped, looking intently through his glasses. *Bantry* would follow astern of the ships of the Second Cruiser Squadron and act as one of them; they had to weigh and pass her first and she'd tag on behind. Tomorrow – Admiral Heath had passed the information by light some while ago to Wilmott – the Scapa force would be joined at sea by the ships from Cromarty, and when the rendezvous had been made *Bantry* would transfer to the first Cruiser Squadron, to which she now belonged.

'*Minotaur*'s under way, sir.' Nobby Clark spoke quietly. The whole movement, the whole Flow, was quiet. A watcher ashore, even if he should be on a shore as close as Flotta's, might not become aware before tomorrow's dawn that a single ship had sailed. Clark added gruffly, 'And *Hampshire*, sir – and *Cochrane*—'

'I see them, thank you . . . Tell the foc'sl stand by to weigh anchor.'

The sailor manning the navyphone to the cable-party said sharply into his mouthpiece, 'Stand by to weigh!' David called less urgently into his voicepipe, 'Slow astern starboard.' *Bantry* had over-swung a little. 'Slow ahead port.' His own orders floated back to him as the quartermaster re-intoned them, and he heard the clash of engine-room telegraphs down there in the steering position, felt the vibration through the soles of his half-boots as the ship's engines were put to work. But not much was needed: he called down, 'Stop both engines'. One could imagine the engineers glancing at each other: *what the 'ell they playin' at, up there?* He heard the commander's voice from the bridge's wing: '*Shannon* is about to pass ahead, sir.'

'Weigh anchor.'

A muffled shout from for'ard; clanking resumed, as the last shackles were hove in. *Shannon* loomed ahead, her four tall funnels duplicates of *Bantry*'s – visible against the night sky as she passed.

'Anchor's aweigh, sir!'

They were waiting for the next report, and it came soon enough.

'Clear anchor!' Meaning that the anchor was out of water, in sight from the foc'sl and not fouled by anything such as another ship's wires or cables. *Bantry* was in fact clear of the seabed, a free agent.

Wilmott muttered, 'Carry on, Everard.'

'Slow ahead together.'

'Slow ahead together, sir! Both telegraphs slow ahead, sir!'

Straightening from the voicepipe, David raised his binoculars to watch *Bantry*'s bow and *Shannon*'s track ahead of her. He felt the churning of the screws, a vibration right through the ship as she gathered way; fifteen thousand tons of her, and twenty-seven thousand horsepower inside a six-inch armour belt to overcome the vast inertia and then drive her – when speed might be called for, later – at her designed rate of twenty-three knots. At a pinch, she might manage a shade more than that.

Wilmott was impassive, immobile, watching *Shannon* through his glasses but leaving the handling of the ship to his navigator. David called down, 'Port fifteen.'

Bantry's bow swung to starboard just inside the wake left by *Shannon*; her forward momentum as she turned would carry her right into it, so that she'd finish precisely astern of that next-ahead. He stooped again: 'Half ahead together.'

'Half ahead together, sir!' He ordered revolutions for twelve knots.

Astern of the cruisers would come Admiral Hood's

Invincible, *Inflexible* and *Indomitable* – they were up here from Rosyth, for gunnery practice, and *Nile* with her squadron of Queen Elizabeths had been sent south to take their place temporarily in Beatty's force – and then the battle fleet led by Jellicoe in *Iron Duke*. While at this same moment Vice-Admiral Sir Martyn Jerram would be leading the Second Battle Squadron and Arbuthnot's cruisers out of the Cromarty Firth, Invergordon. Beatty, presumably, would be putting out from Rosyth with his battle cruisers and the Fifth Battle Squadron, including *Nile*: and young Nick's destroyer with them.

Nick's pierhead jump into *Lanyard* still infuriated David. Obviously Uncle Hugh had arranged it somehow. Otherwise that bloody-minded little tyke who'd been about to go under report – which effectively would have put a stopper on his naval career – could never have been even considered for a destroyer job!

They ganged up – Hugh, Nick, Sarah . . .

Would Captain Hugh Everard, Royal Navy, have lifted as much as one finger to help his older nephew, David Everard? Would he, hell!

David bent to the voicepipe and called down, 'Steer three degrees to port!'

Uncle Hugh, and Sarah. His own brother's wife, for God's sake. It had been skirt-chasing that had wrecked Hugh Everard's career and marriage, years ago. Whatever he *said*, everyone knew that was the truth of it . . . Wilmott spoke suddenly out of the darkness, 'Which side of the Skerries do we go?'

'South of them, sir.'

They were passing through Hoxa Sound now, beacons flashing dimly on each side; no stars visible; wind south-east, force three. *Bantry* trembled under her engines' gentle thrust; she'd begun to pitch a little, as if sensing the open sea ahead and lengthening her stride for it. Below, in stifling-hot boiler-rooms, stokers would already be glistening with sweat as they swung their shovels with piston-like rhythm into the banks of coal and slung it into roaring furnaces . . . The boom-vessels, trawlers which operated the net defences by hauling them to and fro to allow ships to pass through them, loomed up suddenly out of the dark. For a moment or two they seemed so close that one might have reached out and touched them before they fell away astern and disappeared. As *Bantry* passed the second pair, the outer gate, David called, 'Porter – note the time, in the log.'

'Aye aye, sir.'

A useful lad, David's 'tanky'.

Wilmott ordered, 'Secure the foc'sl.'

They'd be shivering with cold down there by now, but until a ship was clear of harbour an anchor had to be kept ready for letting go, in case of some emergency. Now it would be cranked home into its hawse-pipe, the screw-slip hammered on and tightened, Blake slip secured and lashed, lashings and securing tackles would be rigged between the two cables, port and starboard, hove taut and secured. *Bantry* was out now, her pitching to the long, smooth swell more pronounced as she steamed in *Shannon*'s wake towards Swona Island five miles ahead. It was in the vicinity of Swona that one felt the impact of the Pentland tide-rip, a current of as much as ten knots which, if the bridge and quartermaster weren't alert and ready for it, could take a ship's bow as she steamed into it and swing her clear around through sixteen points.

A new arrival on the bridge approached Wilmott. David saw that it was Harrington, *Bantry*'s first lieutenant, up from his duties as cable officer.

'Foc'sl secured for sea, sir.'

'Thank you. Pilot, are we falling astern ?'

David bent to the voicepipe and ordered an increase in revolutions. He hadn't noticed the slight widening of the gap between *Bantry* and the ship ahead of her. He told himself, *Come on, wake up*. It was an illusion that Wilmott had left it to him to take the ship out of harbour; the man was at his elbow, watching each move, every detail. Discovering – as a new CO had to, of course – whom he could rely on, who might need watching. He'd only taken over just over a week ago, and he'd not had his fourth stripe much longer than a month; he was a man bent on further swift strides up the promotion ladder, and David was aware that the coat-tails of a young, ambitious post captain weren't bad things to snatch a tow from. So far, touch wood, Wilmott seemed to approve of his young navigating lieutenant. David told himself, *I don't need my damned uncle's help, I don't even want it! I detest the lot of them!*

They'd see, one day – Hugh, Nick, Sarah – who had the whip hand. It might not be all that long before they saw it, either. As elder son and therefore heir to a baronet – father currently occupied in – or at least not far behind – the Flanders trenches, one was fully aware of the possibilities. The French were saying *Ils ne passeront pas*: but a Hun breakthrough at Verdun, where the bloodiest fighting of the war had been going on for months now, wouldn't surprise anyone. Wilmott broke into his thoughts.

'How many miles to Swona, Pilot?'

'Roughly ten, sir, but I'll—'

'That's near enough. What's course and speed after we pass the Skerries?'

'South seventy-three east, sir, seventeen knots.'

'And our disposition?'

'Number one, sir, with ourselves added on the starboard wing. But we're to remain in close order ten miles ahead of the battle fleet until daylight, and then spread out.'

'Ah.'

Wilmott had known the answers before he'd asked the questions; the orders for the cruisers' disposition had been passed by light from *Minotaur* while the fleet had still been raising steam. David bent his tall, thin body again, to put his mouth to the voicepipe. 'Quartermaster.'

'Sir!'

'In a few minutes we'll feel the Firth tide. Watch your steering very closely.'

'Aye aye, sir.'

'Pilot—' Wilmott again 'what revolutions will give us seventeen knots?'

'One hundred, sir, near enough.'

'Damned odd!'

'Yes sir.' The ratio of revolutions to speed was unusual, in this class of ship. Wilmott paced over to stand beside Clark, his second-in-command, and David heard him mutter, 'I'd like to be past Swona before we fall out special sea-dutymen.' He was coming back now. 'Whose watch will it be?'

Aubrey Steel, who'd been loitering somewhere at the back of the bridge, answered the question.

'Mine, sir.'

'Who's that?'

'Lieutenant Steel, sir.'

'Oh, Steel . . .'

When Swona was astern, and *Bantry* pounding along at seventeen knots on the new south-easterly course, David handed the ship over to Steel and went down to the wardroom. He'd have a cup of coffee, he thought, before turning in. As navigator one had no watch to keep, but one did have to put in a fair amount of time on the bridge – particularly with Wilmott watching like a bearded hawk . . . It was warm here in the wardroom. Overhead lights shone on white-enamelled bulkheads and on the high polish of the mahogany mess table; *Bantry* quivered as she rose and fell, driving rhythmically into a low swell and light headwind. Her padre, the Reverend Pickering, was dozing on the sofa, Maudsley and Laidlaw – both watchkeeping lieutenants – were playing a game of *Attaque*, and Rutherford the surgeon lieutenant was fiddling half-heartedly with a jigsaw. Other officers dropped in and drifted out again while the ship relaxed into her cruising routine. There was an air of boredom; this was just another sweep, and the Grand Fleet would draw another blank, and then it would be Scapa again and next week another sweep . . . For the Grand Fleet this war seemed to be a matter of fighting not Germans so much as boredom. The Hun didn't care to face the fire-power of the British dreadnoughts; he'd make his occasional sneak raid on the English coast, lob shells into Hartlepool or Scarborough and kill or maim a few civilians, but he'd always nip back quickly to his bases in the Elbe or Jade before anyone could make him pay for it. Time and again Jellicoe had led his fleet in sweeps across the North Sea, hoping to catch Germans in his net; or on coat-trailing exercises on the Hun doorstep, tempting him to come out and fight. The Hun was wary; his strategy was to lure the Royal Navy over mines or submarines, or trick some detached squadron into facing the full weight of the High Seas Fleet. The Germans wanted odds clearly in their favour, in order to whittle down the superior British strength without risking losses of their own: and Jellicoe, who knew that the continued existence of British naval power was as vital to Britain and her Empire as a heart was vital to a living body, wasn't being had. It was difficult to see much prospect of real action for the Grand Fleet's big ships.

'Hello, David.'

Johnny West, *Bantry*'s gunnery lieutenant. Plump, balding, cheerful. In a few months he'd be putting up the extra half-stripe that would make him a lieutenant-commander. It was still a bit of a novelty, a rank introduced in 1914 for lieutenants of eight and more years' seniority. He'd flopped into an armchair next to David's, and reached back to the table to grab yesterday morning's *Daily Mail.* The wardroom door banged open again and Commander Clark came in, pushing the door shut behind him with his heel. A stocky, aggressive-looking man, he walked with a kind of strut. Blue-eyed, and red-faced from the cold night air, he stared round at each officer in turn. His glance swept over David, barely pausing; he nodded to Johnny West.

'Anyone done anything about coffee?'

'Not yet, sir.'

West had answered. David shook his head; he was reading a report about the forthcoming trial of Sir Roger Casement. Clark banged his fist on the sliding hatch to the wardroom pantry. It opened, and a young steward's pale face was framed in the square of it.

'Coffee in here, steward!'

One forty am, 31 May: *Minotaur*'s searchlight split the pre-dawn light as it winked out an order to the cruisers to spread into screening formation. Sunrise wouldn't be until after three o'clock, but even now one could see two or more miles through the misty, salt-laden air.

Sub-Lieutenant Denham was officer of the watch. David had just arrived on the bridge; Denham had sent his midshipman to shake the captain and at the same time had warned the engine-room that more power would be called for presently.

Wilmott appeared from his sea-cabin alert and immaculately dressed. His short, jutting beard gave him a cocky, terrier look. 'No executive signal yet?'

'No, sir.' Denham said, 'I've warned the engine-room.'

Wilmott trained his glasses on the flagship. 'Do we have a course to open on?'

'Yes, sir.' David had worked it out on the Battenberg, Prince Louis' invention that solved so instantly all kinds of station-keeping problems, the triangles of relative velocities. He'd given the course to Denham.

Wilmott muttered, 'You seem to have matters reasonably well in hand, Everard.'

That was a compliment, presumably.

'Executive signal, sir !'

'Carry on, Denham.'

The sub-lieutenant called down, 'Port fifteen! One hundred and ten revolutions!'

'Port fifteen, sir. Fifteen o' port helm on, sir. One hundred an' ten—'

Bantry was sheering too sharply away to starboard.

'Midships!'

'Helm's amidships, sir. One-one-oh revolutions on, sir.'

Denham gave the quartermaster the new course to steer. The cruisers were dividing, fanning out to their new stations. They'd end up in line abreast with a gap of five miles between each pair of ships and the centre – *Minotaur* – ten miles ahead of the battle fleet. Another ten miles in front of *Minotaur*, Admiral Hood with his three battle cruisers screened by two light cruisers, *Canterbury* and *Chester*, spearheaded the advance.

David, crouching at the binnacle, watched the line of bearing as the squadron spread. Wilmott stood a yard away, feet apart, hands pushed flatly into reefer pockets, chin belligerently thrust forward. Might it have been conscious, David wondered, the adoption of that Beatty-type stance ?

Wilmott spoke suddenly, gruffly.

'We'll meet no Huns this time, Pilot.'

'Shan't we, sir?'

'Hipper's scouting force may be out. But the Admiralty's just wirelessed the C-in-C – Scheer's flagship's still in the Jade River. Flagship'd hardly be in port if the battle fleet were at sea, now would it?'

Hugh Everard stood with his back against the port for'ard corner of *Nile*'s fore bridge and listened to reports arriving by navyphone and voicepipe as the ship's company closed up at their action stations and went through the routines of testing gear and communications.

It was two forty-two am, and in thirty minutes the sun would rise – technically speaking – on this last day of May. Technically only, because it would not itself be visible through the mist and low cloud which obscured horizon and sky alike; but its growing brightness during the next half-hour would still produce the confusing, varying visibility which made it essential for ships to stand-to, on the alert against surprise attack.

Nile's fifteen-inch turrets had been trained out on the beams: A and X to starboard, B and Y to port. Brook, the gunnery lieutenant, was at his station in the control top, fifty feet above this platform, and he'd just reported that all quarters were closed up and circuits tested. Knox-Wilson, the torpedo lieutenant, had reported similarly from the torpedo control tower aft. Tom Crick, the commander, had been receiving reports on the closing of watertight doors and hatches and the readiness of his damage control parties, below decks. Lieutenant-Commander Rathbone, the battle-ship's navigating officer, was all this time at the binnacle, where he'd taken over ten minutes ago from Mowbray, conning the ship as she kept up her anti-submarine zigzag astern of the others of her squadron on a mean course of south eighty-one degrees east.

Almost due east, in fact. Beatty's force had cleared the Forth Estuary by eleven last night, and had held this course at eighteen knots since then. Jellicoe had given Beatty a position some eighty miles off the Skaggerak which he was to reach by approximately two pm this afternoon, and then, failing a sight of the enemy, turn north to rendezvous with the main body of the Grand Fleet.

Hugh stared down over his ship's port side. The secondary armament, the six-inch batteries, had been trained outboard too; their barrels pointed menacingly towards the black-hulled torpedo craft which, in line ahead, steamed on the same course two thousand yards away. On this side were five destroyers of the first flotilla; to starboard four others were trailing their flotilla leader, the light cruiser *Fearless*. The destroyers were lifting and plunging heavily to the swell which *Nile*'s immensity merely thrust aside.

'*Lion* signalling, sir!'

Hugh turned and raised his binoculars, focusing on the distant, winking light. Beatty's *Lion* and the five other battle cruisers were about five miles south-east; Beatty had the ninth, tenth and thirteenth destroyer flotillas with him, and three squadrons of light cruisers disposed in screening formation another eight miles ahead. The seaplane-carrier *Engadine* was up there with the cruisers, too; with them, or ahead of them.

It wasn't for *Nile* to acknowledge Beatty's signal. *Barham* was this battle squadron's flagship, and Admiral Evan-Thomas would take care of it. Hugh lowered his binoculars.

'What's it about, Chief Yeoman?'

'Speed alteration, sir.' Chief Petty Officer Peppard, the chief yeoman of signals, had his telescope at his eye. 'Speed of the fleet nineteen and a half knots, sir!'

'What revolutions will that call for, Rathbone?'

The navigator's round, yellowish face turned to him. 'Two-three-oh, sir.'

Hugh told Crick, 'Warn the Engineer Commander, will you?' He raised his glasses again. One could make out – just – grey smudges against an unclearly defined horizon: Beatty's battle cruisers. Two groups of them, slightly separated, and the speed signal had been flashed from the right-hand group.

'Executive signal for nineteen and a half knots, sir.'

Sallis, that had been.

'Carry on, Rathbone.'

If you were slow on it, you'd drop astern of station, and then you'd need even more revs in order to close up again. Rathbone had passed the order to the quartermaster; he was watching *Malaya*, the next ahead, through narrowed eyes; to get inside the distance would be as bad as to fall astern of it. Hugh turned away, rested his eyes on the grey specks that were Beatty's battle cruisers. He was remembering how after the Falklands battle he'd met Jellicoe – who'd been persuaded to leave his Grand Fleet in other hands while he attended some conference or other, at the Admiralty. The small, quiet-mannered commander-in-chief had asked him some questions about the Falklands action then he'd put another: 'What views, if any, Everard, have you formed on the subject of our enemy's capabilities ?'

Hugh had mentally taken a deep breath. There were quarters in which it was not thought seemly to respect the Hun.

'I think we should forget all we've been brought up to believe, sir, about our unquestionable superiority at sea. The Germans' shooting is first class, and they're as brave as lions.'

Scharnhorst had sunk with her starboard batteries still firing. *Gneisenau* had fought on until all her guns were wrecked and she'd no steam in her boilers; then she'd blown herself up. Nearly all *Leipzig*'s crew had died with her, fighting.

'I'm inclined to agree with you, Everard,' Jellicoe had nodded. 'We must never for a moment underestimate them; and we must make our own shooting *better* than first class.'

He and his battle squadrons had been working at that, ever since; doggedly, persistently; practice after practice, in all weathers, week in and week out.

Had Beatty? Or did Beatty trust more to his 'cavalry's natural élan and dash'?

Never underestimate them. He could still hear Jellicoe's dry, emphatic tones. And the recollection triggered something else which had been lurking abrasively in the back of his mind . . .

'Captain, sir.'

Tom Crick loomed beside him, bat-ears stark against a lightening sky. 'Secure from action stations, sir?'

'Yes, please. Secure.'

But still thinking . . . The bugle-call was sounding as he moved aft, down the three port-side steps from monkeys'

island to the lower fore bridge. He pulled back the sliding
door of the chartroom, and went in. The chart, spread over
the long table which took up exactly half the space, had been
marked by Rathbone with positions, courses and times
which he'd obtained from Admiral Evan-Thomas's staff
before they'd sailed. There was the position off the south-
western tip of Norway where Jellicoe intended to be at two
thirty this afternoon; and here was the spot, a hundred miles
south-east of that, which Beatty had been told to reach at
roughly the same time – and then, failing a sight of an
enemy, to turn northwards and link up with Jellicoe.

The Grand Fleet was operating, as usual, right in the
Germans' back yard. Which corresponded with Jacky
Fisher's dictum, that Britain's frontiers were the enemy's
coastlines. Hugh Everard frowned as he stared down at the
chart and allowed the last few hours' orders and signals to
filter through his brain.

It came to him, suddenly. That Admiralty signal telling
Jellicoe that Scheer was still at Wilhelmshaven; it had stuck
in his mind like a piece of grit, mentally indigestible, and
now with time to think about it he knew why. Hadn't there
been an item in an Intelligence summary, at that time when
he'd been kicking his heels in the Admiralty in London,
about a German trick of transferring their C-in-C's call-sign
to the shore signal-station when he took his fleet to sea? So
that a wireless bearing on the transmitter which was
continuing to use that call-sign would seem to indicate that
the flagship hadn't moved?

If the Admiralty had blundered – Scheer might be at sea
now with the whole of the High Seas Fleet, while Jellicoe
was being assured that he was still in port!

Hugh leant on his elbows on the chart table, with his chin
resting in his hands, and put his mind to it. If that was the
situation, what difference might it make?

The chartroom door slid back. Able Seaman Bates's wide
shoulders filled the gap. Hugh didn't move, or look at him.

'Captain, sir?'

If Jellicoe realised Scheer *might* be at sea – and if the Germans had pulled that trick it would suggest some kind of trap was being laid – if Jellicoe knew it, wouldn't he want to be closer to Beatty, close enough to move quickly to his support?

'All right, sir?'

'Eh?' Hugh glanced round. 'Oh. What is it, Bates?'

'I've put some tongue sandwiches and a pot o' coffee in your sea-cabin, sir. Case you was feelin' peckish.'

'Thank you, Bates.'

There was a gleam in the monkeyish eyes.

'Reckon we'll get a bit of a scrap this time, sir?' It was the fact that they were out with Beatty, of course, that was making everyone imagine this sweep might be different from all the others that had drawn blank. Beatty was supposed to be the fighter, the man who got to grips with Germans.

Hugh shook his head, 'Damned if I know.' He stared down at the chart, and said again, more to himself than to his coxswain, 'Damned if I know.'

Chapter 4

Bantry was starboard wing ship in an extended cruiser screen sixteen miles ahead of the battle fleet. She was steering south fifty degrees east at fifteen knots, which allowing for the anti-submarine zigzag was giving a speed-of-advance of fourteen. The smear on her port beam was the cruiser *Black Prince*.

David had been working in his chartroom since lunch-time; he'd come up on the bridge for a look-around and a breath of air. Aubrey Steel had the watch; it was just after two pm, with a flat, grey sea and low cloud and a light south-east wind; there was nothing in sight except one attendant destroyer zigzagging astern like a dog on a lead, and that smudge in the north-east.

She – *Bantry* – belonged to the First Cruiser Squadron now, and her consorts were *Black Prince*, *Duke of Edinburgh*, *Defence* – who was Sir Robert Arbuthnot's flagship – and *Warrior*. *Defence* was in the centre of the fifty-mile spread of cruisers. *Warrior*, three miles astern of her, and *Hampshire* six miles astern of *Minotaur*, were link-ships for visual signalling purposes with the battle fleet. And the battle fleet was now a huge concentration of power: six divisions of battleships, the divisions disposed abeam of each other and each consisting of four dreadnoughts in line ahead; a great square of armour and big guns: *King George V* leading *Ajax*, *Centurion* and *Erin*, *Orion* leading *Monarch*, *Conqueror* and *Thunderer*, Jellicoe's flagship *Iron Duke* leading *Royal Oak*, *Superb* and *Canada*. On Jellicoe's starboard beam *Benbow* was followed by *Bellerophon*, *Temeraire* and *Vanguard*; then the Fifth Division with *Colossus* leading *Collingwood*, *Neptune* and *St Vincent*, and the Sixth comprising *Marlborough*, *Revenge*, *Hercules* and *Agincourt*. There had been sixteen battleships when he'd sailed from Scapa, and Admiral Jerram had joined him with the other eight this morning.

Light cruisers formed an inner screen. And twenty miles ahead, Rear-Admiral the Honourable Horace Hood's three battle cruisers were still the vanguard of the fleet.

It was more than a fleet: it was an armada. To David Everard it all seemed rather pointless – so much effort, such vast expenditure of fuel and other energies, all in the vain hope of encountering an enemy who hadn't left his anchorage. When it was *known* he hadn't!

David mooted this thought to Captain Wilmott, who'd just come back to the bridge after a snack lunch in his sea-cabin. Wilmott had seemed to be in a jolly mood; he'd cracked a joke with Steel, and now he'd commented to David in his brusque, clipped manner that the fleet was an hour astern of schedule.

'Of course, having to stop to search those trawlers hasn't helped.'

Neutrals, who might turn out to be disguised enemy scouts, had to be examined whenever they were met, and Jellicoe had slowed the whole fleet several times for this purpose. If he hadn't, the destroyers conducting the searches would have needed to have raced at full power to catch up again, depleting fuel reserves which were never more than barely adequate.

David suggested, 'We could as well go home, sir. Since Scheer's not coming out?'

Wilmott's head turned slowly. One eyebrow rose. Then he looked away again, as if he wasn't going to answer. Finally he growled, 'Hipper may be at sea, mayn't he? Scheer's not the only Hun there is, is he?'

'Of course not, sir.'

David tried to make himself sound agreeable; afterwards, he wished he'd kept his mouth shut. 'But aren't Sir David Beatty's battle cruisers a match for Hipper's?'

Wilmott sighed. He made a thumb-print on the compass glass.

'Here's Beatty, Everard, close to the Hun bases. And here, let us say, might be Hipper, out ahead of him. D'you see?'

David nodded. Wilmott's fingernails, he noticed, were jagged, as if he bit them.

'We'd have him caught between our—'

'God's sake, man, d'you propose the Commander-in-Chief should leave the route northwards open to him? D'you think a Hun battle cruiser force should be let out into the Atlantic? What d'you imagine our blockade of the German ports is all about, for God's sake? Why d'you think we sit in *Scapa*, of all places, month after month? To count sheep?'

David's face burned and it embarrassed him acutely to know that he was blushing. In front of Steel and the snotty of the watch – Ackroyd – and the bridge messenger, duty signalman, captain's coxswain . . .

Wilmott had swung away from him.

'Keep the lookouts on their toes, Steel.' His arm scythed, a gesture covering miles of grey, empty sea; grey-green, with a dull shine on it from the steely, cloud-filtered light. David was taut, sweating with resentment of his captain's unnecessary rudeness. He told himself as he moved out into the unoccupied port wing of the bridge, with his back to Wilmott, that henceforth he'd remain correct in manner and as efficient as any navigator could be, but socially, Wilmott would not exist. His nerves were racked tight; he felt as he did when he thought about his family. He told himself to forget it – think about something else . . . the next leave, for instance: Ellaline Teriss in *Broadway Jones* – he'd see that – and *The Bing Boys* at the Alhambra, with George Robey in it. Pat Johnson, who was now Nick's first lieutenant, had told him the other day that *The Bing Boys* had made him laugh his head off.

'W/T signal, sir, urgent !'

The yeoman, Petty Officer Sturgis, was taking it to Wilmott. Sturgis had come pounding up the ladder from the signal bridge like an elephant run amok. He looked dishevelled, as if he'd buttoned his jacket and stuck his cap on his small, round head on his way up. It was warm in the signals office, of course; they did sit around in shirt-sleeves, because they had the heat of the foremost funnel within a few feet of them. Wilmott had taken the clip-board from his yeoman's hands. Perusing the top signal, he'd glanced up at him, then down again; a hand rose slowly to stroke his beard while he read the message for a second time. Flipping back, now, over signals that he must have been shown earlier . . . David, aware of the act that was being put on and of his own disdain for it, could hear Midshipman Ackroyd squeaking away, lecturing the wretched lookouts.

Wilmott glanced his way and beckoned. The zigzag bell rang; Steel told the quartermaster, 'Port ten, steer south forty east!'

The quartermaster was repeating the order as David read the signal. It was from *Galatea*, flagship of the First Light Cruiser Squadron, which was part of Beatty's scouting force, and it was addressed to Beatty – Flag Officer, Battle Cruiser Fleet – and to C-in-C. Time of Origin two twenty pm. It read: *Two cruisers, probably hostile, in sight bearing E.S.E. course unknown. My position Lat 56 degs 48' N Long 5 degs 21' E.*

Wilmott called, 'Midshipman Ackroyd. My compliments to the commander, and would he kindly join me on the compass platform.'

'Aye aye, sir!'

Ackroyd scuttled away. Wilmott cocked a bushy eyebrow: 'Still think we should "go home", Everard?'

At nineteen knots, *Lanyard* felt to Nick as if she were doing forty. It was like a bumpy, windy, exhilarating canter; noisy too, with the wind thundering on jolting steel and the crashing of the destroyer's bow as she met and smashed through the ridges of the low swell. And there was the throbbing clatter of the ship herself driving forward, ploughing a broad white streak across leaden-tinted sea, stumbling, shaking herself like a dog and plunging on, an answering pendant cracking like a whip in the wind as it raced to her yardarm, acknowledging the preparatory order to turn north. *Lanyard* and the rest of the thirteenth flotilla, led by the light cruiser *Champion*, were grouped closely around *Lion* and the other three ships of the First Battle Cruiser Squadron. They were clustered so closely that, looking to his left as he clung to the port-side rail – this was the side of the destroyer's bridge, all there was to it, just a single rail supported on corner stanchions and with a painted canvas screen lashed to it – Nick could see the cluster of gold-peaked caps on *Lion*'s high compass-platform. Sir David Beatty, and his staff . . . Astern of *Lion* pounded *Princess Royal*, *Queen Mary* and *Tiger*, the four great ships hemmed in by the two lines of destroyers, while the close, solid phalanx of grey steel hid from *Lanyard*, for the moment, the other battle cruiser squadron which, surrounded by destroyers of the ninth and tenth flotillas, thrashed eastward on the same course six thousand yards north-eastward.

Lieutenant Reynolds had the watch, and Mortimer, *Lanyard*'s captain, was also on the bridge. Nick stared up at the wildly fluttering answering pendant; looking down again, he found Mortimer watching him, half-smiling. Nick, still holding tight to the port-side rail, returned the stare, and Mortimer shouted, his voice high and with a cutting edge to it to beat the bedlam of sound around them, 'Think you'll make a destroyer man, do you, Everard?'

As it happened, that *was* what he'd been thinking. If being a destroyer man involved this kind of thrill, this heady feeling of swift movement, exuberance – in a way, a kind of freedom – well, yes, why not? Mortimer was yelling down a voicepipe now. Nick took another look at *Lion*'s bridge; he knew how it would be up there. Ritual, deference, pomposity. Middle-rank officers murmuring, junior officers whispering; cold eyes staring down noses under gilded peaks . . .

When that signal at *Lion*'s yard came fluttering down, the battle cruisers would swing north and steer for the rendezvous with Jellicoe and the battle fleet. Beatty had already re-disposed his cruiser screen. The centre of it lay south-east from here, and it extended on a line north-east, south-west; so he'd have the screen astern of him, spread across twenty or thirty miles of sea between him and the German bases. And he'd put the Fifth Battle Squadron five miles on his port quarter, in other words north-west; when he swung his whole force to a course of north-by-east it would find itself in a V-formation with the battleships in the port wing, Beatty and his First Squadron behind in the V's apex, and the Second Squadron on the starboard wing.

Mortimer had explained it to Nick ten minutes ago, down in the chartroom. He'd said, 'Damn shame, no Huns this time. This is the limit of the sweep, you see . . . Never mind, young Everard – we'll find ourselves a skirmish for you, one day!'

Nick wondered what he'd done to deserve such decent treatment. Did destroyer men become human beings at sea? Or might Mortimer be a friend of his uncle's? He hadn't mentioned him. Nor had Johnson. And most startling of all was what Johnson – supposedly brother David's friend – had said earlier this morning, when they'd been on watch together. It was still difficult to believe . . . Nick's eyes were on that flag-hoist above Beatty's battle cruiser; suddenly he saw it jerk and begin its downward rush. He shouted, 'Executive!' He realised that Leading Signalman Garret had yelled it almost simultaneously. The answering pendant was falling like a shot bird. Nick grinned at Garret and the signalman wagged his head, a sort of wink. Reynolds was shouting down to the quartermaster, 'Four hundred revolutions!' Not full power, but not much short of it; the starboard-side destroyers had to race now to maintain their station on the outside of the turn. Noise rising, the rush of the wind increasing, *Lion* swinging, foreshortening as she went round, Reynolds yelling down the voicepipe, 'Steer five degrees to port!' Cutting the corner, *Lanyard* was thrashing forward like a racehorse, trembling with the effort or with eagerness. That was it, she did feel eager, and here on her bridge in the rush of air and spray Nick shared her keenness. A surprise, a revelation, almost!

'What?'

He looked to his right. The Captain had his ear to the voicepipe from the chartroom. He looked, Nick thought, astounded. He'd turned his head to shout into the pipe again, 'Bring it up here, Number One!'

The destroyer ahead of *Lanyard* – it was *Nomad* – suddenly looked too close. Reynolds saw it too; he'd called down for a cut in speed. Nick craned out, looking astern; *Narborough* seemed to be in perfect station. Mortimer shouted to Reynolds, '*Galatea*'s made an enemy report. Two Hun cruisers!'

'*Galatea*?'

Mortimer pointed a bit north of east. He told Reynolds, 'About fifteen miles away. Wing of the screen.' Reynolds bent to the voicepipe, 'Three-six-oh revolutions.' *Lanyard* had just about regained her station. Mortimer snapped, 'Too close. Come out a bit.' He snatched the sheet of signal-pad from Johnson's hand; when he'd read it, he looked round for Nick, and shouted above the noise of the wind and the ship's motion, 'May get that skirmish after all, Sub!'

Hun cruisers, fifteen miles away? There must be, Nick thought, six or even eight – yes, two squadrons – of our own light cruisers out there in the screen with *Galatea*. Widely spaced, but a lot closer to the enemy than this battle cruiser force was. If the German presence was as little as two cruisers, it would be dealt with long before *Lanyard* got a whiff of cordite . . .

A voicepipe squawked, 'Bridge!' It was tinny and remote. Johnson, who'd been on the point of leaving the bridge and was nearest to the pipe, answered it. 'Bridge?' He was listening to the rapid gabble, and Nick, staggering as the destroyer rolled – the swell was abeam, and it didn't take much of a crosswise sea to roll a ship whose beam measurement was eight feet nine inches – shifting his feet and grabbing at the rail again, Nick saw it was the voicepipe from the wireless office, which was immediately below the bridge on the starboard side.

Johnson straightened. Mortimer, with an elbow crooked round one of the binnacle's correcting-spheres, was watching him, waiting for the news.

'Well?'

'*Galatea*, sir.' Johnson looked puzzled, as if he could hardly believe whatever it was they'd told him. 'Two more signals to *Lion* and C-in-C. First one saying *Engaging the enemy*, and the other reports—'

'Speak up, man !'

'Other one says *Large amount of smoke as though from a fleet bearing east-nor'-east*, sir !'

'*Lion* signalling, sir!'

Leading Signalman Garret's shout had a cutting, penetrating quality. Bunting was rushing upwards to the flagship's yardarm. Nick heard Johnson say, 'Addressed to destroyers!' At the same moment he recognised for himself that the top flag of the hoist was horizontally striped yellow-blue-yellow, the destroyer flag. Garret already had *Lanyard*'s red-and-white answering pendant at the dip, meaning 'Signal seen but not yet understood,' and he was using a pair of binoculars one-handed to read that string of flags half a mile away. He was in profile, one hand on the halyards half-hitched on their cleat, and his lips were moving as if he was trying to read print, not flags. He muttered, to himself, '*Destroyers take up position – as anti-submarine screen—*'

Nick moved over to help him, flicked quickly through the pages of the signal manual. Garret should have had one of his three signalmen up here to help him, but there'd hardly have been room.

He'd got it, '*– when course is altered to sou'-sou'-east!*'

Garret sent the answering pendant whipping up to the yard: *Signal understood.* He turned, stared into Nick's face, hissed, 'We're goin' after 'em, sir! *Fleet*, that said!' Nick stared back at those craggy features illuminated by a glow of joy. He felt it too. He was suddenly delirious with happiness. Every face in the destroyer's bridge was either grinning broadly or tense with expectation, and Mortimer, her captain, suddenly waved his cap above his head and screamed like a banshee at the grey overlay of cloud – 'Tally ho – o!'

Hugh Everard left young Lieutenant Lovelace at the binnacle and walked out to the starboard wing of *Nile*'s bridge to look back over her quarter at the battle cruisers, or rather, at the smoke that hid them.

'Make anything of it, Chief Yeoman?'

Peppard had a telescope at his eye. He was about six feet away, on the lower level of the bridge and with his back against the handrail of the ladder that led down to it. The support helped him to keep steady while he concentrated on the difficult business of making out *Lion*'s signal.

Beatty's last flag-hoist, forewarning the destroyers of a change of course to south-south-east, had been readable from *Nile*'s bridge, but a minute or two earlier Beatty had ordered all ships to raise steam for full speed; as the battle cruisers' engineers drew their coal fires forward the funnel-smoke had thickened, blackened, so much so that from this five-mile range now one had only brief and partial glimpses of them.

'Can't read it at all, sir.' The chief yeoman hadn't given up, though. 'If they'd use a light—'

'Keep your eye on it. It might clear.' Hugh told Greenlaws, the midshipman of the watch, 'Keep in touch with the wireless office. I want to know if anything even *starts* coming through.'

'Aye aye, sir.' Greenlaws' rather burly figure moved aft; the W/T room reported by telephone to the signals office, which was next to the chartroom at the back of the bridge. Hugh leant on the binnacle as *Nile* ploughed northwards astern of *Malaya*, *Warspite*, *Valiant* and the flagship *Barham*. Admiral Evan-Thomas in *Barham* would, he knew, be staring astern just as he had been, trying to guess Beatty's intentions. If that signal had been an order to alter course to south-south-east, it might be addressed to the whole force or it could be intended only for the battle cruisers. One would hardly have expected that; but one was not supposed to guess an admiral's intentions – he was supposed to control his squadrons, not confuse them!

Surely he'd realise his flags couldn't be seen through smoke at this range? And therefore, if he wanted his signal to apply to this squadron, would have passed it by searchlight?

Nile, all thirty thousand tons of her, was as steady as a rock: as she forged on in *Malaya*'s broad, white wake. The battleships of this Queen Elizabeth class being entirely oil-fired, they weren't fouling the sky as Beatty's coal-burners were.

'Signal's hauled down, sir!'

Whatever it had been . . .

Lovelace, the officer of the watch, was calling down a helm order, maintaining the ordered zigzag which had not as yet been cancelled. Commander Crick was on the bridge; and the navigator, Rathbone, was in the chartroom, trying to make some sense or lucid pattern out of the welter of enemy-report signals which had been intercepted by *Nile*'s tele-graphists. Hugh had alerted his officers to the possibility of an action developing, but there'd been no point in sending the ship's company to their battle stations – not yet. And if Beatty allowed the squadron to continue steaming *away* from the enemy, most likely not at all.

'Battle cruisers are hauling round to starboard, sir!'

He nodded, watching them. You could see, in gaps in the drifting smoke, the long, grey ships shortening as they turned; destroyers racing past them. You could see their smoke too, and the white of their bow-waves, but the general picture, from this distance and obscured as much of it was, was of a jumble of ships all going different ways. If one hadn't known what was happening, it would have been impossible to make it out.

Did Beatty intend to leave his most powerful ships steaming northwards? Perhaps he did. His alteration of course to east-south-east, when the enemy had been reported to be somewhere roughly north-east, would be aimed at putting himself between that enemy and his escape-route southwards, south-eastwards. It wasn't inconceivable that he wanted to leave the battleships out here, so that the Germans would find themselves between the two forces, hemmed in while Jellicoe bore down from the north? But it would have been a very strange, even dangerous – in fact *highly* dangerous decision. And remembering the Dogger Bank action, the confusion of misunderstood signals – might history be repeating itself here? Hugh wondered whether, if he'd been in Evan-Thomas's place in *Barham*, he wouldn't have assumed an error on Beatty's part and led the battle squadron round after him without waiting for any orders.

'Wireless signal, sir, *Tiger* to *Lion*. *Tiger*'s asking whether the alter-course signal should have been passed to *Barham*.'

Someone had woken up, at last.

Perhaps *Tiger* was supposed to have passed it on anyway? But the fact she hadn't, and that she'd had to ask, suggested an element of confusion in the vice-admiral's grasp of communications problems. Already the gap between the battle cruisers and the QE's was more like nine miles than five. And Beatty would be cracking on at his 'cavalry's' best gallop – twenty-eight knots, when these more heavily armoured battleships could only make twenty-five at most. So if there should be a significant enemy force over there, he'd be charging at it without the support he should have had and might badly need.

'*Lion* has replied, *affirmative,* sir!'

And there it was. Dogger-Bank type manoeuvres!

'*Tiger* is signalling by searchlight, sir.'

Hugh stared out at the flashing light. Closer, destroyers of the first flotilla thrashed white paths through the grey-green sea. Hugh saw Tom Crick watching them with a kind of hunger in his face. Crick's heart was in destroyers, where he'd spent his younger days.

Barham – Evan-Thomas – would be answering that signal. It was completed now. Hugh had caught the signing-off letters 'AR'. The chief yeoman called, 'Flags from *Barham* sir: *alter course in succession sou'-sou'-east,* sir!'

'I'll take over, Lovelace.'

'Aye aye, sir.' The young officer of the watch stepped aside. Peppard reported, 'From *Barham*, sir: *speed twenty-five knots.*'

Admiral Evan-Thomas wasn't wasting any more time, but he had to re-dispose his destroyers ready for what would be almost a sixteen-point turn. The swift black hulls were curving out to port and starboard, heeling almost on to their beam-ends as their helms were flung over and they wheeled like a cavalry squadron scattering and then re-forming; or like wasps disturbed and now settling again, settling in screening formation on the battleships' starboard quarter where, when the big ships turrned, they'd be in the right place to screen them on the new course. Astern, the two battle cruiser squadrons, grey dots recently in two separate groups, had merged into one.

'Executive signal, sir !'

'Very good.' *Barham* was sheering off to starboard. Her squat grey profile loomed, lengthening as she swung out-wards, shortening as her swing continued and *Valiant* followed in the same white crescent of churned sea. Now *Warspite*'s move: *Barham* passing, steadying on the south-easterly course, destroyers falling into their positions round her . . . 'Port fifteen.'

'Port fifteen, sir . . . Fifteen of port helm on, sir!'

Nile began to turn: six hundred and fifty feet of battleship leaning to the swing of it, her stem carving, slicing round inside *Malaya*'s track. 'Ease to ten.'

'Ease to ten, sir . . . Ten of—'

'Midships!'

'Midships, sir. Helm's amidships—'

'Steady!' Now the quartermaster would keep her in the wake of the next-ahead. Hugh saw the speed signal drop from *Barham*'s yard, and he anticipated Peppard's report of it.

'Two hundred and eighty revolutions.'

Now at least they were pointing the right way; perhaps it might be possible to get some idea of what had been happening elsewhere. Hugh looked over towards Crick: 'Tom. Take over for a minute, would you.'

In the chartroom, Rathbone had translated a whole wad of cryptic signals from the scouting forces into positions and courses on a plotting-diagram

'*Galatea*'s been hit, sir. Must be somewhere about here. She's in action against a cruiser believed to be the *Elbing*. She got one hit below the bridge, but the shell didn't explode.'

'Be nice if all the Hun shells were that kind.' Hugh

pointed at the plot. 'Explain the rest of it?'

'Reports of enemy cruisers and destroyers here, here, and here, sir. *Galatea* had turned north-west, with *Phaeton* in close company and *Inconstant* and *Cordelia* not far off. She reported a few minutes ago that the enemy's following her north-westward.'

Trying to draw the Hun towards Beatty – which was not a scouting cruiser's job. A hatch slid open, and a signalman passed a message through to Rathbone.

'*Galatea* to *Lion*, sir.'

Hugh read the signal. *Galatea* was reporting that the enemy had turned north, and that more smoke indicated the approach of heavier ships . . . Now another signal: Beatty was ordering *Engadine*, a seaplane carrier with the cruiser screen, to send up an observer 'plane.

One couldn't envy any admiral having to dispose his fleet in the light of this haphazard scattering of information. Those light cruisers should have been pressing through to discover what lay behind the enemy light forces, not playing some decoy game. And a screening force wouldn't be there to screen nothing.

'Well.' He pulled the door open. Then he paused and looked back at Rathbone. He was a shy, quiet man, this navigator, with his round face and alert, quick eyes. 'Pilot, come out and take over.'

He went outside, and up the three steps to the compass platform. Evan-Thomas was grabbing a chance to close up slightly on the battle cruisers by cutting a corner instead of following astern of them. Wouldn't make all that much difference, but every yard was one in the right direction. If it should turn out to be the High Seas Fleet that Beatty was charging at on his own, the sooner this squadron could bring its fifteen-inch guns and heavier armour up, the better.

Jellicoe would have had all those signals – for what they were worth. One could imagine his impassive, steady manner covering a desperate longing for useful, detailed information. He'd be working his battle fleet up to full speed, hurrying down to Beatty's aid, still convinced that Scheer was in harbour and unaware that Beatty had managed to put twenty thousand yards, ten miles, between himself and his supporting battleships!

Rathbone had taken over the handling of the ship. Crick stepped down from the central island. He nodded in the direction of the battle cruiser squadrons.

'Unfortunate we're so far astern, sir.'

Hugh nodded. The situation, and what had caused it, was plain to both of them, but one did not, in conversation with a more junior officer, criticise one's admiral. Crick murmured phlegmatically, pulling at one of his large, pink ears, 'Want it all to themselves, perhaps.'

A signalman saluted: 'W/T signal, sir.'

It was to Beatty and commander-in-chief, from the cruiser *Nottingham*, who reported *Have sighted smoke bearing east-north-east. Five columns.*

Hugh showed it to Crick. *Nottingham* was only a few miles from Beatty, and 'five columns' sounded like Admiral Hipper's scouting-group of battle cruisers.

'Getting warmer, Tom.'

Crick looked up from reading it; he pursed his lips as he gazed out towards Beatty's smoke. 'Shall I get the hands up, sir?'

'Not yet.' As he said it, a light began to flash from that hazy, far-off line of ships. This time he'd been looking that way as it started, and he read the message for himself. Crick did too, muttering the words one by one as each burst of dots and dashes was followed by a second's pause for the acknowledging flash from *Barham*. Beatty was telling Evan-Thomas: *Speed twenty-five knots. Assume complete readiness for action. Alter course, leading ships together, the rest in succession, to east. Enemy in sight.*

Hugh told Crick, 'Belay my last order. Get the hands up.'

'Aye aye, sir.' The commander faced aft; tall, bat-eared, as benign and calm as an umpire at a cricket match: 'Bugler, sound action stations!'

Below, in the battleship's messdecks and compartments, the bugle call produced an effect similar to that of a stick pushed into an ant's nest. Men were streaming from their messes to battle stations above and below decks; some only half-dressed, pulling jumpers on as they ran; expressions were tense, excited, joyful. This ship's company had been called to action stations a thousand times, for exercises, target practices and so on, but in the last half-hour a buzz had flown round the ship that German units were at sea and perhaps not far away ... Bit of luck, to be with David Beatty, who had a nose for Huns ... Damage-control and fire parties stood back out of the rush as they assembled at key points, and were sworn at when they didn't; they waited for the last of the rush, so that watertight doors could be shut and clipped and the quarters reported closed-up and ready.

Petty Officer Alfred Cartwright, gunner's mate and cap-tain of 'X' turret, heard the bugle in his sleep and was out of the POs' mess before he'd really woken; up a ladderway between S3 and S4 casemates to the foc'sl deck, emerging near the screen door into the bridge superstructure. A destroyer racing past seemed almost alongside. He noticed a sailor on her after searchlight platform who was doing some sort of jig with his arms up above his head and his mouth opening and shutting – singing, or shouting for joy. Cartwright thought, *daft bugger* ... He raced aft – past the funnels, the lashed-down cutters, whalers, pinnaces, and the captain's gig with the sixteen-foot dinghy nestled against it like a baby just below the torpedo control tower and near the ladder – which he shot down, using his hands on the rails more than his feet on its steps – to the upper deck and the rear of his own 'X' turret. He swung himself up into it and pulled the hatch shut.

He saw at a glance that his crew was complete; Dewar,

number two of the right gun, grinned at him cockily, and Cartwright scowled at the Scotsman's impudence. They'd less distance to come than he had: and he had them trained, he'd have booted a man from here to Flamborough Head if he'd not come running like a greyhound to *that* call.

'Turret's crew, number!'

Cartwright's sharp Yorkshire eyes checked each man as he sprang into position. Gunlayers, trainers and sightsetters in their places; number ones at the loading-cage levers, facing the breeches, number twos in line with their breeches and facing the muzzles; number threes in front of number twos and number fours at the sides, facing inwards to the breeches. The second captain-of-turret and numbers five and six were below, in the working-chamber. Civilians, Cartwright knew, outsiders, thought a turret was a round thing with a pair of guns stuck in it; they had no idea until you told them that below the gun-house – which was what they thought was the whole thing – was a lower part, a working-chamber below decks which was about as big as the gun-house; or that a great armoured tube called a barbette extended right down into the bowels of the ship – five decks down – and contained the revolving hoist, cages in which projectiles and charges were fed up to the gun-house, plus a magazine, a handling-room and shellroom. There were eighteen men under another petty officer in the magazine, and one more petty officer plus eighteen in the shellroom.

The numbering was complete, and Cartwright nodded, satisfied. It was a happy thought that perhaps he'd be blooding his guns, by and by. He turned about, went to the cabinet at the rear of the turret. Its sound-proof door was open. It had to be sound-proof, so that the turret officer could hear and speak over his navyphones to the control top and transmitting station.

Captain Edwin Blackaby, Royal Marines, nodded affably. 'Well, Cartwright? Got your shooting boots on?'

Peculiar fellow, Mr Blackaby. Looked like a younger

version of old Kitchener, and spent more time cracking his own idea of jokes than he did making sense. The men liked him, though. Behind Blackaby was Midshipman Mellors, his assistant.

'Turret's crew numbered and correct, sir.' *Nile* heeled, and he realised she must be altering course. Blackaby put his eyes to the lenses of his periscope; he murmured from that position, 'Right you are, GM. You'd best test loading gear, hadn't you. And be quick – but for heaven's sake don't let 'em go mad, eh?'

'Aye aye, sir.'

Over Blackaby's shoulder, young Mellors grinned at him. Mellors liked Cartwright. When he'd joined *Nile* – green as grass, and fresh out of Dartmouth – and been detailed as an assistant turret officer, he'd come to this gunner's mate for advice and information, and Cartwright, showing him round the turret's workings and then the cabinet's fire-control equipment, navyphones and so on, had summed up what his function would be by telling him, 'Captain Blackaby is turret officer, sir; if we're ordered to independent control 'stead o' director-firing, it's him as controls us. Tha' sits up there wi' him, and tha' works the rate clock, and tha' takes charge if he should be killed; but 'appen if Captain Blackaby's killed sir, so'll tha' be theself . . .'

He was back behind his guns now, bellowing, 'Test main loading gear!' Number one of the right-hand gun yelled it down to the crew of the working-chamber, and like a hollow echo the voice of number six below there took it up and passed it down to the magazine and shellroom. The number twos meanwhile had grabbed the breech levers and swung the breeches open; number threes roared in unison, competing with each other for sheer noise, exuberance, 'Gun run out, breech open!' Tripping the air-blast levers, since of course nothing had run out, while number ones were trying rather perfunctorily to raise the gun-loading cages while the telegraphs showed 'not ready' and the pedals were pressed down. It couldn't be done; if it had been possible it would have proved some failure in the mechanism. Now they'd put the telegraphs to 'ready' and they were trying again with the pedal not pressed. It was as it should be; they were reporting this to Cartwright; and the number fours, who'd checked meanwhile that the chain-rammers wouldn't work when the cages weren't up, were confirming this point just as loudly. They were enjoying themselves, bawling out their reports and slamming the gear about. Cartwright warned them, shouting the whole lot down, 'Steady, lads, now *steady*!' Nobody wanted a jam-up, not at a moment such as this.

'Out rammers, free the cage!'

You couldn't do that, either. So many things you couldn't do. Safety precautions, all of them. With fifteen-inch guns you weren't dealing in weights of pounds or hundredweights, you were handling moving steel parts that weighed *tons*.

'Withdraw rammers!'

Not halfway through, yet. But routine they knew by heart, orders which they'd die – as old men if they were lucky – still knowing. After main loading gear, there was secondary gear to be tested. Then the firing circuits to be checked, and training- and elevation-receivers to be lined-up with the director-trainer's transmitter in the director tower.

'What're we fightin', GM, d'ye know?'

Number two of the right gun, Able Seaman Dewar, was glancing round over his shoulder. Cartwright ignored the question. He pointed: 'Interceptor there, ye gormless clown!' Dewar snatched at the interceptor switch, broke it, and the right gun-ready lamp went out. He looked round again, rather furtively; Cartwright told him, glaring, 'Tha'd best stay awake and lively, Dewar!' He went back to the cabinet, where Midshipman Mellors had synchronised the turret officer's receivers with those of the director and the guns; Blackaby told his turret captain, 'Load the cages with common shell, GM, and then stand by, and *don't* let 'em play that gramophone!'

'Aye aye, sir.'

Blackaby hated Dewar's gramophone. His main complaint of it had been that Dewar always put on the same record, a well-worn hit called *Everybody's Doing It*. But when Dewar had borrowed a couple of other ragtime records from some pal of his, Blackaby had been just as discouraging. *He* should worry, Cartwright thought; all *he* needed to do was shut his cabinet's sound-proof door!

'Stand to!'

Laughter and banter died away. He faced them at attention; a tallish man, deep-chested, black-browed, with a strong-boned, open face. Glancing round the turret, he met each pair of eyes in turn, asserting an essentially personal control.

'Wi' common shell, load the cages!'

Dewar jumped to the voicepipe to the working-chamber, and number three grabbed the handle of the magazine telegraph and whirled it round to rest at the word LOAD.

Three thirty-five pm: the enemy battle cruisers were in sight from *Lanyard*'s bridge. There was a mass of smoke in the north-east, and under it five grey, ship-shaped objects. They were about fifteen miles away, and steering roughly east-south-east.

Lanyard's turbines normally whined but now, at full power, they were screaming. Her bridge was juddering, jolting, wind-whipped as her funnels belched black smoke to mingle with her flotilla's and the battle cruisers'. She felt like some creature that was alive and suffering, panting, dragging each last ounce of effort out.

This fleet and the distant, silent procession of Hun warships might have been two fleets passing, without contact!

In fact they were converging on each other rapidly. Looking to his right as *Lanyard* clawed painfully up the port side of the British battle cruisers Nick saw that their turrets had been trained round to point at the far-off enemy, the great gun barrels cocked up to maximum elevation, ready to send their projectiles whirring skyward and away. Everything was silent, now; the silence of waiting, the silence of eyes at range-finders and periscopes, of guns loaded and waiting only for the fire-gongs' clang. It was a tense, not a peaceful silence; but what struck one as incongruous was the sense of detachment between the two converging fleets, the feeling that neither had anything to do with the other. It was difficult to convince oneself that in that remote grey battle line on the north-eastern horizon there were eyes watching instruments, indicator-dials clicking the ranges down, down . . .

The sky had cleared a little, or was clearing. Clouds still drifted in the light south-easterly breeze, but there were gaps now through which the sun was greening and glossing the sea's flat surface. But the sun was westering already, and the Germans would have their targets silhouetted against its brightness.

Lanyard felt and sounded as if she'd tear herself apart if she kept this pace up much longer, straining her steel guts to keep up with her flotilla and get into station ahead of the battle cruisers. Nick – Johnson had told him to stay on the bridge for the time being, although his action station was at the after four-inch guns – could almost feel the strain in his own muscles as the destroyer struggled on, overhauling the big ships easily enough but slipping back in comparison with her sisters. They were not sisters, that was the trouble; *Lanyard* was an L-class destroyer, the only one of that earlier type in a flotilla consisting otherwise of more modern, faster craft, N's, O's and P's. She was supposed to be the fastest of the L's, and that was the reason for her having been included in such scintillating company. Theoretically, according to the results of fairly recent speed-trials, *Lanyard* could work up to almost her designed speed of thirty-five knots.

The theory wasn't exactly being proved today. If she was making thirty-five, then *Nestor*, *Nicator* and *Nomad* must have been making thirty-seven, which nobody could have claimed for them.

The ensign whipped overhead in the wind, mast and rigging hummed, the deck trembled and jolted and the canvas lashed to the bridge rail thrashed and boomed. Every loose fitting rattled and they were all, apparently, quite loose. But *Lanyard* had passed Beatty's flagship now and she was thrusting on to take up her station in the flotilla's port division astern of *Champion*, their leader, who was waiting for them now two miles ahead of *Lion*. The ninth and tenth flotillas had been ordered to get up there too, but that group's four L-class weren't making it at all; they were well astern, fouling the battle cruisers' range with their smoke. At any minute now Beatty would tell them to drop astern and clear the range, and Nick could see in the grim anxiety in his captain's face the recognition of that frightful hazard; that if *Lanyard* failed to keep up, she might be relegated, forced to join those others. It might seem logical, to some minds, to lump all the L's together. But *Lanyard* was making it, or seemed to be. So long as she didn't bust a gut.

There was one plain purpose in sending the destroyers up ahead, and that was to dispose them in a situation from which, when the vice-admiral considered the time was ripe, they could fulfil their destiny, perform the function for which they'd been designed and built and for which their officers and crews had been trained – to attack the enemy battle line with torpedoes.

Nick checked the time: three forty-five. And almost there. Mortimer had just shouted down, 'Four hundred revolutions!' He was easing her speed almost to twenty-five knots, the speed of the fleet, as *Lanyard* closed up astern of *Nicator* in the port column. Ahead of *Nicator* were *Nomad* and *Nestor*, who was the leader of this division. In the centre, *Champion* led *Obdurate*, *Nerissa* and *Termagant*; to starboard *Narborough* led *Pelican*, *Petard*, and – closing up now – *Turbulent*.

Off on *Lanyard*'s beam as she settled into station in the port column Nick saw two boats from the ninth or tenth flotillas; two M's who'd left the slower L's and pushed on to join this faster group.

Two flag-hoists had broken simultaneously at *Lion*'s yards. Mortimer straightened from the voicepipe – he'd reduced the revs again, to three hundred and eighty – and pointed: 'Garret?'

'Aye, sir, I'm—'

Having problems, by the look of it. Nick snatched up the signal manual and moved over, ready to help. Garret had binoculars pointed at the bright clusters of flags; his legs were braced apart against the ship's jolting, pounding motion . . . But he wasn't, after all, going to need the manual.

'Line-of-bearing signal to the battle cruisers, sir. Can't make him out, not—'

'What's the other?'

The glasses moved fractionally. 'Alter course east-sou'-east, sir!'

'Very good. Doesn't matter about the first one.' Nick realised that a course of east-south-east would be parallel to the enemy's; Beatty was squaring-off for the fight. That signal was fluttering down, and up ahead *Champion*'s wake grew an elbow in it as she put her helm over. Glancing back at the battle cruisers, expecting the thunder of the first salvoes to come at any moment, he saw the line-of-bearing forming as the great ships swung to their firing course; the line-of-bearing 'staggered' them, so that instead of following directly in each other's wakes, their tracks were spread. It meant that no ship would be steaming entirely in her next-ahead's funnel-smoke, and this should make it easier for the gunners. Nick stared out to port, at the distant line of Germans. He was watching them in that second as they opened fire.

A ripple of sharp, red flashes blossomed and travelled from right to left down the line of ships.

'Enemy's opened fire, sir!' Johnson had reported it.

Nick was aware of an extraordinary feeling of detachment. One heard nothing, yet. One had seen those red gun-flashes, and now ... nothing. All silent, and those enemy ships so far away. One knew what it was about, what it meant, what would be happening here in a matter of twenty or thirty seconds, yet it seemed to be utterly remote from what was happening and visible here now.

But there was also a sense of enormous satisfaction – *relief*, it might be. This, finally, was battle.

More flags were showing from *Lion*, and Garret shouted to Mortimer, 'Distribution of fire signal, sir!' Beatty had six ships to the Germans' five; he had to tell his captains which targets each of them should aim at. Johnson had come to the after end of the bridge, where Blewitt crouched beside the Barr and Stroud transmitter; Nick had opened his mouth to ask whether he should go down now, when the sound of that distant gunfire reached them. A booming roll of far-off thunder, but it was lost immediately in a tearing, ripping noise as if the atmosphere was being forced apart, torn open, and the sea began to spout great mast-high columns of white water with dark tops; a forest of yellowish foam. All short, but already the red flashes of a second salvo were rippling down the German line, red spurts out of what looked now like a lumpy layer of smoke. Simultaneously the air astern erupted, split and split again as first *Lion* and then the ships astern of her opened fire.

You could actually see the shells, like scratch-marks against the pale-grey sky, as the battle cruisers' guns lobbed them away towards the Germans. Nick got his question through to Johnson when the volume of noise lessened. Johnson shouted, 'No, I'll tell you when to go down.' He'd explained earlier that it was preferable for Nick to stay on the bridge until the last moments before action, so that when he went down to his guns he'd know as much as possible about the tactical situation and the CO's intentions. Nick had thought perhaps that the time had come, but of course it hadn't, there was no enemy anywhere within range of the destroyers' little four-inch guns. This was a duel between giants, and it was continuous now. That reply of Johnson's had been squeezed into the last oasis of comparative silence there'd been – perhaps the last there'd *ever* be? Gunfire was no longer a matter of separate percussions or even separate salvoes, the noise of guns firing and shells falling was continuous, both fleets shooting steadily and rapidly and the fall-of-shot thick, closing-in, the German salvoes creeping closer as their gunners adjusted range, and – *Lion* had been hit! And hit *again* . . . That second hit had struck her centre turret, 'Q' turret: not just the shell-burst but a larger explosion and a shaft of flame and smoke that leapt to the height of her funnel-tops. Nick watched, fascinated, horrified: it was a blaze now, orange flames and thick, black smoke pouring back across the flagship's upperworks as she thrust on at twenty-five knots, her other three turrets all still firing. One had to remind oneself that shells would be raining down also on the enemy: in fact *that* had been a hit! He'd glanced over at the German line as the thought had come to him, and he'd seen the red-and-black explosion on their leading ship: and the third ship too, that third one might even be on fire . . . But in Beatty's squadron *Lion* wasn't the only one getting knocked about: her next astern, *Princess Royal*, had been hit on her foc'sl and the flash of the explosion had erupted from *inside* the ship. Extraordinary – horrible – to stand and watch: men must have died in there at that second, there'd be others wounded, mutilated, and the two fleets steaming on, side by side and ten miles apart and – as it seemed – indifferent . . .

Tiger was being hit now – so was *Indefatigable*. Nick whispered inside his skull, *please God, may the Hun be getting as much as he's handing out! Indefatigable* had been hit again. The sea was a mass of leaping shell-splashes, the churned foam yellow, even the air yellowish with the explosive reek; the line of battle cruisers astern was almost entirely hidden now under the absolute smothering of German shells and – even more obscuring – their own funnel-smoke. But it was blowing clear again: suddenly he could see the whole line, and it looked as if *Indefatigable* was badly hurt.   Smoke pouring from her after super-structure but no sign of any flames...

Lion was altering course to port – to close the range? The next ship to her, *Princess Royal*, going round too; and *Queen Mary*, and *Tiger*, and *New Zealand* and – Garret, the leading signalman, had turned to draw Nick's attention to the fact that *Indefatigable* didn't seem to have put her helm over. She was ploughing straight on across the other battle cruisers' tracks – already she was two cables or thereabouts out on *New Zealand*'s starboard quarter, and she was still steaming straight ahead. Her steering might have jammed, Nick thought; perhaps steering engine smashed; smoke billowed from her afterpart. As he watched her – with Johnson close beside him in the starboard after corner of the bridge – two more shells hit her. Nick felt himself cry out: or he thought he had. He'd felt his gut convulse and all the muscles of his body clench. But *she was all right*! The first shell had landed on her foc'sl and the other one on 'A' turret, and both had seemed to burst on impact. Had *seemed* to . . .

Indefatigable blew up.

There were those two hits, which hadn't seemed to penetrate her armour. Then perhaps half a minute in which nothing seemed to happen; he'd only continued to watch her because she held her course and still hadn't altered round with the other ships. He kept his eyes on her, aware of bedlam all around, of the continuing roar of gunfire and the fall of German shot, the sound of it screeching through the sky and then its impact mostly, but not all, in the sea, foul black water from near-misses sheeting across ships' decks.

And then suddenly great flares of orange flame were leaping
from *Indefatigable*'s forepart, spreading aft in a blazing
mass with black smoke as well as flame, the smoke
spreading until everything else had been blotted out, until
that ugly, sickening pall hid the ship entirely. Above the
smoke, in clear air, a fifty-foot picket boat soared, spinning
like a toy. Other debris too. As it fell, the smoke was already
dissipating and blowing clear, and *Indefatigable*, nineteen
thousand tons of battle cruiser and more than a thousand
men, had gone.

Leading Seaman Garret's mouth was open, his eyes wide
and glazed with shock. His hands, up at chest-level, opened
and shut convulsively, as if they were trying to find
substance in thin air.

Hugh Everard told his gunnery lieutenant, speaking into the
navyphone to the control top, 'Open fire when you're ready,
Brook.'

'Aye aye, sir.'

Replacing the telephone, Hugh joined Rathbone at the
binnacle.

Nile heeled slightly under rudder as she followed the
others of her squadron in a sharp turn to starboard, on to a
firing course.

It was five minutes past four. The Fifth Battle Squadron
had been straining eastward to close the gap between
themselves and Beatty's battle cruisers, and even more
essentially to get into hitting-distance of the enemy. Now the
German battle cruisers were in sight, at a range of something
like eleven miles, and Admiral Evan-Thomas was opening
his squadron's broadsides to that distant target.

A minute ago, Hugh had seen *Indefatigable* blow up.
He'd been watching the battle cruisers through his binoculars at the time; there'd seemed to be some alteration of
course in progress, but it was a confused, smoky picture and
he'd been trying to sort it out while he chatted briefly to Tom

Crick. During the short exchange of conversation Crick had been standing with his back towards Beatty's ships, and consequently hadn't seen the sudden and total destruction of the battle cruiser. Probably very few men had. Indeed, hopefully . . .

Hugh had continued with the conversation. He'd kept the glasses at his eyes, hiding the shock he'd felt.

Now Rathbone was steadying *Nile* on the new course. The turrets were all trained out to about forty degrees on the port bow, which was where the Hun was. That far-off smoke, that cloudy suggestion of a line of ships was the enemy. From the top, where Brook was, the view would be much clearer, of course. But the Germans had the light on their side, and there was nothing Beatty could have done about it.

How would the Germans enjoy their first taste of fifteen-inch shells? The long barrels jutted menacingly, upward-pointing; silent, but ready to erupt. One could envisage very easily the interiors of the turrets; the warm, slightly oily atmosphere, the gleam of polished brass and steel, the quiet, and the tension in the guns' crews as they waited. The range was long, certainly, but that was no great drawback. These ships, like all those in Jellicoe's Scapa squadrons, had been trained to standards of excellence which one knew would be difficult to improve upon.

The Germans could shoot, there was no doubt of that; in the last few minutes the evidence of it had been incontrovertible. But in the next few minutes, they'd be getting experience of Jellicoe-type gunnery.

Hugh lowered his binoculars, stared up at his ship's masthead and then back at her after struts . . . It was all right. He might have known Crick would have seen to it. No less than three white ensigns and one union flag were fluttering up there. One or more might be shot away and *Nile* would still display her colours.

Barham opened fire. The thunder of that first salvo rolled back like thunder and brown cordite-smoke clung for a few seconds round her turrets. Now *Valiant* had begun: and that was *Warspite* joining in. Hugh left Rathbone, and moved out again to the port side – which shortly would be the engaged side – of the bridge, and levelled his glasses at the far-off enemy. The rearmost pair of them, the two grey shapes to the left, flickering with the red sparks of their own gunfire, had been identified as *Von der Tann* and *Moltke*, and on them – once the nearer cruisers had been dealt with – this squadron's fire would be concentrated.

Malaya had opened fire. Hugh swallowed to clear his ears from the percussion-effect of it. He put his glasses up again, and watched for the fall of *Barham*'s shells.

Five minutes ago the guns had been loaded; since then, range and deflection had been passed electrically from the TS to the director-sight in the top; and in the turrets, pointers followed the director settings.

The TS, or transmitting station, was a small compartment deep in the belly of the ship. In it, Royal Marine bandsmen fed numerous items of information into a computer called a Dreyer fire control table, which then churned out the settings that were to be applied to the guns.

In 'X' turret, Blackaby had ordered 'Salvoes! Right gun commmencing!'

For the moment, that was his job done. Now it was up to the captain of the turret, PO Cartwright, out there behind the gleaming oiled steel of the great breech mechanisms, with the crew he'd trained and over whose every movement he now watched eagle-eyed. Number three, for instance; if number three had shut the interceptor switch before he'd seen the gunlayer raise his hand to confirm the pointers were in line – All right. The layer had put his hand up and three had slammed the switch shut and bellowed 'Right gun ready!'

In the TS, and in the control top where the lieutenant (G) hunched tensely at a binocular sight, and in the director tower where the director layer had his eye at the cross-wired telescope and a hand hovering close to the firing key, four out of eight 'gun ready' lights glowed brightly as in each of the four fifteen-inch turrets the crews stood by one loaded and cocked gun.

Brook, the gunnery lieutenant, who'd already had the order from Captain Everard to commence firing, spoke clearly and unexcitedly into the mouthpiece of his telephone-set.

'Fire.'

The director layer waited a split second, until his sights rolled on. Then he pressed the key.

Moorsom, one of the tenth flotilla destroyers, had closed up astern of *Lanyard* so that the port column of the thirteenth flotilla now consisted of *Nestor*, *Nomad*, *Nicator*, *Lanyard*, *Moorsom*. It was twelve minutes past four. Almost unbelievably, that meant it was less than two hours since the first enemy report had been made by *Galatea*.

A long way astern, perhaps almost ten miles, the Fifth Battle Squadron was in action. One could hear nothing, of course, at such a distance and when the noise here was so great and so constant, but one could see the Queen Elizabeths back there in a grey clump hazed by smoke that was pierced intermittently by the spurting scarlet flashes of their guns. With binoculars you could also see their fall of shot. The fifteen-inch shells made such enormous splashes that there was no question of confusing them with the battle cruisers' smaller-calibre projectiles, and it looked as if they were straddling and hitting with impressive frequency. Their first salvoes had fallen short, but now they'd found the range and the Germans must have been feeling the effects unpleasantly; in fact the enemy rate and accuracy of fire had fallen off, or seemed to have, and the third ship in their line was clearly burning. The British battle cruisers had suffered badly enough, meanwhile; *Lion* had had the roof of one of her turrets blown clean off, and all the ships had been punished, hit time and time again. But no one would have guessed it from a quick inspection now – no one who hadn't seen the shells hitting, or didn't know that where five ships steamed now there'd been six ten minutes ago.

'Signal from *Champion*, sir!'

Garret had his glasses up, but hardly needed them. That signal whipping from the light cruiser's yard was one familiar to all destroyer men. It was the order they longed for, dreamt about.

'*Flotilla will attack the enemy with torpedoes, sir!*'

'Number One! Tell Chief I'll be calling for full power!'

'Aye aye, sir!'

Johnson started yelling into the engine-room voicepipe, and at the same time he was beckoning to Nick to come for'ard ... 'Chief? Full power any second now. We'll be carrying out a torpedo attack on enemy battle cruisers. You'll—'

Interruption. Something about fuel? Johnson cut in again: 'Just everything we've got, Chief. *Everything*.' He straightened, nodding to Mortimer. Then he looked at Nick. 'Sub, listen. When we—'

Garret called, '*Champion* to thirteenth flotilla, Sir: *Speed thirty knots – three-oh knots*, sir!'

'Very good.'

'Sub,' Johnson turned sideways, blocking one ear with his palm; Reynolds was bawling into a voicepipe to Pilkington, the torpedo gunner. Johnson told Nick, 'What'll happen is this. We'll push on ahead a mile or two first, and then—'

'Executive signal for thirty knots, sir!'

Mortimer was shouting now, on Nick's other side, for increased revolutions. It would be a relief to Worsfold, the engineer; *Lanyard* could manage thirty easily enough. Johnson yelled, 'When we're far enough ahead we'll haul away to port and aim for a spot out there somewhere.' He was pointing ahead and into the no-man's-land between the

British and German squadrons. 'Up there on the Hun's bow, you see, for the attack. But when he sees what's happening, the Hun'll almost certainly send a flotilla or two out to meet us halfway. Perhaps light cruisers too. Understand?'

Nick nodded. *Lanyard* had the shakes again; thirty knots, and the whole flotilla in its three line-ahead divisions was racing forward on *Champion*'s heels. The first lieutenant told him, pitching his voice high above the din of increasing speed and of battle from astern, 'There'll be some high-speed gunnery before we can launch our torpedoes. Impossible to say which side the action'll develop on. Most likely both sides at once. You'll just have to watch out and shift fron side to side; it'll be too fast for me to control from here.' He stared at him questioningly. All right?'

It was as 'all right', Nick thought, as it ever would be. The tight feeling in his stomach wasn't anything to take notice of; nor had the appalling dryness in his mouth anything to do with what was going on. Such fear as one was conscious of was – well, ninety per cent of it – was fear of not measuring-up, not doing the thing right.

Suddenly that mattered more than anything had ever mattered in his life.

Chapter 5

'Destroyers of the 13th Flotilla . . . having been ordered to attack the enemy when opportunity offered, moved out at 4.15 pm simultaneously with a similar movement on the part of the enemy. The attack was carried out in the most gallant manner and with great determination . . .'

From Vice-Admiral Sir David Beatty's report to
Commander-in-Chief

Champion was flying the signal for the port column, this division, to attack, and over Nick's head at the after end of the bridge *Lanyard*'s answering pendant thrashed enthusiastically at the yardarm. Ahead, *Nicator*, *Nomad* and the divisional leader *Nestor* also had their pendants close-up; astern, *Moorsom*'s ran up now.

Mortimer was hugging the binnacle in an ape-like stance with his arms spread and hooked around the spheres. Reynolds was making an adjustment to the port torpedo sight. Johnson, close to Nick on the port side farther aft, was looking through his binoculars at the head of the German line.

Behind them, Garret's yell was like a seagull's screech:

'Executive, sir!'

That signal had dropped from *Champion*'s yard; a new one climbing off the other side would be the order for the next division, the centre column, to follow this one. Mortimer, in that hunched-up position, had his face right down on the voicepipe, and he'd called down to the quartermaster for full power before Garret had had time to haul in the answering pendant. *Nestor* had put her helm over and she was careering away to port, leaning to the turn and digging her bow deep, flinging back a bow-wave like a great white scarf streaming from a runner's throat, the wave lengthening and curling aft down her sleek black side and her wash sluicing away in a heaped-up curve of foam with *Nomad*'s stem sheering into it, and then *Nicator*'s into hers; and now it was *Lanyard*'s turn, Mortimer shouting 'Starboard twenty!' into increasing noise as the stoke-hold fans roared and her speed built up. Nick grasped for handholds on the base of the searchlight platform to steady himself against the force of the turn and the suddenly slanting deck, the sharp heel to starboard as she swung fast to port; Garret, coiling halyards with the pendant bundled temporarily under one arm, lurched round and crashed against him, muttered terse apologies as he struggled back up the sloping deck. But she was levelling again now, straightening into the straight lines of the other destroyers' wakes. Reynolds shouted into a voicepipe close to the torpedo sight, 'Stand by all tubes!' His voice, snatched away by the wind, was sharp and thin. Nobody had said anything about the guns yet; Nick was watching Johnson, who had his glasses up again to stare out over miles of grey-green sea to the dark shapes and heavy smoke-trails of Hipper's battle cruisers.

'Ah!' – Johnson from . . . *Lanyard*'s funnels were pouring smoke; it curled down to brush the welter of sea astern, stream over *Moorsom* and spread wider, drifting in the slow-moving haze of all five destroyers' smoke; it might just help to hide the next division until they burst through it, perhaps confuse the picture to German eyes. The distance between

Lanyard and *Nicator* seemed constant so far, although down below there Worsfold and his engine-room staff must have been squeezing every ounce of pressure out of her. The sounds of battle were only a distant thunder now; the noise that ruled here was all ship-noise, sea-noise, wind-rush, the turbines' scream and the fans' roar and the thrum of vibration in the destroyer's plates, mast, rigging: not separate sounds, but one great orchestra of movement urgency.

'Take a look. But be *quick*!'

Johnson was holding the binoculars out towards Nick. He took them, leant back against the searchlight mounting to steady himself on the jolting bridge. It didn't work: the mounting, solid as it appeared to be, was shaking like everything else. The only way was to balance on feet spread well apart and avoid contact with bridge fittings. He saw what Johnson had wanted him to see, had prophesied; a flotilla of destroyers was moving out from the head of the enemy battle cruiser line. The counter-move. Judging by the smoke pluming astern of them, they were moving, like this flotilla, at high speed.

Nick nodded as he handed the glasses back. The first lieutenant stooped slightly to shout into his ear. 'Set the gunsights at ten thousand yards and I'll tell you when to open fire.' He pointed at the Barr and Stroud transmitter dials; 'I'll give you the early ranges too, on the leading ships. After that you'll have to select your own targets and carry on in "rapid independent". Understand?'

'Aye aye, sir.'

He was anxious to get on with it, do it instead of talk about it. Johnson pointed: 'Looks like we'll have 'em approaching on the starboard bow, unless they cross over. Their object'll be to force us to turn away – which of course we shan't do.' He grinned. 'Down you go, Sub.'

Nick wondered, as he climbed down the ladder, its metal runners singing like guitar-strings, whether that had been the first real smile he'd ever seen on Johnson's face. He couldn't remember seeing one before. Was this – action – what *everybody* lived for? Down here on the destroyer's upper deck the ship's motion, the sensation of her battering herself to destruction against sea, wind, and her own reluctance to move at such a speed, was even more pronounced than it had been up on the bridge. The sea's surface was so much closer, the steel of the deck less remote from the actual motion than the bridge was, stuck up there on top of it. The highest curve of the bow-wave was higher than the actual deck, so that one felt less 'on' the sea than 'in' it: and the sound of the sea matched that of the ship, like the sound of a mill-race magnified a dozen times ... Nick moved aft, past the slung whaler and the foremost funnel, and up on to the raised platform of the midships four-inch gun.

'Layer! Leading Seaman Hooper?'

'Sir!' Hooper was a tall, thin sailor, stooped and narrow-shouldered, with a strangely triangular, narrow-eyed face. On his left arm he wore the killick-emblem of a leading hand above two good-conduct badges; on his right, the crossed gun-barrels and star of a gunlayer. He'd been peering over the top of the gunshield while the rest of the gun's crew stood waiting in its shelter ... From the bridge, Johnson timed it perfectly: as Hooper and his men turned towards Nick, the buzzer sounded. Hooper ducked to his receivers, and a second later shouted the order 'Load!'

Nick stood back and watched. He saw that the shot-ready racks and cartridge racks had already been uncovered; shells lay nose-down, their brass bases gleaming. The number three snatched out the first one and slid it into the open breech; number four – a stout, one-badge seaman with tattoos on the backs of his hands loaded a cartridge in behind it; number two – young, fresh-faced, no badges – slammed the breech shut.

'Ready!'

They all looked cheerful, eager. Nick checked the readings on the receivers against those on the sights: range ten thousand – on the dial that looked like a hundred – and deflection fifty right. It might become more, firing at a destroyer going flat-out in the opposite direction; at the full rate of crossing it could be at least sixty knots. But they'd most likely be approaching at an angle.

'Layer. Here a minute.' Out beside the gunshield, standing in the platform's saucer-shaped rim, Nick found he could just see the oncoming German boats. They were pointing straight at the thirteenth flotilla now, while in the distance way behind them, several miles farther away and indistinct in the smoke-haze left by the speeding enemy destroyers, Hipper's battle cruisers still pressed southwards.

'See 'em there?'

'Aye, sir!' Hooper grinned. 'I got me eye on 'em!'

'You'll get your open-fire order from the bridge. Follow receivers to start with, but when they're really close you'll have to shift from target to target and make your own corrections. Right?'

'Aye aye, sir!'

He dropped down to the upper deck and headed aft, to see that the quarterdeck gun's crew knew what was happening. Passing the ventilators, the roar of fans was almost deafening. It wasn't much short of a miracle that *Lanyard* was keeping up with the more modern N-class boats ahead of her; under his feet – in the engine-room and in the two boiler-rooms which he'd just passed over – was where that miracle was being worked.

He looked astern, and saw *Moorsom*, well back from her station. She'd lost a cable's length since he'd left the bridge. Beyond her – but not far beyond – the second division of the flotilla was coming flat-out on this division's heels. If *Moorsom* didn't watch out, they'd soon be overhauling her. Between him and those ships astern and in the same line of sight *Lanyard*'s wake was piled like a great heap of snow, higher than her counter; it managed the trick of staying that high while at the same time it melted constantly away.

'Hey, Sub!'

Mr Pilkington, the gunner (T), was peering down at Nick from the searchlight platform between the two sets of tubes, the for'ard pair of which had been trained out to starboard and the after pair to port. Pilkington looked weird: at the best of times he had a gnome-like appearance – small, short-legged, with a large head and fiercely bristling eyebrows – and now he'd jammed his cap so hard down that its peak was almost covering his eyes. Nick nodded to him, 'About a dozen Hun destroyers, Mr Pilkington.'

'So we bin told, Sub,' the gunner nodded. 'An' so I seen. What I want you to tell me, 'owever, is would there be a light cruiser wi' em, leader sort o' thing?'

Had there been one larger shape, to the right of the flotilla, in support of it?

'There might be. I—'

'Might be!' Pilkington stared skywards, muttering his dissatisfaction. Now he was looking down – for sympathy perhaps – at his torpedo gunner's mate, an outsize petty officer squatting toad-like between the tubes of the for'ard mounting. The same position on the after tubes was occupied by a leading torpedo-man, while the number twos, lacking fixed seats, leant beside their training handwheels. Nick moved on aft, and found that the stern gun was loaded and had the right settings on its sights. He explained the general situation and intentions to Stapleton, the grey-haired gunlayer, a three-badge able seaman. Stapleton told Nick, pointing along the barrel of his gun – it was trained round as far for'ard as it would go – 'First customer's pretty near in range now, sir.'

It was a fact. But *Nestor*, *Nomad* and *Nicator* would be the first to open fire; there'd be that much forewarning. Looking for'ard there, *Nomad* was in sight out to starboard, on what was going to be the engaged side; and she was closer, as if she'd fallen back, perhaps changing places with *Nicator*? Or she might have swung over to try a long torpedo shot at the battle cruiser line before the German flotillas got in the way ... Nick looked around him, checking that the ammunition-supply party was ready with the trap open. It was a circular hatch in the deck behind the gun, and it led down into the wardroom, which was the compartment immediately underneath. There was a similar trap in the deck of the wardroom, and below that were the after four-inch magazine and shell-room; the ammunition was passed up through the first hatch and through the wardroom, where a sailor on a steel ladder pushed it through to the supply ratings here on the upper deck. There were half a dozen of them, since the cartridges and projectiles had to be delivered to the midships gun as well as to this one.

And they ought to get some up there now, not wait for the midships gun to empty its shot-ready racks ... He told the leading seaman who was in charge of the party, 'Get a dozen rounds up amidships, before the shooting starts.' He saw the movement start; a shout down through the hatch, and shells coming up, it was like pressing a switch and starting an automatic process ... 'Sub-Lieutenant, sir!'

A bridge messenger. 'First Lieutenant says, when we engage the enemy would you start the upper deck fire-main, sir.'

'Right.'

'Shall I stand by it, sir?'

Why not. And then report back to the bridge. As Stapleton had observed, the fight would be starting at any moment now. He told the messenger, 'Yes, please.' But there was no sign of the enemy destroyers now: he started looking out on the port bow, thinking they might be crossing ahead; or perhaps this division had altered course just slightly, putting the Germans dead ahead? The purpose of opening the fire-main would be to have a continuous flood of water over the upper deck, thus making it less easy for fires to start. Nick wondered whether Johnson had had the boats' tarpaulin covers filled with water too. Strangely, it seemed quite

natural, now, to be going into action. As if one had done it
before, and knew all about it. Maybe because one had
imagined it so often, in one's daydreams, since the age of ten
or so?

Crashes were coming suddenly from ahead. *Nestor*, he
guessed, had opened fire. More gunfire now, quite rapid, and
the wind into which *Lanyard* was thrusting had a stench of
cordite in it. Ammunition, he noticed, was flowing for'ard
smoothly. But that tightness had returned to the pit of his
stomach: it was infuriating, he'd thought he'd got rid of it:
he told himself, *Ignore it. Probably just physical, it's not* –
A waterspout leapt, shattering the introspection; a second
one; no, *three* – forty or fifty yards abeam to starboard, and
still no enemy in sight; the gun was trained to its foremost
stop and there was nothing for it yet to bear on. It sounded
like the two leading destroyers firing now, the crashes were
too frequent to come from just one ship. The ammunition
party had come to a halt again, having built up supplies at
the other gun. Nick went inside the cover of the gunshield
and stood behind Stapleton to see what, if anything, might
be coming through on the receivers from the bridge. To his
surprise, the range was showing as 060 – six thousand yards
– well inside effective range. He went out again. He was out
there just in time to see the stern gun of the next ship ahead
fire on a for'ard bearing, and a second later he saw the
leading German destroyer sweep into sight. The Hun must
have been right ahead, or almost right ahead, and now swung
a point or two to port to pass on a more or less parallel but
reciprocal course to the British flotilla, which meant, if he
held that course and the ships astern of him did too, they'd
be shooting at each other as they passed at something like
point-blank range. *Lanyard*'s bow gun fired, Nick opened
his mouth to shout to Stapleton, and thunder cracked right
beside him as the gunlayer let rip without waiting for an
order. The midships gun had opened up too. There were
three enemy in sight now; Nick could see the flashes of their

guns, hear the almost continuous shooting from the thirteenth flotilla ships ahead, see waterspouts all round the
Germans and the glow of hits too; the orange flare of
bursting shells and black smoke streaming aft. The leading
destroyer had been hit two or three times and she was
swinging away, her bow down and her bridge – no, her
waist, between the funnels – pouring black smoke. The
range was about four thousand yards now and water was
sluicing over *Lanyard*'s iron deck, her guns firing as fast as
they could load and fire again, the deflection increasing as
the distance lessened and the bow-on angle opened. You got
used to noise; it became simply what you had around you.
Shell-splashes surrounded the next-ahead. This was *Nomad*,
not *Nicator*, for some reason they'd swapped places and
Lanyard was swinging out to starboard suddenly, closing-up
on *Nomad* as if Mortimer intended passing her. Well, *she'd*
gone out to port, or *Lanyard* had swung to starboard, before
this – otherwise she wouldn't have been in sight from aft
here. And she'd been hit: amidships, where her boilers were.
Lanyard raced past her as she slowed; the action was all to
starboard and the leading German destroyer – no, the
second, the first was out of it, she'd turned away and
stopped, she was still being hit and she looked as if she was
sinking: the nearest German was less than fifteen hundred
yards away, all her guns blazing. The ammunition party's
leading seaman was bawling down into the hatch: Nick saw
that the flow of shells had stopped, this gun's crew snatching
what they needed from the ready-use racks. Nick stooped,
yelled in the man's ear, 'What is it?' His face turned,
mouthing something frantically, his words lost in gun
crashes and the screech and explosions of enemy projectiles. Nick repeated his question, and this time he got an
answer that he could hear, 'Tryin' to find out, sir, they don't
seem—'

Enemy destroyers abeam now, point-blank, waterspouts
all round, the gaff with the ensign on it shot away and

hanging, but *Lanyard* had been lucky, *Nomad* was stopped back there astern and someone was using her for target-practice. Nick had an idea that *Lanyard* had been hit for'ard; meanwhile her own guns had sent number four in the German destroyer line reeling out to port and listing. The guns' crews were cheering as he flung himself into the deckhouse over the wardroom hatchway; he took the ladder in a single leap and crashed in through the latched-back wardroom door. He saw the trouble at a glance. The ladder to the ammo exit had come adrift, so they hadn't been able to reach that deck-head hatch, and the two men who comprised the supply-link in here – stokers, he saw, by their insignia, and both very young – were struggling frantically to fix it. The bar which ran through its top and through two eye-bolts in the deckhead by the trap hadn't been pushed through properly, so one end had come out and it had buckled. What they were trying to do was hopeless. Nick told them, 'Leave it. Get the table under, and that chair on the table, quick now!' They'd jumped to obey him. Remembering Johnson's remark about new hands in the supply party he wondered whether they'd been trained at all. He helped them slide the table into place; then the chair was on it, and one of them up there while the other handed up ammunition from the lower hatch. Nick saw the stream re-started, then he ran for the ladder to the upper deck.

Halfway up it, the blast hit him. There was a moment before he realised that he'd been knocked backwards off the ladder. Dazed, bruised, scrambling back to it and starting up again. Torpedo? The explosion had been big enough. It was already, within seconds, indistinct in his memory, but it seemed to have taken time, to have had a certain duration to it. Behind him a voice asked, 'What's happened? What was that?' Nick looked back and downwards, and saw the surgeon, Samuels. The dressing-station and emergency operating theatre was Mortimer's cabin, a dozen steps from the ladder's foot; but ten minutes ago Samuels had been up near the midships four-inch; Nick had seen him there, just before the action started, when he'd been talking to Hooper.

'I don't know yet.'

At the top of the ladder he found that the steel hutch, the superstructure over it, had changed shape, its vertical walls concave, pushed in by the blast. He could hear guns firing, but the stern four-inch wasn't – wasn't *there*! The deck was ripped where gun and mounting had been torn off it. Jagged, upturned edges of the deck itself, and littered wreckage of steel that might have been twisted around in giant hands and then flung down and stamped on. And there'd been men in it when that had happened, there were bodies and parts of bodies held in it, like animals caught in traps. The rush of water from the fire-main entered this strewn, smashed area as clear water and flowed out bright red.

Samuels stood beside him, clutching his dark, curly head between both hands . . . 'My God, what *did* this?'

'Sir, I—'

A torpedoman – the number two of the after tubes. Bent sideways as he staggered aft, holding his left side: all blood, ripped cloth and flesh. 'I been 'it, sir, I—'

Samuels caught him as he fell. Nick felt as if he woke up at that moment; to the fact that the action was at its hottest and no ammunition could be getting to the midships gun. Also that those jagged holes in the deck, which were above the store compartments immediately aft of the wardroom, had water from the fire-main pouring into them; the fire-main had to be shut off. Ammunition for that gun was what mattered most. He crouched down beside the trap; the deck around it had been scoured, grooved, its bare steel shone like silver. One of the young stokers peered at him through the hole and began, 'Sir, is—'

'Ready, sir, they're wantin' it!'

Whipping round, Nick found two of the ammunition supply party; they must have just returned from delivering shot to the midships gun. He'd thought of them all as being dead. Nick told the stoker down below, 'Come on then, get it moving!' He stood up, and one of the two sailors said, 'It all begun to come up fast, sudden like, faster 'n we could take it from 'em. I reckon a shell hit a lot of 'em as was stood there, sir.' The other man looked winded, sick. Nick grasped his arm, and told them both, 'Only two of you now. You'll just have to damn well run with it.' The surgeon's helpers, one sick berth attendant and one cook, had come up to help; they were carrying the wounded torpedo man down through the hatch, all three of them soaked already in his blood. As Nick started for'ard a shell dropped alongside, exploding as it hit the water. He heard the rattle of splinters on the ship's side and the whirr of others whizzing past and overhead, but all that hit him was a douche of black, foul-smelling water. He located the fire-main, and shut it off. He headed for Pilkington now, who had the use of the searchlight crew's voicepipe to the bridge. The noise had slackened, there was still a lot of gunfire but it seemed to be all astern. 'Mr Pilkington!'

'What, you still alive?' Crouching on the platform, the torpedo gunner had only glanced down briefly. He had his torpedo-firing disc in his hand. Nick asked him, 'Would you tell the first lieutenant – stern four-inch blown overboard, crew all killed and—'

'Bloody 'ell I will!' Mr Pilkington's small eyes gleamed with anger under the jammed-down peak of his cap. 'Fill up the voicepipe wi' bloody chatter?' He stood up, pointing out on the port bow and yelling down to his beefy TGM, 'Port side only, one an' two tubes only, get 'em round!' Looking round just as the midships four-inch fired, Nick saw a shell-splash leap up astern of what must have been the last of the German flotilla. Farther back and broader on the quarter he could see two others stopped and sinking; the after part of one of them was on fire. How long had the whole action taken, from start to finish? Four, five minutes? *Lanyard* was still steaming flat out, the roar of her fans unchanged, funnel-smoke pouring astern thick and black. He could see three, four – no, *five* more destroyers following astern there, their guns still engaging the German boats: and the Germans seemed to be fanning out, disengaging. They'd still have the thirteenth flotilla's starboard division ahead of them, of course, and it was possible they'd had enough. He climbed up behind the midships gun; there was nothing for it to shoot at now, and as the supply party came panting to and fro with charges and projectiles they were refilling the ready-racks. Nick told Hooper, 'Train round to the other side. We'll be turning to starboard in a minute to fire torpedoes.' The Barr and Stroud, he saw, was showing a range of 080. He told the gunlayer as the four-inch pivoted round through the stern bearing and up the other side, 'Set range oh-eight-oh—' Shells screeched overhead. He finished, 'And deflection zero.' Shell-splashes went up astern. Shellfire was thickening now, the noise of it rising and the sea spouting like a pond from heavy rain, the air alive with the scrunch and screech of overs. He felt *Lanyard* begin her turn, deck tilting, screws pounding, wake curving crescent-like to starboard. A range of 080 meant eight thousand yards, four sea miles; good torpedo range but hardly a comfortable distance at which to loiter round five German battle cruisers whose secondary armament of six-inch guns was reserved exclusively for just such moments. Each of those ships had six six-inch on each side, which meant that now *Nestor* and *Nicator* had made their runs there'd be no less than thirty six-inch banging away at *Lanyard*. A clanging crash came from the foc'sl and a smoke-cloud that flew aft and left a stink of high-explosive as it passed told of a hit for'ard. Now water rained down from some near miss or misses, and Nick saw the Germans suddenly as the destroyer's bow swung and they came into view while her turn continued until she was broadside-on to all of them – a sitting duck, and the deck's slant lessening as Mortimer eased her helm, levelling her for the convenience of Mr Pilkington and his torpedoes. The enemy was five vast

silver-grey juggernauts with what looked like a hundred
guns spitting fire and fury under a long, unbroken shroud of
funnel-smoke; Hooper was firing steadily as *Lanyard* still
swung and his gunsight travelled from the third in the line,
past the second, to the leader – Hipper's flagship. Nick
shouted in the gunlayer's ear, 'Bridge! Aim at her bridge!'
A hit on the person of Vice-Admiral Hipper with a four-inch
QF Mark IV might be worth scoring. But it was hard to see
now through the density of shell-spouts and falling spray. A
piece of the for'ard funnel suddenly flared, smoked, flew
away in the wind and fell astern, and the gun was training
slowly aft now – faster – Hooper keeping the flagship's
bridge as his point of aim. There'd been no sign of any
torpedo hit, but Nick realised that while ten seconds ago the
big ships' firing had been rising to a hideous, merciless
crescendo – he'd thought, as they hit that funnel, *Now this
can't last* – it had just as suddenly slackened off. And the
German ships were turning! Swinging away together to
port, to avoid *Lanyard*'s torpedo. *Lanyard*, eight hundred
tons, making a whole squadron of twenty-five-thousand-ton
battle cruisers turn away! Then he saw the error in that
boast, for it wasn't only *Lanyard*, but here were three – no,
four others racing in, perhaps more, at this moment out of his
view. The situation wasn't orderly, there were ships here,
there and everywhere . . . and *Petard* seemed about to cross
astern as she swung over to make her attack; Nick shouted
to Hooper to hold his fire.

Nile's broadsides roared again: and since the Fifth Battle
Squadron had opened fire fifteen minutes ago there was little
doubt that the enemy were suffering. To start with, the
screening cruisers had been sent scurrying; now *Moltke* and
Von der Tann had both been hard hit and their rates of fire
reduced, and it looked as if the leading ships of the squadron
were reaching *Seydlitz* now as well. Hugh Everard swung his
glasses to the left, to what had been the battlefield and was

now once again just a grey acreage of North Sea. There, well abaft the battle squadron's port beam now, a sailing barque – tall, square-rigged – lay becalmed with all sails set. A lovely craft; a peaceful, restful and utterly incongruous sight, a total contrast to the destructive violence which during the last half-hour had thundered past on either side of her, shells hurtling in their low trajectory over her white, idle sails. With his glasses resting on her for a moment, Hugh found himself thinking of Sarah. No, not thinking of her, but forming a picture of her in his mind; her smile and her calm, friendly manner; a combination of vulnerability and quiet self-confidence. The vulnerability was something one saw oneself, of course, because when one thought of her one tended to have *him* in mind. How she'd accepted him in the first place was – well, there was no answer to it! John could turn on his charm, of course, and hide his more natural attributes. And he was a baronet, which would have delighted Buchanan, who would have used his influence . . .

Nile's guns crashed out again, just as a close pattern of German shells thumped into the sea sixty yards short. Nothing had touched *Nile* yet, and there'd been no hits so far on any of the ships ahead of her. All the shells fired at this squadron had fallen short, while their own fifteen-inch guns had had the range to hit the two rearmost Germans time and time again. The range was closing now, though, as the lines converged, and before long one might expect a taste of one's own medicine, a share of the hammering which Beatty's ships had been enduring for about forty minutes – a hammering which Beatty had positively invited by rushing in without waiting for this squadron. But meanwhile, with Rathbone piloting *Nile* in *Malaya*'s wake, and Brook up in the control top sending salvo after salvo thundering from her guns, there wasn't a great deal for her captain to be doing.

He thought he might tell Sarah, one day, how the sight of that becalmed sailing-ship had turned his thoughts to her in the middle of a battle . . .

Extraordinary, that one could reach years of discretion and still behave like an adolescent. Blurting that out to her, as he had yesterday . . .

Damn it, I meant it! I feel it now!

As she must too. Otherwise, would she have telegraphed an answer to his letter, to arrange a meeting? Well, *would* she?

He bit his lip. He'd got cold feet, that was all. He'd begun to express a fraction of what he felt for her, and then baulked at it, backed off. Career? And the idea of stealing his brother's wife? *Morality?* Where was the morality in leaving her in John's hands, for God's sake?

Tom Crick touched his arm.

'Sir.'

Drawing his attention, privately, to something on the starboard bow . . . To Beatty's ships – fine on the bow, almost right ahead. Hugh raised his glasses and focused them on the battle cruisers – still some five miles distant, still pressing southward, their guns flinging out a brownish cordite haze that mingled with clouds of heavier funnel-smoke.

He saw what Crick was showing him. Twenty minutes ago, *Indefatigable* had blown up. Now he was watching the same thing happen to *Queen Mary*. A dull, red glow faded almost before he'd seen it: another glow spread for'ard: her hull was opening, expanding outwards, and as he watched – hardly letting himself believe he was seeing it – her masts and funnels toppled inward, as if a great pit had been opened for them to fall into. Then the eruption: he saw the roofs of all four turrets blow up like corks from bottles: smoke spread, built up, a column piling, rising in great circling folds to a height of about a thousand feet. The ship astern of her had vanished into that vast cloud's base: they'd be in darkness, pieces of their sister-ship would be raining down around them as they steamed through the stench of her destruction.

Like *Indefatigable*, *Queen Mary* would have taken about

a thousand men with her to the bottom. Some would have been trapped, and at this moment still alive, not even knowing yet what had happened ...

Jellicoe, Hugh thought, must be getting close now. *Please God, lend him speed: Beatty has already lost his battle.*

'Signal, sir!'

Hugh took the clip-board from his chief yeoman's hand.

Jellicoe had given Beatty this Fifth Battle Squadron to support him, and Beatty had stupidly or arrogantly (or *both* adverbs might apply) left it astern and taken Hipper on alone. All right, so there must obviously be some structural defect that allowed the battle cruisers to fall such easy victims to a few hits, but they *were* lightly armoured, as Beatty well knew, and if the Queen Elizabeths had been with them the German fire would have been spread over more targets, and the German gunners would have had a much less easy time of it, because there'd have been fifteen-inch salvoes pouring down on them.

Over there in the German line, they'd be cheering themselves hoarse now.

Sick at heart, he gave his attention to the signal. It was from senior officer Second Light Cruiser Squadron – which meant Commodore Goodenough in *Southampton* and addressed to C-in-C and FO, BCF. The message, prefixed URGENT, read: *Have sighted enemy battle fleet bearing approximately south-east. Course of enemy north. My position lat 56 degs 34' N long 6 degs 20' E. Time 4.38 pm.*

Hugh looked up at Crick. He told him, 'Scheer's coming north with the High Seas Fleet. He's already almost on top of Beatty.'

'Flag signal flying from *Lion*, sir!'

Midshipman Ross-Hallet had reported it. The chief yeoman whipped his telescope to his eye as he hurried out to the bridge's starboard wing. It wasn't an easy string of flags to read, at a distance of five miles and with the flags blowing this way, end-on, and in smoke.

'What's he saying, Peppard?'

More shells were falling just short of them.

'Can't quite make—' The chief yeoman's face was screwed up in concentration. Yeoman Brannon, one of his four assistants, was beside him with another telescope. 'Looks like an alter-in-succession signal, sir, but—'

'It's coming down.' Hugh was behind the binnacle, where Rathbone had made room for him, and he had his binoculars trained on Beatty's ships. 'Doesn't matter, Peppard. He *is* turning.'

The battle cruisers were going-about, reversing course, by the looks of it. And in the circumstances, Hugh thought, that was wise enough. In fact there was nothing else Beatty could have done – short of committing suicide with all his ships and men. But there was more to it than just survival. Just as Jellicoe, misled by the Admiralty, hadn't known Scheer was at sea, so the probability was that Admiral Scheer had not the slightest idea that Jellicoe was either. Certainly not that the Grand Fleet was only fifty miles away, and coming closer at every minute. He couldn't know, because if he did he'd be steaming south, not north!

Jellicoe steaming south at, say, twenty knots – of which his slowest battleships were capable – and the ships here going north at twenty-five; in an hour, there'd be no gap! But Scheer and Hipper must be thinking they had Beatty trapped and running for his life; they could hardly guess he'd be leading them into a *British* trap.

The four surviving battle cruisers had completed their northwards turn; they were returning this way, now, towards the Fifth Battle Squadron, which Evan-Thomas was still leading south. Beatty had had quite a mauling; no doubt he wanted the more powerful battleships astern of him, where the brunt of the fighting would now be. That was reasonable and fair. Unlike the battle cruisers, these super-dreadnoughts were armoured to take punishment as well as gunned to hand it out.

'Rathbone.' Hugh passed his navigator the clip of signals. 'Put the last one on the plot, will you.'

'Sir.'

'You know, Tom—' he kept his eyes on *Malaya*, the next ahead – 'this is an odd situation. Scheer thinks he's got Beatty's goose cooked. Whereas with any sort of luck, he's practically in the oven himself!'

Crick pulled thoughtfully at an ear. 'Let's hope so, sir.'

Geoff Garret held on to the rail in the starboard after corner of *Lanyard*'s bridge and wondered how long he'd live.

It was necessary, vitally necessary now, that he should survive; but could Fate or the Almighty be counted on to recognise the necessity?

Blood – not just stains, but pools of it – in certain parts of the bridge suggested that no particular element of Divine protection was being extended over this destroyer. Against that, one might take comfort from the theory that lightning never struck twice in the same place. He told himself, *Best not to think about it. Me going soft won't help her.*

Ahead of *Lanyard*, *Nestor* and *Nicator* zigzagged to and fro, dodging like snipe; *Lanyard* followed in the water they'd slashed and churned, whipping to and fro just as wildly, under almost constant helm one way or the other, salvo-dodging, flinging herself from tack to tack so savagely that she was permanently on her beam ends, her deck bucking as she flung herself from side to side while the pair ahead were often hidden from sight in foam, spray, the height of their own wakes and the spouts of German shells – and battleships' shells now. The Hun dreadnoughts had only hove into sight ten minutes ago, when *Lanyard* and her two N-class consorts had been heading westward to rejoin Beatty's force, and Geoff Garret had read in other faces that he wasn't the only one who felt distinctly relieved, at that point, to be getting out from under. But relief hadn't lasted long. *Nestor* had suddenly veered out to port and begun flashing to the two boats astern of her. Garret, as he concentrated on reading the first words of *Nestor*'s morse, had heard Sub-Lieutenant Hastings exclaim: 'It's the Fifth Battle Squadron, sir. They're off on our port bow now!' After the attack, the turning and twisting to and fro, he'd been confused, as most were; whichever way you looked the sea was grey, planted here and there with groups of ships or single ships at varying distances, with patches and streaks of smoke. Those three German destroyers, for instance, two of them sinking, and *Nomad*, whom they'd had to leave, shrouded in steam escaping from her shattered boiler-rooms . . . Hastings had thought that line of big ships which had just shown themselves out of the mistier section of the horizon were the Queen Elizabeths, but the misconception was quickly dispelled. *Nestor*'s signal said *Enemy battle fleet bearing S.S.E. Intend attacking with remaining torpedoes.*

Garret had read it, calling the words out one by one as he clashed the shutter of the searchlight to acknowledge them; and during the recital of the last few words, he'd begun to wonder whether the intention which was being expressed could possibly be in his own best interests.

He'd never thought in such terms before. He'd been in action three or four times, in another boat down in the Harwich flotilla, and he'd always rather enjoyed it, same as most of the lads did. You couldn't swing round an anchor or prop up a jetty and hope to win the war; fighting was what the fleet was *for*. But he'd changed. He felt entirely different. Part of his unease was that he recognised the change and disliked it; he was uncomfortable, and the fact he was uncomfortable made him more uncomfortable.

Returning a wink from Blewitt, Garret hoped his fear didn't show. He wished he could recover the sense of excitement and anticipation he'd felt when they'd had the signal about altering course to go after the enemy. He wasn't the same man now that he'd been then.

There was a six-foot hole in the port fore corner of the

bridge. There'd been steps there and a door; now it was just a pit. And three men were dead. Two of the for'ard gun's crew had been wounded, and soon after that there'd been an enormous explosion aft. It had felt and sounded like a torpedo hit. Number One had tried to find out what had happened but the voicepipes didn't work, and then he'd been busy with the for'ard gun and Blewitt's machine. It had been during the run-in to fire torpedoes that a German light cruiser's shell had smashed into that corner where the bridge connected, with three steps down and a wooden door and a short ladder inside, with the steering position. The blast went both ways: it killed the coxswain, CPO Cuthbertson, at the wheel, and Lieutenant Johnson and Lieutenant Reynolds in the bridge, and a splinter from it had cut the throat of the bridge messenger, aft on the other side.

Entrance to the lower bridge – the steering position – was through that hole now. The second coxswain had brought up a rope ladder and rigged it there.

'Hard a-starboard!'

'Hard a-starboard, sir!'

Geordie Alan was on the wheel now. He'd pulled the coxswain off it, and taken over. *Lanyard* stood on her ear as she skidded round to port, with her captain clinging to the binnacle and watching for the fall of shot; he'd order the wheel over as soon as he saw shell-spouts rise; he seemed to head *towards* each salvo.

'Midships! Meet her!'

'Meet her, sir!'

Pandemonium: the ship was jolting, crashing, swinging from side to side: you braced yourself – then you had to shift, brace differently as she flung over the other way. Mortimer had somehow jammed his body at the binnacle, and looked nowhere except ahead, at the grey shapes of the enemy with their white bow-waves looking big now as the distance lessened, and at the destroyers ahead, and the splashes of shells scrunching down right, left and – Mortimer never saw the overs, because he never looked astern.

'Hard a-port!'

'Hard a-port, sir!' The for'ard gun fired; it couldn't shoot much, with the other two destroyers in the line of fire half the time and *Lanyard* doing acrobatics when they weren't. No gunlayer on earth could have kept his sights on, the way she was throwing herself about. Near-misses shot up close to port as she sheered away to starboard; they'd gone in the drink but you felt the blow of them, and water cascaded black across the bridge. Filthy reek lingering . . .

'Midships! Starboard twenty!'

Nestor was performing a long swing to starboard. Shell-spouts hid her, then she was in sight again, pouring black smoke from her funnels, her starboard side visible almost as far down as her bilges as she heeled to the turn, but the heel lessened as she eased her wheel, and Geoff Garret realised she must be about to fire, steadying the turn so that her torpedo gunner'd be able to hold his aim on the enemy long enough to send a fish away. *Nicator* swung over, lancing through white water, dashing after her leader now to add her torpedoes to the attack.

'Hard a-port!'

Lanyard swivelled, flinging over as starboard rudder bit into the sea: 'Midships! Meet her!'

Nestor would be firing about now, and *Nicator* with her, both firing to port as they swung to starboard. Mortimer had moved, grabbed a hold on the bridge rail by the torpedo voicepipe where canvas screening flew in tatters behind splinter-mattresses which were also ripped: 'Mr Pilkington! I'm turning to port now so you'll fire to starboard. Train round to *starboard*!'

Garret heartily approved. He'd expected Mortimer to turn *Lanyard* with the others, fire on the same curve in sequence, same as it was done in practice firings; he'd been thinking that if that happened, the Germans would only have to keep dropping shells in one spot.

'Hard a-starboard!' Mortimer yelled at Hastings, pointing at the torpedo voicepipe, 'Tell Pilkington to fire when his sight comes on!'

'Aye aye, sir!'

Sub-Lieutenant Hastings looked as cool as anything. Garret hoped he looked like that. He was trying to. *Lanyard* was lifting to the turn, riding across the wall from the other two. She was going to almost scrape *Nicator*'s stern as she peeled-off to the left and *Nicator* to the right; they'd be almost on the same spot together for a moment, then they'd be dividing and you could hope the German gunners might think they were seeing things – like one ship splitting into two, and wonder which half to shoot at . . . But *Nicator* had suddenly reversed her wheel!

She'd checked her starboard swing, and begun to turn back – across *Lanyard*'s bow. Garret held his breath and thought, *Oh God, we're going to hit her . . .*

He heard Mortimer almost scream, 'Hard a-port!' Garret thought it was too late, he wouldn't make it. And he could see the reason for *Nicator*'s suicidal change of course: *Nestor* had been hit, so *Nicator* had had to reverse her wheel or run into her. *Nestor* had swung broadside-on, with her after-part pouring smoke; she'd lost all her way, and she was down by the stern. *Lanyard*'s only hope of avoiding collision had been to reverse her helm – which Mortimer had done – and try to turn inside her, the other way.

Shell-splashes spurted everywhere and within seconds *Lanyard*'s stem was going to embed itself in *Nicator*'s stern. What was more, Pilkington's tubes would be trained out on the wrong side, now. Garret whispered in his mind, *please God, please . . .*

Nicator's stern shaved past with about a foot to spare.

Mortimer yelled down, 'Ease to ten!' Garret's breath rushed out like air from a balloon. *Nicator*'s turn had flattened; she was going over to starboard again, towards the enemy, and Mortimer had steadied *Lanyard* on a course to pass close to *Nestor*. *Nestor* was done for, the German gunners were concentrating on her, she was stopped and helpless and taking the whole weight of their fury. The small mercy of it was that for the moment there was very little coming *Lanyard*'s way.

About as much as an hour ago, one might have felt she was in the thick of it. After the last eight or nine minutes everyone knew better: this was nothing.

Mortimer called down, 'Port twenty!'

'Port twenty, sir! Twenty of port helm on, sir!'

Turning away: leaving *Nestor* to her fate – which could only be that of a target for gunnery practice by Admiral Scheer's High Seas Fleet, which within the next twenty minutes or so would be steaming past her in its stately progress, battleship after battleship, keen to draw British blood.

'Midships! Steady !'

The midships four-inch fired.

'Steady, sir! Course west by south sir!'

'Steer west.'

That midships gun fired again, and at the same time spouts from enemy shells went up fifty yards on the bow.

'Starboard ten!'

Salvo-dodging again; Mortimer began to alter towards each lot of splashes as they leapt. There was another salvo scrunching over now, and the gun aft fired again. Garret edged out as far as he could, and leant over, peering aft; the south-east wind was carrying *Lanyard*'s smoke to starboard, and on the port quarter – almost right astern – he could see a grey line of battleships, their two leaders spitting fire. *Nestor* was out there entirely alone now, surrounded by shell-spouts and smoke; *Nicator* was speeding after *Lanyard*.

Mortimer turned his head, yelled at Hastings, 'Tell 'em aft to cease fire. And get Everard up here.' He ducked to the voicepipe: 'Midships . . . Steady!'

Garret heard him mutter then, glancing aft, 'Waste of

ammunition. We may well need it, later.' Garret thought, *Oh God, please don't make us need it* . . . He had to jump aside then as the engineer officer, Mr Worsfold, climbed into the bridge. Mortimer, stooped at the binnacle, didn't know Worsfold was there until he spoke.

'Captain, sir.'

'What?'

Mortimer's head jerked round . . . 'Oh. Hello, Chief. What're you doing up here?'

'I needed a word with you, sir.' Worsfold's narrow, small-boned face was set hard, and his deepset eyes were anxious. Mortimer stared at him for a second or two, then he turned to Hastings. 'Pilot, take over for a minute. Mean course west, and for God's sake keep her zigging.'

'Aye aye, sir.'

'What's up, Chief?'

'We can't keep up this speed, sir. If we try to, we'll—'

'Chief. Wait.' Mortimer held up one hand. 'There's no can't about it.' He cocked a thumb over his shoulder. 'That's the leading division of the High Seas Fleet coming up astern of us. We need every knot we've—'

'It wouldn't help us to break down, then, sir. And that's what's going to happen unless—'

'Chief.' Mortimer licked his lips. It seemed to Garret that he was making an effort to control himself. 'Listen to me. We have no option, you have no option, none whatever, but to continue at our maximum—'

'Sir. With respect, I—'

'*Damn* your respect!'

Control had been forgotten. A finger pointed, shaking, in the engineer's face. Mortimer's face seemed swollen with his rage. He shouted, 'I'll keep going at full power, Worsfold, because I bloody well have to! D'you understand? Eh? Well, understand something else, if in the next half-hour we either ease off or break down, I'll have you *shot*! I'll shoot you myself, by God!'

Hastings called down to the quartermaster, his face low on the rim of the voicepipe so that his voice seemed quiet, 'Port twenty.' The engineer's dark eyes were fixed on Mortimer's. He might have been wondering whether this was some kind of joke. Mortimer said in a more even tone than he'd just used, 'I mean it, Worsfold, I mean exactly what I say. Don't doubt it for a moment. Get back to your engines, and keep 'em going!'

Garret, not wanting to meet Mortimer's stare if he happened to glance this way, directed a professional stare at the ensign, flapping furiously at the masthead. He felt Mr Worsfold's shoulder brush against his own as the engineer came back aft without another word and climbed over on to the ladder. Garret thought, *Skipper's gone off his chump.* Glancing down again, he saw that *Nicator* was moving up to take the lead, steering a straight course to overhaul *Lanyard* on her starboard beam. Astern, the sound of gunfire hadn't slackened, while ahead, where they were going, it was like continuous, rolling thunder.

Poor old *Nestor.* She was the second of *Lanyard*'s flotilla mates they'd had to leave behind: two static, helpless targets for the Huns to knock to smithereens. Geoff Garret closed his eyes. A few minutes ago he'd foreseen, almost as if it was happening, a similar fate for *Lanyard*: he'd seen her and *Nicator* interlocked after they'd collided, lying stopped with *Lanyard*'s bow locked in the other's quarter; and the shells locating their helpless target, raining down. And Margaret, back there in Edinburgh, Margaret, for whom he needed now to live.

He shook his head, to clear away the imagery. It hadn't happened, had it. He remembered a thing he'd had to memorise at school: *The coward dies a thousand deaths, the brave man dies but one.* He knew what it meant, now.

Nick climbed off the ladder into the bridge; Hastings had sent Blewitt to him with the captain's message. Nick nodded to Garret, as the leading signalman made way for him; 'All right, are we?' Garret, he thought, looked out of sorts. Mortimer half-turned his head: 'Everard. Come here.' Hastings reported, with binoculars at his eyes, 'I believe the battle cruisers have gone round sixteen points, sir.' Mortimer, forgetting Nick, used his own glasses to check this statement. He agreed. 'But the Queen Elizabeths haven't gone about.'

'No, not yet, sir.' Hastings pointed, '*Nicator*'s mean course seems to be a point or two to starboard, though, sir.'

'Well, keep astern of her, of course!'

Lowering his glasses, Mortimer turned to Nick.

That blown-out corner of the bridge: Nick stared at it, seeing the canvas screen and the splinter-mattress ripped and charred black at the edges, and the paintwork blackened; but in the distortions of the steel deck there was a dark, glistening spillage. Like oil – but he knew it wasn't oil. He could smell it, and see its reddish tinge. A sweet, sickly smell, mixed with the stench of burning and explosive. Nick felt dazed; there was no sign of Johnson, or . . . He shook his head, and he was staring at that mess again when Mortimer told him evenly, 'Lieutenants Johnson and Reynolds have been killed, Everard.'

Nick had heard it, but there was a sense of unreality.

'Sub.' He met Mortimer's eyes. Mortimer asked him, quite pleasantly, 'Be a good fellow. Try to listen to what I'm telling you ?'

'I'm sorry, sir.'

It was bewildering. Johnson, dead . . .

Johnson who'd astonished him this morning, in the darkness of the four to eight am watch on the bridge; first by becoming chatty and friendly, and then by launching what had amounted to a thunderbolt when the subject had turned to David. Nick's mind went over it all now. He'd said that David had done as well as he had in the Service – and at Osborne and Dartmouth – because he had some sort of terror of not doing well, so he'd always swotted, 'pushed himself' . . .

'Don't get on with him, do you?'

'No. But —'

'I guessed not. Nobody does, really.'

Nick had stared at him through the pre-dawn gloom. He'd never spoken on any sort of personal level to any of David's friends or term-mates. One had learnt in one's first weeks at Osborne that one did not consort with one's seniors, except on formal terms.

Johnson murmured, 'Sort of — edgy, isn't he. You say something quite harmless to him, and as often as not he thinks you're getting at him or criticising. I've always felt a bit sorry for him, really.'

Nick shook his head. 'And I've always thought it was just me that didn't get on with him!'

'I'll tell you what I expected you to be like. Like your brother — in other words difficult — and on top of that ignorant and useless.' Johnson smiled. 'Frankly, it's quite a relief that you're fairly normal.'

Meaning, Nick had wondered, that he thought David was abnormal?

Well, he was. But not in any way that Johnson knew.

He came back to the present with a jolt. Mortimer, staring at him, was looking considerably less than patient. Nick shook his head, as if to clear it; it was Johnson who was dead, not David.

'I'm sorry, sir.'

Mortimer told him, 'Sub-Lieutenant Hastings becomes my second-in-command. You'll assume the duties of gunnery control officer. Understood?'

'Yes, sir.'

'Now tell me what's been happening aft.'

'Excuse me, sir.' Hastings interrupted. '*Nicator*'s ceased zigzagging.'

'Then do the same, for God's sake!' Mortimer's voice had been sharp, surprised. He closed his eyes for a second, opened them, and repeated more quietly, almost apologetically, 'Do what she does, Hastings.'

'Aye aye, sir.'

'Now then, Everard.'

Nick told him: the stern gun and mounting blown overboard, that gun's crew were wiped out, three of the ammunition-supply party killed with them – probably by a shell hitting projectiles standing loose behind the gun. He added that one torpedoman had been very badly wounded at the same time.

'Why didn't you report this earlier?'

'Wasn't possible, sir. The voicepipes to the guns have been shot away, and Mr Pilkington wanted to keep his voicepipe clear for torpedo-control purposes, and I couldn't leave the other gun when we were still in action.' Mortimer turned, stared towards the smoke and grey shapes which could only be the Fifth Battle Squadron. He looked back at Nick. 'Where were you when it happened?'

'In the wardroom, sir.'

Mortimer started as violently as if he'd been kicked. Hastings glanced round and Nick caught a look of astonishment before the pock-marked face turned away again. Garret and Blewitt exchanged glances which were extraordinarily devoid of expression. Mortimer said grimly, 'Will you explain that?'

'Ammunition had stopped coming up, sir. Both guns were in action and something had to be done. I went down, put things right, and—'

'What had been wrong?'

'The ladder had carried away, sir, and the two hands in there are young stokers, new to the job, I think. They were – well, confused. I had them push the table under the hatch and forget the ladder. So it only took – well, a second or two, and I was on my way back up when—'

'I see.' Mortimer turned away. Nick resented, still, the implication which had lain behind the question, behind the way they'd all looked so shocked. Then he thought of

David, and Johnson's saying, 'He thinks everyone's against him.' Their surprise had been perfectly normal; there was nothing whatsoever to resent. Mortimer added, with his eyes on the smoky mass of Beatty's battle cruisers and the Fifth Battle Squadron as they passed each other on opposite courses, 'Two men of the for'ard four-inch's crew were hit. The first lieutenant replaced them and sent them aft to the surgeon, but you'd better check the replacements know their jobs. Also, I want to know how much ammunition we've used and how much is left. Have gunlayers clean guns and refill racks. Get flexible hose from engine-room stores and rig it in place of the damaged voicepipes. And tell Surgeon Lieutenant Samuels I'd like a report from him as soon as possible.'

'Aye aye, sir.'

'Tell Mr Pilkington I'm waiting for a report from him too. D'you know how many torpedoes we have left?'

'One, sir.'

'Only one?'

'Two were fired at the battle cruisers, sir, and Mr Pilkington managed to get one away at the head of the battleship line during our final turn away.'

'Firing to port? Weren't the tubes trained starboard?'

'We got them round in time, sir.'

'We ?'

Nick hadn't meant to say that. He corrected it. 'Mr Pilkington did, sir.'

Mortimer looked pleased. 'One more thing, Sub. The ensign seems to've been shot away, aft there. Have the staff struck, and re-hoist it.'

'Aye aye, sir.'

'And see those – stokers, did you say? See they don't gum up the works next time we're in action.'

'They won't, sir.'

As he turned away, Nick found Garret and the steward watching him; they looked away. He wondered what they were thinking. Perhaps his own thought, which was when would that 'next time' be?

As it happened, he, Nick Everard, had got the tubes round. He'd seen what was happening and roused the crabby little gunner to it, and they'd been in time to get one fish on its way. Some time later Pilkington, who'd never taken his beady eyes off the enemy battle line, had seen what he'd thought might be a hit.

Pilkington could tell Mortimer, if he wanted to. The tubes were his affair. Nick began to check over in his mind, as he pushed past Garret to the ladder, the various things he had to see to. What had been done with the bodies, anyway?

'Enemy battleships have opened fire with their main armament, sir!'

Hastings had seen it, as he'd swept round to the quarter with his binoculars and seen the flashes of gunfire from the leading German ships; the head of Scheer's battle line had now crossed *Lanyard*'s stern from her port quarter to starboard. Mortimer swung round, raising his glasses to take a look, and at the same moment they all heard the whistling roar of high-calibre shells passing overhead towards the German fleet.

Hastings observed, 'Fifth Battle Squadron's engaging 'em.'

Garret thought, *right over our bloody heads!*

Chapter 6

'At 4.19 a new squadron consisting of four or five ships of the Q.E. class . . . appeared from a north-westerly direction, and took part in the action with opening range of about 21,000 yards ... . The new opponent fired with remarkable rapidity and accuracy.'

Admiral Scheer's official Despatch.

The guns of the Fifth Battle Squadron fell silent as the battle cruisers rushed towards them. In half a minute Beatty's ships would be passing between these battleships and the enemy. Hugh Everard moved out to the port wing of his bridge as the gap between the squadrons closed at roughly fifty sea miles per hour. *Lion*, with foam streaming from her enormous bow and black smoke pouring from all three funnels rushed by *now* ... too fast for any detailed assessment of what Hipper's guns had done to her: but certainly her 'X' turret was out of action – it was trained to the disengaged side with the guns tilted up to maximum elevation – and the smoke of an internal fire was pouring from her after superstructure, while great black splashes of charred paintwork showed here and there on her port side.

Now a string of flags broke at her port yardarm, close

enough to read easily with the naked eye: *Fifth Battle Squadron alter course in succession sixteen points to starboard.*

Rathbone's yellowish face showed concern as Hugh came back to him at the binnacle.

'A *red* turn, sir?'

Hugh had been considering exactly that point. A turn in succession, each ship following her next ahead and turning on virtually the same spot, and the German gunnery officers knowing, once *Barham* had led round, that each of her squadron would be paddling round after her like tame ducks . . . well, *sitting* ducks!

The Huns would make a meal of it. Hugh didn't answer Rathbone, or look at him. What could he have said – *Our Admiral's an idiot?*

A 'blue' turn, all ships turning at once and ending on a reversed course in reverse order, would have been far better in these circumstances; and that signal should in any case have been hauled down by this time. It couldn't be acted on while it was still flying, and even if the turn was started now, this second, the interval needed for reversing the course of a squadron of battleships would mean there'd be a gap of several miles between this squadron and Beatty's. It wasn't just the time it took to turn, but the loss of speed involved in it: every second's delay now was increasing that ultimate distance apart. German shells were falling into the sea ahead and short, and those were salvoes from Scheer's battleships, from guns that had never before been fired in anger. Hugh had his glasses trained on the enemy as *Nile*, rearmost of the squadron, drew clear of the last of Beatty's smoke. Just as he was wondering why Brook hadn't yet opened fire, *Nile* shuddered from the concussion of her first salvo at the High Seas Fleet.

'Executive signal, red sixteen points, sir !'

About time . . . Hugh stepped up on to the central platform, and took over again from Rathbone.

'Shift down to the conning-tower, Pilot. Then you can take over when I call down.'

'Aye aye, sir.'

The conning-tower, lower down, was the action control position. You could only see out through a periscope and through slits in the protective armour, but it would be senseless to stay up here, exposed, when things warmed up. Hugh told his second-in-command, 'You'd as well go down too, Tom. It's likely to get fairly brisk, presently.'

Crick eyed Scheer's distant battleships – mile upon mile of them, pouring northwards. He enquired, 'And you, sir ?' As calm, Hugh noticed, as a parson at evensong. He nodded. 'I shan't be long.'

Ahead, shells pock-marked the sea round *Barham* as she swung away to starboard. One hit her, when she was halfway through her turn; starboard side for'ard, that sickeningly *pretty* orange glow, black smoke rising to enfold it like foliage around a flower; then the flame was disappearing, smothered, and the smoke dissipating astern. If only Beatty had signalled, 'Follow me' or 'Alter course to north', Evan-Thomas could have exercised his own judgement on the method and the timing. His flag – white, with the red St George's cross and the two red balls in the cantons next to the halyard – stood out as stiffly as a weather-vane as *Barham* – hit again – steadied on the new course. *Valiant* was going round now, through a barrage of falling shell; it was going to be worse for each ship in turn, worst of all for *Nile*, the last. *Warspite*'s helm had gone over and she was turning into a forest of shell-spouts, a curtain of high-explosive shrieking down, raising the sea in fountains. She'd been hit for'ard, two hits together and both on her foc's'l; the Hun salvoes came closely spaced, so if you got hit at all the chance was you'd get hit hard. Their gunners were firing fast, seeing this opportunity and loth to let it go, but *Malaya* was showing good sense, turning half a cable's length before she should have. If she'd held on, she'd have run into a real plastering. You could see now exactly what she'd managed to avoid, the sea leaping, alive with falling shell just off her bow as she hauled round. As it was, she'd suffered; as he bent to the voicepipe he'd seen the sudden gush of smoke. He called down, 'Starboard ten!'

'Starboard ten, sir! Ten of starboard helm on, sir!'

A diversion to port. An impromptu zigzag to throw their range out before *Nile* became the next Aunt Sally.

'Midships!'

'Midships. Helm's amidships, sir.'

He watched *Malaya*'s turn. You had to do it right, when it was a 30,000-ton battleship you were handling, mistakes couldn't be corrected easily or quickly. He told himself, judging it by eye while fresh salvoes lacerated the sea on *Malaya*'s starboard quarter, *now . . .*

'Port fifteen!'

'Port fifteen, sir!'

Round she goes . . . The gunners over there in Scheer's battleships, with their sharp eyes on *Malaya* until about this moment, might not have noticed *Nile*'s small excursion out to port. If they hadn't, their shots as she went round now would – hopefully – be 'overs' . . .

Hearing them tearing the air like ripping calico as they passed overhead, a degree of satisfaction helped him resist the urge to duck.

'Ease to five!'

'Ease to five, sir!'

By prolonging the turn, he'd slide his ship back into line astern of *Malaya* . . . Smoke drifting in streaks and patches at masthead height might be confusing, he hoped, to Scheer's spotting officers. Another salvo crackled over, and spouts rose like the fingers of a dirty hand poked up through the surface forty yards to port.

'Midships!'

'Midships, sir. Wheel's—'

'Meet her!'

Beatty's ships were seven or eight thousand yards ahead, sparking with gun flashes as they continued to engage the German battle cruisers. Hipper had altered course, reversing it to accompany Beatty northwards and at the same time placing himself ahead of Scheer's battle squadrons. There was a gap of six miles between the two German forces: and neither could have any idea yet that Jellicoe was coming south like Nemesis.

A flag-hoist was climbing to *Barham*'s yard, curving on an arc of halyard in the wind's force and straightening as it was hauled taut. Peppard, the chief yeoman, reported that it was a distribution of fire signal. He used the manual to get its meaning: that *Barham* and *Valiant* were to engage Hipper's battle cruisers while the others took on Scheer's battleships.

Hugh called down to the conning-tower, 'Pilot?'

Rathbone answered. Hugh told him, 'Take over. I'll be with you shortly.'

'Aye aye, sir.'

'Quartermaster, obey your voicepipe from the conning-tower, now.'

'Aye aye, sir!'

He used the telephone to talk to his gunnery lieutenant in the control top.

'Brook, concentrate all your fire on the quarter, second battleship in the line. If you have to shift from him take the third.'

'Aye aye, sir.'

'Your shooting's looked good, so far. Keep it up, Brook.'

'I do believe we've scored a few, sir.'

'Score some more, a lot more.' He hung up the navy-phone. Now Beatty's four surviving battle cruisers, plus the two leading ships of this squadron, would be engaging Hipper's five ships – leaving *Nile*, *Warspite* and *Malaya* with Scheer's leading division of nine or ten dreadnoughts to hold off . . .

He ought, he knew, to go down to the protection of the conning-tower; and he would, in a moment. He wanted to see first what sort of practice Brook might make against those looming, pursuing battleships. He went out into the starboard wing of the bridge – it seemed particularly spacious, with only himself and the chief yeoman sharing it – and trained his binoculars on the leading ships just as *Nile*'s four turrets roared and smoked; he began to count, reckoning on a time-of-flight of something like twenty-five or thirty seconds. To his left, *Malaya* sent off a salvo, and the concussion of it with her guns firing as it were past one's ear was indescribably powerful. It wasn't only noise that split your head; it was like being hit on that ear with a sandbag at the same time. He put his hand to it, and found the plug of cotton-wool still in place; he'd thought it might have been blown into the eardrum. Focusing on the German battle-ships, it seemed to him that the range had closed somewhat. If it had, either Scheer's ships had more speed than was officially credited to them, or their course and this squad-ron's were converging . . . Twenty-six, twenty-seven – *there*! Brook's salvo spouted between the first and second ships. So there was no clue to range, you had to get the line right before you could usefully correct up or down. The guns fired again, *Warspite*'s did too, while at the same moment *Malaya*'s salvo fell, short and in line with the leading ship. Hugh decided to stay where he was for just one more salvo; he wanted to see *Nile* straddle her target, and from the tower his view would be so restricted, the tower itself so crowded. Still watching the line of Scheer's battleships, he was thinking of that shortening range: if he was right and it *was* shortening. And looking harder, taking advantage of an improving light as the mist in that quarter thinned, he saw that Scheer was indeed converging; this squadron was following Beatty on a course of about north, while those inimical grey shapes with white flecks at their stems and gun-flashes rippling constantly up and down the steadily oncoming line, must have been steering something more like north-west-by-north.

It would make sense from Scheer's point of view. His ships didn't have the guns to shoot effectively at the long ranges with which these QE's could cope. Just as it would have been making the best use of the British advantage in long-range gunnery to have kept the enemy at arm's length.

Well, you couldn't sheer off westward when the object was to lead the Germans north, into Jellicoe's embrace.

Scheer's dreadnoughts were getting the range. In the last minute two salvoes had fallen close but short, and one had gone over. Hugh watched *Nile*'s – he thought it must be hers – straddle the second ship in Scheer's line; two spouts went up short, one only showed its top beyond her quarterdeck, and the fourth struck a spark and then a flare on her stern turret. *Nile*'s guns roared again – that *must* have been her effort – and again within half a minute; Brook was firing double salvoes now he had the range. *Warspite* and *Malaya* were also keeping up the pressure, each getting a salvo into the air at about one-minute intervals. Now two or three German salvoes had gone over, and out of the corner of his eye Hugh saw a burst and blossom of flame on *Malaya*'s stern and another between her funnels. Lowering his glasses he swivelled round to look at her and saw that her after superstructure had been hit. Smoke was pouring out of both sides – from the entry-hole, probably, and another the shell had made when it exploded.

He was feeling sorry for *Malaya* when a lone shell came whirring like a bluebottle and burst on *Nile*'s foc'sl.

It didn't penetrate. It had landed close to the port cable-holder and burst against the armoured deck. All ships were firing fast now and there were practically no intervals between the falls of German salvoes; by the time one lot of spouts had collapsed back into the torn sea, another lot were leaping in their places. And hits were being scored; with any luck the Germans were being walloped too, but at this end one couldn't have denied it was becoming reasonably uncomfortable. Hugh decided that the time for loitering in such an exposed position was past: he'd go down now.

'Peppard – carry on down on the conning-tower.'

Chief Petty Officer Peppard looked surprised. 'All the same to you, sir, I'd as soon—'

'That was not an invitation, Chief Yeoman.'

'Aye aye, sir.'

With an entire division of battleships letting rip at one squadron – and probably concentrating, at that, on *Nile* and *Malaya* who were their nearest targets – one could hardly expect to emerge unscathed. He picked up a different navyphone and at the same time, glancing round, saw Peppard hesitating at the top of the port ladder, looking back at him. Then the chief yeoman started down. At the same moment a sailor's cap rose into view on the other side. Hugh stared at it exasperatedly: Bates . . .

His coxswain was carrying a tray.

'Torpedo control tower!'

'Torpedo Lieutenant, please.' That had been the midshipman who worked the plotter for Knox-Wilson.

'Lieutenant (T) here, sir.'

'Knox-Wilson, are you ranging on the quarter?'

'Yes, sir. Down to sixteen thousand, closing quite fast.'

'We're in a good position on their bow to try a long shot. This visibility's none too reliable, so don't wait for ever.'

'No, sir. But—'

'But ?'

'Starboard for'ard tube's stuck, sir. They can't shift the bar.'

'Use the starboard after tube, then. And keep 'em working to clear the other.'

'Aye aye, sir.'

Knox-Wilson would have wanted to clear his for'ard tube for action before he took a long-range chance, so as to make sure of having one of the two starboard tubes functioning in case a much surer chance cropped up. But the enemy was there; you couldn't always play safe, you had to take your chances. Hugh told Knox-Wilson, 'Send Mr Askell to see what they're up to down there.' He hung up the navyphone. The action was getting hotter all the time: six to eight salvoes a minute were dropping round them. He'd felt a hit aft and seen another for'ard, and *Malaya* had been hit three times in succession, all amidships. But all guns still fired, which was not the case with the enemy. The fire from the battle cruisers had been considerably reduced – as a result, one imagined, of *Barham*'s and *Valiant*'s influence. Looking that way, he couldn't see Hipper's ships now: they'd vanished, swallowed in the mist. It freed the two leading Queen Elizabeths to join the three astern of them in this rather uneven fight with Scheer. But mist – falling visibility – Hugh murmured in his mind, *please, God, don't let it get worse*! Just when Jellicoe should be on the point of joining in, if Scheer at just that moment should be presented with a mist to run away and hide in . . . Whose side would the Almighty seem to be on, if *that* happened?

Bates said, behind him, 'Cup o' coffee, sir. Thought you was likely gettin' a bit—'

Hugh whipped round. 'For God's sake, man, get below.'

'Aye aye, Sir.' Unruffled, cheerful. 'Leave your coffee 'ere sir, shall I ?'

Nile trembled to a double explosion aft.

'I could leave it 'ere, sir, or—'

'Yes.' Hugh made himself speak levelly: his ship's guns crashed out another salvo, and Bates's hands, he noticed, holding the tray with the coffee on it, were completely steady. 'Yes, thank you, Bates. Leave it here.'

He remembered – perhaps inconsequentially – as he turned for'ard again, that Bates couldn't swim. A salvo screeched overhead. He didn't see it fall, because he'd glanced round to make sure his coxswain had left the bridge, almost dreading, as he turned his head, that he'd find those brown monkey-eyes still watching him.

The coffee was there, steaming on the ledge below the starboard Battenberg. Bates had gone below.

This patchy mist: Jellicoe wouldn't pursue an enemy at night or in bad visibility. He'd put this to the Admiralty, and their Lordships had approved the principle that the Grand Fleet must not be put at risk in circumstances where pure chance might play too great a part. The Germans had equipped their cruisers for mine-laying, they could lay a field of mines, unseen, ahead of a pursuing fleet, actually during the course of battle. And the newer destroyers with their new long-range, high-speed torpedoes were an unknown quantity. Britain's survival depended on the continued existence of her fleet; the way to handle it was not to handle it the way the Germans would like it handled, in conditions which gave advantages to the techniques of sneak-attack.

Barham was altering course to port, as Beatty had at that same point. She seemed to have a fire amidships, but it could be just her boats that were being incinerated. *Valiant*, following her in the two-point turn, had blocked off his quick view of her. *Warspite* had taken a lot of hits, and *Malaya* was suffering again as she put her helm over. *Nile* was surrounded with shell-splashes. Hugh felt her shudder, heard the explosion and the deep clang of metal striking aft: looking back there he saw a seepage of smoke drifting down-wind from her quarter but no evidence of damage. A navyphone buzzed harshly, and he crossed over to it, waiting for the guns to fire before he answered.

'Bridge. Captain.'

'Crick here, sir. Shouldn't you be coming down, sir?'

'I'm on my way. Tom, we had a shell hit us aft, just then. It might have been below the waterline.'

'I'll find out, sir.'

Against twice their own number of ships, the Queen Elizabeths were hitting at least as often as they were being hit themselves. Beatty had been out of the action for the last twenty or thirty minutes; with Hipper's ships hidden in the mist, there'd been nothing for his guns to shoot at. No doubt he'd have been using the respite well, getting fires under control and repairing damage. Hugh focused his glasses on the battle cruisers and saw they'd just altered to starboard again, steering north, by the looks of it. To head off Hipper, or perhaps just to get back in sight of him. A salvo plunged just short, its tall spouts lashing a black salt rain across *Nile*'s forepart; then came two explosions in quick succession down near S1 and S2 casemates. He realised he'd forgotten that intention of going down to the tower.

'Captain, sir!'

Crick, at the top of the ladder, had a look of disquiet on his normally unruffled features.

'It must have been a near-miss aft, sir, the one you mentioned. It seems it—' He had to shout, as a salvo crashed overhead and raised spouts thirty yards from *Nile*'s side – 'didn't hurt us, sir!' That close, on the disengaged side and with the flat trajectory of ships' guns, those shells must have passed between her masts. Hugh hadn't looked out to port much in the last ten minutes, but he did so now, and paused to watch destroyers streaming up on the squadron's beam and bow. This must be the flotilla which had been across and made a torpedo attack on the enemy battle cruisers, an hour or so ago. And the nearest boat seemed to have lost her stern gun, so that her oddly levelled afterpart gave her the look of an attenuated tug. Training his glasses on her, he saw the rips and scars in her quarterdeck. She was one of the half-dozen L-class boats that had only two funnels instead of three; and it looked, from the lump which had been shot out of her for'ard funnel, as though she'd done her best to get down to one.

Crick, judging his moment for it between shell-bursts and gunfire, cleared his throat loudly. Hugh glanced round at him, and nodded.

'Yes, Tom. You're right.' He turned aft and went down the steps to the lower end of the bridge. Five forty-five now. On his way down to the next level of the superstructure, he thought that it would be as well for Jellicoe to get here soon. Otherwise he wouldn't have enough hours of daylight left in which to do the job for which his Grand Fleet had been built and trained . . . He was two levels down with one more to go when he heard the crash, felt the shock and the reverberation of an explosion somewhere close below the bridge; then a sound like hail lashing a tin roof – splinters from that shell-burst, raking the compass platform. He didn't bother to look round at Crick, who'd be wearing his told-you-so expression.

Bantry pitched rhythmically to the low swell as she followed astern of *Warrior* and the First Cruiser Squadron's flagship, *Defence*. A grey, faintly lumpy sea, and greyish, rather hazy light with clearer patches here and there. The cruiser screen had fallen back closer to the battle fleet on account of the deteriorating visibility. *Bantry* was less than five miles ahead of the fleet's starboard column, and looking back over her port quarter David could see quite clearly that concentrated mass of armoured and destructive power, as Jellicoe held on grimly south-eastward at the speed of his slowest dreadnought.

His ships were still in their cruising disposition of six columns. Soon – if they were to come into contact with the enemy, which David was convinced they would not – that solid phalanx of ships would have to be re-formed into a single line ahead, which was the only way a fleet could bring all its guns to bear. But in order to deploy in the way which would give him the most advantage when he met the enemy, Jellicoe needed the one thing he wasn't getting: information.

There'd been a smattering of it, which *Bantry*'s W/T operators had picked up. It amounted to only the facts that Scheer's as well as Hipper's ships were coming north, and that the battle cruisers and the Fifth Battle Squadron and the light forces with them had been heavily engaged.

Bantry ploughed on south-eastward behind the other two. Four miles on the starboard beam was *Duke of Edinburgh*, and four or five beyond her, *Black Prince*. If anyone was going to sight the enemy or establish contact with Beatty's cruiser screen as he came northwards, it would be *Black Prince*. But for half an hour now, there'd been no reports at all. Nothing. All the earlier information, sketchy and even conflicting as it had been, had been put on the chart – by David – and he'd set Midshipman Porter, his 'tanky', to work producing a large-scale plot of it. It still made very little sense.

Not, David thought, that it mattered. There'd be no action, for the Grand Fleet. It was too late now; he felt sure of it.

Wilmott came forward and stopped beside Nobby Clark. He said irritably, 'C-in-C must be beside himself. Why don't they tell him what they can see, for heaven's sake?'

Clark shrugged agreement. David was at the binnacle, conning the ship while Wilmott drifted about the bridge like a cat on hot bricks and paid visits to the chartroom and signals office. *Bantry* had been at action stations for nearly four hours, now, and the only intelligible enemy reports had come from Commodore Goodenough in the light cruiser *Southampton*. Goodenough must have been almost along-side Scheer's battleships, at one point, to have sent back as much information as he had!

But in the jumble of reports from this source and that, positions and bearings and reported courses conflicted – confused, more than informed. Beatty, for instance, had told Jellicoe nothing that could be of any real use to him . . . But then, Beatty would be in the thick of it – as he always was, which made one wonder about Nick; might he have been in the thick of it too?

A few minutes ago Jellicoe had betrayed his impatience by signalling his own position to Beatty; and long ago he'd sent Hood away with his three battle cruisers to join Beatty and support him. There'd been no word of Hood since then – he might as well have vanished into thin air. Or – David thought, taking a look round the horizon – thickening air. The light was getting very patchy indeed. Drifting mist kept changing things: one minute it was clear in one direction and hazy in another, and next time you looked the conditions might be reversed. Visibility might drop to four or five miles, or open out to twelve. It wouldn't be the first time the North Sea's unpredictability had helped Germans out of the way of British guns. He looked astern again. As well as this squadron of armoured cruisers, and Rear-Admiral Heath's Second Squadron, with which *Bantry* had sailed from Scapa, there were ten light cruisers and thirty-nine destroyers in Jellicoe's inner screen. One could imagine him, in the centre of that mass of steel, the fleet he'd created, trained, prepared, pacing his bridge, cloaking anxiety behind a mask of imperturbability, silence and *sangfroid*, and knowing that with an armada of this size whichever of the methods of deployment he chose, it would from the moment that he ordered it become irreversible, unstoppable. It had to be not a gambler's throw, but a tactician's masterstroke.

Or if he acted on incomplete or wrong information, a tactician's blunder.

At four fifty-one – getting on for an hour ago – he'd wirelessed four words to the Admiralty: *Fleet action is imminent.* That pre-arranged message would have resulted by now in an alert being flashed to dockyards, tugs, hospitals, all the emergency services which large-scale damage and casualties would call for.

Action imminent. They'd be saying it excitedly even in London now, let alone on this cruiser's bridge; but David couldn't believe in it; his instincts denied it, he couldn't feel it as something that could ever happen.

Not to himself. If anything happened to David Everard – it wouldn't, but just imagining it, supposing – and with one's father in France, with the big push intended to relieve the pressure on Verdun expected any day now ... Even a brigadier couldn't last for ever, you'd only to glance at the daily Roll of Honour in *The Times*. Just thinking about what could, but wouldn't, happen – well, young Nick would inherit the title, Mullbergh, everything!

The idea of that was simply – grotesque ... One could only dismiss it, put it out of mind and replace it with an entirely contrary thought – that Nick, having through Hugh Everard's influence got himself to a destroyer, might well get his come-uppance. The torpedo craft did tend to get knocked about, and it was a fact that Nick was behind steel plating one-eighth of an inch thick, instead of the twelve-inch armour belt worn by the battleship he'd left. Nick's destroyer might well be in action at this moment. It was a tantalising thought!

'*Duke of Edinburgh* flashing, sir!'

From four miles to the south a rapid series of dots and dashes cut through the haze. In fact the visibility down there looked better, at the moment.

'W/T signal, sir.' It was a leading signalman who'd come pelting up from the office. 'To C-in-C from *Black Prince*, sir.' Commander Clark took the clip-board and passed it straight to Wilmott – who scanned it, raised his thick eyebrows and told Clark, '*Black Prince* is in contact with *Falmouth*, in Beatty's screen.' He let the signalman take the board out of his hand. Narrow-eyed, beard jutting very much like a wire-haired terrier's, he was watching that distant, flashing light. He murmured, 'We'll be at 'em soon.'

A snapshot of Nick flashed suddenly in David's memory, of Nick staring at him; an accusing, condemning stare, not only judgement but dislike, contempt even, in his steady scrutiny. Insufferable little – pig! what did he know about—

'Pilot!'

Snapping out of nightmare: 'Sir?'

'What's the—'

Wilmott had checked, with his question unasked. Every head in the bridge had jerked round, faces turning to the sound that had come rumbling on the south-east wind. The sound of heavy guns.

It was so loud that it was surprising it hadn't been audible before. A voice squawked distantly, metallically, 'Bridge!' It was the voicepipe from the fore top, and Commander Clark was nearest to it. He bent his thickset body jerkily, like a tubby marionette, and barked, 'Bridge!'

'Ships in action on the starboard bow, sir! Looks like battle cruisers and cruisers!'

Another voicepipe call: from the wireless office, this time, and Porter took it.

'Commander-in-Chief to Admiral Beatty, sir: *Where is the enemy battle fleet?*'

Wilmott muttered something angrily into his beard. Defence was flashing a signal to *Iron Duke*, reporting ships in action south-south-west, course north-east. Wilmott began a conversation over the navyphone to Johnny West, the gunnery lieutenant, in the control top, asking him what he could see, and where, and what it was doing; and that whole southern sector of the horizon was suddenly full of ships and the flashes of their guns. Petty Officer Sturgis, the yeoman, reported to Wilmott, 'C-in-C to SO, BCF by W/T sir – *Where is the enemy battle fleet?*'

'We've already had that one, Yeoman.'

'No, sir.' Sturgis looked hurt. 'He's asked it again, sir. Repetition, sir.'

Bedlam increasing, as reports flowed in . . .

Wilmott had moved up close to the binnacle; he was staring ahead at *Warrior* and *Defence*. He extended his left arm with the hand open, and said to David without looking at him, 'Hand me my glasses, Pilot.' David unslung them from the brass cylinder that enclosed the flinder's bar, and placed them in the outstretched hand. Midshipman Porter, straightening from the fore top's voicepipe reported, 'Fore top can see shells falling close to the light cruisers, sir, but they can't see where they're coming from.' They were referring, presumably, to light cruisers in Beatty's screen.

David felt quite calm – not so much disinterested as detached, waiting for the visibility to clamp down. He was still sure it would.

Wilmott snapped suddenly, with the binoculars still at his eyes, 'Revolutions for twenty-three knots, Pilot!'

'Searchlight signalling starboard, sir!'

It was on the bow; a distant, winking light . . . David called down for maximum revs, full speed. And now he saw why Wilmott had ordered it. *Defence* and *Warrior* had surged forward, pushing out ahead, and from out to starboard *Duke of Edinburgh* and *Black Prince* were converging to join up with them. Sir Robert Arbuthnot was gathering his squadron together and speeding to close the enemy, leaving the battle fleet astern. South-eastward at full speed, towards the sound and flashes of the guns. There was an impression suddenly of things speeding up, a sense of urgency and impending action developing; David resisted it, feeling that it was only a kind of hysteria in which one should not allow oneself to become involved. The yeoman was reporting to Wilmott with a touch of excitement in his voice that the searchlight flashing from the south was Beatty's, *Lion*'s, and that the message was one answering that repeated question about the enemy battle fleet. Beatty was telling his commander-in-chief, *Have sighted enemy battle fleet bearing south-south-west.*

So now Jellicoe knew the direction of his enemy, even though he'd no information at all about distance, course or speed. And *Bantry* was picking up speed now, her steel trembling as she pressed forward, her bow rising and falling as it cut through the combined wakes of the other cruisers.

Arbuthnot, David guessed, must be watching the falling visibility and trying to hurry his squadron into action. One had not foreseen this, but had thought rather in terms of the cruisers remaining in company with the battle fleet.

'All right, Pilot,' Wilmott nodded, 'I'll take her.'

'Sir.'

Turning away and looking astern towards the broad front of the battle fleet as they began to draw away from it, he saw specks of colour sliding up to the flagship's yardarm. The yeoman had seen it too, and he whipped up his telescope. David, using binoculars, identified the blue-and-white stripes of the equal-speed pendant above the quartered black, red, blue and yellow of flag C and the red St Andrew's cross of flag L. The yeoman confirmed his accuracy.

'Equal-speed, Charlie, London, sir . . . Battle fleet deploying on—' he hesitated, staring astern still – 'on the port column sir!'

Twenty-four dreadnought battleships were about to form into a single fighting line. Deploying on the port column meant that the leading ships of the six columns would all turn simultaneously ninety degrees to port; each division would follow its leader round, until the six divisions had thus fallen into line-ahead. Finally, the battleships would file round to starboard, a follow-my-leader turn which would bring the whole line back on to their course towards the enemy. It meant that Scheer, coming north-eastward, would find several miles of dreadnoughts across his intended line of advance: Jellicoe would have 'crossed Scheer's T', and the Grand Fleet's massed broadsides would be able to hammer Scheer's leading division into scrap-iron before more than a few German guns could be brought to bear. And Jellicoe would have the light-gauge; the westering sun would throw the German line into sharp relief while the British battleships remained invisible in the mist!

The light had not failed, after all. It was patchy, but Jellicoe had seen how he could take advantage of it. David was beginning to realise that his instincts had tricked him. Meanwhile, he had nothing to do except stand ready in case

Wilmott wanted him to take over at the binnacle again.

A navyphone buzzed and flashed; he snatched it up, forestalling the commander, who'd started towards it.

'Bridge.'

It was Johnny West, calling from the control top again. David turned his eyes up towards that swaying, box-like construction on the foremast as he listened to West telling him, 'Our own light cruisers bearing south, course north-east, and the battle cruisers are in sight astern of them, same course, and in action. They're under fire from an enemy I can't see. Look as if they're going to pass ahead of us.'

David passed the message verbatim to Wilmott. Wilmott glanced at his second-in-command.

'It's going to be like a bloody circus ring, in a minute.'

David thought about it; Beatty, storming up from the south, steering north-east now to head-off Hipper's battle cruisers and force him round ahead of the deploying battle fleet. It was rather spectacular, really; Beatty was doing his job perfectly, he'd not only led the Germans up to Jellicoe but now he'd be screening the sight of Jellicoe from them until the very last moment, and Wilmott's meaning was clear: in a few minutes there'd be something like a hundred ships all rushing in different directions as Beatty with his screening cruisers and destroyers ahead and around him raced across the front of the battle fleet.

With binoculars, you could even see it all developing from the bridge now. The light cruisers, and behind them the dark mass of the bigger ships. Shells falling among them, and more than anywhere round the battle cruisers. No sign of where they came from; just that great spread of ships all racing north-eastward, bow-waves flaring, guns flashing. They must have an enemy in sight. And *Defence* was under helm, swinging to port, with flags rushing to her yardarm.

'*Defence* to squadron, sir: *Engage enemy starboard!*'

'Tell West to open fire when he has a target.'

'Aye aye, sir.' David passed the order. *Warrior* was going

round astern of the flagship. Wilmott, stooped awkwardly at the binnacle, watching *Warrior*'s piled wake gleaming as it flowed curving away behind her, kept his face low beside the voicepipe's copper rim, waiting for the exact moment to put the helm over; crouched like that, he looked to David as if he was about to defecate.

There'd hardly been time to think about how wrong he'd been. It was only about six o'clock, there were several hours of daylight left, and *Bantry* would shortly be in action.

'Starboard fifteen!'

Swinging over . . .

'Ease to five!'

'Ease to five, sir . . . Five o' starboard helm on, sir!'

The two ships ahead opened fire. Smoke burgeoned out of them to starboard, then the sharp percussions cracked astern with the stink of cordite. David put his glasses to his eyes – German cruisers. He saw three, and one other which seemed to be stopped. Everything was greyish, wrapped-up in mist. It came clear for a moment, then hazed-up again. He found himself wishing that the visibility would hold up, give Jellicoe time to get to grips with Scheer. He heard a fire-gong ring, and before the clang had lost its echo *Bantry*'s nine-inch guns flung out their first salvo.

'Midships!'

'Midships, sir—'

'Meet her, and follow the next-ahead!'

'Aye aye, sir!'

It was the nearest of the enemy ships that was lying stopped. She must have been damaged – by a destroyer's torpedo, perhaps – but her ensign was still flying. Another salvo roared away; the splashes from *Defence*'s and *Warrior*'s salvoes went up a long way short. *Defence* was hauling round to starboard; one could guess that Arbuthnot had decided to close the range and try again. She was steaming directly towards the still motionless German cruiser; *Warrior* was following her, and in *Bantry*'s bridge

Wilmott was once again lowering himself into that undignified knees-bend position.

Light cruisers of Beatty's screen were on the quarter and astern, and closing rapidly at high speed. On the beam the battle fleet was extending north-eastward as Jellicoe made his deployment. The Second Cruiser Squadron – *Minotaur*, *Shannon* and company – was in sight in that direction too. Wherever one looked there were ships and smoke, and the smoke was mingling with the mist to create banks of impenetrable fog.

'Port fifteen!'

Wilmott turned his cruiser's bow into the swirl of *Warrior*'s wake. With the change of course, David saw that the light cruisers would now pass astern. In every direction there were ships racing at high speed, crossing each others' bows, swinging under each others' sterns, destroyers passing through cruiser squadrons and cruisers combing down between the lines of the deploying battle fleet. There was purpose in it all, and it was a display of high-speed ship-handling such as had never been seen before, but it looked like a free-for-all, a mass of ships in the hands of madmen, while shell-spouts leapt in clumps here and there between them and funnel-smoke hung and drifted everywhere.

Astern of the other two, Wilmott was turning *Bantry* to starboard in order to open fire again. But David was counting ships and there seemed to be only four battle cruisers in Beatty's force, instead of six. He decided he must be mistaken, two of them might be with that group astern? It was difficult to count them. The four battle cruisers were making an enormous amount of smoke, and it was all piling astern in that direction, and the ships were – from this angle – overlapping. His eyes ached, the glasses kept getting steamed-up from his rising breath and he couldn't hold the damn things steady.

'Midships!'

'Midships, sir . . . Wheel's amidships—'

Bantry's guns fired; the four nine-inch, and this time the broadside of seven-point-fives joined in too. David lowered his glasses as the dirty-brown cordite fumes flew back in the wind. Defence and *Warrior* were firing steadily, synchronising their salvoes; as a newcomer to the squadron, *Bantry* was the outsider. Looking over at the German cruiser, which was now about forty degrees on the bow and still stopped, he saw shells hitting all down her length. The shots were landing rather like match-heads hitting and striking on emery-paper, one after another and in twos and threes as *Bantry* too found the range and began to strike home. Now white smoke – no, steam, they'd hit her in a boiler-room – gushed skyward. He took his eyes off her, looked back to see a squadron of light cruisers racing past astern. Those were part of Beatty's screen, and within seconds, he realised, this squadron, *Bantry* and the other two, would have crossed the battle cruisers' bows, which meant – the position suddenly clarified in his mind – they'd be out in no-man's-land, between the battle cruisers and the German fleet!

Did Wilmott realise it? David turned back to look at him. He was standing with his eyes on that German cruiser; his fingers were caressing that beard of his, and there was something admiring in his expression, David thought. The main armament weren't firing now; it had evidently been decided to finish the Hun off with the seven-fives, but it was amazing that she hadn't already sunk.

Did Wilmott understand the position they'd put themselves in ? Destroyers flashed past astern, and just abaft the beam now came Beatty's battle cruisers, bow-waves high and creamy under bleak steel bows, jutting guns flaming intermittently to starboard, black funnel-smoke pluming up and rolling astern like coils of tight black wool. *Lion*, their leader, with Beatty's flag and half a dozen ensigns whipping in the wind, had smoke belching from an enormous hole in her for'ard superstructure – but she looked magnificent: proud, angry, indestructible. David was staring at her when he heard a tearing, howling noise and shell-spouts shot up just short of *Warrior*'s quarterdeck, and half a second later another salvo crashed into the water sixty yards over, abreast *Bantry*'s second funnel. A navyphone buzzed; Commander Clark had snatched it up, but his voice sounded calm, less brusque than it did normally.

'Bridge here, West. What is it?'

Listening, his expression was bland, unworried as he glanced at Wilmott. A salvo fell short and foul water fell solidly across the for'ard nine-inch turret. They'd bracketed her now; David thought, *This isn't happening – is it?* He realised suddenly, for the first time ever, what his most compelling fear was. It wasn't just the thought of being killed, but of being killed and Nick left alive to inherit Mullbergh, the title, everything, with Uncle Hugh there as an honoured guest – and he and Sarah – No! David told himself, *It couldn't happen. It simply could not happen ...* Himself, David, gone, and never mentioned, while they all—

'Enemy battle cruisers on the bow and stern, sir.' Clark was reporting to Wilmott what West had just told him. 'He says he only gets glimpses of them, but their course seems to be north-east.' The Commander pointed, 'You can see their gun-flashes now, sir.' Nobby Clark's tone had never been so mild.

More shells ripped over. A salvo raised the sea just short of *Warrior*'s stern; the gap between her stern and *Bantry*'s stem was two cables, four hundred yards. All guns were firing now. *Defence* had been hit; there was a spurt of bright orange flame and a puff-ball of black, oily smoke. She'd swung away to starboard, but *Warrior* seemed to be holding her course so Wilmott, who'd started his curtsey to the voicepipe, straightened again. Wilmott's clownish movements had ceased to be amusing. Minutes ago, David recollected, everything had been calm and easy, they'd been coming up to take some pot shots at a disabled cruiser and there'd seemed to be no danger in it at all. Now in some extraordinary way they'd found themselves acting as targets for German battle cruisers. The heavens had opened, and the stuff raining out of them was explosive, steel, destruction, death. The sea was a forest of shell-spouts, and the stinking splashes of near-misses carried with them steel splinters, shell-fragments which screamed whirring across the decks, tore holes in funnels, cut halyards, brought rigging and wircless gear crashing down. A shell hit aft, and then two in quick succession for'ard. *Warrior* was all smoke and *Defence* was ploughing out to starboard, burning, smoke pouring from shell-holes below her bridge.

The navyphone called again. The commander had left the bridge, to take charge of damage-control below decks after those three hits. Had there been three – or more? David wasn't sure. Porter was answering that 'phone; he'd glanced enquiringly at David, and David hadn't moved; he was close to Wilmott, a couple of feet from the binnacle, and he hadn't felt like moving. So the midshipman had nipped over and taken the navyphone off its hook. *Warrior* had turned away about two points to starboard, and Wilmott was conning *Bantry* round astern of her. Midshipman Porter reported, 'Control top says we're being fired at by enemy battleships bearing due south, sir.'

'Thank you, Snotty.' Wilmott glanced sideways at David. 'Can't say I'd noticed the difference. Had you ?' He bobbed down, 'Meet her.'

'Meet her, sir!'

'Steady!' He'd looked up, pointing, 'Oh, no . . .' A second ago he'd been smiling; now it was shock that David glimpsed before he looked where he was pointing, staring . . . *Defence* was reeling from a full salvo which had burst on her. Smoke was everywhere: her fore top swayed, and crashed down into the sea. A second salvo hit at that moment, as they watched: she seemed to check, like a shot animal before it drops, and then she blew up. A sheet of flame ran horizontally along her length, and then opened, swelling upwards into smoke as the ship disintegrated into blackness. Wilmott, knees bent, called down 'Port twenty!' *Warrior* had sheered away to port – towards the enemy battle fleet. She was still being hit, and shells were plastering the sea all round her, and it wouldn't have done her the slightest good if *Bantry* had gone that way and shared what she was getting. Wilmott was taking his ship to starboard... 'Midships!'

'Midships, sir!'

She'd be heading roughly north now; David wasn't close enough to the binnacle to see. At least it was a course away from the High Seas Fleet ... Porter came to Wilmott from a voicepipe he'd been answering: 'Commander says there are heavy casualties between decks, sir, and several fires which he hopes he'll shortly have under control.'

'Thank you, Snotty ... Steady!'

'Steady, sir! Course north by west, sir!'

'Steer that, quartermaster.'

'Aye aye, sir!'

Wilmott straightened, and looked round. *Warrior* was some way off on the port beam, and she seemed to be on fire; but there were no shell-splashes there now, and it looked as if she was coming round to starboard, perhaps to follow *Bantry*. David heard Wilmott mutter to himself as he turned to watch the Fifth Battle Squadron coming up from the south-west, 'Find the other pair...' David guessed he was expressing an intention of joining *Duke of Edinburgh* and *Black Prince*, who'd sheered off somewhere on their own. Beyond the Queen Elizabeths, who were still heavily engaged, David saw destroyers, a pack of them tearing along on the disengaged side. Ahead, where that squadron was going, the air was like soup, layers of haze drifting and mingling with banks of funnel-smoke from the dozens of ships which in the last twenty minutes of skilfully-managed chaos had dashed across this acreage of sea. The water still bore the tracks they'd made; it seethed where wakes met and clashed, swirled in whirlpools where ships, squadrons and flotillas had turned or ploughed through each others' washes ... But in fact, David saw as the picture changed even while he was watching it, in the space of just a few minutes, the haze was splitting up. It was dividing, like curtains opening on a stage; and suddenly its drab, milky greyness was punctured by red stabs of gunfire, massed gunfire, where a minute ago one would have sworn there'd been nothing but a North Sea fog.

Wilmott announced, 'Jellicoe's at 'em, at last. Now we'll see a thing or two.'

Still in the process of deployment, the Grand Fleet's battleships had opened fire. You could see the ships behind the gun-flashes, now; this was the Sixth Division, the end of the line, opening fire as it swung in to form the tail. Wilmott raised a hand, pointing at the clouds, his eyebrows rose too, and his beard cocked. David listened to the hoarse rush of shells hurtling overhead. The main action, the trial of strength which would decide which fleet won or lost the battle, was just about beginning.

'Starboard ten!'

They were getting *Bantry* out of it, turning to pass up ahead of the Queen Elizabeths who, with their fifteen-inch guns still firing steadily, were swinging away to port – a 'blue' turn that would get them into position to form astern, presently, of Jellicoe's long battle line.

But one of the QE squadron – the third in the line – had gone on turning, on her own. Instead of steadying on the squadron's new course she was circling on, all by herself and getting closer at every second to the German battleships, whose shells were already straddling her.

The third in line; that would be – *Warspite*? Wilmott had seen it too; he had his glasses up, watching her as she swung into the enemy's welcoming arms. The German gunnery officers were grabbing their chance of an easy target: alone, close, and out of control. It was a reasonable supposition that her steering-gear had jammed: and anyone's bet whether her engineers would clear it before the Germans finished her.

Wilmott had shouted something at David, he was pointing. He shouted again as David turned to look at him; he got one word '– *Nile*!'

But *Nile*, Hugh Everard's ship, was the last in that QE line, not the third. This one in the trap was *Warspite*: if Wilmott thought it was *Nile*, he was wrong. David turned his glasses, just to make sure, on to his uncle's ship.

Nile had put her helm over. She was steering out to join – or cover – *Warspite*. All her guns were blazing; she was a fantastic, splendid sight. All *Warspite*'s guns were firing too, in spite of the smothering she was getting, in which *Nile* any minute now would be sharing. David's glasses were jammed against his eyes, and his teeth were clenched. He was watching something marvellous, stupendous, and he felt he was part of it and yet wasn't; it was an extraordinary feeling. The sea all round *Nile* was spouting with shell-bursts and splashes, columns of water and black blossomings of smoke: at times you could only see the scarlet flashes of *Nile*'s guns, not the ship herself at all. She'd drawn two-thirds of the enemy's hate from *Warspite*, and she still had a long way to go: she was geting everything they had to offer now, she'd snatched a victim from their claws and they were making her pay for it with her own blood. David stood spellbound, fascinated; he heard Porter answer a navyphone and then tell Wilmott, 'Commander reports fires not yet under control, sir, and Lieutenant-Commander Harrington's among those killed.' David thought *Harri dead*? That meant Johnny West was third in command now. Wilmott had taken no notice of what Porter had told him; he'd just shouted down to *Bantry*'s quartermaster, 'Starboard twenty!'

It was confusing. Another turn to port made no sense. Wilmott was crouched over the voicepipe in that silly squat of his; he told David, 'We'll get him out of it, now.' He pointed at the cluster of navyphones on the for'ard bulkhead: 'Tell the engine-room I want smoke!'

Bantry's head was falling off fast to port. As David jumped to the 'phone, Wilmott called down, 'Midships!'

Suddenly it was obvious what he was about to do. He was taking this cruiser and her smoke between *Nile* and the half-dozen dreadnought battleships that were shooting at her.

Chapter 7

'**M**idships!'

Rathbone repeated Hugh's order into the voice-pipe. Hugh was watching through the conning-tower's periscope, and passing helm orders to his navigator. He heard the quartermaster's dirge-like repetition of that last one; immediately, instead of giving him a 'Steady' for a course to settle on, he ordered the helm the other way: 'Port fifteen!'

Rathbone's quick snap, the quartermaster's hollow bleat ... Constant helm. And erratic too. He was planning to weave *Nile* like a picket-boat, take a leaf out of the destroyer men's book and dodge between the Germans' salvoes, even if a thirty-thousand-ton battleship *was* a somewhat ponderous dodger. Hugh wondered whether his decision to turn out of the line and cover *Warspite* might have been the one truly appalling decision of his career; whether it could even be thought of as a 'decision' at all; whether it hadn't been pure reflex.

Destroyer captains, a high proportion of whom were generally acknowledged to be raving lunatics, could be allowed such aberrations. A battleship's captain was another animal altogether – or should be.

'Midships! Starboard ten!'

He'd started it, and he and *Nile* – which meant not just an expensive heap of steel but about a thousand men – were out on the limb he'd opted for. You couldn't turn back, you had to see it through. And if of course you had the luck – tempered by a bit of judgement and timing – to pull it off, bring *Nile* back into the line intact and operative as a fighting unit with *Warspite* at least afloat, then the taking of the risk would have been justified. It was a biggish 'if'.

'Midships ... Ask the control top what's up with "X" turret.'

'Midships—'

'Control top!' Ross-Hallet's voice was shouting.

'Wheel's amidships, sir!'

'Port fifteen!'

The enemy were out of sight sometimes, from this level, the view of them obscured by the rain of their own shell-splashes and bursts. From the control top, of course, Brook shouldn't be getting any such interference; all he had to do was keep his guns bearing, and cope with the wild zigzag. The noise was tremendous, and almost uninterrupted by any periods of quiet. It was like trying to keep one's brain working normally while trapped inside a steel drum that was being beaten continuously with sledge-hammers.

Midshipman Ross-Hallet reported, 'Lieutenant Brook says "X" is back in action, sir.'

'Good. Ease to five!'

'Ease to five, sir!'

'*Warspite* seems to be getting out of trouble, sir.' That had been Rathbone's voice imparting good news. Hell of a long way to go yet, though. Hugh told him, 'Midships the helm, then put on twenty of starboard.' The tower seemed to lurch, in a huge, close explosion, and there was an immediate tattoo of splinters or debris clanging against its armour; through the slits, there'd been an impression of a white-orange flash, more *surrounding* than localised. Among those who'd been knocked off their feet was the Secretary, Paymaster Lieutenant the Honourable James Colne-Wilshaw, whose action job was to keep the written 'narrative'. His notes of times, movements, orders and observed events were strewn about the iron deck under everyone else's feet.

'Twenty of starboard wheel on, sir.' The ship heeled under so much rudder . . .

Crick was down below; he'd be reporting, when he had a chance, on the state of things. Damage-control was a second-in-command's main responsibility. Hugh said, 'Midships, Pilot.'

'Midships!'

Rathbone, Hugh had noticed, was very cool and steady. He'd rather thought he might be, when it came to it.

'Ross-Hallet!'

'Sir?'

'Use the navyphone, tell Lieutenant Brook that within a few minutes I'll be turning away so he'll only have his after turrets bearing.'

Run for cover. If the next few minutes saw a continuance of good fortune . . .

'Captain, sir, message from the Commander, sir—'

'Wait.' It was a seaman boy, one of Tom Crick's party. Hugh said, 'Port ten, Pilot.' He looked back and down at the young messenger. 'Yes?'

'Shell burst in the W/T room, sir—'

Hugh interrupted him: 'Chief Yeoman?'

'Aye aye, sir.' Chief Petty Officer Peppard was already on his way. Hugh told him, 'Bring me a report as soon as possible.' The W/T cabinet was inside the bridge superstructure but on about its lowest level, the shelter deck. Hugh looked back at the messenger, who rattled on, 'It blew up into your sea-cabin, sir, and that's all wrecked—' Hugh thought, *Oh, God* . . . He wasn't thinking of the loss of his sea-cabin, but of the fact he'd told Bates to wait in it until he sent for him. The seaman boy concluded his report: 'Superstructure's on fire, sir, but commander says 'e'll soon 'ave it in 'and, sir.'

'Very good.' He looked round at Rathbone. 'Starboard fifteen.' By making the turns to port tighter, sharper than the ones to starboard, he was gradually easing her round; he wanted to get *Nile* round to a north-west course without making the intention so obvious that the German gunners might anticipate her movements. He also wanted news of Bates. 'Midships.'

'Captain, sir.' He looked round quickly at CPO Peppard, who told him, 'It's like the lad said, sir. W/T room's all smashed, and your cabin's gone too, sir. The fire's spread a bit but they're gettin' on top of it now.'

'Casualties?'

'One telegraphist killed, sir, three men 'urt. They've been took below, sir. Lieutenant Sallis was 'urt too, sir, an' the PO Tel, they've been took down to—'

'Ross-Hallet. Able Seaman Bates was supposed to be waiting in my sea-cabin. Go and—' he paused, while the guns fired and fresh spouts of German shells went up on the bow: he was about to finish what he'd been saying to the midshipman when something big clanged into *Nile*'s starboard side. He met Rathbone's calm, round eyes, and commented, 'That one was a dud'n.' Behind him, several men laughed. Amusement wasn't difficult to trigger. Hugh said, 'Port ten.'

Rathbone passed the helm order into the copper tube.

'See what you can find out, Mid.'

'Aye aye, sir.'

The chief yeoman finished his report: 'I was to tell you the commander's gone aft now, sir. Spot o' trouble – one in through the quarterdeck I believe, sir.'

'All right, Peppard.'

Crick would tell him, when he could, what was happening below. In the meantime, nobody could handle 'spots of trouble' more ably than Tom Crick . . . A shell exploded on the roof of 'B' turret, which was only a few feet from this conning-tower's hood and periscope. The smoke cleared: with his eardrums hurting, Hugh saw paintwork charred black but no other visible damage. Rathbone shouted, fiddling with his earplugs, 'Still have ten of port helm on, sir.'

'Midships!'

'B' turret had just fired, with the others, and it was comforting to think that some of *Nile*'s fifteen-inch shells would be smashing down into German ships . . .

'Starboard fifteen!'

He glanced, round at the hatch. But it was too soon for that midshipman to have got back yet.

Lanyard rang dully, sporadically, with the percussions of the Grand Fleet's salvoes. It was a distant sound, and intermittent. With the easier motion of the destroyer at this greatly reduced speed there was a sense, at least down here in the chartroom, of a lull in the storm of battle; a false lull, perhaps, which might be shattered at any moment. Meanwhile, this job was hardly a pleasant one. Nick dumped the contents of Johnson's pockets in a heap on the chart-table. There wasn't much; a wallet with some letters in it, a notebook, some stubs of pencil, a pocket-watch and a ring of keys. Reynolds' small possessions were similar, but included a silver cigarette-case and a metal match-container.

Nick weighed it for a moment in his hand. He'd seen Reynolds using this, in the wardroom, earlier this very day. Now it was an object to be packaged for transmission to the lieutenant's next of kin, so that the body could before long be 'committed' to the sea. For the time being it was outside on the foc'sl, together with the body of Pat Johnson – who'd seemed at first to be something of an ogre but who'd astounded Nick, this morning, with totally new aspects of his brother.

He'd never thought deeply about David; it had never occurred to him to try to understand him. Unpleasantness was all one had been conscious of. Coldness, hostility; resentment of his – Nick's – existence. And since in any dispute David had always had their father's backing, Nick had learnt to walk alone and avoid them both. Birds of a feather...Well, they were! And since that time in London, when he looked at his elder brother, what he saw in his mind's eye was a girl's face – bruised, swollen, pulpy...

He put Johnson's and Reynolds' keys aside. They'd be ship's keys – safes, pistol and rifle racks, the spirit store, and so on. Nick told Garret, who was helping him, 'Grab a couple of those old charts and make parcels, would you? Put their names on 'em. This pile's Lieutenant Johnson's.'

Garret complied wordlessly. Mortimer had told Nick to see to this, and as an afterthought he'd sent Garret down to help him. *Lanyard* was on the disengaged side of the battle fleet, and it was a good time for patching up, clearing away, making good. And for such tasks as this.

There'd be five men for burial, when the time for that came. Two men aft, as well as these; the torpedoman had died, and one of the for'ard gun's crew, and the coxswain, CPO Cuthbertson.

The guns had been sponged-out and greased, ready-racks refilled, ammunition stocks counted. Jury voicepipes, halyards and wireless aerials had been rigged. A collision-mat had been spread on the quarterdeck and lashed down with a steel-wire hawser laced to and fro over battens across the damaged area. Spare splinter-mattresses had been secured around the bridge. Finally, Nick had organised the cooks and some of the ammunition-supply ratings into a canteen service to provide tea and bully-beef sandwiches to all hands at their stations.

Lanyard was lazing along now at no more than fifteen knots, keeping station on the port side of the battle fleet. The fleet had slowed, in the course of its deployment, to avoid 'bunching' as the squadrons slid into place in the great, unwieldy line. Six miles of battleships . . . And coming now was the crucial phase, the duel between the dreadnoughts. Destroyer and cruiser actions had drawn blood, cost lives and ships, and there'd surely be more of the same – more dead, and more destroyed – before darkness fell; but the heavyweights were in the ring now and the big fight, the contest for the world championship, was about to follow that earlier sparring and jockeying for position.

He'd seen his uncle's ship, when *Lanyard* had overhauled her some while ago. *Nile* had suffered some hits, but looked none the worse for it; and the Fifth Battle Squadron would be out of harm's way by this time, because the way Jellicoe had deployed his other squadrons had left the Queen Elizabeths no alternative but to tag on at the rear. But Nick could understand his uncle now, understand the strength of his feeling for the Navy; a few hours of action, some moments of fear followed by longer periods of extraordinary exhilaration: the sight of the flotilla attacking, that wild charge against the line of blazing guns: the entire experience of these last hours had convinced him that the Service was – or could be, at times – what he'd been told it was, believed it to be: and he had the key now to the riddle of Hugh Everard's having retained enthusiasm for the naval service in spite of its having kicked him in the teeth.

'My own fault . . .'

Hugh had said that to his brother, Nick's father, at luncheon at Mullbergh, one day about four years ago. Nick, David and Sarah had been there too; Sarah had become the second Lady Everard only a few months earlier. She'd asked Hugh how he'd been forced to give up his career, and he'd answered briefly, quite dispassionately. She'd been indignant, cross with him, even, for 'taking it lying down'. He'd smiled at her angry face, and Nick had seen the effect of that smile and the quick glance she'd immediately thrown at her husband. Hugh had murmured, 'My own stupidity, perhaps

I should say. Jacky Fisher being the man he is, I should have – oh, been less ingenuous. Genius and rationality shouldn't be expected in one individual, you know.'

'Are you saying Lord Fisher's irrational?'

It was Sir John who was indignant now, glaring down the table at his brother. 'Surely Fisher, of all men, is the most practical, down-to-earth—'

'In directly professional matters, yes. But where personalities are concerned – why, Jacky'd smell treachery from a brick wall at a hundred paces with a clothes-peg on his nose!'

'One of the greatest men of this century, in my view.'

'I agree, John. Entirely.'

'But you feel free to blame him for your own failure?'

At the time of this conversation Nick had been seventeen, and a midshipman, not long at sea. Nineteen-twelve . . . He remembered the impression he'd had at that luncheon table that his father was trying to belittle Uncle Hugh in order to reduce him in Sarah's eyes; as if he didn't want his new, young wife to think anything of her brother-in-law. In fact they'd become the best of friends – not more than that, as David had been spiteful enough to suggest, but – well, friends. Which hadn't been enough, and still wasn't, for brother David . . . But anyway, it had been some trifling indiscretion, a social thing and quite meaningless, that had aroused Lord Fisher's displeasure. Displeasure and distrust: and Fisher was proud of his own ruthlessness. In 1904 Hugh Everard had been a member of the 'Fish Pond', a group of outstandingly promising young officers whom Fisher had inducted to the Admiralty and given influence and authority out of all proportion to their ranks or years; high-flyers all: and he promoted them over the heads of older, more experienced men, making enemies for himself and them in the process. 'Favouritism', declared Fisher, 'is the secret of efficiency!' With favouritism went despotism; at thirty-three, in 1904, Hugh had been a commander; in 1906, the year of his marriage, he was promoted to post captain, eight years ahead of the most favourable normal expectation. In 1907, Fisher broke him.

The damage hadn't been permanent, as things had turned out now. For some years Hugh had worked for a shipbuilding company, but the war had brought him back to active service and the Falklands victory had re-established him as an up-and-comer and led to his being offered the command of *Nile*. Fisher, of course, had gone. He'd built this fleet, bulldozed it into being. But a year ago his quarrels with the First Lord, Winston Churchill, had reached a climax, primarily over the Dardanelles issue. Fisher had been opposed to the Gallipoli adventure right from the beginning. A year ago, goaded beyond an old man's endurance by the young politician, he'd stalked out of the Admiralty for the last time, not so much defeated as bemused, an old dog snarling through broken teeth at enemies real and unreal.

Garret scrawled *1st Lieut* on one package, and *Lt Reynolds* on the other. He asked Nick, 'Reckon we'll come off best, sir?'

'Good God, yes! Of course!'

Garrett nodded. Somewhere ahead and to starboard a battleship's guns fired one broadside, and fell silent. One could visualise the shifting mist-banks, the eyes pressed against periscopes and range-finders, searching constantly for targets. The signalman hardly seemed convinced; Nick explained to him that Jellicoe's course was now roughly south-east, and that Hipper's battle cruisers in the van of the German fleet had been bent off-course, eastward, first by Beatty and more recently by the deploying battle fleet. It was doubtful whether Admiral Scheer yet appreciated how powerful an enemy lay across his line of advance. The poor visibility was maddening to the Grand Fleet, but it might also be a blessing in disguise, hiding Jellicoe from Scheer. Meanwhile the German line, as Scheer's leading division followed Hipper round, was an arc, a curve that started

northwards and sheered away east as it flinched from the
wall of advancing British dreadnoughts.

Garret reached for his enamelled mug of dark-brown tea.
Nick asked him, 'Rough up there, was it, when we—' he
glanced down at the parcels on the table – 'when we got that
hit?'

Garret nodded as he put his mug down. 'It's the standin',
wi' no work to do. Just waitin' – you get time to think – like
about if – if you're a married man, say . . .'

'Yes.' The tea tasted like liquid boot-polish. 'I'm lucky,
that way, with no ties. But you only just got married, didn't
you.'

Garret bit into a thick sandwich. The packages in front of
them kept their voices low, reminded them of the bodies
outside on the foc'sl between the for'ard four-inch ready-
racks and the rattling steel bulkhead of this chartroom.
Garret chewed thoughtfully, glancing at Nick and away
again while his thoughts made a quick trip to Edinburgh,
took a look at Margaret, and came back.

'Don't you have any—' he hesitated, as if having
embarked on the question embarrassed him – 'Any young
lady, as it might be, sir?'

Nick thought about it. Chewing the last of his door-stop
sandwich while Garret swirled dregs of tea around the
bottom of his mug. Young lady . . . Did Greta Magnusson,
the Orcadian crofter's daughter, rate as a 'young lady'?

It wasn't the social aspect he was questioning. It was just
that he didn't think of her in such terms, any more than he'd
think of Sarah, his stepmother, as a 'young lady'. They were
both well, different . . . 'Young ladies', as he'd understood
the words, were the giggly creatures one met, danced with,
played tennis with, and so on, in other large Yorkshire
houses. He'd never yet met one he'd found at all interesting
or more than passingly attractive, and in any case they'd
always directed all their interest at his brother David. He was
the heir, of course, and the good-looking, taller one; the one

who danced better, played better tennis, and who didn't keep falling off the horses which he was more or less forced to ride.

But Greta Magnusson belonged in the setting of the Orkneys. It struck him as he thought of her that if he was back there, next week, say, and told her all about this battle, how it had seemed and felt, and how he was suddenly feeling that he belonged, that this was the Navy he'd wanted, dreamed about and had begun to think didn't exist at all – well, Greta would have said something like, *Och, is that so?* and changed the subject at once, to fish, or sheep, or what her father had said yesterday.

Finishing the crust, he swallowed hard, making an effort of it to justify the length of time it had taken him to produce an answer. He shook his head.

'Not really.'

In *Nile*'s 'X' turret, everything had been running as smoothly as it ever had, until the loading rammers jammed.

Cartwright had been feeling proud of his men: and not unproud of himself, for the way he'd trained them. However hard you worked at it, and however good a performance looked when it was a wood-and-canvas target you were shooting at, you always wondered how it would pan out when it was a live target that shot back at you. And this had gone off, so far, like the best of the practice shoots; except that there was excitement, elation and a terrific sense of satisfaction in them all. Not just because this at last was action, justification for all the weary months of training and waiting; but also that they were measuring-up, matching-up to the high standards of their Service, fleet, ship. Those standards had seemed intimidatingly high, sometimes, but nobody was falling down on the job now. Nobody would, either; you could see it in their faces, in the swift, confident, skilful way they worked, keeping the guns firing – firing fast and hitting.

Information came now and then from Lieutenant Brook in the control top to his turret officers, and here in 'X' turret Captain Blackaby passed it on to the men who worked the guns.

They'd been told during the last half-hour that the German battleships *Grosser Kurfürst* and *Markgraf* had each been hit several times. Those were the two at which *Nile*, *Malaya* and *Warspite* had been shooting mostly, during the run northwards. Also the battle cruisers *Seydlitz*, *Lutzow* and *Derfflinger* were in poor shape now; *Seydlitz* particularly: she was on fire, four of her turret guns had been silenced, her secondary armament had been completely smashed, and shell-damage to her foc'sl had left her down by the head and losing speed. *Von der Tann* had no turrets left that she could shoot with; she was still in the line with the other battle cruisers, but she was toothless . . . And now *Lutzow*, *Derfflinger* and *Markgraf* had all been hit again, during the last few minutes. 'X' turret's crew cheered as the right-hand gun fired, flung back; the cage came up – left gun fired – number two of the right gun swung the breech open and Cartwright roared 'Right gun STILL!'

He'd seen number two – Dewar, of course – open the breech too soon, before the gun had finished its run-out; the carrier arm of the breech had struck the rammer head, and metal-bound it. So the rammer had stuck and now the port rammer had too. Cartwright swore loudly and articulately as he flung himself off his seat. Until this moment, everything had gone so smoothly, easily; there'd been none of the silly over-eagerness which could be counted on to lead to this sort of jam-up and consequent delay. Up in the control top, Lieutenant Brook would be cursing when 'X' turret's gun-ready lamps failed to light; *Nile*, for the moment, would be firing three-gun salvoes, and Captain Blackaby, normally quite a patient man, would very shortly be exploding with Royal Marine-type fury. Cartwright shoved Dewar out of his way, taking some satisfaction in using a considerable degree of force; he snatched up a steel pinch-bar, and shoved its end in behind the rammer head. Then he jerked the lever over to the 'Run Out' position; and the rammer slid out, sweet and quick and no more bother. Cartwright brought it back again and out two more times, and there it was, gay as a lark again, right gun back in action.

'Load!'

He passed the steel bar over to the captain of the left gun, and went quickly back to his seat to lay the gun by pointer, following the director's. The gun was ready just in time, and the second the interceptor switch was shut, it fired. They were loading again: cage up, rammer thudding over, projectile up the spout and then the charge hard up behind it. Cartwright thought he'd take a look, see what was happening out there; he got up, and put his eyes to the periscope.

Nothing. They'd heard a few German shells hit, from time to time, and one of them had blown muck of some sort over the outer glass. He could see some sort of wreckage; could be anything, just black. He felt *Nile* turning. He was back on his seat quickly, he kept the pointers lined up; gun ready – fired – recoiling – running out ... loading again, and no problems now. He spoke to Captain Blackaby on the telephone.

'Cartwright here, sir. Don't matter so bad, since we're in director-firing but this periscope's fouled up outside, sir. 'Appen we'd go in local control, wouldn't be too easy, sir. Dunno we might send a hand out?'

Blackaby peered through the cabinet's periscope. *Nile* had turned to port, and so had the ships ahead of her. It was a 'blue' turn, which had left the squadron in quarter-line, but the turrets had trained round on to the starboard quarter and still bore on the enemy.

'If we get a chance, I'll see to it.' He hung the navyphone back on its hook. Midshipman Mellors suggested, 'Say the word, sir, and I'll nip out. Shouldn't take a second.' Blackaby was using the periscope again, and for a moment or two he didn't answer. *Warspite*, for some reason that was difficult to fathom, had suddenly gone off on her own. She'd hauled out between the squadron and the enemy; and *Nile*, for the moment, couldn't shoot at all. If there was ever going to be a moment to clear that periscope, this was it. He buzzed the gunner's mate.

'Cartwright, I'm sending Midshipman Mellors out. Break both interceptors.'

'Aye aye, sir! '

With interceptor switches broken, the guns couldn't be fired. And if 'Y' turret did – which was unlikely, in the next half-minute – it would be on that after bearing, pointing the other way. It might frighten the snotty, but it wouldn't hurt him.

'Both guns at half-cock, sir!'

'Right . . . Go on, Mellors. Be damn quick, eh?'

The boy scuttled out, and the hatch clanged shut behind him. Blackaby watched through his periscope, wondering what *Warspite* was up to. She certainly couldn't be doing it for fun: she was being hit hard and often. It occurred to him that she might be out of control, with steering jammed, or – *Christ*, but the Huns were going for her! He felt *Nile*'s lurch as she began a sharp turn to starboard; checking on *Malaya*, the next ahead, he realised that this was yet another solo effort. The turret trained exactly as fast as the ship swung, since the director kept its sights trained on the enemy and the turrets followed the director. *Nile* was still under helm; still swinging, anyway: and Blackaby guessed that she was going out of the line to cover *Warspite*, who was quite obviously in bad trouble. There wasn't any other explanation.

Where the blazes was that snotty? Blackaby bit his lip; time was a peculiar thing, in action. Fifteen seconds could seem to take five minutes. But surely—

'A', 'B' and 'Y' turrets all fired.

He heard salvoes hitting, as German gunners switched to the new target which was being presented to them. Shut in an armoured turret it was difficult to know where the hits had been; there'd been savage, penetrating clangs and the deep thuds of detonations below decks. Three – four – and the other turrets had all fired again . . . Brook was calling on the navyphone from the Control Top.

'What's wrong, Blackaby?'

Blackaby told him he'd sent a man out to clear an obstructed periscope.

'Well, for God's sake get him back inside!'

'Right.'

How? Panic stations up there, by the sound of it. The moment had not, after all, been such a good one to clear that damn thing. How long had Mellors been outside – a minute? Less? Two salvoes, that would account for a minute and a third one now . . . *Nile* had steadied, but she'd begun a new turn, the other way; there was a thunderous explosion which seemed – felt – to have been astern, and Blackaby had nothing in front of his periscope but smoke.

Cartwright, waiting for his glass to be cleared, was just as anxious. He was thinking they ought to shut the interceptors and get back into action. Things were much too brisk up top for a turret to be standing idle, and it seemed obvious that the midshipman must have come to grief. Even if he hadn't, the guns would only break his eardrums.

The periscope was clear, suddenly. There was smoke, where before there'd been something solid; smoke, swirling thickly. *Nile* was being battered and that smoke was from shell-bursts; if you were out there, it'd be enough to gas you if you weren't already dead. He put a hand on the navyphone and saw Midshipman Mellors' face in the smoke. The boy's eyes were staring at him – into the glass of the periscope – wide, dead eyes. Mellors was crouched on the roof of the turret, kneeling, bent over, staring at the periscope and his arms clamped across his belly. He seemed to be clasping a mass of blood and as he toppled sideways Cartwright saw it all just fall away . . . He – Cartwright – had the navyphone in his fist: he raised it, and reported, 'Midshipman Mellors is dead, sir. Periscope's clear.' Mellors' remains slid, vanished over the turret's edge. Blackaby snapped, 'Salvoes – director firing – right gun commencing – recock!'

Back to four-gun salvoes . . .

In the torpedo control tower, just above 'X' turret and for'ard of it, Midshipman Greenlaws had been watching the movements of his friend Mellors and he'd seen everything that had happened to him. Greenlaws was leaning with his face against the starboard sighting hole; he felt sick and weak. He was leaning there when the first detonation of 'X' turret's guns for two minutes flung him backwards against the corner of the range-finder, and knocked thoughts of sickness out of his head. Knox-Wilson, the torpedo lieutenant, said sharply, 'And that was your own damn fault, Mid!'

He'd spoken roughly – out of impatience and also because Greenlaws was a bright lad, by no means wet or soft, and he needed reminding of it. There was also the question of setting an example to the other members of this control tower's crew. Knox-Wilson told Pugh, the communications rating, 'Ask Mr Askell what progress he's making.' Pugh was putting his hand out to the navyphone when its light began to flash; Knox-Wilson muttered, his words lost in the screech of a salvo tearing overhead, 'Speak of the devil . . .' His eyes were on the smoke pouring out of *Nile*'s bridge superstructure, streaming away over her port quarter; sparks flew in it . . . But he was right, it was the torpedo gunner on the navyphone, and he was telling Ordinary Seaman Pugh, 'The bugger's clear now. You can use it when you want.'

'Wait, sir, please.' Pugh passed the message to Knox-Wilson, who nodded. 'Good. Tell him—' he paused, as the guns crashed out, lobbing another fifteen-inch salvo at the enemy – 'tell him—' Deep thuds and the crack of hits came from somewhere for'ard; shell-spouts leapt in a close group flinging black water at the funnels. Knox-Wilson roared, 'Tell him I'm firing soon, he'd better stay there!'

Askell was in the for'ard torpedo flat, which was way down below the waterline – six, seven decks below the air and daylight and just for'ard of 'A' turret's revolving hoist. The torpedo flat occupied the full width of the ship, with one tube aimed out on each side. The starboard one had run into trouble some while ago; they'd fired from the after torpedo flat at longish range, and as they were now a lot closer to the enemy it seemed a good time to take another shot.

'Range?'

A salvo ripped over and burst just off the quarter. *Nile* had taken a fair number of hits; there'd have been far more if it hadn't been for the way she'd been handled, the erratic dodging. Knox-Wilson wondered how many shells had penetrated, what things might be like below decks ... 'What's the range, Kilfeather, damn it!'

He was trying to line-up his torpedo-firing disc, and being under constant helm wasn't making it any easier ... Leading Torpedoman Kilfeather, the range-taker, reported finally, 'One-double-oh, sir.'

'So if we take their course as north-east by east, the distance off track will be ...' he was muttering to himself, fiddling with the disc, and now peering over Greenlaws' shoulder at the plotter. 'H'm.' He nodded, and yelled at Pugh, 'Stand by!'

Greenlaws had worked out the deflection. Kilfeather, with his eyes at the lenses of the range-finder, called suddenly, 'Range about to be hobscured, sir!' Knox-Wilson leant to the sighting hole, and stared out; he saw a cruiser laying smoke, coming southwards at high speed; she was about to pass and hang the curtain of her smoke between *Nile* and the tail end of the German line. Within seconds they'd be cut off from each other's sight; and with the cruiser where she was there was no chance of getting a torpedo away quickly, before that happened. Arriving on an opposite course as she had, she'd less approached than suddenly appeared.

The enemy's salvoes were already thinning out. But the

cruiser was about to pay for interfering in the Germans' sport. Ahead of her the sea was alive with shell-fire. They were smaller splashes, probably from the battleships' secondary armament, but it amounted to a rain of fire, an explosive hailstorm she was steaming into. From the shape of her forepart, which except for the brown cordite haze flung out by her own guns was clear of smoke, he guessed she was one of the *Minotaur* class. She'd almost passed now; watching her, Knox-Wilson found himself willing her to turn, praying she'd put her helm over *now*, retire behind her own smoke-cover. She'd done the job: he whispered in his mind, *Now go on, get out of it, for God's sake!*

At last . . . He realised he'd been holding his breath. He let it out, and sat back a bit.

Nile was getting out of it, too; turning away. There'd have been no chance now of firing that torpedo. She was swinging her stern towards the Germans, who would probably still have her masts and upperworks in sight above the smoke; but they wouldn't have for much longer. In any case it was the cruiser they were bombarding now. He saw a salvo hit her as she altered round; two hits amidships, twin orange bursts of flame that seemed to split the swirling smoke, and then a streak of fire that shot up the side of her bridge superstructure. Seeing it, imagining what it might be like to be on that bridge, he winced; and in the same instant a new salvo came whistling down on *Nile*.

Lieutenant-Commander Mortimer was staring aft, with his binoculars levelled at an area of smoke way out over his destroyer's starboard quarter. He was trying to catch some glimpse of *Nile* or *Warspite* or of the cruiser *Warrior*.

There was still a vast quantity of smoke down there, and he couldn't see any of them; it was only that in these changeable conditions of visibility one did from time to time get a clearance, an unexpected view through haze which as suddenly clamped down again. He'd seen *Defence* blow up;

in fact her destruction must have been witnessed from as many as fifty different ships, when the battle fleet had been starting its deployment and every Tom, Dick and Harry had been rushing across its van. He'd also seen *Warrior* reeling from salvo after salvo, burning, slowing to a crawl, trying to creep away somewhere like a wounded animal to lick her wounds. That German cruiser – he'd thought she might be the *Wiesbaden* – which *Defence*'s squadron had rushed out to attack, had been still afloat though burning from end to end, and a destroyer – *Onslow*, from *Lanyard*'s own flotilla – had had a crack at her with torpedoes, and scored a hit, but got badly smashed-up herself in the process; she'd lain stopped, licking her wounds, then incredibly got going again for a solo attack on the Hun battleships. He'd lost track of her about then, because it had been at this stage that he'd seen *Warspite*'s helm jam.

Lanyard had been on the Fifth Battle Squadron's port bow, then, shaping course to get round astern of the battle fleet. There'd been no shells falling near them – which had made a pleasant change, a breathing-space – and there'd been no visible prospect of action in the immediate future; so when Everard came up to the bridge to report he'd completed various jobs, it had been a good moment to send him down to do another. Consequently Everard hadn't seen *Nile* come out and charge the enemy: and that might be just as well.

Considering all things, *Lanyard* herself had been lucky, so far. When one thought of *Nestor* and *Nomad*, left behind. . . *Nestor*'s captain, Bingham, had waved a 'leave-us-to-it' signal to *Nicator*. It wouldn't have made sense to have hung around and there would have been no time to take her in tow. Even to have attempted it would have been a matter of throwing away another ship; it would have cost lives, not saved them. But it still hadn't been easy, to steam away and leave one's friends in the lurch.

'Sir. You sent for me.'

Mortimer glanced round, and saw Worsfold, his commissioned engineer.

'So I did.' Worsfold's face was set, inscrutable. The man had that kind of face anyway, but there was also the circumstance – which was in both their minds – that the last time he'd appeared on the bridge Mortimer had threatened him with death.

It was when he'd just left *Nestor* sinking, and lost two officers and *Lanyard*'s coxswain. Worsfold had picked a bad time to come up with his bleat about how the destroyer's engines should or should not be used.

'All right now, Chief?'

'I'd say we eased up just in time, sir.' Worsfold hesitated. 'Used a lot of fuel, of course. But so long as there's no more prolonged high-speed —'

'You know damn well I can't guarantee anything of the sort!'

They stared at each other. Worsfold added, 'Slight leak on one feed-tank, sir. We can cope with it if it gets no worse.'

'What caused it?'

'A hit aft, sir. I think when the gun went overboard.'

'Yes.' Mortimer nodded. He cleared his throat. 'Chief, I'm afraid I lost my temper, earlier on. I apologise, and I congratulate you on the job you've been doing. You and your staff.'

The engineer's thin lips twitched. Mortimer had turned to stare at the destroyer ahead of *Lanyard*; she'd done a sudden jink to port, but it had probably been only a helmsman's momentary aberration. In any case, Hastings had his eyes on her. Worsfold murmured, 'No firing squad this time, sir?'

'Chief.'

'Sir'

'I can't stand having my bridge cluttered-up with bloody plumbers. Get to hell off it, would you?'

Hastings winked at Worsfold as he turned away. At the same moment, the battle fleet's hitherto sporadic gunfire seemed to thicken, solidify and rise to a crescendo, as if every ship in the vast line of dreadnoughts had suddenly found a target.

Mortimer had whipped up his glasses.

'My God, look at that!'

Emerging from thick haze in the south was the head of Scheer's battle line. And the leading German battleship, as she came thrusting out of the murk into clearer air, was being hit simultaneously by *Agincourt, Bellerophon, Conqueror, Thunderer, Hercules, Colossus, Benbow, Iron Duke, Orion, Monarch, Royal Oak,* and *Revenge.*

The leading German ship had burst into flames. Her whole forepart was ablaze, and the rest was smoke.

'She's turning away!'

Mortimer added, murmuring it to himself, 'Can't say I blame her . . .'

The battle cruisers up ahead, who had also felt the rough edge of Jellicoe's welcome, had swung off to starboard, and the front division of Scheer's dreadnoughts was now following them. The entire High Seas Fleet was tightening its curve away to starboard as its leaders flinched from the concentrated fire-power of the British squadrons.

Nick, with Garret close behind him, climbed into the bridge. Blewitt muttered, pointing, 'They're blowin' the 'uns to kingdom come, sir!'

The mist was lifting. Three, four, six German battleships were in sight now, and all of them were being hit repeatedly. Scheer, the layer of traps, must know now – *now*, in what must have been his most terrible moment ever – that what he'd steamed into was the mother and father of all traps. Jellicoe's deployment, the decision he'd taken on no more than scraps of information, had put his squadrons into the perfect position for the destruction of the High Seas Fleet.

The noise of the cannonade was tremendous; and in between the crashes of gunfire and the echoes of bursting shells there was a new sound – cheering. Guns' crews,

bridge and signals staffs, every man on any upper deck –
their cheers rose, swelled, rolled across the grey-green sea
from ship to ship and were drowned only in the renewed
thunder of the guns. The smoke and flames of detonating
shells smothered the German line. They were shooting back,
but compared to the punishment being dealt out to them it
was no more than a token resistance as their line bent,
sheered away. And as the leaders turned, others were
pressing up astern to get *their* rations.

Mortimer, holding his glasses in his left hand and pointing
with the other, shouted, 'They're running away, by God!'

Whenever there was a view of German ships, through
gaps in the British line and where the mist was thinnest,
Scheer's battleships were swinging away to starboard in a
simultaneous about-turn. They were reversing their course,
retreating into the cover of the mist.

One had heard quite a lot of this emergency-turn man-
oeuvre. The Germans had one of their long words for it,
which when translated, meant, 'Battle-Turn-Away' – a
splendidly Teutonic euphemism for 'cut and run'!

Captain Blackaby, struggling out of his cabinet into 'X'
turret's gunhouse, was blinded and half suffocated by smoke
and the acrid reek of high explosive. A shell had come in
through the turret roof. He'd heard and felt it and seen a
great flattish disc of orange flame before his periscope had
shattered. The range-finder was smashed too. In here men
were choking, reeling about; some, dead or wounded, were
still or writhing on the deck. He could hear questions being
asked, men calling their friends' names.

'Cartwright! GM!'

He pushed someone out of his way, stumbled over a man
crawling on hands and knees. Light seeped down from
above, where the hole was. He found Cartwright; the petty
officer was face-down, sprawled in a heap of blue serge and
blood; Blackaby noticed how his boots still gleamed, and

that there was no back to his head. It wasn't necessary to turn him or look more closely to know that he was dead.

'Captain Blackaby, sir?'

It was Dewar, the right gun's number two. Blackaby told him, 'Get the hatch open, Dewar, let some air through.'

'Aye aye, sir!'

It was already clearing, in fact, through the ordinary ventilation and assisted by the hole which the shell had made in the roof, in the centre plate of the sighting hood. It had burst there, detonating as it penetrated the steel armour; you could see that by the size of the hole and the way the edges of the steel were bent upwards. It occurred to Blackaby that if the shell had come right inside before its fuse fired it, things would have been a great deal worse. Men were picking themselves up – those that could – and moving back towards their places at the guns; others were trying to help the wounded. Dewar had the hatch open, and the clearing air was helping stunned men to recover. Blackaby had been slightly dazed, but he was clearer now. He shouted, 'Turret's crew, *number*!'

That way, he got them sorted out. Five men, including the gunner's mate, couldn't answer. Of those, three were still alive. There were seven others wounded, two of whom said they could carry on. Blackaby got the spare crew up from below, and the men he didn't need he detailed to get the wounded to the surgeons and the dead out on the quarterdeck. The second captain-of-turret was a young petty officer by the name of Davies.

'Test loading gear, Davies.'

'Aye aye, sir!'

Both cages were jammed. They freed the right one: the left was immovable. Luckily it had stuck in the 'down' position, where it wouldn't interfere with hand-loading, and Davies sang out, 'Left gun hand-loading in gunhouse!'

Cartwright had drilled them well. Number five had repeated the order to the magazine and shellroom; numbers six and eight of the shellroom came up into the working-chamber to become numbers nine and ten. Meanwhile five had got the main cage door off, and Petty Officer Davies had shut off pressure to the cage mechanism and slammed the door shut in the auxiliary trunk. Blackaby stood back, fingering his moustache, as the wounded were helped and carried out.

'Surgeon'll soon fix you up, you fellows. You'll see, you'll be as right as rain!'

'Aye, sir!' A sightsetter, who looked as if he'd been scalped, grinned at him; he was holding a scarlet, sodden wad of cotton-waste against his forehead. He said, 'Don't you worry about us, sir. We'll be gettin' a whack o' leave, we will!' They all cheered; Blackaby told them, 'By God, I could make Marines of you lot!' His eyes shifted, to watch the men at work around the gun; except for the dead and wounded and that hole in the roof through which steely light probed into a swirl of still faintly yellowish vapour, this might have been a practice.

'I want that right gun back in action, Davies!'

'Aye aye, sir!'

Davies was a pale, fair-haired man with a Welsh lilt and a squinting eye; now he left the left gun's hand-loading preparation to the spare left gun-captain, and shouted, 'Right gun, load!' The cage hissed up and the rammer slid across; projectile in, charge in, rammer clanking back. Dewar slammed the breech shut. The layer put his right arm up, and number three banged the interceptor shut.

'Y' turret fired, but the loaded and cocked right gun of 'X' turret remained inert.

Davies shouted, as was laid-down in the drill book, 'Still! Missfire!'

Blackaby thought it was probably the director firing circuits that had failed; most likely they'd been cut. If so, protracted missfire procedures now would be a waste of time. And since in a moment the left gun would be ready, one would very soon know for certain. The left gun's projectile had come up on the grab, the chain-hoist, and they'd eased it into its loading-tray; now the rammer did the rest, and the charge went in, and Blackaby saw number three on that side shut his interceptor.

'Left gun ready!'

It didn't fire, though, with the next salvo. Two of the spare hands were carrying Petty Officer Cartwright out. The back of the gunner's mate's head was a pulp of bone, brain and blood. The layer of the left gun shouted 'Still! Missfire!'

Both interceptors were now broken; both guns loaded. Blackaby ordered, 'Gunlayer firing, salvoes, right gun commencing!'

The fact the turret had no periscope or sights of any kind now didn't matter. The layers would keep their pointers lined-up with director's pointers, so the guns would remain on target, and they'd press their own triggers when they heard 'Y' turret fire.

The right gun fired, recoiled, ran out. Its crew were reloading as number three of the left gun shut its interceptor and reported 'Left gun ready!'

'X' turret was back in business.

Blackaby went back into his cabinet, to report to the control top. Brook said, 'Well done, Blacko. But we've nothing to shoot at, for the moment. All we can see is smoke . . . Damn sorry about Cartwright.'

'Yes.' The cabinet door opened – from the outside – and Blackaby saw the commander stooping, peering in at him. He hung up the navyphone.

'Got yourselves to rights, eh, Soldier?'

'Yessir. Chaps've done splendidly.'

'Quite,' Crick's pink face beamed. 'Bit of a lull now, too. I should stand 'em down, one gun's crew at a time, if I were you. Give 'em a stand-easy while we're quiet?'

'Good idea, sir.'

Crick, his long frame bent double, withdrew. Blackaby

got on the navyphone to Davies.

'Petty Officer Davies. Five minutes' stand-down for each gun's crew alternately. And let Dewar play his blasted gramophone if he wants to.'

'Aye aye, sir!'

Crick climbed out of the turret, and shut the hatch behind him. He moved aft around 'Y' turret, and banged with his heel on the lid of the hatch beside the capstan; the man inside it, at the top of the ladderway, knocked a retaining clip off and pushed the hatch up, and Crick eased himself down inside. The sailor had to lean out sideways on the ladder's edge to give him room.

'Thank you. Shut and clip it now. I'll go back through the ship.' He'd only come up from here a few minutes ago, when he'd had a message about Blackaby's turret. At the bottom of the ladderway he turned aft, crossed the lobby which was lined each side with cabins – including his own – and passed through the bulkhead doorway to the captain's lobby.

It was all fumes and stink. Charred paintwork, and the reek of burnt corticene; the resin under it ran like viscous, stinking glue. The captain's day-cabin and sleeping-cabin had both been wrecked; there seemed to have been two hits by large-calibre shells, something like twelve-inch, and one of these had burst in the deck of the dining-cabin, opening a ten-foot diameter hole to the secretary's clerks' office immediately below, on the middle deck. The captain's dining-table was charred, wet matchwood, but that cabin hadn't suffered as badly as the others, since the blast had all gone downwards, apparently. The day- and sleeping-cabins had been transformed into one large room in which a herd of elephants might have run amok before someone set fire to it; and a third shell had burst outside the hull at the level of the main deck and carved away most of the catwalk which ran around the ship's stern. The fire brigade had got their hoses in this way, using what was left of the captain's private balcony to stand on while they jetted water in from outside. It hadn't been possible to get in, at first, the way Crick had just come.

But it was all in hand now. Steam rose from fire-heated steel and paintwork, smoking rubbish and the gluey mess of corticene. Water from the hoses, a great deal of it, had flooded down through the holed deck into the offices below, and 'Pay' was down there cursing loudly and continuously while he and some of his writers tried to rescue ledgers and other saturated documents. But the emergency situation here was over now, and Crick had only returned to make sure of one thing: he asked the petty officer in charge of this number eight fire brigade, 'Has Able Seaman Bates gone for'ard?'

He'd found Bates here, trying to rescue the captain's personal possessions, and getting himself more or less cooked in the process. He'd ordered him for'ard; but the captain's coxswain wasn't a man who could be relied upon to obey orders with anything like alacrity – not unless the orders were issued personally by Hugh Everard.

Petty Officer Ainslie grinned, his teeth white as a nigger minstrel's in his blackened face. 'Yessir. Picked up all 'e could lay 'is 'ands on, an' 'opped it.'

'Good.' Crick glanced round the wreck of the captain's quarters. Bates, he thought, was like a one-man dog. He corrected that; a one-man ape . . . 'Nothing much more you can do here, Ainslie.'

'Just makin' sure, sir. Some of the wood's still smoulderin' inside.'

Crick told him, 'I'll send the chief carpenter along to get those holes plugged.' He meant the ones in the deckhead, the quarterdeck. But none of this was serious damage; the ship's fighting efficiency had been hardly scratched, and so far as he'd been able to discover – touch wood – there was no damage at all below the waterline.

He walked for'ard, alternating between the main, middle and upper decks, as ladderways permitted. He'd seen to the damage on the starboard side, on his way aft; there'd been two fire brigades at work there, and he'd left the chief carpenter, Mr Wise, in charge. The after starboard six-inch gun casemate had been penetrated by a shell that burst inside and killed the entire gun's crew; another shell from the same salvo had burst in the casemate lobby and wiped out almost all the starboard ammunition-supply numbers. That gun's crew had been Marines. When he'd been there on his way aft they'd already got the wounded down to the after emergency operating room, and they'd been plugging cut fire-mains, trying to stop water pouring into the ventilation trunks; the trunks had to be kept open or men down below would suffocate. Apart from the broken fire-mains, tons of water had burst in from near-miss 'shorts' deluging into the shattered casemate.

On the port side, everything was intact and happy. Marines of the six-inch ammunition-supply parties were playing cards; a noisy game, which involved flinging the cards down and shouting at each other. A corporal asked him what was happening up top; he told them that everything was fine, that *Nile* had hit the enemy a couple of dozen times and the Huns had barely bruised her paintwork; that she'd come out of it fighting-fit, and now things were so quiet up there it was like being in church. The men cheered, and the cheer was taken up right through the casemates and the lobbies. Crick went on for'ard. There really were no problems; it was astonishing how lightly *Nile* had suffered. This had been the first test, she'd stood a real, hard hammering and sailed out smiling. Casualties were fairly heavy, but nothing like they might have been; and if *Warspite* had been saved, that would put a thousand plus-marks against these minuses.

There was still one area of damage he hadn't checked. There'd been a hit up for'ard, on the starboard side, in the master-at-arms' mess. But he went over to the port side first, and told Mr Wise to transfer his expertise to the damage aft as soon as he felt he could leave this lot to his henchmen. Wise seemed to be well on top of things now, and Crick moved on for'ard, taking the bo'sun, PO Harkmore, and Ordinary Seaman Thompson, his own messenger, along with him. He'd lent them to Mr Wise when he'd had his hands full there; now he led them past the ladderway which ran up to the bridge superstructure. There'd been some hits here too, around S3 and S4 casemates, but no real harm done, just smashed lights and so on – round 'B' barbette and through the foc'slmen's mess on the starboard side. Ahead of him, he could see the damage. The inboard bulkhead of the jaunty's mess had been blown out, ripped. Jagged flanges of sheet-steel jutted towards the centre-line. The mess itself was a ruin, although the fire had been put out before it had taken a real hold. The bulkhead between this section and the ERAs' mess for'ard of it was bulged and charred. But it was all in hand; number two fire brigade were clearing up, collecting debris, sweeping up broken glass, and a party of torpedomen under Mr Askell the warrant officer, were repairing cables on the deckhead. Amidships, the skylight over the sickbay had been shattered. Crick peered in, getting a bird's-eye view of sickberth ratings attending to a queue of lightly wounded men. Some of them looked up and saw him, and there were the usual questions to which he gave the same answers – and again the men cheered.

The glass on the skylight for'ard of this one was intact. It was over the centre of the operating room. There was a man on the table and two on stretchers awaiting their turns; the one on the table was having a leg removed.

Over on the port side, the chief stokers' mess and its pantry hadn't suffered from the blast. And all the men here were exceptionally cheerful, probably because they'd been through an unusually brisk action and come out alive, fit to tell the tale . . . He turned to PO Harkmore.

'Nothing to worry us here, Bo'sun. We'd better go and see how they've managed up top.'

'Aye, sir.' Harkmore was a big man; he'd reached the semi-finals in the Fleet heavyweight boxing competition up in Scapa, and Crick had thought he should have won it. If he, Tom Crick, had been the referee, Harkmore would have.

The bridge superstructure, when he'd last seen it, had been well ablaze from the shell which had burst in the captain's sea-cabin. He went quickly up the ladder to the foc'sl deck, and then the next one to the shelter deck; one more climb brought him and his party to the level of the conning-tower.

The captain wasn't in it. Rathbone was, and a midshipman and some signalmen, and the spare director's crew, but everyone else had gone back up to monkey's island, Rathbone said. Crick walked back the thirty-odd feet to the ladder, and climbed again. The fire had spread, before they'd got it contained and stifled. The superstructure around him as he climbed the ladderways was black, distorted and stinking, but the two upper levels were undamaged. As he stepped on to the fore bridge, he saw Hugh Everard raise a cup to his lips as if he felt he needed it.

'Bates, this stuff's cold!'

Crick saw Hugh's coxswain hurry forward.

'Beg pardon, sir, that's what I give you a 'alf-hour or more ago.'

'Oh, is it.' Hugh pushed the cup into his coxswain's hand. 'Get me some fresh, will you.' He saw Crick, 'How is it, Tom?'

'Not at all bad, sir, considering – except you personally seem to have no home left.'

'So I hear.' Hugh told him, 'I'm taking Rathbone's sea-cabin. He'll doss in the chartroom.'

'On the whole, sir, we've got off lightly.'

'Good.' The wild, zigzagging course had been *intended* to let *Nile* off lightly. Hugh trained his glasses on the other ships of *Nile*'s squadron. They were six or seven miles ahead, but they'd be reducing speed as they formed astern of the battle fleet, and it wouldn't take long to close up on them.

Hugh had a feeling that he'd done a worthwhile job. *Warspite* was on her own, north-westward from here, steaming west at slow speed. Badly hurt, obviously, but at least she was still afloat.

Hugh lowered his glasses, and turned to his second-in-command. A thought struck him; he shouted, 'Bates!'

'Sir ?'

The coxswain's voice had come from one deck down.

'Bring a cup for the commander as well!'

'Aye aye, sir!'

Hugh nodded to Tom Crick. 'All right, Tom. Tell me how lightly.'

Chapter 8

*B*antry was alone. The Germans who'd been battering her, and from whom perhaps she'd saved *Nile*, had gone – eastwards. It was all mist there; grey, impenetrable.

Nile had gone, too. *Bantry* had been zigzagging haphazardly in the spreading drift of her own smoke-screen, and now that it had dissipated *Nile* was only one of several grey smudges in the hazy northern and north-eastern distance.

'Hand me my glasses, Pilot.'

Wilmott was on his left, at the binnacle. He and David were alive, but the men in the bridge's afterpart had been killed by blast or flash or both. Incredible; it seemed like a nightmare from which sooner or later one would wake up.

'*Damn* you, Pilot! Give me my glasses!'

He snatched them up and passed them over.

'Not that side, you fool!'

David turned and stared at him. Wilmott's eyes glared back above a deathly-pale, strained face, a jutting beard with flecks of spit on it.

Looking downwards, David saw the reason for the *not that side*. Wilmott's arm had been wrenched off at the shoulder. There were streamers of blood-soaked superfine cloth, and sort of – *strings*, and . . .

179

David shut his eyes. He felt sick, and above all, out of touch, unreal. It felt as if there was madness in the air . . . Like a robot, he moved round behind his captain and placed the glasses in his left hand. Wilmott said without looking at him again, doubled sideways with his elbow hooked over the binnacle and bent to reach the glasses with his eyes, 'Find out where Commander Clark is, and tell him I want to know what the state of things below is . . .Watch your steering, quartermaster!'

'Aye aye, sir . . .' The voice out of the copper tube sounded normal, steady. 'She's not answering too well, sir.'

The telegraphs weren't working either. Weren't being responded to, anyway. None of the navyphones seemed to be alive. Since the final salvo had smashed down into her, there'd been two reports, both by word of messenger; one from Pike, the engineer, to the effect that the port engine-room was out of action, and then one from the commander to the effect that he'd ordered the evacuation of the maintopmen's messdeck and that there were too many fires for all of them to be coped with adequately.

All magazines had been flooded. The hands in the after steering compartment reported water rising steadily. They were trapped in there, and rescuers couldn't get to it to help from outside.

A voice bleated from a voicepipe: 'Bridge!' David located it: it was the one from the spotting top.

'Bridge.'

'Everard.' It was Johnny West. 'Tell the Captain that all electrical circuits seem to have failed. I can't even contact the TS. And before communications went dead they told me the turrets' hydraulic power's failed. I want—'

Wilmott had sharp ears, still. He snapped, 'Tell him turrets can go into hand-training.' West was saying, '– permission to abandon this spotting top and the director. I want to get the guns into local control and hand-training, and without communications I can't do a bloody thing.'

'Tell him yes!'

'Johnny? Captain says yes. Come down.'

'Pilot!'

'Sir?'

At this slow speed and on one engine, listing and down by the stern, *Bantry* was all shakes and rattles, metal groans. It felt to David as if he was standing on something that was about to fall apart. Wilmott was leaning sideways now against the binnacle, as if without its support he'd have had no balance. His whole right side was a sheet of blood, and he was standing in a pool of it. David wondered if it was possible to be in such a state and not feel pain. Might there be some brain-defeating mechanism in the nervous system, some switch that threw off? Wilmott was paler still now, absolutely white, and there was a weird light in his eyes, but he didn't seem to be aware of the drastic nature of his injury. It added to the sense of unreality, the feeling that one would suddenly be released from all this, that it didn't have to be taken seriously. David asked him, 'Yes, sir?'

'Didn't I tell you to find the Commander?'

'I'll go now, sir.' He glanced round the bridge. He'd no idea where to start – or even, really, where he was. Even the light was peculiar; milky, streaked with duller grey and a sort of khaki haze, while aft there, of course, there was only smoke ... He heard his voice informing Wilmott, 'I'll get the surgeon up, sir. You can't—'

'Don't tell me what I can or cannot do, Pilot. Just *you* do what I've ordered you to do.' It sounded like some sort of game, or a children's argument. 'D'you understand me, Everard ?' David nodded. Presumably the man was numb, and couldn't feel it. It made one ill just to look at him even at his face. *He's dead, and he doesn't realise it ...*

Then: *Signal bridge: there'll be men down there, and I'll send them to find Clark* . . . It was a voice speaking in his head, something he listened to from outside himself. He felt grateful to it; there didn't seem to be any other kind of help around.

'*Everard!*'

'Yes, sir.' He was moving towards the after end of the bridge, to the ladder that would take him down to the signal bridge. He managed not to look at Wilmott again before he'd got past him. But he had to pass the yeoman here, and Midshipman Porter and the Marine bugler, and a signalman named Rouse; they'd all been standing here in the after part of the compass platform when that flash had shot up and enveloped it. He half-closed his eyes, so that he could see his way but not those *things*. Clothes all charred: if you brushed against them by accident they scattered like dust or dead leaves; and the bodies weren't burnt – simply discoloured, horrible.

He started down the starboard ladderway.

'Where the devil are *you* going?'

He looked up. The question seemed to cut through the surroundings, which were too appalling to be believed. There was enough beastliness here to fill a lifetime of nightmares. Commander Clark's blue eyes blazed up at him.

'I was coming to find you, sir. Captain wants a report on how things are below decks.'

'He's about to get one.' Clark came up the ladder fast, pushing past David, hauling himself up with quick, powerful tugs of his short, thick arms. Stocky, balding, belligerent, he looked as if he'd been fighting Uhlans single-handed and unarmed and then been dunked in oily water. He stopped at the top of the ladder: feet apart, hands on hips, glaring at the corpses as if they were so many defaulters.

'What the devil!'

'They're dead, sir.'

'I didn't think they were dancing a bloody hornpipe.'

Clark swung to his right, took a few paces for'ard; his usual aggressive, strutting paces. When David took his eyes off the baked effigy which had been PO Sturgis, he became aware that the commander was standing with his fists on his hips again, facing a deserted bridge.

'Well? Where *is* the Captain?'

David moved up beside him. Wilmott was down beside the binnacle, on his back. His head dangled backwards over the low central step; his mouth was an open pink slit above the beard. His eyes were open too, staring upwards at the sky.

Clark bent down, put a finger to an eyeball. Then he straightened.

'Right.' He took a deep breath, and let it out again. The word and the breath signified his assumption of command. 'Get Lieutenant West down from the spotting top.'

David glanced aloft, and pointed. With his two-man crew following him, West was climbing down the rungs on the foremast. The third man – boy, rather, it was little Ackroyd – was just emerging from the lubber's hole in the base-plate of the top. David told Commander Clark, 'None of the navyphones work, sir, and the engine-room don't answer telegraphs. The quartermaster says steering's difficult.'

'That, Everard, is hardly surprising.' Clark watched as the gunnery lieutenant – who'd just become the executive officer – climbed on the foremast into the after end of the bridge, and came for'ard.

'Sir.' West glanced down at Wilmott, and caught his breath. He looked at David, then back at Clark. He seemed to square his shoulders.

'Listen, West. We're going slow ahead on one screw, but the engine-room's inaccessible, cut off by a fire which we don't seem able to make much impression on. We're badly holed, but we can't get at the holes either, and even if we could we wouldn't be able to stop them up because they're too damn big. I estimate we've about a hundred dead and about as many wounded. And as you can see—' he pointed aft – 'there is no chance whatsoever of this ship remaining afloat.'

West nodded. Clark went on, 'I want all the wounded

fetched up on deck, and then I want all fit men employed making rafts. All the boats are smashed, of course – or burnt. Now listen – we should get some warning, because the main flooding's through the starboard engine-room, and that's the one that's still going. When the water gets to a certain height it'll stop it. Then we'll know time's nearly up. Understand?'

'Might we not have a chance of getting her home, sir?'

'No. Three hundred miles, in this state?' Clark's head jerked sideways in brusque dismissal of the hope. 'If there was a chance in a thousand, I'd have a shot at it. But there isn't, and the best hope of finding assistance is to stay in this area.'

'With respect, sir – might she not float longer if we drew fires in the boiler-rooms, and shut off steam?'

'I doubt if it'd make much odds, West. And if we were completely stopped it'd make us more vulnerable to any Hun that sneaks along. A submarine, for instance.' West nodded. Clark looked at David, 'Everard.'

David was thinking that Clark was right; there must have been as many as two or three hundred ships in this approximate vicinity – say within fifty miles – and that was quite a concentration. As long as one had something fairly solid to hang on to, something that floated well – surely if one could simply stay afloat, alive, sooner or later even a German would stop and—

'Are you asleep, Everard?'

'Sir ?'

Clark peered at him curiously. Johnny West was giving him the same look. The commander sighed, shook his head. 'Go on down, West. Wounded up on deck, then rafts. And send young Scrimgeour up here.'

'Aye aye, sir.' West turned away, towards the ladder. 'You come and help me, Ackroyd.'

'Sir!' Piping treble ... Clark frowned, shook his head, thinking something like *ought to be at home, with his mother* ... 'Now, Everard. I want you to see to the destruction of confidential books and charts.' He pointed to the back end of the compass platform. 'You can organise a bonfire right there.'

It was black and charred, skeletally gaunt where all the wood trimmings had been scorched away; there was only bare steel, blistered paintwork, and those hideous, red-indian-coloured corpses.

'Wait a minute.'

Not that he'd moved yet. Perhaps this fellow thought he had. He stared into the commander's blue eyes, wondering who he was, where he'd met him. The top half of Signalman Rowse's face was white, unburnt, where he'd shielded his eyes by throwing up his hands. David could see Rowse's face as if the image of it was over-printed on his vision as he stared at Clark. Clark said, 'Before you start on the books, go down to the signal bridge and find a flag six and hoist it somewhere.'

He looked up. He could see one or two halyards still up there, flapping loose. Perhaps one of them might be serviceable.

'Flag six, sir?'

'For God's sake, man, snap out of it!' Clark clapped his hands, for some reason, in front of David's face. 'What does flag six mean when it's hoisted on its own?'

He concentrated. Six . . . He could visualise it, all right. Half blue and half yellow . . . He nodded, as the answer came to him.

'*Am in danger of sinking from damage received in action, sir.*'

Clark nodded, angrily. 'What d'you want – congratulations?'

David stared at him, wondering what he'd meant.

'Go on, man, *move*!'

Mr Pilkington, the torpedo gunner, stared up at Nick.

'Spare a minute, can ye?'

Nick had been chatting to Leading Seaman Hooper, the layer of the midships four-inch. Now that he was gunnery control officer, he had a lot to learn, and it was likely he'd pick up more useful information from an experienced gunlayer than he would from any drill book.

He climbed down from the platform, to join Pilkington. *Lanyard* was doing about five knots, using only her starboard shaft, while Worsfold did something in one of the two boiler-rooms. Nick hadn't heard all of it, when the commissioned engineer had come up to the bridge and explained to Mortimer what it was he wanted. Roughly, it was to drain one feed-tank so that his ERAs could mend or patch a leak in it; then he'd refill it from one of the reserve tanks. Mortimer had agreed reluctantly, under Worsfold's threat that a stitch in time, now, might keep *Lanyard* in the battle, whereas otherwise she might well have to drop out with bigger trouble later.

Down in the south-east, Jellicoe's battle fleet was a grey haze topped by smoke. The fleet had altered course to south now, presumably – so Mortimer had surmised, discussing it with Nick and Hastings – to impose its guns between the Germans and their escape-route south-eastwards.

'The 'uns 've turned back agin, Sub.'

Pilkington's eyes were small and bright under the beetling brows. Since he had exceptionally short legs, he was several inches shorter than Nick.

'Are you sure?'

Pilkington jerked his head towards the bridge. One of the gun's crew, prone and dozing on the platform, rolled over and raised his head to listen; up there, the man's head was on a level with their own as they stood on the upper deck below the gun.

'We just picked up a signal from *Southampton*. Wireless signal. *Enemy battle fleet steering east-sou'-bloody-east*, it said.' He pointed, 'Bring 'em up agin Jelly agin, won't it.'

'Perhaps you're right.'

'There's no *per'aps*, Sub.' The gunner demonstrated with his hands. 'Look. Scheer goin' this way, Jelly strung out 'ere. Can't 'elp fetchin' up agin each other, eh?'

'I'm glad our W/T's all right now. That leading tel's pretty good. What's his name – Williams ?'

'Garn!' Pilkington screwed up his nose. 'Don't take much to rig a jury aerial. Like stringin' a bloody washin' line! You don't want to go roun' lettin' these fellers think they're bloody geniuses, you know, Sub!'

'No. I won't.' Nick thought Pilkington was all right in small doses. 'And thanks for the buzz. Let's hope the chief has us fixed up in time.' He turned away, to go back up on the platform. Pilkington's hand clamped on his forearm.

'Wasn't that I want to talk to you about, Sub.' The gunner scowled. 'No 'urry, are yer?'

'Well—'

'Come aft 'ere a minute...'

'All right.' They walked aft together, past both sets of tubes and the distorted superstructure over the quarterdeck ladderway. The gunner halted facing the stern, staring critically at the lashed-down collision-mat covering the gashes in the deck. Beyond it, *Lanyard*'s wake seethed gently, like soapy water seeping from a drain. Quite a difference, Nick thought, from the boiling white cauldron which, an hour or so ago, had been piled higher than the stern itself.

It felt strange that she should be alone now, and quiet. It also felt wrong; down there to the south, the outcome of a major battle was being decided. Or at least, if this little man was right about *Southampton*'s signal, *about to be* decided.

'Well?'

'Listen. Am I right, you didn't let on to the Old Man about it bein' you as got the tubes roun', an' all ?'

Nick thought about it.

No, he hadn't said anything about that. He remembered now. He'd felt it wasn't necessary. And Mortimer had been firing questions at him, one after another, hadn't he. Also – it was coming back, now – Mortimer had been critical, or near-critical, of Nick's account of his movements aft here during that action and the explosion; and one's natural tendency in such circumstances had always been to clam up, say as little as possible and then remove oneself from the presence of the criticiser as swiftly as possible.

'That's so – although I did have to tell him you'd fired, and that there was only one fish left, because he asked me the direct question. Don't imagine I was making your report for you, because I wasn't.'

'I know you wasn't, ol' mate.' The warrant officer nodded his rather large head. It might not have seemed as big as it did if the rest of him hadn't been so small. But then again, he was not – as Nick had thought, on first being introduced to him – anything like a jockey, because if you'd sat him on a horse he'd have seemed quite tall. It was only his legs that the midwife must have taken reefs in.

'Right.' He nodded again. 'But I mean you did it. You could 'a took the credit. An' we scored, old chum, we bloody 'it the bugger!'

'Let's hope so. I suppose it'll all come out, some day. Who fired which way at what time, and who got hit, and all that.'

'Sub, listen.' Mr Pilkington grasped his arm. 'I'm tellin' you. That fish bloody 'it. I *seen* it 'it.'

'Well.' Nick didn't know what he was supposed to say or do. At the time, Pilkington had said he'd *thought* he'd seen a torpedo hit one of the enemy ships. Now he was swearing to it. But at least he'd let go of that arm now. 'Well, good for you. Did you tell the Captain you scored?'

'Course I did!'

'Was he pleased?'

'Christ Almighty, what d'you think?'

'Well, that's fine, then. Splendid.'

The gunner was staring at him.

'You're a rum 'un, you are, Sub.'

'Why?'

'Thought you was a toffee-nosed young sod, when you first come aboard.'

Nick laughed. It would be a bit of a lark, back at Mullbergh, going out to one of those awful parties, if one said to one's giggly little tennis partner, 'I know that at first I give the impression of being a toffee-nosed sod, but *act*ually . . .' He smiled at Pilkington. 'I'm sorry about that. Probably shyness, first day on board, that sort of thing?'

'You're all right, Sub.' Pilkington raised a hand and began to pick a back tooth with its forefinger. Whatever he'd been after, he'd got hold of; he was examining it, now.

He'd flicked it away.

'You want a bit of 'elp, or advice, or what, any time, Sub – well, I bin in this Navy close on thirty bloody years, I oughter know a thing or two.' He slapped Nick's shoulder, suddenly. 'You get problems, you come to me. I'll see you right, old son.'

'Thanks. I'll bear it in mind.' Evidently Pilkington felt he'd done him some sort of favour. He certainly hadn't intended to.

He left the torpedo gunner beside the after searchlight platform, and went to finish his chat with the gunlayer, Hooper. The men of the four-inch's crew were all mad keen to get back into the action; none of them had any doubts of it ending in a resounding British victory, and they wanted to be in at the kill. They'd seen that cannonade, when Jellicoe's battle squadrons had hit Scheer so hard that the High Seas Fleet had had to turn about and escape into the mist, and it had convinced them all that if the Germans could be forced to stand and fight, they'd be annihilated. Nick agreed, of course.

'But it's a very difficult move to counter, isn't it. What can a boxer do if his opponent just ducks under the ropes and legs it for home?'

Hooper pursed his lips, and pushed his cap to the back of his head. 'If you 'ad a few squadrons the other side of 'im, sir?'

Hugh Everard, when he'd told Nick and David about the turn-away tactic which Scheer had been practising in the Baltic had been thinking in terms of a fast destroyer flotilla which, when such a move seemed likely, could somehow slip out to the enemy's disengaged side, so that the turning line would be enfiladed with torpedoes. But that sounded a lot easier than it would be to achieve in practice – or rather, in action. And Jellicoe's view was that the only answer to it was time, and to keep between the enemy and his bases so that sooner or later he'd have to fight.

Probably that was Jellicoe's intention now. But he hadn't much daylight left.

Nick went back up to the bridge. Hastings was alone in charge of it, with a bridge staff consisting of two lookouts and one signalman. Mortimer, Hastings told him, had gone down to see what was happening in the boiler-room.

'He's getting slightly frantic again.' Hastings spoke quietly to Nick, in the forefront of the bridge. *Lanyard*'s stubby bow, below them, was pushing like a snow-plough through dull-grey sea; at this speed there wasn't much movement on the ship, only rattles . . . 'I can't say I blame him. We picked up a signal from senior officer Second Light Cruiser Squadron to the effect that the Huns 've gone about again – so it could all start up again pretty well any time now, and here we are lolling around like something on a spring cruise . . . By the way, you're doing all right. Mortimer likes you . . . You know you replaced a snotty, do you?'

'I replaced a—'

'Keep your wool on.' Hastings bent to the voicepipe to give a helm order. They were altering now and then, not in a regular zigzag pattern but just an occasional change of course to make things slightly less simple for any lurking submarine. 'Steady!'

'Steady, sir . . . Course sou'-sou'-east by south, sir!'

'Steer that.'

'Steer sou'-sou'-east by south, sir.'

Hastings straightened, turned his pock-marked face to Nick. 'Poor old Mike Reynolds was due to move to another boat as first lieutenant. Mortimer had recommended him, and we'd just been deprived of our snotty. So the plan was, since you were suddenly available for some reason, that you'd take over the dogsbody jobs for a month or two, and then when it was considered you could pull your weight, Reynolds would leave us and we'd get a new midshipman. You don't have to feel insulted or—'

'Who said I—'

'All right, then.'

David would have felt insulted, according to Johnson. Nick thought, *I may be like him, in that respect. It's something I must watch out for.* He wondered where David was now, whether *Bantry* had seen any action. 'Hey!' Hastings was using his binoculars, looking ahead, south-ward. 'Hey, it's warming up again!'

Nick grabbed a spare pair – he thought they'd belonged to Johnson – which had been hanging from a voicepipe. As he raised them, he heard the gunfire; now he saw flashes, that now familiar red flickering. Hastings was shouting into the engine-room voicepipe, telling them to ask the captain to come up to the bridge. Nick checked the compass while Hastings was away from it; at least *Lanyard* was pointing in the right direction, at more or less the centre of the arc of flashes. The firing was still only intermittent, but its frequency and spread seemed to be increasing.

Mortimer flung himself into the bridge, and snatched up his own glasses. Hastings told him, pointing, 'Action's resumed, sir. Can we use our engines yet?'

'If we could, we *would* be, damn you!'

Mortimer had snarled it. His hands holding the binoculars shook; Nick could almost feel the voltage of his frustration crackling out of him . . .

'Damn-fool questions. . .' He dropped his glasses on their lanyard, raised his fists and shook them at the clouds. 'It's worse than that fool Worsfold thought. We'll be an hour, at least . . .'

Derfflinger had been hit again; Hugh saw the flames shoot out of her. *Lützow* had dropped out of the action; Hipper had abandoned her, and it wasn't likely she'd float.

The guns of the Fifth Battle Squadron were all firing; their targets were Scheer's battleships as they loomed out of the mist, vanished, reappeared. This damnable mist. But there was always some target in sight, to shift to, and everything that appeared was being shot at and hit, not only by the Queen Elizabeths; *Revenge, Colossus, Neptune, Benbow, Superb, Hercules, Agincourt, Collingwood, Bellerophon, Royal Oak, Orion, Monarch, Centurion*, Jellicoe's own *Iron Duke, Temeraire, Agincourt* and *Marlborough* were all in it. *Marlborough*, who'd been hit a few minutes ago by a torpedo, was maintaining her station at the head of the Sixth Division and had just scored two hits on a König-class battleship which had since disappeared. And once again, the High Seas Fleet was being hit too hard and too often to do much in reply. Hugh was on *Nile*'s open compass platform, because there was virtually no shellfire to take shelter from. Because, also, he disliked the blinkered feeling that one got in the enclosed conning-tower; visibility was bad enough without having to peer into it through a slit in a steel wall.

Tom Crick stood on his right, Rathbone close to the binnacle on his left. The chief yeoman, Peppard, was in the port after corner of the bridge, and Bates was hanging around there somewhere. Hugh was uncomfortably aware of a certain irrational quality in his current anger with Bates; he'd been enormously relieved to discover that his coxswain had not been in the sea-cabin when it was hit, and at the same time annoyed that he'd left it and gone aft without orders. Also at the back of the bridge now was the secretary;

Colne-Wilshaw was taking photographs as well as keeping his diary notes up to date.

It wasn't only mist that was hiding the German dread-noughts, it was the smoke of exploding British shells.

A navyphone flashed and buzzed. Midshipman Ross-Hallet answered it. There'd been no need, in the last ten or fifteen minutes, for communications or conversation; the Germans had appeared, and the fleet had known what to do about it. In *Nile*, Brook in the control top had set his gunnery organisation going without a second's delay or a wasted word; and Jellicoe wasn't a man to waste time with unnecessary signalling. Ross-Hallet called out the message from the control top: 'Enemy destroyers seem about to launch torpedo attack on the bow, sir!'

'Very good.' Hugh got them in his glasses. A flotilla was emerging from the head of the German line, the gap between the four battle cruisers and the battleships; and it looked as if those surviving battle cruisers were turning towards Jellicoe's line now: there were *two* flotillas of destroyers moving out to the attack. Scheer must have ordered offensive action up there in the hope of making Jellicoe turn away.

As he would. If torpedoes were fired, he'd allow an appropriate time for their run and then order turns-away of two or perhaps four points, to allow the torpedoes to run harmlessly between ships and squadrons. When they'd run through, he'd turn back.

Perhaps Scheer was planning another retreat, and using an attack by battle cruisers and destroyers as cover for it?

Nile's salvoes had a different sound to them, now that 'X' turret came later, by a split second, than the other three. And now the noise-level increased sharply as her secondary armament of six-inch guns opened up, to add to the hail of steel that was greeting the German torpedo craft as they moved out. Brook would be keeping up his fifteen-inch salvoes at the battleships; the six-inch guns had their own director towers, one each side abaft the foremast.

Crick lowered his glasses, pointed towards the head of the enemy line, those four already badly mauled battle cruisers. They were steaming directly towards the British squadrons, actually charging them, and not all their for'ard turrets were still functional.

'They're trying to commit suicide!'

'I believe Scheer's about to run for it, Tom.'

The guns of the whole British line were blazing continuously now, and making better practice than they ever did against towed targets. Scheer would be mad if he did not order another 'battle-turn-away'. And those suicidal battle cruisers: *Von de Tann* had just been hit again, aft; Hugh had his glasses on her as she erupted in smoke and flame. *Derringer*, almost finished but maddeningly refusing to admit it, was being blasted from end to end. *Seydlitz* seemed to be about to sink; she was so low for'ard that her foc'sl had hardly any freeboard at all. He'd seen two – now three – of the attacking destroyers hit, and certainly one of them was foundering. And suddenly Hugh saw that his guess had been right. Scheer's battleships were turning – and not all to starboard! *This* retreat was haphazard, a desperate scramble of huge ships to escape that pulverising cannonade.

'They're beaten, Tom.' Hugh lowered his binoculars. He told Tom Crick, 'We've *broken* 'em – they can't stand up to us!'

The torpedo craft were laying smoke. It would cover Scheer's retreat; it would also cover their own – when they'd fired their torpedoes, they could slip back into it. And a third flotilla was launching itself now from the German line; as they were spotted, gunfire rose to a crescendo, until one heard no individual shots or salvoes but only a continuous roar of exploding cordite and bursting shells. Two more destroyers had been hit, and a third and one of the first to be hit had sunk. Astern, Hugh saw four British destroyers racing out to finish a Hun flotilla leader who'd been stopped, disabled, between the lines. He looked southwards again to see that the four battle cruisers had finally turned away, and were limping into the cover of the destroyers' smoke. '*Barham*'s flying the preparative, sir!'

Chief Petty Officer Peppard had kept one eye continually on the squadron flagship, and he'd just seen the blue-and-white striped flag shoot up to Evan-Thomas's port lower yard. It was the emergency-turn signal, to avoid torpedoes. Hugh watched *Malaya*, his next ahead, as *Nile*'s answering pendant ran close-up. *Malaya*'s was up, and *Valiant*'s too now. To starboard there was no German in sight, except for a few destroyers mostly hidden in shell-spouts and smoke, but from the control top Brook must still have had targets in his sights, and all turrets were still firing.

Another destroyer emerged from the belt of smoke; she was dodging to and fro, her bow-wave high and brilliant-white against surrounding grey-black drabness. Hugh saw a jet of flame as the popgun on her foc's'l fired. Then the sea ahead of her gushed up, and the rest of the same salvo smashed down into her vitals. She split open, disgorging smoke and a great pillar of escaping steam. When the smoke cleared, there was no trace left of her.

'Executive, sir!'

'Starboard ten.'

'Starboard ten, sir . . . Ten o' starboard wheel on, sir!'

Nile and the ships ahead of her were swinging away to port.

'Midships!'

'Midships, sir. . .'

Midshipman Ross-Hallet answered a navyphone, and shouted, 'Director tower reports torpedo passing astern, sir!'

'Very good.' Evan-Thomas had timed his avoiding-action well. 'Steady as you go.'

'Steady, sir. Course sou'-west by south, sir.'

Hugh watched the ships ahead, and waited for the signal

to resume previous course. Jellicoe would obviously continue southwards now; or perhaps west of south, to keep
closer to the enemy – who had once again been turned,
driven back, leaving the Grand Fleet massive and remorse-
less between them and their homeland.

'Keep the men busy', Clark had ordered. And he'd sent
David down with the same instruction, after he'd destroyed
the secret charts and books. The commmander had then gone
down himself, to take charge of the fire-fighting, leaving
Lieutenant Scrimgeour on the bridge with young Ackroyd.

Bantry's upper deck was a scrap-heap of twisted steel; it
hadn't been easy to find spaces for all the wounded. Going aft
for the first time since the action, David had been astonished at
the amount of wreckage – the funnels full of holes, mainmast
holed too, the after searchlight blown right into the third
funnel; he'd thought at first it was smoking, but that was steam
leaking where one of the two steam-pipes on the funnel had
been cut through. He saw that someone had lashed a Union
Flag to the top of the mainmast stump. The topmast and
topgallant – which had carried the W/T gear – had been shot
away, and the whole lot of it, with shrouds, stays, aerials and
lifts, had been dumped on the after shelter-deck and across the
stern turret, buckling that screen door. The ship's boats had of
course all been smashed, and the ones for'ard had been burnt;
the superstructure was full of holes and great black stains
where exploding shells had scorched away the paint.

West had set up his raft-factory right aft on the quarterdeck. Half a dozen Carley floats were intact, but that was all,
and for a hundred wounded men the able-bodied ones were
lashing together any buoyant materials they could find.
Timber, boxes, mattresses, oil and paint drums were being
assembled into catamaran-like shapes with sections of colli-
sion-mats, boats' sails from the bosun's store below, sections
of plank – stretched, nailed, lashed across as decking.

West murmured, as they picked their way for'ard, 'A lot

of those contraptions may not float too well with the weight of men on 'em.' David glanced at him, wondering why he didn't tell them so, warn them. West answered the unspoken question: 'Keeps 'em occupied. That's the main thing we must do. Anyway, you never know, until you try it out.'

He'd thought of a new way to keep the hands busy now: ranging the cable on the foc's'l. To make room for it, they were going to have to shift a lot of the wounded from there up to the battery deck.

Petty Officer Toomey looked doubtful. 'Won't get many up there, sir. Dickens of a job hoistin' the badly hurt ones up them ladders, wouldn't you say?'

'I'm afraid it has to be done, Toomey.' West thought about it. Bland, plump, considering nothing but how to make the best of the situation. 'The ones we can't lift, you see, can stay on the foc's'l; just shift 'em aft as far as possible. Here, say, each side of the turret and in behind it. Eh?'

Ranging the cable, which would be the first step to take in any preparation to be taken in tow, meant heaving the great, heavy chain up out of the cable-locker and 'flaking' it to and fro – fore and aft – on the foc's'l. There was very little chance of any ship arriving to take *Bantry* in tow, and there'd be no point anyway in óne doing so; but it would cheer the men to see such preparations being made.

West asked Toomey, 'Blacksmith?'

'Aft, sir, below, helping the chief carpenter.'

'We can do without him if you get his tools. But pipe for the cable party, will you.'

'Aye aye, sir.'

West had a light of enthusiasm in his eyes as he turned to David.

'No hope of getting steam to the capstan, so we'll have to ship its bars and do the job by man-power. Well, that's not such a bad thing, is it. If only someone had a fiddle.'

The old custom was to have a fiddler up on the capstan, a lively shanty to bring the cable up by.

David suggested, with his eyes on the smoky-grey horizon and a rumble of distant gunfire in his ears, 'Why not the Marine band, instead?'

'That's a splendid idea!'

If enough bandsmen could be mustered . . . West pointed: 'I'll put 'em up on the turret there.' He looked round. 'Braithwaite!' Like everyone else, Able Seaman Braithwaite was listening to that gunfire. Someone for'ard shouted, 'The 'un's gettin' it in the neck now, lads!' A cheer went up. West shouted again, 'Hey, Braithwaite!'

'Sir?'

'Go after Petty Officer Toomey for me, ask him to come back here.'

'Aye aye, sir!'

'Sing-song, sir?'

A smoke-blackened face was looking up at him. The man was wrapped in a blanket which was patched dark-brown where his blood had soaked through it.

'If you like, Edwards.' West crouched down beside him. 'But we're going to get the cable up and range it. Then if some decent spark comes along to offer us a tow, we'll be all ready for him.'

They cheered again. A stoker with a bandage round his neck and shoulders called out hoarsely, ''ome by Christmas, lads!'

Toomey came up the ladder at the foc'sl break. 'New orders, sir?'

'Yes, Toomey.' West got up. 'This is the bright-ideas department. I want you to muster all of the Marine band that you can get hold of, and tell 'em to get their instruments up on the roof of 'A' turret here.'

'Reckon that is a good idea, sir.' Toomey rubbed his hands together. From somewhere aft came the shrill note of a bosun's call, and the summons, 'Cable Party muster on the foc'sl!' West nodded. 'Capital.' With his left hand he raised his cap, and used the right one to scratch the bald area which through nine-tenths of his waking hours it hid. 'Things are looking up, Toomey!'

'Aye aye, sir!'

David remembered that down below the engineers were still trying to get through to men trapped in compartments which were steadily filling with salt water.

'Off you go, then.' West stared round at the prostrate or reclining forms of the wounded. 'Surgeon'll get back to you chaps soon, now. He's bound to deal with the bad cases first, of course. He'll get round to you all soon enough, though.'

'Good ol' guns!'

There was more cheering. West knew that in fact the surgeons – the PMO and his assistant surgeon-lieutenant – were working in the for'ard messdeck beside the seamen's washplaces. They'd had to evacuate the main dressing-station aft, and they were labouring in cramped, over-crowded quarters lit by oil-lamps, struggling to ease the sufferings of hideously mutilated sailors and Marines, and knowing that at any minute the ship might founder. It was more than medical skill that doctors needed at such a time, it was – West frowned, baulking at words like *heroism*. They were good people, that was all, and they were measuring-up well to the situation. He heard a sailor ask, 'Anyone got a smoke?'

West didn't smoke anything but cigars, and he didn't carry those on him. He asked David, 'Have you?'

David pulled out his case. It was silver, with the Everard otter's head crest on it. He flipped it open.

'Not many. Half a dozen.'

'Pass 'em out, there's a good fellow.'

Bantry seemed suddenly to lurch; a sudden plunge. For about five seconds there was a total silence on her decks, as if everyone alive or half alive was holding his breath; that thump could have been a bulkhead going, the beginning of the end. David was bent forward with the open cigarette-case out in his left hand. He froze in that position, and the rattling and groaning of the cruiser's fabric and the rush of the sea along her sides were the only sounds anyone could hear. Then a sailor called boisterously, 'Who 'ad beans for 'is breakfast, then?'

A roar of laughter cracked the silence, and an oily hand took David's last cigarette. He snapped the case shut, and felt in another pocket: 'Here. Match . . .'

'Ah, you're a toff, sir . . . Mind lightin' it? Can't see, not too clear . . .'

Not too clear. You could see, under the edges of the strip of bandage, the cordite-burns that had blinded him.

'Look, David.' West was groping in his pockets. 'We've got cigarettes in the wardroom store—' he cocked an eyebrow – 'and I don't think fishes smoke . . . Here. This key, the small one. And this one's the pusser's stores – there's tins of pipe and chewing tobacco, you could get them too. All you can carry. Mind you lock the wardroom store behind you; we don't want liquor circulating.'

David stared at the grey sea sliding past: it was so impersonal that it was terrifying. It swallowed whatever it was given, and afterwards it looked the same: like *that* – secretive, malevolent . . . His hand tightened on the ring of keys, and he felt their edges bite into his palm. It was knowing what was happening down there, what *had* happened. Men trapped, others working to beat the fires and cut through to them: a sweet stench of blood which on its own was enough to make you vomit, and in it the reek of burnt corticene and paint and rubber cables. Pockets of cordite gas. Worst of all, the bodies and parts of bodies. There'd been one in the armoured grating above the for'ard boiler-room; it had been blow half *through* the grating. The surgeons were dealing with the wounded, not the dead, and the engineers were trying to reach the living. The dead stayed where they'd been thrown or dropped or—

David opened his hand, stared at the keys as if he was wondering what they were, or whose . . . West was frown-

ing, looking at him in that odd way again: 'David? Will you
do that?'

'I'm – working out what's the best route.' He pointed at
the base of the bridge superstructure. 'In that way, I suppose,
and down to the middle deck and aft along the port side,
through the messes. If the fires are still mostly on the
starboard side—'

West slapped him on the back. 'That's it! Go on, they'll
bless you for it!

The blinded stoker had eased himself down on to one
elbow. He waved the hand that held the cigarette: 'All
together now, lads! One – two – four – *It's a long way—*'

He had a voice like a rusty hinge, but all his mates were
joining in. David was on his way down the buckled ladder.
He was reminding himself to walk carefully down there: the
torn steel had sharp edges, razor-sharp, and it was easy
enough to pick a safe path where the oil-lamps had been lit,
but with a wrong step or a slip and blood in areas where the
carnage had been worst did make it slippery – where the
compartments weren't fully lit—

Behind him the song rose, swelling: . . . *to Tipperary, to
the sweetest girl I know—*

Chapter 9

'At 9 pm the enemy was entirely out of sight, and the threat of torpedo boat destroyer attacks during the rapidly approaching darkness made it necessary for me to dispose the fleet for the night with a view to its safety from such attacks whilst providing for a renewal of the action at daylight. I accordingly manoeuvred to remain between the enemy and his bases. . . .

'There were many gallant deeds performed by the destroyer flotillas: they surpassed the very highest expectations that I had formed of them.'

From paragraphs 20 and 24 of Sir John Jellicoe's Despatch

*N*ile forged southwards into fading light, astern of the other Queen Elizabeths. In less than half an hour, it would be dark.

Hugh glanced at Mowbray, who was waiting in his usual stolid manner to take over as officer of the watch. The fleet had fallen-out from action stations; they'd stand-to again at two o'clock, just before first light.

'All right, Mowbray. Course south, two hundred revolutions. She's all yours.'

'Sir.'

Hugh wondered what thoughts – if any – passed through the head behind Lieutenant Mowbray's deadpan countenance. He'd never managed to draw the man out at all. His thoughts changed and he forgot him now, wondered what sort of night lay ahead. Jellicoe wouldn't want a night action. But if Scheer tried to break through again, he'd have one anyway.

The sea looked like oiled silk. Shiny, opalescent, with a haze like polish floating on it. Here and there, according to patches of thicker or thinner mist, the shine disappeared, and where that happened you could see that the surface was dimpled, slightly fleck-marked by the wind.

'How's the barometer, Pilot?'

'Down a little, sir.'

A wind would be an ally for Jellicoe. Wind dispersed mist, kept fog away, allowed the dog to see the bone. It was to be hoped – expected – that with the morning light of the first day of June the bone would be there to be grasped and crushed.

There'd been some kind of action about an hour ago, down in the south-west, when the battle fleet had been steaming west to get closer to the enemy. Almost certainly it had been Beatty's battle cruisers brushing against some outlying German squadron. Perhaps a cruiser action: but it had sounded like big guns. It was all quiet again now.

Without wireless – and *Nile*'s equipment was smashed beyond any kind of emergency repair – one knew very little of what was going on. Only what could be seen, and signals passed by light or flags. The destroyer flotillas, for instance, had just been ordered to take up screening stations five miles astern of the battle fleet.

The battleship divisions were each in line ahead and one mile on each others' beams. Jellicoe in *Iron Duke* was leading the Fourth Division, which came roughly in the centre of the fleet, with three files of battleships on his starboard hand and the fifth to port, between him and these

Queen Elizabeths. Outside this squadron – actually on *Nile*'s port quarter, since they'd dropped back by two or three miles now were the Sixth Division, led by *Marlborough*. *Marlborough*, as a result of that torpedo hit on her earlier in the evening, was finding it difficult to maintain the ordered speed of seventeen knots.

'Mowbray – has the commander had his supper, d'you know?'

Mowbray nodded. 'He was in the wardroom for about five minutes, sir. I think he had some sandwiches. He's doing rounds of the messdecks now, sir.'

Hugh turned aft. 'Bates?'

'Sir.' A figure detached itself from the mounting of the twenty-four-inch searchlight. Bates had been chatting to the yeoman of the watch. 'Supper, sir? Ready when you like, sir.'

'Hot?'

''otter 'n that, sir!'

'Right. In my – the navigating officer's sea-cabin, please.'

'Aye aye, sir!'

Hugh paused, looking out to starboard. There, against a dulling sky and a fading sea, was Admiral Gaunt's Fifth Division: *Colossus*, *Neptune*, *St Vincent*, *Collingwood*. The King's son, Sub-Lieutenant Prince Albert, was an assistant turret officer in *Collingwood*. Beyond Gaunt's division was Sturdee's – with Jellicoe leading it in *Iron Duke* – and that was where young Nick must be. There could hardly have been time for anything to have been done about his transfer to a cruiser or destroyer; one could only hope he hadn't yet actually gone under report. And at least he'd been in action, had a taste of fighting, and that might help.

David would know what action felt like too, if the smoke-laying cruiser had been *Bantry*. She'd certainly been one of the Minotaurs, and Rathbone had thought it was *Bantry*. Whoever she was, a natural appreciation of her captain's intention to assist was tempered by a conviction that his judgement had been at fault. By the time he'd made his move, *Nile* had been through the worst of it; the Germans had been about to lose one target, and he'd presented them with a new one.

Nile's gauntlet-running in aid of *Warspite* had been a very different matter. For one thing, the timing had been right, and *Nile* was armoured to withstand punishment, which a cruiser of that class was not. But thinking about judgement, good or bad – in the first minute after he'd put the helm over, hadn't he been wondering whether he might have made a terrible mistake? Judgement – or snatching at a chance?

He told himself, *judgement by instinct*. One had seen what needed doing, and that it could be done. That cruiser captain had followed suit without recognising the differences in their situations.

It was getting really dark now. He looked ahead, at *Malaya*. The gleam of white under her counter was as easy to follow as any stern-light. It would seem strange, when the war ended, to have ships festooned with lights again.

'Pilot – are we on the top line with recognition signals?'

'Yes, sir. They're listed in the chartroom.'

The yeoman of the watch, PO Brannan, said, 'Signal-men've got it all weighed-off too, sir.'

Hugh went down the ladder, to his purloined cabin. Bates was standing by a tray of food. He'd stiffened to attention; he had a tendency, in that position, to rise and fall slightly on his toes. Hands cramped against his thighs, thumbs pointing downwards among the inverted creases of bell-bottoms.

'What's the menu, Cox'n?'

'Beef stew, dumplings, boiled spuds and carrots, sir!'

'In the middle of a battle?' Hugh sat down. 'A few hours ago I was thinking you'd have been wise if you'd gone on with your swimming lessons.'

Bates's brown eyes blinked at him. 'I got 'eavy bones, sir,

that's my trouble. Waste o' time, all that . . . But beggin' your pardon, sir, you done a treat. Reckon we'll be 'oistin' an admiral's flag 'fore long, sir.'

Hugh smiled. 'Looking forward to flag rank, are you?'

'Better 'n a crack on the snout, sir, wouldn't it.' Bates looked down at the tray. 'That's the last o' the good Stilton, sir. . . Coffee after, sir?'

'No. A mug of cocoa, please. Any casualties in the gig's crew?'

'Robertson, sir. Shell-splinter in 'is arse. Must 'a bin facin' the wrong way, I tol' 'im.'

Robertson was a Glasgow man; he was a marksman, and he'd done well in the Scapa rifle-shooting competitions.

'You'll have to replace him, temporarily. Pity.'

Bates looked surprised. ''E's not 'urt bad, sir!'

'You think he can sit on a thwart and pull an oar, with a splinter in his backside?'

'Useful 'and, is Robertson.' Bates wasn't a man to change his mind once he'd made it up. ''E'll soon 'arden, sir.'

Petty Officer Toomey stood aside as they reached the ladder to the foc's'l. David stopped too, looking at him enquiringly. It was more than halfway to being dark now.

'After you, sir!' The petty officer's voice was cheerful, encouraging. David climbed the steel stairway to the higher level.

On the turret roof, Marine bandsmen were churning out their repertoire. It wasn't doing much for anyone; there was a sort of incongruity about it, and West was wishing he'd left the men to their own sing-song. The cable party had finished ranging the cable ten minutes ago, with two shackles – twenty-five fathoms – up on the foc's'l. There'd been no point getting more up, and the light was going. West had had a bar put through one link of cable above the navel-pipe; they'd hove-in until the bar had the cable's weight, then disconnected the capstan and unrigged its bars and swifter.

At least the operation had made the men feel something positive was happening: the worst thing for morale was inaction. He'd told them, 'That's the best we can do, until tomorrow. Be easier in daylight.'

He saw Toomey coming with David Everard, and went aft to meet them.

'Hey, no smokes?'

'What?'

David Everard was gazing up at the bandsmen. They were at about half strength, as a band, and they were playing *Billy Boy*. Toomey told West quietly, drawing him aside, 'Found 'im just wand'rin' about, sir. Talkin' to 'imself and not makin' much sense, sir. I thought I oughter bring 'im along like – well—'

Toomey was embarrassed. West swore, under his breath. He put a hand on David's shoulder.

'Did you go to the stores, David?'

'Stores?'

Concentrating . . . Stores?

He'd been on his way aft, through the messdecks on the port side, trying not to see more than he had to on his way through. This had been the worst, here; shells had penetrated and then burst when the compartment had been full of ammunition-supply parties, damage-control parties, a stand-by fire brigade. None of the dead had been moved – well, who'd have done it? There were parts, bits of bodies, things your foot struck and moved . . . Had to be careful, avoid the sharp edges of lacerating steel, because a leather shoe-sole wasn't proof against them; you trod in a puddle that was dark, looked like oil, and the surface broke and it was red, bright red . . .

'Everard! Everard, my dear fellow!'

Stench . . .

'Everard, old chap?'

Pickering, the padre. Looking more like a fugitive from a chain-gang than a man of God; blackened, blood-stained, hair on end, clothes torn, eyes that seemed to be all whites in a dirty, bruised-looking face. He looked as if he'd been fighting for his life: and there was an excitement – no, desperation – in his manner as he grabbed David's arms and peered into his face.

'You're just the man I need to help me, Everard!'

'I was on my way to get some stuff for—'

'I shan't detain you long, old chap!' The chaplain's action duty was with the first-aid parties, the part-of-ship back-up to the medical organisation. David wondered what he might be doing down here on his own. In the yellowish gleam of oil lamps, there were only horrors here.

'Listen, Everard – there's someone still *alive* in this compartment! I *know* it for a fact! We were bringing the last of the stretchers through – we were using the wardroom and officers' cabins as an emergency hospital, you know, but with the water coming in aft naturally we had to move the chaps, you see – well, the last time we passed through this messdeck, just about this very spot, I heard some poor fellow cry out "Help, help me".'

Pickering had waved an arm, indicating the whole length of the compartment. David stared at that hand as it fell back to the padre's side; it was wet, gleaming red, with blood. He looked down at his own sleeves, where the man's hands had grasped him: the dark stains looked like mourning bands.

If one had to pick through bodies, heaps of dead, pieces—

'I must try to find him, Everard, d'you see? Or at least be *certain* . . . The thought that some poor creature might be lying here alive, under—' the hand waved again, and the padre smiled, a fierce, determined, almost threatening smile: 'You *will* help? My dear chap, thank you, thank you!' He'd pointed: 'I've got as far as – there . . . From the after bulkhead. If you were to start on that side, perhaps at the other end?' He seized David's arm again. 'It's not – not a pleasant task, Everard.' His voice had a shake in it. 'One needs all – all one's strength. Or it may be – God's strength?'

That fanatic's smile again and then it faded. 'Well – I cannot begin to express my gratitude . . .'

Corpse by corpse. The foul, sweet stench, and everywhere the – the detritus . . .

West leant forward, peered into David's face.

'You were going to bring up some cigarettes and things.'

Everard looked surprised.

'Was I?'

'Did you not go to the store?'

'Store?' David shook his head. 'Look here.' He showed West his hands. 'It's *everywhere*.' He began to laugh.

'Oh, Christ . . .' West turned away, and spoke to the petty officer. 'All right, Toomey, thank you. I'll look after him.'

'Right, sir. But – sir—'

'Yes?'

'Commander Clark's down there, sir, where they're tryin' to get through to the engine-room, an' he's just about done in, sir.'

'I'll go down, in a minute.' Johnny West looked up at the bridge, at the black ridge of its forefront silhouetted against the comparative lightness of the sky. There was more wind than there'd been all day; he could feel it on his face. He wondered if he could get Everard up there, out of the crowd, where he might be able to pull himself together. This ship's company was marvellous; disciplined, brave, cheerful, more impressive than he thought he'd ever be able to express. The last thing one wanted was to have an officer wandering among them in this condition. Shock or madness – the label you put on it made no difference. Everard had seemed peculiar earlier on: then he'd seemed to get better . . . West took his arm and drew him towards the ladder.

'Let's go up on the bridge, David. Up where it's—'

The starboard engine stopped.

Sound, vibration, had abruptly ceased. There was a thin hissing sound from a steam-pipe on one of the funnels and you could see the whiteness pluming out. Like ectoplasm: *Bantry* giving up her ghost. As she lost way, she seemed to slump lower in the sea. The bandsmen stopped playing; they stopped one by one, so that the music died disjointedly, and now the silence was emphasised by the swish of sea alongside and that leaking steam.

West looked round, at the pale faces of men patiently awaiting orders, guidance.

'Lieutenant West!'

Clark, the commander was using his short arms to haul himself jerkily up the foc'sl ladder. 'Lieutenant West here?'

'Here, sir.' West met him, and saluted. Toomey had been right, Clark did look just about all-in. He could hardly stand. He panted, clinging to the handrail of the ladder for support, 'Put lines on the rafts you've made, and get 'em over the side. Hold 'em there. Drop a scrambling-net over – then get the wounded into the rafts.'

'Aye aye, sir. Petty Officer Toomey!'

'Here, sir!'

'Bosun's Mate?'

Toomey bellowed aft, 'Bosun's Mate, report for'ard!' He edged past Clark and rattled down the ladder. 'I'll send him to you, sir.' West called after him, 'I want him to pipe all hands on deck. And send some men to the dressing-station, bring up the last of the wounded. Tell the Surgeon-Commander we're about to abandon ship.'

'Aye aye, sir.'

'Listen to me, all of you.' Clark, still clutching the handrail, struggled for breath as he turned to and fro, addressing the men on the foc'sl and those below him in the waist as well.

'Listen . . . There's no rush We've time to do this in an orderly manner. All wounded men will be helped into the rafts. *Un*wounded men will stay *out* of 'em, and help tow 'em clear of the ship as soon as they're filled. There are plenty of ships about – or will be, by daylight – so you can reckon on being picked up quite soon. Right then – good luck to you all.'

Nick leant in a rear corner of *Lanyard*'s bridge listening to her thrumming, thumping clatter as she tore southwards through the dark. Not at full power; Worsfold had finished his repairs at about half-past eight, and he'd implored Mortimer not to use maximum revolutions unless action situations demanded it. Mortimer, who'd been getting more and more bad-tempered during the long delay, had been so relieved at getting his ship moving again that he'd accepted the recommendation.

Worsfold had muttered as he passed Nick, behind the binnacle, 'Wonders'll never cease!'

Mortimer had half-heard him.

'What's that, Chief?'

'I said, "Now for a bit of peace", sir.'

'Meaning?'

'We've been at it pretty hard down there, sir.'

'Oh, yes.' Mortimer's suspicion faded. 'I dare say you have. Well done, Chief.'

Worsfold had then winked at Nick and left the bridge. They'd been pushing south ever since at about three-quarters speed – twenty-six knots – which should bring them up astern of the Grand Fleet's flotillas in an hour or not much more. The jury-rigged wireless aerial could receive, after a fashion, but not transmit; the telegraphists had picked up Jellicoe's course-and-speed orders, and his order to the destroyers to take station five miles astern of the battle fleet, and that was all Mortimer had had to base his calculations on. Hastings had demurred, suggesting that they didn't know which way the fleet had steered between the time they last saw it and the time – nine twenty, roughly – Jellicoe had ordered the course to be changed to south. Mortimer had told him that it didn't make much difference, a point or two this way or that; you couldn't *not* come up astern of a fleet that size, with no less than four destroyer flotillas spread out astern of it.

Nick had taken over on the bridge for about an hour before the boiler-room repair had been completed. Hastings had needed a break. And during that time, the dead had been buried. Each had been given a few prayers from the 'Form for the Burial of the Dead at Sea', the shrill pipe of a bosun's call, and a volley from half a dozen rifles. The simplicity of the ceremony had emphasised its sadness. And the destroyer alone here in gathering dusk, with the sea's reflective quality fading under a slowly darkening sky: there had been an acute sense of solitude, and loss . . .

Alone on the bridge except for Garret and the helmsman and telegraphman down there below them, Nick had listened to Mortimer's voice intoning the simple prayers, and to the high, thin wails of the pipe, the rattles of rifle-fire, the splashes. He'd felt a tightness in his throat, a depth of personal sorrow which astonished him.

He'd attended only one funeral in his life. His mother's. Mary Everard had died in 1906 of pneumonia, which had grown out of a chill caught when she'd got soaking wet out hunting. Nick had been eleven, and he'd felt he was attending the funeral of a stranger. It had been so cold, so impersonal; he'd thought, *that's how she was* . . . He remembered his father's tall, black-clad figure and set, stern face; there'd been the same clothes, the same faces, everywhere Nick had looked. He'd hardly known his mother; she'd seen to her sons' wellbeing in an efficient, supervisory manner, and he'd thought of her in that way – as a kind of supervisor, or 'higher authority'. The woman who'd mothered him had been 'Old Nanny'; he knew what her real name had been, now, but he hadn't then, and she'd died recently at Harrogate, where she'd gone to live in her retirement.

David had been fourteen, and a cadet at Osborne, at the time of their mother's funeral, and he'd attended it – on orders from their father – in his uniform. Nick had been surprised, and their father had been embarrassed, when David had started weeping. It had never occurred to Nick that either of them might be so affected. When they got back to the house, their father had sent for David, and he must have given him a ticking-off; David had been sniffling again when he'd come back upstairs to the schoolroom. He'd stopped in the doorway, and glared at his smaller brother out of reddened eyes: 'You don't *care*, do you!'

'Care what?'

'That she's dead! You never loved her, like I—'

'No, I—'

'There! You admit it! You little beast, you—'

'I was trying to say I didn't *not* like – love her.' He remembered being totally confused. He didn't *know* how he'd felt about her, or even how he felt about her being dead.

Uncle Hugh had come up from London for the funeral. He'd got married only a few months before, and he'd brought his wife up with him. Nick remembered being sent down to the big drawing-room at Mullbergh, and introduced to her. She'd drawled some comment which he didn't understand, and she'd shrugged, laughing at his embarrassment. He'd always hated that room.

'Starboard ten.'

'Starboard ten, sir!'

'Steady on sou'-west by south.' He turned, met Garret's eyes as they heard yet another rattle of shots and yet another splash. Garret muttered, 'Must be the last. Poor devils.'

'They may not be feeling poor, perhaps?'

He'd just said it without thinking and immediately wished he hadn't. Garret put the thing back in an easier perspective; he said, '*I* would be.'

An hour later: twenty-five sea-miles farther south. It was pitch dark now, and an empty sea. There'd been some signals which *Lanyard* had intercepted from light cruisers reporting sightings of the enemy; it seemed fairly plain that the Germans were to the westward or south-westward of Jellicoe's southbound battle fleet.

Mortimer had said, 'He's got 'em where he wants 'em. Given any sort of luck, he'll have Scheer over a barrel in the morning!'

It was a satisfying thought that one was taking part in a major battle that was likely to end up as a major victory. Nick wondered where David was, whether his cruiser had been in action – and if so, how he'd reacted to the experience. David would come out of it all right; not that anyone could 'arrange' what happened in a battle, but simply that David would take care he personally different come to grief. If his ship sank, he'd survive, in any situation . . . Like getting over tall hedges, out hunting – David invariably picked his spot, and usually one that a few other riders had been over first, whereas he, Nick, tended to charge the obstacle at its nearest point – and come off, yet again . . . He enjoyed it, but he usually managed to make an idiot of himself; he wasn't the right shape for a horseman, as David was, with his length of leg, balance and slimness. David's great disadvantage was his nervousness. He'd always been scared, even as a small boy. But according to their father, David was the horseman, the one who was mad keen on riding to hounds, who looked right on a horse. Nick had never heard his brother argue the point – but he'd seen his hands shaking, seen the tremble of his lips. And David, the heir, had to do it well. Sir John Everard expected nothing less, from his elder son. Was that part of David's trouble? It matched what Johnson had said about him the idea of his being scared of not succeeding – didn't it?

Nick frowned as he thought about it. The possibility of getting some insight that might help one to like – or *cease to dislike* – one's own brother had obvious appeal, and this was why what Johnson had said had interested him so much.

Then when one thought about it – about, for instance, David's concern for his own person, and in contrast, what he'd done to that wretched tart – he had *done* it, and he'd tried to pretend he hadn't, tried to suggest some other man might have been with her after he, David, had left her: he'd been desperate, almost grovelling in his attempts to persuade Nick to accept his denials, evasions. But Nick had just returned from the girl's lodging, he'd seen her, heard her: now he saw his brother's white face and frightened eyes, and it had been an effort to keep his fists at his sides.

David had begged him to go to her address. The morning after: Nick had a bad hangover from the party – a mutual friend's bachelor night, the eve of his wedding – and David had something more than hangover. Nick hadn't realised that; on his way to see the girl he'd construed that all that was wrong with his brother was an excess of alcohol the night before and a degree of shame at having spent what had been left of the night with a prostitute he'd picked up in the street. It had been in character, that David shouldn't want to face her sober and in daylight, and Nick, on his way there in a cab, had felt no more than a familiar, mild contempt for him. It had been no more than that – until the girl opened her door to his knock and he saw her bruised, smashed-up face.

David had left his wallet, cigarette case and silver-topped cane in her room. Whatever had happened between them, he'd panicked and run away. The girl, with one eye completely closed and the other a slit in bruised flesh, stared at him through the partly-opened door. She shook her head: he saw her wince.

'Not up to it, dear. See that, carn'ya?'

He'd explained. He'd wanted to fetch a doctor.

'Get one to *'im*!'

'Why, what d'you—'

'*Brain* doctor . . . Is'n 'e ravin' bloody mad?'

There was quite a lot of money in David's wallet. Nick emptied it on the chest-of-drawers. The girl almost didn't

take it. When he asked her why or how it had happened, she
shrugged and turned away.

'I laughed at him. Drunk, were'n 'e – I mean, 'e could'n
– you know . . .'

Nick handed David back an empty wallet. He told him,
'You'll find it's empty. I gave her all you had.'

'*What*?'

Nick stared at him, seeing not only his brother but his
father too. And he could have hit him, even then, before the
excuses and denials had even started. David was thumbing
angrily through the wallet; he muttered, 'Damn near a whole
month's pay! For God's sake, Nick—'

'Leave God out of it!' David seemed to be in shock. Nick
said, 'You're lucky the police aren't looking for you. I
suppose she thought they wouldn't take her word for it. . .'

Like father, like son. Nick thought, on *Lanyard*'s bridge as
she thrust southwards through the night, *perhaps they can't
help it. Perhaps it's in the blood. In mine too, then?*

'Everard?'

Mortimer had his binoculars at his eyes. His back was
resting against the binnacle. Nick moved up beside him.

'Sir?'

Hastings was over on the port side; looking past the
captain, Nick could see him and his glasses silhouetted
against the night sky. Heading into such wind as there was,
and into the low, choppy sea which during the last hour it
had begun to push up, *Lanyard* was thumping a bit now,
smashing the small waves down but making quite a fuss
about it. The damage she'd suffered had of course added to
her rattles. He looked down and for'ard, saw her bow-wave
gleaming white, fading into a vaguer lightness and finally
merging, abaft the beam, into the surrounding blackness of
the sea.

Mortimer finally condescended to lower his binoculars
and turn towards him.

'Yes, now then. Not because we're short-handed, Sub, but

because I'm satisfied you're reasonably sensible – which to some extent compensates for the fact that you're still wet behind the ears and haven't been with us much more than half a dogwatch – I'm declaring you competent to take charge of a watch at sea. When time permits you may type out a watchkeeping certificate, and I'll sign it. Copy the wording from the screed I gave Hastings last year.'

'Thank you very much, sir!'

'Don't let me down, that's all.'

Nick felt wonderful. It was like being let out of the nursery, or given the key of the door!

He blinked: something had flashed, out there, a long way off.

Mortimer had whipped up his binoculars: 'What the—'

Gunfire. There'd been that single flash, and then a lot of it, flickering to and fro out there on the horizon; now its sound reached them too. Nick heard movement behind him as someone else arrived in the bridge. Mortimer was conning *Lanyard* around two points to starboard, to steer straight for the action. Behind Nick, the torpedo gunner demanded in a stage whisper, 'What's that lot, then?' Nobody was in a position to enlighten him. The gunfire was increasing, and the stabs of flame were yellowish, not red as they'd been in daylight. A searchlight beam – no, several, a whole battery of them sprang out blinding white, held for a few seconds and then went out as suddenly as they'd come on.

That flickering, ruddy-coloured point of light might be a ship on fire. The gunfire died away, and ceased altogether.

Mortimer asked without lowering his glasses, 'What is the state of the guns, Sub?'

'Midships four-inch closed-up and ready, sir. The crew of the for'ard gun are resting under the midships gun-platform. The two crews are working watch-and-watch, and ammunition parties are at their stations but standing easy, sir.'

'Have 'em all stand-to, please.'

'Aye aye, sir.'

'Mr Pilkington, is that you?'

'Yessir. After tube is closed-up, sir.'

'Our last torpedo must not be wasted, Mr Pilkington.'

'I'm countin' it won't be, sir.'

Nick had alerted the guns' crews, by voicepipe. He moved past Garret, to see what settings Blewitt had on the Barr and Stroud transmitter. 'Put zero deflection, Blewitt. And range – well, say two thousand yards.' He thought any action in the dark would most likely be fought at fairly close quarters.

'Oh-two-oh set, sir.'

'Check that the guns have the same readings.'

'Aye aye, sir.'

'Everard.' Mortimer told him, 'If we meet any Huns, my first consideration will be to use that torpedo effectively. So I don't want any guns blazing away without orders. The object will be to get in close and make as sure as possible of a torpedo hit. Make sure the gunlayers understand this.'

'Aye aye, sir.'

It was all quiet, up ahead where that brief action had taken place. The fire, if that was what it had been, had gone out too, and it felt as if *Lanyard* was entirely alone in a great emptiness of night and sea. Mortimer said to Hastings, 'Might have been ten miles away, could've been six or seven. Anyone's guess.'

'I'd have thought at least ten, sir.'

And by the time *Lanyard* got down there, Nick thought, whoever it had been might well be another ten miles away in any direction at all . . . He went down to instruct the gunlayers. On his way back a few minutes later, abreast the whaler on the port side, he met Pilkington coming aft.

'We'll be stuck in agin soon, Sub. Got yer rubber weskit on?'

But *Lanyard* was well astern of the fleet, and the Germans were down somewhere in the south-west; there seemed no reason for either fleet to turn north. The farther south Scheer went, the closer he'd be getting to his bases. With luck,

Lanyard might come up astern of her flotilla and rejoin it, or tag on to one of the other flotillas and locate the thirteenth at daylight. One felt that Jellicoe knew there'd be no night fighting; he'd so to speak appealed against the light and drawn stumps.

Apart from which, things felt quiet . . .

A few seconds later, as he climbed up to the bridge, he heard Hastings shout, 'Port bow, sir, more—'

'I'm not blind, Pilot!'

Nick, joining them quickly, saw the new outbreak of gunfire on the port bow. Mortimer said angrily, 'It's damnable, not knowing what's going on . . .'

Whatever it was, it was happening a long way off again, much too far for it to concern *Lanyard* in any immediate sense. There was more of it than last time, though. Searchlight beams and the flashes of explosions lit lightning glimpses of ships, miniaturised silver shapes behind blazing guns. Mortimer announced, 'Light cruisers. God knows which is what.' Keeping his glasses at his eyes, he performed a long knees-bend to the voicepipe.

'Starboard ten!'

'Starboard ten, sir!'

Again he was aiming *Lanyard* towards the action; towards toy ships firing tiny guns, making sparks and pops instead of blinding flashes and the thunder of destruction. That was what one knew it was, but its remoteness and the impossibility of reaching it in time to play any part in it gave one a sense of detachment; men were being killed down there, but one couldn't *feel* it . . .

Mortimer repeated, 'Light cruisers, wouldn't you say?' Hastings mumbled something. This action was taking place much farther east than the last one had. German scouting forces – cruisers – shadowing the Grand Fleet, perhaps, probing for information to pass on to Scheer, and running up against our own cruisers or destroyers?

'Midships!'

It was a much larger-scale action than the first. Gunfire was continuous; brilliant white and softer, yellowish flashes lit the clouds. Now to the left – eastward – there was a blaze of searchlights and more rapid shooting. Smoke, illuminated by sudden flashes from inside it, vanished as the flashes ceased, then reappeared as it rolled across the searchlights, dimming them. A ripple of gunfire came from farther to the right; the spread of the action was wider, as well as its pace being hotter, than the other one.

'Steady as you go.' Mortimer slowly straightened. 'Good God, look at that!'

A ship's tall grey funnels had been lit suddenly in an enormous gout of white flame: a second column, also white, shot up close by it. Her foremast showed black against it for a moment: and then it vanished, all of it extinguished as neatly as doused candles, and there was only a peculiar glow left, pinkish and showing through smoke like a picture-postcard sunset by a rotten artist. A moment ago searchlights had been blazing: now they'd gone out with a suddenness that left sea and sky black, empty. And the guns had all ceased fire.

Hastings said to Mortimer, 'Someone met a sudden end *there*, sir.'

'You could be right. Are we on the top line with our recognitions signals? Because with all this lot barging around the North Sea we'd damn well better be!'

'I have the current signal letters, sir, and Garret has too, I think.'

'Yessir.' Garret spoke from the far side of the searchlight mounting, 'Got 'em in mind and wrote down too, sir.'

'What about you, Everard ?'

'Well, sir, if Garret—'

'Look here – suppose we were to get blown up. You're left in charge. Garret's knocked out too. Now you're challenged by – *Southampton*, say. She'd have a broadside of five six-inch guns trained on you before she made the challenge, ready to blow you out of the water if you don't give the right answer *immediately*. Well, what arc going to do about it?'

There really wasn't any answer.

'Everard, you're *dead*, by now! So's every man of your ship's company!'

'I – I'll make sure I do know the signals that are in force in future, sir.'

'How ?'

'I'll—' He didn't want to say 'I'll ask someone'. . . 'I'll look it up, sir.'

'D'you know how to? Sure you can do it accurately? It's not a thing you can allow yourself a mistake in, you know!'

The book was in the chartroom. But nobody had ever shown him how to check a recognition signal. In the ships he'd served in before they'd always been chalked up on a board; he'd never given much thought to how they got there. And that book might not be simple to work from without instruction.

'I know where the book is, sir. I imagine it's fairly easy to look up the—'

'Now we approach the truth . . .' Mortimer looked round, a quick check that *Lanyard*'s surroundings were still all peaceful. He turned back, and pointed.

'Leading Signalman Garret – do *you* know how to extract the recognition signal of the watch from the appropriate CB?'

'I do that, sir.'

'Then go down to the chartroom with Sub-Lieutenant Everard, and show him how to.'

'Aye aye, sir.'

To have him instructed by a leading signalman was intended, no doubt, as a small humiliation, to serve him right for not knowing such a simple procedure. He should have made it his business to find out, long ago. There were quite a number of things which he should have done, in the past eighteen months, and hadn't done; such as putting in some study and practice of the taking and working-out of sun- and star-sights. He was cack-handed with a sextant, and invariably got muddled with the figures. But he could, with a bit of effort, teach himself to do it properly. And he would, now.

He swung himself on to the ladder, and climbed down, using the ladder's sides, not its rungs, as handholds, for fear of Garret's knuckle-crushing boots coming down close above him.

Hastings, sweeping the sea and horizon with his binoculars, was working to a system. From right ahead he'd sweep down the port side to right astern; then at about twice the speed he'd sweep back up to the bow. He'd do the same thing then on the starboard side, but in between he'd give extra attention right for'ard, about two points to port and two to starboard. That was the way the ship was travelling, where an enemy would appear most suddenly, be most likely to appear.

He heard Nick and Garret leave the bridge behind him, just as he paused with his glasses trained right ahead. He murmured to the Captain, 'With respect, sir, it was always Lieutenant Reynolds's job. None of the rest of us ever looked it up.'

'I know.' Mortimer was wiping sea-dew from the lenses of his binoculars. 'Matter of keeping Everard on his toes. If we push him a bit, I believe we could make a useful—'

Hastings choked; his body jerked as if he'd had an electric shock: 'Ships, starboard bow, sir! They're – *not British*!'

Mortimer whipped up his glasses . . .

A light cruiser; two of them. The twin searchlights on their foremasts above the spotting tops was a distinctive German feature and it was plain to see against the sky.

'Port ten!'

'Port ten, sir!'

'Tell Pilkington stand by to fire to starboard, target the leading cruiser!'

'Ten o' port wheel on, sir!'

Lanyard had begun a swing to starboard. Mortimer's intention was to slip in towards the enemy, close the range enough to ensure a hit, and then come round to port, firing on that turn-away.

'Midships!'

Hastings had alerted Pilkington.

If *Lanyard* could get in there undetected, and get the fish away before they woke up and blasted her into scrap, she'd have a good chance of a kill. She was well up on the Germans' bow – a perfect situation, and no need even to increase speed. Not until after she'd fired: *then* there'd be the little matter of getting away from two angry cruisers' guns . . . For the moment, all one had to think about was getting in there and firing.

There was every chance she'd make it. Low speed, very little bow-wave, no risk of the glow which at full power showed at funnel-tops. They certainly hadn't seen her yet: and she was low, and black-painted to match the night, and at this moment almost bow-on to them, presenting very little silhouette.

Mortimer said quietly, tensely, 'Tell Pilkington I'm about to turn to the firing course.'

Hastings passed the stand-by message. Raising his head from the voicepipe, he happened to glance out on the starboard bow.

For a split second, while he confirmed that he wasn't imagining what he was staring at, he froze . . .

'Starboard bow – battleship – about to *ram*!'

Mortimer had sprung round, and seen it. Too late. A third ship – a dreadnought battleship following astern of those cruisers: she'd swung out to port, her vast bulk was rushing at them out of the dark, and she'd take *Lanyard* on her ram with as little trouble as it might take a rhinoceros to horn a dog.

'Hard a-port! Full ahead together!'

If he'd attempted to evade by turning to port – which would have allowed him to fire his torpedo on the way round – the German would only have needed to adjust his course by a few degrees and he'd still have got her. But a turn to starboard – turning *inside* the dreadnought's own swing to port, and probably scraping paint off her as they scraped by – that was just – *might* be – possible . . .

Fifty-fifty chance? No. Two to one against.

'Helm's hard a-port, sir, both telegraphs full ahead!'

The turbines' whine rose to a scream: the vast shape of the oncoming ship loomed bigger, closer, towering overwhelming. . . And *Lanyard*'s bow seemed to be coming round so *slowly*!

'Stop starboard!'

He'd needed speed; now he needed swing. The sea might have been treacle, she was turning so sluggishly . . . They were finished. In seconds they'd be smashed, ridden under, ploughed into the sea. But she was getting round: with the starboard screw stopped she was fairly whistling round! Her stem pointed at the German's foc's'l – at his bridge superstructure – amidships – round, round . . . You could have touched the bastard with a boathook!

The night split. The world exploded in their faces.

Hugh Everard lowered his binoculars. Mowbray had sent the midshipman of the watch to him, and he'd come out to see the latest of several flare-ups which had lit the blackness astern of the battle squadrons. This one had ended almost before it had started.

'Short and sweet.' He thought about that: he added, 'Though perhaps not for everyone.'

Destroyer actions, probably. Something bigger, possibly.

Having no wireless, one could only guess. Reports might

well be flooding in to Jellicoe in *Iron Duke*; it might be quite plain to the commander-in-chief, and to subordinate admirals and captains whose ships still had wireless equipment in working order, what was happening astern.

The 'something bigger' possibility wasn't a comfortable thought to entertain. If the Germans were not where they were believed to be; if Scheer was attempting to break through astern of the Grand Fleet and run for the minefield-gap at Horns Reef . . ..

One could only dismiss the thought. Jellicoe must know where Scheer was, and where he'd find him in the morning. And Jellicoe would be able to see that fighting astern just as easily as he, Hugh Everard could.

'I'm going to get a few hours' sleep now, Mowbray. Shake me if you need to, otherwise at one forty-five.'

'Aye aye, sir.'

He found Bates waiting in the sea-cabin.

'Afraid your kye'd get cold, sir.'

'Doesn't look like it.' The mug of cocoa was steaming; he reached for it. 'Hot, all right.' He put it down again, and asked Bates, 'Where's the stuff you salvaged?'

'In 'ere, sir.' Bates dragged a suitcase up on to the bunk. 'Not much, sir. Just odds an' ends, this is. But there's some shirts as'll want dhobyin' – an' your best suit o' number fives, an' our other pair of 'alf-boots – that's in the commander's day-cabin, sir.' He saw Hugh's quick glance, and added, 'I did ask 'im, sir.'

'Good.' Hugh opened the case. He found a litter of correspondence, bank-books, ornaments, a silver cigarette-box, the case he kept his cufflinks and studs in; and one leather folding photograph frame.

Hugh looked at his coxswain, 'Your own personal selection, Bates . . .'

'Yessir. Lot o' stuff was spoiled, sir. An' I only 'ad the one case 'andy, for these bits.'

When Bates wanted to look blank, he knew how to. Hugh

surrendered. 'I'm – much obliged to you.'

'No need, sir.' With his hands on the case, to put it back on the deck, he looked at the frame in Hugh's hand. 'Keepin' that out, sir?'

Hugh nodded. He watched Bates stow the suitcase away. 'Tell me. What made you go aft when you did? When I'd told you to wait in the sea-cabin?'

Bates straightened.

'Sorry about that, sir. Didn't 'ave time to think, not really. I felt them 'its aft, an' I looks out and there's smoke comin' out where our quarters is, so I says to meself, that's us, that is, best takee look-see, sort 'o thing.'

'As well you did, in view of what happened to the sea-cabin in your absence.'

Bates nodded phlegmatically. 'One way o' lookin' at it, sir . . . Be gettin' your 'ead down now, sir, will you?'

'Yes.' He'd finished the cocoa. Bates stooped, pulled out one of the bunk drawers. 'I borrowed some gear for you to be goin' on with, sir. Sweater, scarf, pair o' gloves – well, this 'ere, sir, spare socks 'n—'

'You've done well, Bates. Thank you.' Someone knocked on the door. 'Come in!'

Tom Crick peered in. Bates said quickly, tapping that drawer with the toe of his boot, 'Commander's gear, sir.'

'Oh, *is* it.' He saw enquiry in Crick's face. 'All right, Bates, I shan't need you for a couple of hours. Get some sleep.'

'Aye aye, sir.' Bates slid out. Hugh nodded to Crick. 'Kind of you to lend me your things, Tom. I hear there's some junk of mine in your day-cabin too?'

Crick pulled the door shut. 'That's so, sir. Your coxswain has what one might call a persuasive manner.'

'You don't like him, do you, Tom?'

'Only hoping he won't let you down one day, sir.'

'If you'd care to bet on it, I'll take your money.'

Crick smiled and shook his head. Then he cleared his

throat. I've come to report we're in reasonably good shape below decks now, sir. We'll need a couple of weeks in the dockyard, of course, but there's nothing need concern us for the moment. The PMO asked me to tell you he'll have a detailed casualty list ready in the morning; looks like four officers and thirty-one men killed, and two plus twenty-eight wounded.' His eyebrows rose. 'Might 've been a lot worse, sir.'

'Considering the chance I took.'

'You saved hundreds in *Warspite*, sir.'

When Crick had gone, Hugh took his reefer and half-boots off, loosened his tie and collar and stretched out on the bunk. He pulled a blanket up over himself. Then he opened the leather frame that Bates had had the remarkable percipience to rescue.

Sarah smiled at him from her photograph. A gentle, rather wistful, lonely smile. Hugh had picked this one – stolen it – from a bunch of prints which a photographer had sent to brother John so he could choose one for mounting.

The puzzling thing was, there'd been quite a number of framed portraits displayed openly in the day-cabin; but this one he'd kept more discreetly in a drawer. Had Bates reasoned that it made Sarah's portrait more important than the others or did he have second sight, in those monkey eyes of his?

Hugh closed the frame and pushed it under the pillow. He thought, with his hand out to the light switch, that he had two stories now for Sarah. This indication of his coxswain's intelligence would make one, and the other was the incident of the sailing barque which, caught between the embattled fleets, had made him think of her.

If he told her of those two things, wouldn't he be telling her everything there was to tell?

He hoped he'd have the nerve to. To let her know how he felt. Not to funk it as he had the other day.

Chapter 10

He was alive. Mortimer and Hastings were dead.

Lanyard was still afloat, and for the time being, so far as one could tell, out of any immediate danger.

So far as one could tell: the qualification was a real one. Uncertainty, a sense of detachment and confusion, was the residue of shock, upheaval. It had to be fought against. It was as if one's mind had been switched off for several seconds, or minutes – a period of indeterminate length during which one had seemed to be struggling to retain awareness of one's surroundings, and making no headway. Now the struggle was for renewed power of thought, judgement, decision.

He was in command!

'Four hundred revolutions.'

'Four hundred—' MacIver gulped – 'revolutions, sir.' MacIver's mouth was open, and his breath whistled through the gap of a missing tooth. He looked dazed still.

'Port ten.'

'Port ten, sir.' CPO Glennie, the chief bosun's mate, span the wheel. After Cuthbertson's death earlier in the day Glennie had become the destroyer's senior rating. Steady as a rock: he was built like one, too. Nick told him, 'Ease to five, and steady on south.'

Lanyard's sudden lurch to starboard had sent Nick and Garret flying across the chartroom. Nick had hauled himself up the slanting deck to the starboard-side door, got out through it and started climbing the ladder to the bridge. He'd been some of the way up when the German dreadnought's port batteries – her secondary armament of six-inch guns – had crashed out a broadside at point-blank range and maximum depression. For him and Garret the blast had been an incredible volume of sound and a great sheet of flame which swept across above their heads as the ship lurched back against the natural heel of her swing. For about two seconds a scorching heat radiated downwards. Then she'd heeled back again, and she'd still been turning; he'd climbed a few more rungs, and stopped again when he'd discovered that *Lanyard* no longer had an upper bridge. The top part of it – with binnacle, railings, flag-lockers, everything – had been shorn off.

The steering position – lower bridge – was roofless but otherwise intact and operable as a wheelhouse. The searchlight had gone – simply wiped off. So had the for'ard gun, both boats, and several feet of the already damaged top of the for'ard funnel. The roof of the galley, the superstructure between the boats, had been stove in. Mr Pilkington, who'd arrived in the steering-position a minute ago, had told him about the funnels and the boats, and apparently that was as far aft as the area of damage extended.

Nick and Garret owed their lives first to Mortimer having sent them down to the chartroom, and second to their having been below the reach of the guns' blast, and sheltered from it by the superstructure. Otherwise they would have been dead, blown away in that blast of flame – like Mortimer, Hastings, Blewitt and the entire crew of the for'ard four-inch.

The only shell to have hit *Lanyard* had sheered through

her foremast without exploding, and passed on. The foremast had toppled, snapped, and crashed overboard. All the other projectiles had passed overhead too; the battleship's six-inch guns hadn't been able to depress far enough to reach her. According to Pilkington, the two ships had been almost alongside each other at that moment.

There'd been only that one broadside. The Germans must have thought they'd finished her; she'd reeled away, and they'd steamed on into the night.

Nick's first question to Chief Petty Officer Glennie, when he'd reached the steering-position – climbing into it, through the now completely open corner where *Lanyard* had been hit during the torpedo attack in the afternoon – had been, 'Does she answer her helm ?'

'Aye, sir, she does.' Glennie had shown considerable initiative in the seconds after the cataclysm. He and MacIver, the telegraphman, had been lifted off their feet and thrown at the starboard bulkhead. Recovering, with his head ringing from the explosions and from being bounced off a steel wall, the chief buffer had put the starboard telegraph to full ahead and then grabbed the wheel to steady the ship on a north- easterly course. Finding himself on his own, with nobody up there to direct him, it had seemed sensible to steer her away from the source of trouble.

It was a stump of a bridge, now, like a broken tooth. The after part of its deck – which was also the roof of some of the chartroom and all the signals office – was still there, but all the for'ard part had been peeled off. Apart from jagged edges, it had been done quite neatly, with no bits or pieces left behind. Nick was standing now in the steering-position between Glennie and MacIver; his head was in fresh air, cold wind, and he looked straight ahead over an edge of ripped steel at the destroyer's bow thrusting through a low, black sea.

'Does the engine-room voicepipe still work, MacIver?'

'I'll test it, sir.'

'Well, get Mr Worsfold on it, if you can.'

'Aye aye, sir.' The voicepipe was on the starboard bulkhead. MacIver put his mouth to it and shouted, 'Engineroom!'

Nick asked Pilkington, 'Is that last torpedo still in its tube?'

'Course it is!' The torpedo gunner squeezed up beside him. Space was tight in here; Nick thought perhaps MacIver could be dispensed with. He had a half-inclination to keep Pilkington here with him; but he had the other half, too, which was to keep him at a distance.

Pilkington asked him, 'What d'you reckon on doin' now, Sub?'

'I'll tell you when I've had a word to Chief ... What about the midships four-inch – is it still there ?'

'I *told* yer – nothin' touched us, aft!'

'Engineer Officer's on the voicepipe, sir.'

'Thank you.' Nick thought, as he squeezed over behind Glennie, *no, I do not want Mr Pilkington with me* ... 'Chief?'

'Yes. What have you been *doing* up there?'

'The Captain and Hastings have been killed, the top of the bridge has been shot off and we've lost the for'ard gun. Can you tell me if there's any damage to machinery or hull?'

'I've no reason to think there is, Sub.'

That was good news, indeed, and Worsfold sounded pretty cool, down there.

'What d'you intend to do now?'

'Carry on as before. Find our flotilla.'

He couldn't see he had much choice. *Lanyard* had steam, and a gun and a torpedo. If there was action in the offing, that was where she ought to be. All he had to do was find it.

He turned to Pilkington.

'You're second-in-command, and I want you aft, where you can look after the gun as well as your own department. We'll have to do something about communications—'

'Action on the starboard bow, sir!' CPO Glennie's eyes were slits in his squarish face. He'd seen the start of another firework display. A flash, white like a magnesium flare, and the familiar flickering of guns. It was a long way off.

'Come round a point to starboard.'

'Aye aye, sir.' Glennie's hands moved on the wheel. Nick called out through the open corner of the wheelhouse, 'Garret?'

'Sir?'

'There are some binoculars in the chartroom. If there are two pairs, bring them both, please.'

'Aye aye, sir.'

Nick turned back to Pilkington. 'Perhaps you could get some flexible hose and join it to the bridge voicepipe – the one from the bridge to the after searchlight platform. It'll have been cut through of course, you'll have to find the end. Join up a length of hose and bring its other end down here.'

Pilkington nodded his large head. 'I'll 'ave a shot.'

'The other thing, Mr Pilkington, is to let the ship's company know what's going on. Would you see to that?'

He wondered if he was being too polite; whether he should be telling, instead of asking. But he was, really; and at the moment he needed the gunner's help, more than his obedience. He'd already gone; and Garret arrived now with the binoculars – Johnson's, and Reynolds's.

There was no time to mourn the dead. You could only try to fill their places. As Mortimer had filled Johnson's place with Hastings, so Nick was now replacing all three of them. Johnson had been killed about six hours ago, but he was already a name and a character from the past, his death eclipsed by the more recent ones.

'Chief Petty Officer Glennie.'

'Sir!'

Nick had cleaned and focused the binoculars, and he was sweeping the sea and horizon ahead. There was no clear-cut horizon: only a fuzz, a layer that could have been either sea or sky and might have been two miles deep or five. The unobstructed arc of lookout from here was roughly beam to beam.

'I need Garret in here for signalling. We might be challenged, or need to challenge someone else.' He thought, immediately he'd said it, *I shan't do that. Not with one gun. We'll mind our P's and Q's* . . . 'But there's not much room, is there. Could you manage the telegraphs as well as the wheel?'

'Easy, sir.'

'Fine. MacIver – from here we can't see abaft the beam. And there's nothing left to stand on higher up. So take that pair of glasses and go aft to the searchlight platform and keep your eyes skinned. You'll have a voicepipe to us as soon as Mr Pilkington's got it rigged.'

'Aye aye, sir.'

'Off you go, then.'

Garret coughed. 'No searchlight for'ard here, sir. For signalling. You said you want me here ?'

'Oh, damn . . .'

He did need him here, under his immediate control. Answering challenges at night was a split-second business.

Glennie suggested, 'Use an 'and-lamp, sir?'

'Garret?'

'One in the signals office, sir. Well, there *was*—'

'Get it, or get something else.' He called after him, 'Those recognition signals—'

'I've got 'em, sir.'

He'd gone. Nick said, with binoculars at his eyes, 'You did extremely well, Glennie. You probably saved the ship.'

'Oh, I dunno, sir.'

'That's how it'll read in my report.'

'Let's 'ope you get to write one then, sir.'

He'd half-smiled, with his eyes on the compass-card, on the lubber's line shifting a degree or two each side of south-by-west. The wheel's brass-capped spokes passed this way and that through his large, practised hands as he corrected, more by feel and instinct than by design, the ship's tendency to roam.

Garret came back with a brass-cased hand lamp.

'Is that going to be bright enough?'

'Be all right while it's dark, sir.' The leading signalman moved round to Glennie's other side, where MacIver had been. The space was about adequate, for three men. He added, 'When it's light we can use the after searchlight sir.'

The priority now, Nick told himself, was to be prepared, to decide now, in advance of an emergency situation suddenly confronting him, what to do in this, that or the other circumstance. An unidentified ship there, coming straight for them; or a German there, broadside-on; or an enemy challenge on the beam. One knew nothing about the positions now of either one's own or enemy forces; whatever turned up, it could be either friendly or hostile, and one or two seconds in making a correct identification could spell the difference between survival and extinction. It seemed, too, that the situation might be more complicated than Mortimer had thought it was. His view had been that the Grand Fleet was near enough due south, and the Germans in the south-west. But *Lanyard* had very recently passed the time of day – in a manner of speaking with an enemy battleship and two cruisers, and they'd been steering south-east, across the rear of the south-bound Grand Fleet . . .

Well, it had been only one battleship; and as one swallow didn't make a summer . . . But she might have been damaged, or suffered some machinery breakdown; she could have been detached to make her own way homewards with a cruiser escort.

It didn't seem likely, on reflection. Would a fleet commander in Scheer's position spare two cruisers to take a lame duck home ?

It made no difference. *Lanyard* had no wireless; she couldn't send reports, any more than she could receive them.

There was only one plan of action, Nick told himself; to get her back to her flotilla, add her one gun and one torpedo to its strength. En route, to attack any enemy that showed up, and to avoid either being taken by surprise by an enemy or attacked in error by one's own side.

'Garret, those recognition signals. Have you—'

'All in my head, sir. I've a note of 'em, too.'

The sea ahead was blackish-grey, patched with mist and touched here and there with whitish flecks. It wasn't a broken sea; there was just enough breeze to knock the edge off the little waves, and to whip a few drops of spray now and then from *Lanyard*'s stem to spray this rattling, foreshortened bulkhead. She was pitching just a little, but there was no roll on her at all. The slight wind, plus her progress through it, had the wreckage of the superstructure round them groaning as if it was in pain; the rattles had settled into a rhythm which one might have missed if it had stopped.

Something clanged suddenly, overhead, behind them.

'Voicepipe 'ose, sir. Someone catch it an' 'aul it in, can they?'

Garret grabbed its end and hauled in about a fathom of it; it dangled behind CPO Glennie's head.

'Shall I lash it to the bulkhead, sir?'

'Yes. Leave a couple of feet loose at the end.'

With a voicepipe rigged to the gun and that tube, *Lanyard* would be fighting fit again. Nick thought, *now it's up to me.*

Hanbury Pike, the engineer, spat out a mouthful of North Sea, and pointed.

'She's going.'

'What? Who's—'

'*Bantry*, you damn fool!'

Everard seemed simple, child-like, and he didn't appear to realise what was happening. He was like someone having a bathe for the fun of it. They'd been in the water half an hour;

Pike was cold right through to his bones and he was wishing to God he'd refused Johnny West's request that he should keep an eye on him.

Bantry was on her way to the bottom.

Black against dark-grey sea and a lighter shade of sky, the cruiser's forepart was rising, tilting up as her stern went under, deeper into the sea.

Cold . . . Pike groaned, 'Oh, God in heaven . . .'

'What's the matter, Hanbury?'

The engineer began to swim away. Towards *Bantry*, as it happened, because he'd been watching her and therefore facing that way; his only purpose, apart from needing to use his muscles before they froze solid, was to get away from Everard. He wished he hadn't said he'd stay with him; he was too tired, mentally and physically, to put up with him, let alone look after him.

They'd managed, half an hour or so ago, to cram all the badly wounded men into rafts and floats, and less serious cases had had to go in the water and hold on to the rafts' sides. When they were all down there, West had told the fit men who'd been waiting on the upper deck, 'I want two dozen strong swimmers to tow them clear and stay with them. Volunteers?'

There'd been too many. He'd picked men who had friends among the wounded. The padre and the surgeon commander had gone with them. They climbed down the net into the sea, and pushed and towed the rafts away into the darkness. West called after them, 'Keep close together – you'll be easier to spot and pick up if you stay in a bunch. Good luck!'

Cheers had floated back to him. Someone shouted, 'Lovely boatin' wevver!' Laughter mingled with fresh cheers. They began to sing:

> '*Oh, a life on the ocean wave*
> *Ain't fit for a bloomin' slave* . . .'

They weren't only keeping their spirits up. There'd been a mood almost of carnival since Hanbury Pike and his party of artificers and stokers, helped by the fire brigade who'd worked with them, had brought seven men alive out of the starboard engine-room. The break-through had come within minutes of the pipe 'All hands on deck'; they'd ignored it, because by that time they'd fought their way to one of the armoured hatches and got a tackle rigged to lift it. They'd dragged it up, and the men – seven out of the nine who'd been trapped down there – had been hauled out.

Pike had told West it was the first time in his life he'd seen a stoker petty officer cry. Not the one they'd rescued: the PO who'd been working with him.

Apparently the shell had burst in the port engine-room, wrecking it completely and killing everyone in there; and it had burst low down, close to the base of the centre-line bulkhead. The door between the two engine-rooms had been buckled, and couldn't be shifted, and in the starboard engine-room the water began to rise quite fast. After a bit it was held down to some extent by pressure in the top of the compartment, but it was over the floor-plates, which were dislodged so that the ladders weren't accessible. Two men were drowned; the other seven, before their rescue, had found themselves trapped with the gratings above their heads and the water still rising below.

West asked the men still waiting, 'Any non-swimmers?' A voice answered at once, 'Sparks 'erbert 'ere can't swim a stroke, sir!'

Telegraphist Herbert's friends began pushing him about. Another man owned up – a stoker. . . 'I never made much of an 'and at it, sir.'

'Petty Officer Toomey – make sure they've got swimming collars on. Oh, damn it, here . . .' West took off the inflatable waistcoat which he'd bought from Messrs Gieves in Bond Street. 'One of 'em can wear this. I'll use a swimming collar.'

'No, sir, you don't go givin' me your—'

'I don't need it, Herbert, I'm like a fish in that stuff. And you should bloody well've learnt to swim, anyway, d'you hear? Toomey, the lifebuoys are abaft the second funnel. One each for these two men, and hand out the rest to weak swimmers.'

'Aye aye, sir.'

'Scrimgeour?'

The torpedo lieutenant came forward. 'Yes?'

'Is Commander Clark still on the bridge?'

'Intends to remain there.' Scrimgeour added, 'For the time being, he says.'

Toomey was distributing lifebuoys. West heard David Everard refuse the offer of one. 'My dear Toomey, I swim like a blooming otter!' He had his inflatable waistcoat on, anyway. West sent Scrimgeour to sort out a group of snotties who seemed to have neither waistcoats nor collars. Everard told Hanbury Pike, 'My brother Nick didn't cry when our mother died. Can you believe that?'

Pike stared at him open-mouthed: West put in quickly, 'David *there* you are, old man. Now look—'

'Not even at the funeral. Not one tear! If that doesn't prove he's—'

West patted his shoulder. 'Hang on a minute, David ... Hanbury, a word with you?' He beckoned the engineer, and they moved away from the group of waiting men. He told him, 'Everard's round the bend. Cracked. Would you keep an eye on him – I mean in the 'oggin?'

'If you think it's necessary.' Pike shrugged, without much enthusiasm. 'Are we all set now?'

'I want the rafts well clear first. Not that one expects there'd be competition for them, but—'

'Of course there wouldn't be!'

'No.' West agreed. 'Just playing safe. But I'll go and see Nobby, before we leave her.'

Ten minutes later, he'd come down from the bridge alone.

Pike had been chatting to Clarence Chance, the paymaster. West told them, 'Can't budge him. He says he wants to see everyone away first. I think he means to go down with her.'

Chance removed the monocle from his left eye. 'What would that achieve?'

West couldn't tell him. Nobody had known Clark well; but he'd never seemed a happy man.

'Come on. Time we went.'

Hanbury Pike watched *Bantry* hang for a moment with her stem pointing at the sky and her stern buried in the sea.

He hoped the four men in her after steering compartment, which it had not been possible to reach, had died before this. He tried not to think of the black water rushing through her; There was not only a dreadful sadness in the last throes of a great ship; there was also a terrible malignancy in the sea that swallowed her. And he felt so damn tired . . .

She'd begun to slide. There was a roar of displaced air, like an enormous sigh.

'Sub.' It was Worsfold on the engine-room voicepipe. 'We've been burning a deuce of a lot of oil. D'you think we might ease off a bit now and then?'

Nick thought about it. There was an argument for keeping *Lanyard* plugging along at thirty knots, and two at least against it.

'All right, Chief. Make it three-six-oh revs.'

Twenty-five knots would still be eight knots faster than the speed Jellicoe had ordered for the night. So *Lanyard* ought still to be catching up. But one might have expected to have been up with the fleet by now, and if it hadn't been for the repeated outbreaks of gunfire ahead and on the bows as they'd been steaming southwards he'd have been worried that he might somehow have passed by, diverged from the Grand Fleet's course and missed that not inconsiderable target. The fleet could have altered course – might easily have done – and without wireless *Lanyard* wouldn't know of it. The desire to link up as soon as possible with other destroyers astern of the battle fleet, which was an argument in favour of maintaining a good speed, was not entirely impersonal. Nick was conscious of feeling lonely; he had a strong inclination to be in company and have other ships to follow. But at the same time that nervousness made him glad, in another way, to reduce speed. He'd had a feeling of rushing into darkness and unseen dangers at a breathless, headlong pace; he wasn't frightened, but he was unsure, aware of his inexperience and the responsibility which had dropped on him so suddenly. A few hours ago he'd felt a glow of satisfaction in being told he could have a watch-keeping certificate, for God's sake: and here he was in command; not only in command in a detached situation and in action!

Inactivity made it worse. One had time to think. He wished he could feel more confident. And the one thing which was absolutely imperative was that nobody should be allowed to see or guess how *un*confident he did feel.

He chuckled as he came back to his position on the port side of the wheelhouse. 'Odd how engineers hate their engines being used.'

The chief buffer nodded. His eyes rose from the compass-card to glance for'ard at *Lanyard*'s short, punching bow.

'Think of 'em like mothers with babies, don't they, sir.'

The course was due south again. Nick had given up the business of altering this way and that whenever some distant exchange of gunfire illuminated the horizon. The battle fleet's ordered course, or at any rate the last one they'd heard of, had been south, so that was the heading one should stick to. Those sporadic actions, almost surely clashes between scouting and screening forces, were sometimes in one direction and sometimes in another; there was no point zig-zagging about like a donkey constantly switching carrots.

Another aspect of Nick's current feeling of having lost his

bearings was that the sensation was entirely new to him. The start of his naval career hadn't been exactly brilliant, but he'd never had any sense of fright or personal inadequacy in any given situation. He'd often dug his heels in, or slacked, when he'd found surroundings or subjects irksome, but he'd never thought to himself *I doubt if I can see this through . . .* To be unsure, off-balance, was foreign to him and extremely uncomfortable, and it was making him think again now, from time to time and in the back of his mind while he tried to concentrate it on the immediate situation, of David and what Johnson had said about him. Because if Johnson had been right, this might be how David had felt pretty well all his life. And what it felt like – this situation, now – was being on a horse which you knew you wouldn't be able to stop if it decided it didn't want you to.

'Starboard—'

Nick had jerked his glasses up; since he'd seen it, CPO Glennie saved his breath.

'Hell . . .'

To start with there'd been some stabs of gunfire; just three or four. But within seconds the sea and sky out there to starboard were ablaze with action; with a barrage of noise and flame, the sea spouting geysers of white water and the black shapes of destroyers darting, thrashing through them and between them, racing like greyhounds through a deluge of shellfire towards a solid line of flaming guns. The impressions – the picture which had sprung up out of nothing, out of a dark void of night and sea and mist – registered and resolved themselves into the fact that a flotilla or part-flotilla of destroyers was making an attack on a line of five, or six, much larger ships. . . Which were in line ahead on a south-easterly course. Seven or eight thousand yards on *Lanyard*'s bow, and the head of the enemy line about right ahead: the gunfire was continuous, spouting and rippling the whole length of the line as the destroyers raced in towards it; one saw them in flashes and as they appeared for no more than seconds between the leaping columns of white water. They were British destroyers, obviously . . . Well, check . . . Focusing on one of the enemy he made out a battleship; she was too big to be anything else. It was misty, though, down there, one felt one should be wiping the lenses of the binoculars twice a minute, but it was sea-mist, not the glasses fogging-up. That could only be a squadron of Scheer's High Seas Fleet beating off a determined destroyer attack.

'Four hundred revolutions!'

'Four hundred revolutions, sir.'

'Garret, tell the gun and tubes to stand by. Then get ready with that lamp.'

'Aye aye, sir.'

It looked like the fiercest engagement of the night. The Germans were using every sort of gun they had – turret guns and beam armament and quick-firing weapons flickering higher up. The destroyers were turning, Nick saw, to starboard, to a course opposite to the enemy's; when they'd fired they'd be heading west or north-west. Consequently if he altered *Lanyard*'s course to starboard there might be a danger of collision when the shooting stopped and the night went dark again, with lookouts and captains half-blinded temporarily by the flashes of their own guns and the enemy's.

'Starboard ten.'

'Starboard ten, sir.'

He was taking her round to port; to steer south-east, in order to converge on to the enemy battle squadron. They'd hardly be expecting a new attack from one solitary, shaved-off destroyer. Come to think of it, there wasn't much of *Lanyard* to see now, with no foremast and no top to her bridge.

'Midships. Steer south-east by south.'

'Sou'east by south, aye aye, sir.' Glennie sounded as calm as ever, not in the least excited.

'Garret. Tell Mr Pilkington we may be firing his torpedo at a battlcship in five or ten minutes' time. I can't say which side.'

'Aye aye, sir!'

Garret *did* sound excited.

'And tell him the gun is not to open fire without my order.'

He caught his breath . . .

In the middle of that display of fireworks, he'd seen a sudden splash of dark-red flame on one of the battleships; the third in the German squadron's line. The flame gushed upwards; now it had shot back the whole length of her, and in its savagely bright light he saw that she had three funnels and a large crane-derrick between the centre one and the third. She was German, certainly, and he thought Deutschland-class. The red blaze leapt higher, a soaring mass of incredibly bright fire, and sparks were flying out of it like rockets; sparks, and burning debris tracing arcs into the darker sky. Smoke grew at the fire's base and billowed upwards, folding itself outwards and around the ship, engulfing the brilliant flames, darkening thc night by stages until it was all smoke and the shooting from the other ships had stopped dead, totally, as if at one signal – *finis*.

Nick still had his glasses at his eyes, but all he could see now was the thick, grey blanket of the mist. CPO Glennie allowed himself a comment.

'They done 'er, all right, sir.'

'Let's see if we can't get another.'

Glennie nodded, with his eyes on the steering-compass. 'Never know till you try, sir.'

On this slightly converging course, Nick reckoned, he ought to pick up the Germans at about thirty or forty degrees on the bow and at reasonably close range in perhaps five minutes. He'd first seen them at about three-and-a-half miles; the next meeting should be at a distance of perhaps one mile. Allowing for a further slight closing of the range, he might be able to fire the torpedo at something like fifteen hundred yards. This, of course, depended on the battleships having held their course, not turned away to avoid the other torpedoes which must have been fired at about the same time as the one which had hit.

What would Mortimer have done, or be doing now, if he was in command?

Nick put his mind to it. The only alternative to going after the enemy as he was doing now would, he thought, have been to try to join that flotilla after they'd fired and broken off the action. But they'd vanished – to start with in a north-westerly direction, but they could afterwards have gone round astern of the enemy, or northwards, or any other way. But the Germans had been on what had looked like a straight, determined course.

Why did one have that impression? Because their course had been south-east – the same course as that of the battleship which had blown *Lanyard*'s bridge off. And south-eastward was the course for Germany via Horns Reef.

Nick wiped his glasses' lenses and put them back up to his eyes. At any second, those battleships might reappear. He decided he'd fire to starboard; close in, turn away to port, firing on the turn. But if he'd miscalculated and they should turn out to be abaft the beam, he'd turn towards, close in to a good killing range, and then put her round to starboard, firing to port as those others had done.

He was pleased to find that he could think coolly and logically. It would surely make it a lot easier, when one saw the enemy, to have the alternatives clearly in one's mind.

Still nothing in sight. He was beginning to think that the squadron must have altered course, after the torpedo hit.

Well, which way?

South, most likely. But he decided he'd hold on, steer this course for another five minutes. If by that time he hadn't—

There they were!

On the starboard bow, and in line ahead, steering just east of south. So *Lanyard* was coming up astern of them, but with about one point of difference between their course and hers, so that if she held on without any alteration she'd cross their wakes.

Peculiar. How they'd got into this position, and on that course . . .

'I'll be damned!'

He'd seen it, suddenly. He'd assumed these were the ships he'd been expecting to find, and he hadn't until this moment looked at them at all closely. These weren't battleships at all, they were destroyers. This was the bunch who'd carried out that attack!

Whatever the Germans had done – and it was still puzzling – these five ships must have swung around to port, right round, and then steered due east, and had now altered to something like south by east. They must have been searching for the Germans, too; most likely had torpedoes left, and aimed to make a second attack – encouraged, no doubt, by having knocked out one battleship half an hour ago.

'Steer five degrees to starboard. Three-six-oh revolutions.'

Glennie was repeating the orders. Nick's slight adjustments of course and speed were designed to add *Lanyard* to the tail-end of that flotilla.

'Garret, tell Mr Pilkington we're approaching friendly ships. Train the tube fore-and-aft.'

'Aye aye, sir.'

'Then stand by with your lamp.'

In a minute, they'd have to identify themselves. *Lanyard* was closing-up and edging-in, still a bit out on the other destroyers' starboard quarter. About half a mile between her and the boat she was going to tag on to.

Garret had passed that message aft. He told Nick, 'Ready with the lamp, sir.'

'They're bound to challenge, soon.' He was surprised they hadn't before this. He kept his glasses on them. 'Three-four-oh revs.'

'Three-four-oh, sir.'

A light flashed: from the *head* of the ·destroyer line. *Lanyard* wasn't tucked-in astern of them yet; in another minute she would have been, and that challenge wouldn't have been visible.

'Give 'em the answer, Garret.'

'Sir, that *can't* be one of our—'

From about sixty degrees on the starboard bow, an answering light flashed. Garret was right: all Nick had seen was the letter 'K'. He hadn't thought about it . . . But they hadn't been challenging *Lanyard*; they'd been talking to that other ship – whatever ship it might be – almost on the beam now. Nick swung his glasses on to her.

Not 'her'. *Them.* There were three ships, closing-in at right-angles, more or less. Meanwhile *Lanyard* had fallen into station astern of the main bunch.

'Three-two-oh revolutions.'

'Three-two-oh, sir.'

Nick's mind seemed suddenly to jump, to come alive. . . Inside his skull, a voice screamed protest.

Holding his breath – his hands had begun to shake and his breathing had become rapid, short – he focused on the new arrivals as they came slanting in under helm to add themselves one by one to the line astern of *Lanyard*.

He'd seen the possibility when he'd realised that the challenge was that single letter 'K', the long-short-long; then Garret's cut-off cry had put substance to the wild suspicion. It had still been a long moment of resistance before he'd surrendered to the truth of it.

Now he saw each of the three ships clearly, in profile as they turned to slip in astern. The first was a destroyer with two funnels rather far apart, the for'ard one seeming to be almost a structural part of the stunted bridge. The second funnel was set much farther aft – almost as far as the mainmast, which was just about amidships and had a boom-derrick mounted on it. He looked at her bridge again; there was hardly any foremast.

It made her a 'G' class destroyer. One of the Krupp-built boats. And the second – turning now behind the leader – was another of the same class.

The third ship was a three-funnelled light cruiser. Rather a pretty ship, with delicate, yacht-like lines. Twin search-lights on her foremast, at funnel-top height above the bridge, and another pair on the mainmast, a bit lower.

A Stettin-class cruiser.

All three of them had formed astern now. And the destroyer ahead of *Lanyard* seemed to have accepted her without question. Nick realised – guessed – that they wouldn't have been examining her closely because they'd known they were being joined by other ships anyway; and to the newcomers *Lanyard* would have been just one of that flotilla who'd fallen slightly astern of station. Also, with her shorn-off foremast, low bridge superstructure, cut-down funnel and clean-swept stern she might well, to a careless eye, pass for one of the German 'G's.

His heart was beating so hard that he thought Glennie, beside him, might be hearing it.

'Three-one-oh revolutions.'

Might as well keep good station. The last thing one wanted was to attract the attention of the other ships.

This was a nightmare. The worst he'd ever had . . .

'Three-one-oh revs on, sir.'

Chief Petty Officer Glennie's voice was low and even. Nick looked at him, wondering if he'd caught on to the situation. Glennie must have seen his head turn; he glanced at Nick fleetingly, expressionlessly, before his eyes went back to watching the stern of the German destroyer ahead. He murmured, 'Bound for Wilhelmshaven, are we, sir?'

Chapter 11

Pilkington's wizened face was pale. .
'D-ye know what you bloody *done*?'

Nick said quietly, 'Three-one-five revolutions.'

'Three-one-five. Aye aye, sir.'

'Sub—'

'If you're thinking of swearing at me again, Mr Pilkington, you can get back aft, and quick.'

'Sub.' The gunner pointed. 'Those are 'uns. Those are bl—' He checked himself. The next bit came in a hoarse whisper: 'Germans, Sub. We're poncin' along with a whole pack—' His control broke; he ended in a shout – 'of bloody *Germans*!'

Nick lowered his binoculars.

'If we'd done anything but take station here quietly as we did, Mr Pilkington, they would have *looked* at us. And if they had, they'd have seen who we are and blown us out of the water. That happened to be the situation we were in.'

Pilkington nodded. 'So now we're up the creek. What 'appens when they start signalling at us? Which way're we bloody goin', anyway?'

Glennie glanced sideways at Nick, as if he too had some interest in the questions. Or perhaps he was wondering how much criticism Nick would take from the warrant officer before he shut him up.

'If you'd remained at your action station, Mr Pilkington, you'd have had orders from me by now. Don't come for'ard again without my permission, please. But since you are here, just stop belly-aching and *bloody well listen, will you?*'

He'd shouted that last bit. Now he leant over, checked the compass-card. Their course was south by east; so the reciprocal would be north by west. He told Garret, 'Warn the engineer officer that in a few minutes I'll be calling for full power, and when I do I want him to give us everything he's got.'

'Aye aye, sir.'

By the way Garret glanced at Pilkington, you could see he didn't think much of him.

'Listen. You too, Glennie. Remember that if I get knocked out, Mr Pilkington here would take command, and you're next in line. So you'd better have a grasp of what's happening.'

CPO Glennie nodded. His eyes didn't leave that German destroyer's wake.

'When you go aft, Mr Pilkington, train your tube out to starboard and stand by, and report to me when you're ready. When I hear that from you I'll crack on full power and put the wheel hard a-port. We should take 'em by surprise – they'd hardly be expecting an attack from one of their own ships, would they.'

Pilkington just stared at him.

'We'll circle out to starboard and you, Glennie, will steady the ship on north by east. That's the reverse of this present course. When your tube sight comes on, Mr Pilkington, you're to fire at the last ship in the line, which is the light cruiser. I want a report down the voicepipe as soon as you've fired, so I can alter course again as necessary. We'll be close enough for you to make sure of a hit, I imagine?'

Pilkington nodded. 'Should be.'

'*Very* close . . . So what about the safety range?'

'Oh . . .' Pilkington scratched his head. 'That's a problem, ain't it.'

The pistol in the warhead of a torpedo wasn't armed until the fish had travelled far enough for a small vane, propellor-shaped, to wind down, bringing the firing-pin to within one sixteenth of an inch from the detonator.

'Only one answer. You'll have to wind it halfway down before you train the tube out. Dangerous, but—'

'*Christ*!' A yelp . . . '*I'll* say it's bloody—'

'How long will it take you?'

'Couple o' minutes. But—'

'Once we start to turn out, you'll have to be damn quick. We'll be in the firing position in no time at all. And once we've passed it, that's the chance gone, finished. Right?'

'Aye aye.'

The stroppy little bastard wasn't going to say 'sir', Nick noticed. But that was the last and least thing he'd time to worry about now.

'Go back aft, then, and report when you're ready. And tell Hooper he'd not to fire unless someone shoots at us first.'

Pilkington left. Nick asked the chief bosun's mate, 'Make sense to you, does it?'

'Clear enough, sir.'

'Garret, did you warn Mr Worsfold?'

'Yessir. Says he'll be ready, sir.'

'Good.'

It wouldn't do any harm to move ahead a little, and gain fifty yards or so before the turn. No more than that, because he'd want to put some speed on too, when the time came.

'Three-two-five revolutions.'

'Three-two-five, sir.'

The farther ahead she started, the longer there'd be – in terms of seconds – before the torpedo sight came on. Nick wondered what the rest of the German ships would do. Turn and give chase? One reason he'd decided to take this action immediately was that in a couple of hours it would be dawn; in an hour, even, the sky might begin to lighten. After *Lanyard* had made her move, she'd be needing all the dark there was to hide in.

But if she sank that cruiser, or crippled her, she'd have earned her keep, and he, Nick, would have made up for his idiocy. He'd passed it off rather well, he thought, in his explanation to the gunner – and it was true that if he'd turned away they most likely *would* have sunk her. A point might be made, however, by a more agile brain than Pilkington's, that she shouldn't have been in that position in the first place.

The jury voicepipe squawked. Nick answered it. 'Wheelhouse.'

'Tube's trained out an' ready, Sub.'

'With its pistol near armed?'

'I said, *ready.*'

Nick thought he could spare one minute, just to get a simple matter straight.

'Mr Pilkington. In your Drill Book, does the report "Ready" indicate anything whatsoever about that safety-vane being wound down?'

'Well, no, but—'

'Don't be so bloody stupid or so bloody insubordinate, then! Now stand by!'

Mortimer, he thought, would be proud of me . . . He told Glennie, 'Full ahead together!'

'Full ahead together, sir!' The chief buffer, Nick noticed, had a smile on his usually immobile features. He felt the surge of power as the destroyer's screws bit into the sea and thrust her forward. He waited; the more speed she could pick up before he gave the helm order, the more sharply she'd answer her rudder when it banged over.

But it would be a mistake to wait too long. For one thing, *Lanyard* would get too close to the ship ahead, and for another the piling foam under her counter would catch the eye of her next-astern.

'Hard a-port!'

'Hard a-port, sir!'

The wheel span through Glennie's fingers; *Lanyard* leaned hard as she sliced her bow into the sea to starboard.

Already, at least the next astern and probably some of the others too would have seen her swing out of line.

One had to hope they'd be tired, and not too quick-witted.

Lanyard trembled, rattling like an old tin can as her engines thrust her forward and her rudder dragged at her stern. Nick, using his binoculars, saw that the five leading destroyers were holding on exactly as before; then, as *Lanyard*'s turn continued, he could see only four – three – two – now only the leader . . . And then *she* was blanked-off from his sight. Ahead of *Lanyard* was dark, empty sea with the woolly greyness of drifting mist. He could feel the taut thrumming of her steel under his feet, the shake in her as she battered round. He checked the compass-card: her head was coming up now to due west – past it now, and swinging on: west-north-west . . . He gave no orders, left it to Glennie, who knew his business and what was wanted. North-west by west; Glennie span the wheel to bring the rudder amidships as the ship still skidded round, and as the lubber's line touched north-west by north he wrenched on opposite rudder to meet and check the swing. Now he was centring the wheel again. Nick put up his glasses, and out to starboard the last of the destroyers was just passing: Pilkington should be firing about *now* . . .

'Course north by west, sir.'

'Very good.'

A shout in the voicepipe: 'Wheel'us!'

Nick grabbed it. 'Wheelhouse!'

'Torpedo's gone!'

'Right.' He told Glennie, 'Starboard ten.'

'Starboard ten, sir . . . Ten o' starboard—'

'Steer west-nor'-west.'

'West-nor'-west, sir.'

He held the cruiser's dim shape in the circle of his glasses while *Lanyard* slewed round to port. His object was to point her stern at the enemy flotilla, so that she'd be more difficult to see. As she swung, and the Germans ploughed on southwards, he realised that the cruiser would almost certainly be out of his arc of visibility before the torpedo reached her. Or passed her . . .

Please God, guide it!

'Course west-nor'-west, sir.'

The cruiser was out of his sight now. Could the Germans have guessed that a torpedo would be on its way across that strip of sea? In that situation, he asked himself, would one think of such a possibility? He thought probably not. They'd have first to cotton-on to the fact that *Lanyard* wasn't one of their own side; and that idea would take a bit of getting to, to start with.

A white flash, like a glimpse of sheet-lightning, lit sea and sky for a brief instant before the thudding, reverberating thump of the explosion reached them. The flash lingered, brightened, died away . . .

'Nice work that, sir.'

Nick glanced at Chief Petty Officer Glennie's rock-like silhouette. He thought, *The point now is do we get away with it* . . .

A crash of gunfire astern added weight to that question.

'Starboard twenty!'

'Starboard twenty, sir . . .'

Glennie flung the spokes round. The voicepipe gurgled with a call and Nick snapped, 'Garret, answer that.' He heard the flight of a shell or shells overhead, and as the destroyer swung to port a fountain leapt within a few yards of her bow. She swung on into it as it collapsed, and stinking black water drenched down across her foc'sl; half a ton of it dropped into the roofless wheelhouse, soaking

them – and worse than that blinding, suffocating with its
acrid reek: it was like a heavily concentrated stench of spent
fireworks.

All three of them were coughing, and streaming at the
eyes; Nick breathed out to empty his lungs, and then held his
breath, hoping the gas would clear by the time he had to
breathe in again: but he was out of luck.

The shell burst below them – aft, but it felt as if it was
close below their feet: one looked for the deck to bulge, split
. . . A deep, ripping crash. It was almost like something
tearing one's own gut, the way you *felt* it. Its echoes rang
through the ship, boomed away into the surrounding darkness. *Lanyard* had checked as if she'd steamed into a brick
wall and through it and been slowed by it: it felt to Nick as
if she was slumping, wallowing.

'Midships.'

'Midships, sir.' Behind Nick, Garret shouted into the
voicepipe, 'Yes, I *am* still here . . . sir.' *Lanyard*'s engines
were slowing, and that roar from aft was the sound of
escaping steam. Boiler-room, then. Nick thought, *Finished*
. . . He told himself, hang on. *May not be all that bad.*

He wanted to scream out to somebody to tell him what
was happening, what had happened. But he knew he'd hear
from Worsfold as soon as the engineer could manage it.
Coping with damage had priority over talking about it.

One waited, meanwhile, for the next salvo . . .

'Garret, what the hell's he—'

'Sir.' Garret let the free end of the flexible hose clang back
against the bulkhead. 'Mr Pilkington says we hit the cruiser
under her bridge and she looked like sinking. But that was
her stern guns that fired at us, and we've been hit in the after
boiler-room, sir.'

The racket of escaping steam was dying away. So was
Lanyard's speed. She wasn't just slowing: both engines had
stopped completely.

Stopped, Nick thought. *With one gun left.*

Might as well get her round, while she still had a bit of steerage-way.

'Starboard fifteen. Steer due west.'

'Steer west, sir.'

Nick heard a call on the engine-room voicepipe; but Garret was there, and he held himself in check while the leading signalman moved over with what seemed like maddening slowness and answered it. He told Nick, 'Engineer officer wants a word, sir.'

Now that the engines were silent, one noticed other sounds. The wind humming in the broken structure of the bridge, a rhythmic creaking as *Lanyard* rose and fell, and the slapping of the sea against her bow.

If the Germans knew they'd disabled her, they'd be along, in minute.

Johnny West had been swimming slowly, without hurrying or using up much energy, from group to group, trying to jolly them all up a bit, have a chat and a joke and then paddle away to some other lot. He went by sound; if he heard voices, he swam towards them, or he'd call 'Hello!' and then head in the direction of any faint reply.

In the last half-hour the incidence of men giving-up and allowing themselves to drown had increased alarmingly. Men seemed suddenly to lose their grip, the will to live.

'Why, if it isn't the mechanical genius himself!'

Hanbury Pike revolved slowly in the water, and peered at him through the dark.

'Johnny?'

'Well done, Hanbury! And how're you keeping?'

'I'm damn tired, if you want to know.'

'And that's because you drink too much gin, you know, old lad.' West told him, 'It weakens the muscles of the brain. I'd give it up, if I were you.'

'Since when did—' Pike spat – 'brains have muscles?' He groaned. '*Christ*, but this stuff's cold!'

'I'm lucky, there. I've a few pounds of extra insulation.'

'A *few*!'

Pike had closed his eyes. West peered closely: 'Hey!'

'What?'

'Don't let yourself drop off. If you do, you won't wake up. I've seen it happen – just now, several—'

'I have not the least intention of—'

'Good. Is David Everard somewhere near us?

'Frankly, I hope not.'

'I thought you were going to keep – hey, what's this, searchlights?'

He tried to raise himself in the water to see better. It was like a moon rising; some huge source of approaching light . . .

No moon: that was the leap of flames. A great concentration of – of fire, lighting that part of the horizon, and growing fast, or—

'What the devil?'

He saw suddenly that it was a ship, in flames. Enveloped totally in fire. You could hear her now, roaring, crackling, pounding through the sea at twenty knots or more, and she'd pass close . . . Flames sprouted the whole length of her, from foretop to waterline. The roar of them, fanned by her speed, was like the noise from an open furnace door. The edges of the blaze were jet-black with smoke darker than the night, and streaked with trails of burning, flying debris, while the sea – the waves on either side and the spreading wake astern – was lit by the yellow flames so that she steamed in the centre of a brilliant circle of her own weird light. She was passing now – a cable's length away: West felt the heat of her, heard the flames eating her as she thundered by: she'd passed, and her wash was spreading, coming to them, a great round-topped swell with curling, breaking waves behind it. Close-to he saw the black blobs of men's heads as the piling sea lifted them, rocked them and set them down again for the follow-up waves to play with. Within a few moments of her first appearing, the doomed ship was a rosette of fire dwindling northwards.

Pike gaped after her. 'Battle cruiser – German?'

'No. *Black Prince* —'

'Oh, stuff and—'

'– with her two middle funnels shot away.'

And there could not, he thought, have been a soul left alive in her. For their sakes, he hoped to God there couldn't be.

A hundred yards away, David Everard had watched her pass. She'd come closer to him than she had to West and Pike; he'd had to shield his eyes from her heat, and lumps of burning wreckage had splashed into the sea all round him, hissing as they struck the water. Now from the direction in which she'd disappeared, he heard the thunderclap of an explosion.

He was tired. Really exhausted. And so cold . . .

He'd seen several men go off to sleep, and he'd envied them. What they'd done was simply to stop swimming or treading water, and lie back in the sea.

They'd looked so *restful*. The thought that he might follow their example had infinite appeal.

He pushed his long legs out in front of him. The Gieves waistcoat was an excellent support. He let his head fall back into the softest pillow he'd ever known.

'Bloody daylight!'

He'd whispered it. Dawn, silvery-grey, was leaking from a quickly brightening sky to grey the black waste of sea in which *Lanyard* lay helpless. Mist drifted in shifting patterns and layers, like some kind of insulation adding to the surrounding quiet in which this ship, with men hammering and clattering down in her steel belly, was the only source of noise.

Garret nodded, sharing Nick's distaste for the approach of day. Another hour of darkness might have seen them through. *Lanyard*, disabled and almost defenceless, badly needed the cover which yesterday had twice saved the German battle fleet from destruction.

She wasn't entirely helpless; she did have the one four-inch left, and plenty of ammunition for it. Its crew were sitting and lying around it, muffled in coats and scarves and wool helmets. Some of them lay flat out, dozing. Hooper, the gunlayer, was on his feet, leaning against the shield and using the binoculars which Nick had given him so he could help with the looking-out. Nick and Garret were farther aft. There was a good all-round view from this position, and for extra height of eye one could get up on the torpedo tubes. Also, Garret was handy to the twenty-inch searchlight in case some friendly ship might appear and challenge.

Nick had armed as many of the ship's company as possible with small-arms and cutlasses. He was wearing a revolver himself, and Garret had a rifle beside him. Pilkington and Chief Petty Officer Glennie and a few hands with them up for'ard were similarly equipped; below decks, a couple of dozen sailors lay around or snoozed with cutlasses strapped to them. If any Germans should imagine *Lanyard* was done for and try to board, they'd get a warm reception.

In fact, since she'd been crippled nothing had approached her. The destroyers must have gone on south-eastward. Either they'd been under orders not to deviate from their course – and if that was the case it would suggest the High Seas Fleet was running for home – or they hadn't realised that *Lanyard* had been hit, and had thought it would be unprofitable to chase after her.

The noise the engineers were making down there was getting on his nerves. He knew it couldn't be helped – and that unless a submarine picked it up on her hydrophones there was no enemy near enough to hear – but it still seemed to aggravate the tension. One tended, oneself, to be ultra-quiet, speaking in whispers – while that clattering and scraping got louder all the time. Nerves were jagged with the tension of inaction, the waiting.

The cruiser's shell had smashed in through the starboard side of the after boiler-room and exploded about amidships, further for'ard. The entry-hole was nothing to worry about, being small and well above the waterline, but the shell had wrecked the boiler-room, smashing both boilers and blowing a large piece of one of them out through the hull on the port side. The hole it had made was large, and extended almost to the waterline: it had to be plugged, patched and shored. The other job was longer and more complicated: the steampipes and other connections between the undamaged for'ard boiler-room and the engine-room passed through the wrecked after boiler-room, and a lot of them had been cut or damaged. Worsfold had forecast that the work would take him a good two hours – *if* he ran into no unexpected snags; and that thereafter, all things being equal, and given continuing calm weather, *Lanyard* should be able to make eight or ten knots on her two for'ard boilers.

They'd been working for an hour and a half already.

'If we do get fixed up an' away home, sir—' Garret spoke quietly as he wiped his binoculars – 'if we go westward like you said—'

Pilkington had asked Nick, when the issuing of arms had been in progress, 'Sub – you better tell me, 'case we get in some bust-up and you get 'it, what course we'd steer for 'ome. North-west, is it?'

Nick had shrugged.

'Can't tell you, really.'

'Fine navigator you are!'

'I've never pretended to be a navigator.' His inclination had been to add, *you silly little shyster* . . . He was sick of the torpedo gunner and his chip-on-the-shoulder manner. He added, 'But even if I was a very good one, I couldn't tell you where we are now. We've been all over the shop, haven't we. With no plot kept and nothing to take a sight of . . .' He'd glanced up at the overcast, starless sky, and thought, *thank God for small mercies* . . .

'Tell you what you do, though. What I'll do if Worsfold succeeds in getting us wound up again. Just steer west, until we hit something. When we hear a crunch, that'll be dear old England.' He'd thought, or *Scotland*.

But with any luck, he might fall in with some other ship or ships which he'd be able to follow or take directions from. The first thing to think about was getting out of this hole, getting under way again. After that, one could start worrying about a course to steer.

But Garret's mind, as he reverted to the same subject, was more directional.

'Any chance we'll finish up in the Forth, sir?'

'Not much, really. I think we're probably too far south.'

'Couldn't we sort of point up a bit, sir?'

'I think I'm bound to take the shortest route home, you know, now we've got that hole in our side. Could get tricky if a gale blew up, for instance. I should think the Tyne's about our best bet, on that score. And you see, if I'm wrong and we're farther north now than I think we are, and we – as you say "point up a bit" well, that way we might miss Scotland, even!' *Hopeless navigators*, he thought, *have to play safe*.

Garret had sighed, and mumbled something in a gloomy tone.

'What?'

'Not much good to me, sir. The Tyne, I mean.'

Nick caught on to the reason for the anxiety. He told him, 'There's a perfectly good train service to Edinburgh, you know!'

Garret's head shook in the gloom. His gloom, too. 'They'd likely keep us there, sir. An' s'pose they don't, s'pose we pay off. I'm a Devonport rating, sir, they might send me down there.'

He stopped talking about it: it was too much for him. He muttered, 'I'd – skin off, sir, I would.'

'Don't be bloody daft, Garret. Talking to me about deserting?'

'Well, I'm sorry, sir, but—'

'After we dock, I'll send you on leave. How's that?'

Beside him the signalman took a deep, hard breath.

'Can you do that, sir?'

'I'm in command, aren't I?'

'I've no leave due, sir, that's the trouble. Before I got married I took it all.'

'If your commanding officer says you have leave due, you have leave due. You'll be issued with a railway warrant – and the base paymaster'll come up with an advance of pay.'

'D'you mean this, sir?'

'No skin off my nose, Garret.'

And where, he wondered, would *he* go?

First – when they let him – to Mullbergh. See Sarah. Try first to see Uncle Hugh, and ask him to help with wangling a permanent appointment to some destroyer, anything rather than getting shanghai'd back into some battle-wagon . . . Have to put it a bit tactfully; the old boy was proud of that vast thing *he* drove around.

Nick wondered how the day and night had gone with Hugh Everard and *Nile*, and how things had been for David, too. There'd been a new line of thought, hadn't there, about David. Coupling what Johnson had said about him with the undoubted fact that their father had always looked to David, as his eldest son and the future baronet, to do brilliantly – or at least do well – at everything he was supposed to do . . . Well, hence the horsemanship. Scared half to death – still an accomplished horseman, much better in the saddle than he, Nick, was – but nervous, which Nick had never been. Had David ever really *enjoyed* a day's hunting?

Nick wondered whether he could persuade David to listen to some advice – if he suggested to him, for instance, that instead of forcing himself to continue riding to hounds, he should tell their father, 'I don't enjoy it. I don't intend to hunt in future.'

He couldn't be disinherited. He was the first-born, and the estate was entailed, and the principle of primogeniture protected him completely. Their father wouldn't like a non-hunting eldest son – he'd raise hell – but did that matter? If David could be encouraged to face up to him – or in a way, face up to himself – mightn't he find himself a lot happier and perhaps in the process become easier to get on with?

The biggest 'if' of all was if David could screw up enough guts to face his father. He'd never done so yet. The old man had him cowed. Whereas he'd realised years ago he'd never scare his younger son into subservience, and as a result got into a habit of ignoring him.

The last time he and his father had faced each other in mutual anger had been a couple of years ago, at Mullbergh. Two o'clock in the morning: Nick had been woken by a succession of loud crashes: they'd been part of some dream, but as he'd woken he'd heard another and realised they'd been real: and as the realisation had taken root, he'd heard Sarah scream. He'd sprung out of bed and raced down the long, ice-cold corridor, stone-flagged and about as cheerful as a crypt: then into the central part of the house where his father and Sarah slept. He'd rushed down the half-flight of stairs to their floor.

'What the blazes are you doing here?'

His father was still in evening clothes: he was also half-drunk, and crazy-looking. Behind him, the top half of a bedroom door had been smashed in. A heavy case – it was the dumpy leather one in which the shoe and boot cleaning things were kept – lay on the floor there. Obviously his father had just used it to break down the door.

'Oh, *Nick* . . .'

He saw Sarah, as she came out into the passage. The shoulder of her dark-green evening dress had been ripped, and she was holding it up on that side.

'Is there—' he ignored his father, who was in a rage and shouting at him to go back to his room – 'anything I can do?'

'No, I – no, Nick, there isn't, thank you.' She'd smiled at him. Brown hair, all loose, fell across her face and had to be brushed back. 'I promise you, I'll be all right now. You go back to bed before you catch cold.'

Nick remembered – relived this incident every time his thoughts turned to Sarah and his father: The torn dress and her hair flopping loose and the half-frightened, half-defiant expression . . . It had marked a turning-point in his relationship with his father. From then on, his father had stopped bullying him and taken to ignoring him: as if he'd realised suddenly that Nick wasn't going to change or, in anything that really mattered, give way to him.

But whether he'd stopped bullying Sarah was another matter.

Watching the sea, the coming of the dawn, he sighed . . . The light wasn't grey now, it was silver. Overhead there was a vaguely pearly colour which became brighter, sharper in its reflection in the sea; this was probably what was producing the silvery effect. There were no waves now, only ripples, which in the middle-distance had a streaky look – one side silver, the other black. Mackerel-colour. Mist hung over everything; compared to the radiance of the sea's surface it looked dirty, colourless like sheep's wool in a thorn hedge.

Cold . . . Nick checked that the collar of his reefer was still turned up. It was, but it hadn't felt like it. And he had a sweater on, but he wished he'd put on two, now.

Worsfold had exceeded his ration of two hours, but the hammering was still going on. Nick pulled out his watch; it was light enough now to see the positions of the hands. He told Garret, 'Two thirty-five.' And at that precise moment, the noise stopped. Nick stood still with the watch in the palm of his hand, thinking, *any second, they'll start again.*

Garret murmured, 'Got it done, sir, by the sound of it.'

Garret had grown a lot of beard, for one night. Nick touched his own jaw: it felt about as bad. He remembered Reynolds warning him, referring to Mortimer's idiosyncracies, 'informality is not encouraged in his officers. . . .'

Forty-eight hours ago, Reynolds had said that! It felt as if half a lifetime had passed. For Reynolds and Mortimer, *a whole one* had.

'I think I'll go below and see what's what.' Nick stretched, yawned, and moved out towards the ship's side. There still wasn't any noise emanating from the boiler-room. He warned himself, *don't count your chickens!*

Chief might have run into one of those snags he'd mentioned. He might be squatting there staring at it, wondering what to do about it. Nick stared out over the quarter, at the beginnings of a purple-ish glow, low down where the horizon must have been – if one could have seen it – and blanketed in the mist. That glow would harden, redden, flush upwards and resolve itself eventually into the brilliance of a sunrise, and probably that would be all they'd see of the sun all day.

But it was none too soon, he thought, for *Lanyard* to be getting under way.

He told Garret, 'I'll be back in a few—'

His mouth stayed open.

Out of that tinted mist astern, a ship was looming up towards them.

German.

At a glance, and beyond a doubt. German light cruiser.

Well, that's that . . .

She was bigger than the cruiser they'd torpedoed. She had the typically low bridge and the pair of searchlights on her foremast; the searchlights looked like a crab's eyes stuck up on stalks above its head. She might be one of the Karlsrühe class – Germany's latest in light cruisers.

Not a damn thing, he thought, that one could do. The ball

would be in that Hun's court, entirely. He edged back into the shadow of the searchlight platform and told Garret, 'Hun cruiser, coming up astern.' He'd whispered it. Silly, really: she was still a mile and a half or two miles away. Coming up from the quarter, steering to pass close on *Lanyard*'s starboard side.

He put his glasses on her again. She was closing at a slow, steady speed; unhurried, purposeful. She'd have a broadside – he delved into his memory – of five or six four-point-ones.

'Leading Seaman Hooper!'

'Sir?'

'Enemy light cruiser approaching on the starboard quarter. Keep your gun's crew out of sight. Everyone, keep down!'

'Aye aye, sir!' There was a quick scurry of movement across the destroyer's deck up near the gun.

'Hooper: load, set deflection six knots left and range . . .' He thought, *she'll pass within spitting distance. . . .* 'Set range five hundred yards.' He told Garret, 'Go for'ard and tell Mr Pilkington what's happening. Then below, and tell Mr Worsfold I don't want a pin dropped anywhere. I'll be at the gun.'

Garret shot away. Nick called after him, 'No movement on deck either, tell 'em.' He joined Hooper on the gun platform, and crouched down beside him. 'If they think we're a wreck it's just possible they may decide to leave us alone.' The gunlayer raised an eyebrow, as if to say *fat chance of that*. Nick added, 'Or they might send a boat, a boarding party.'

He thought of the men he had waiting below with cutlasses. He *hoped* the cruiser might send a boarding party.

In a greenish, cold-looking sea, bodies in lifebelts rose and fell amongst other flotsam. The areas of dead came infrequently but there'd be as much as an acre or two of them at a time; sometimes the black and sodden uniforms were

British, sometimes German. When you saw them through binoculars at a distance, the humped shapes had the look of drifting mines. One saw them always on the bow, because by the time *Nile* was close to them they'd been caught in the bow-waves of *Barham*, *Valiant* and *Malaya* and lifted, pushed aside to form an avenue of clear sea through which the Grand Fleet's battle squadrons in line ahead and led by these Queen Elizabeths steamed north in search of the enemy.

An hour ago Jellicoe had wheeled his dreadnoughts round and disposed them in line of battle; since two am the fleet had been closed up at action stations.

Rathbone was conning the ship. Hugh left him, and joined his second-in-command in the port wing of the bridge.

'I'm sorry to say it, Tom, but I think Scheer's got away.' He pointed out towards a scattering of black dots, the last colony of drowned men they'd passed, still visible on the quarter. 'Those are the only Huns we're likely to see today.'

Crick nodded.

'It's a – a disappointment, sir.'

Understatement was a habit, with Tom Crick.

Nile still had no wireless, so one couldn't know what reports had reached Jellicoe during the night, or on what knowledge or lack of it he'd based his decision to hold on southwards. Hugh knew only that throughout the dark hours there'd been flare-ups of action astern, and that there was no sign of any enemy in the area now. The two observations weren't difficult to link.

All right – the Grand Fleet held the ring, kept the sea. Here they were, close to the German coast, ready and more than willing to resume the battle, while Scheer had run home to safety. Wisely, even cleverly; but running was still running. The victors were those left in the field. But by escaping homewards, Scheer had denied to Jellicoe the kind of victory which the Grand Fleet had sought and which it had been expected to achieve.

'Best keep the hands closed-up, Tom, for the time being. You could send 'em to breakfast by watches?'

'Aye aye, sir.'

Hugh was hungry, too. Bates, no doubt, would have something ready for him.

There'd be post-mortems, he thought, till the cows came home. The loss of ships wouldn't be well received: and there had to be some structural defect that had led to the battle cruisers blowing up. Flash to their magazines, almost certainly. By comparison, it was extraordinary how much punishment the German capital ships had been able to absorb without blowing up or sinking. And it could be that there was some deficiency in the British shells, or in their fuses. One had seen so many explode on impact instead of penetrating.

It might be asked why Beatty had rushed into action without the support of this battle squadron; whether it had resulted from the same lack of control of his ships which had made the Dogger Bank action such a fiasco, or whether Sir David's over-confidence and pursuit of fame had urged him to hog the glory for himself and his battle cruisers. But when it came to post-mortem time, the biggest question that would be asked would be how had the Germans been permitted to escape, why it hadn't ended as a twentieth-century Trafalgar.

The public wouldn't understand that at Trafalgar Nelson had drifted into action at about two knots, that once the fleets had grappled the battle had had to be fought out to its conclusion; they might not want to understand that it was a different matter to annihilate an enemy who couldn't move from the mouths of your cannon than it was to smash one who could turn and run away into fog at twenty knots.

The Navy would know what had been proved, and so would the Germans. Twice Scheer had thrown his squadrons against Jellicoe's, and twice they'd had to turn and run. What had been proved was that the High Seas Fleet was no match for the Grand Fleet.

But still – Hugh thought – if he, Everard, had been in Jellicoe's shoes, and seen the night-fighting in the north, wouldn't he have steered for Horns Reef and shut off that escape route?

Hugh remembered the post-mortems inside the Admiralty after the Falklands victory. The arguments had all been of Jacky Fisher's making. Fisher, giving Admiral Sturdee command of the operation, had had his own personal, Fisher-type aim in mind; his hope had been that Sturdee, whom he regarded as an enemy, should fail. Doveton Sturdee had been Lord Charles Beresford's Chief-of-Staff in the Mediterranean and in the Channel, and had naturally shared his chief's anti-Fisher attitude. So Fisher still wanted Sturdee broken: and to have Hugh Everard go along on the same operation made it even better – two birds with one stone!

But Sturdee had had luck – which at one stage he'd surely needed – and he'd destroyed Von Spee's squadron. So Fisher had tried to prove he should have done it better, or more quickly, than he had. Hours, days, weeks had been wasted on an exercise of malice.

Of course, Hugh thought, for years I've loathed Fisher! Who wouldn't – unless he was some kind of saint – who'd been a victim of that brand of hate?

Fisher had broken him, in 1907, because he'd suspected him of having a foot in the Beresford camp. The Navy had been split into factions by the mutual loathing between Fisher and Beresford who'd virtually provoked mutiny in other senior officers against the thrusting, forceful First Sea Lord who'd come up from nothing and rode rough-shod over anyone who opposed him. Fisher was the son of a planter in Ceylon and he looked as if he had more than a dash of Singhalese blood; 'the gentleman from Ceylon' had been Admiral Beresford's way of referring to his First Sea Lord. It hadn't been unnatural for a man of Beresford's stamp to have loathed Fisher's methods and manners; he'd done his best to thwart him, destroy him. So when the Beresfords appeared as guests at the wedding of Commander Hugh Everard, Royal Navy, and Lady Alice Cookson-Kerr, Fisher discovered that he'd been harbouring in his 'fish pond' an officer who consorted with his enemies and had therefore to be eliminated.

The Beresfords had been invited, of course, by the parents of the bride. Hugh, hearing at the last moment of their inclusion in the guest-list, had seen the danger; but it would have been impossible to have done anything about it. Even then he hadn't – or so it seemed now, looking back on it – appreciated the depth of Fisher's paranoia. But he should have known what to expect; Fisher had boasted openly of his readiness to break rivals or opponents; he'd make widows of their wives, he'd promised, and dung-heaps of their houses. The Bible had always been a source of his verbal inspiration. And he'd decided within a week of Hugh's wedding that Commander Everard had 'run out of steam'. Hugh found himself shunted off, and offered appointments which the most dead-beat officers would have regarded as insulting. Within a year he'd resigned his commission. Within a further year, Alice had made it plain that being his wife was no longer to her taste. She'd married a rising star, a future Nelson, and now she found herself with a husband who worked for a firm of shipbuilders. Her friends' husbands, if they did anything except hunt foxes, were in politics or the Services.

Hugh gave her the divorce she wanted. But the story went about – and it still held water in the minds of some of his contemporaries – that his fall from grace in the Service as well as the reason for his wife divorcing him had been 'woman trouble'. Technically, a woman had provided the grounds for the divorce; and before his marriage he'd made no pretence of being a plaster saint. After the divorce – well, he'd been his own man, and there'd been *some* advantages in that unlooked – for 'freedom'.

Fisher had done him more harm than it should have been possible for one man to do another. For nearly ten years, one had been constantly aware of it.

He'd kept his feelings to himself, though, knowing that protests and recriminations couldn't improve his situation in any way, certainly wouldn't add to his chances of recovery, and could only be counted on to make him look ridiculous and sound a bore. And now that Fisher had gone, and was himself ridiculous in his senility, he could actually feel sorry for the old man, feel the sadness of former greatness lapsed into impotence, and remember the great achievements. The reforms of sailors' pay and conditions of service were probably the most important; and this – Hugh looked astern at the line of dreadnoughts extending southwards into the morning mists – this was Jacky's creation. One could recall too that Fisher, whose own nomination to naval service when he'd joined in 1854 had been signed by the last of Nelson's admirals, had been personally responsible for the grooming and appointment of Sir John Jellicoe as C-in-C of the Grand Fleet.

The torch came from hand to hand. Ships, weapons, tactics changed. Nothing else did. Oh, conditions, certainly. One could remember Fisher's own account of joining his first ship, at the age of thirteen, in that year 1854. On the day he joined, he saw eight men flogged, and he fainted. Hugh could still hear the gruff, disjointed reminiscences emerging from that ugly, even brutish face: *Midshipman of four-foot nothing – keeping night watches, and always hungry. No baths – belly always empty* . . . He'd remembered a quartermaster of the watch once giving him a maggoty biscuit, and a lieutenant of the watch who'd sometimes let him have a sardine, or an onion, or a glass of rum . . .

'Spot o' breakfast, sir?'

Hugh nodded to his coxswain.

'Thank you, Bates. I'm ready for it.'

*

Lanyard drifted; silent, inert, misshapen, wreck-like.

The gun's crew, and others with weapons in their hands, lay motionless, almost held their breaths as they watched the German cruiser approaching steadily across the dawn-lit sea.

She'd closed to about a thousand yards, half a sea mile, off *Lanyard*'s quarter. She still slid closer at the same slow speed; she'd pass about two cables' lengths to starboard.

Pass – or stop.

If she saw no sign of life, and sent a boat across, *Lanyard* might have a hope? If one let the boarding party come aboard, and then captured them, would a German captain fire on his own men ?

No. He'd probably send more men.

It was the tension of this waiting, and the fact of being so utterly at that ship's mercy, that made one clutch at straws.

Nick put his glasses on her again. She might have been a a ghost-ship creeping up, slipping closer through a silvery-greenish sea with a feather of white at her stem and only ripples spreading where she'd passed. There was no sound at all from her; all that could be heard here was the slap of water against *Lanyard*'s sides and the creak of loose gear shifting as she moved to the sea's own movement. But nothing shifted or even seemed to live on that cruiser's bridge or about her decks; she only came on steadily with her air of purpose and those twin crab's-eyes up above her bridge as if she herself was some kind of monster watching them. He shook the fantasy out of his mind. He wondered whether there might in fact be men in that bridge who were invisible from here but who'd have binoculars trained on *Lanyard* – German optical instruments being far better than British ones – revealing these men lying doggo around the gun. If so, this would be their point of aim when they opened fire; and since Hooper had built up a large reserve of cartridges and projectiles handy to the gun, it wouldn't be a healthy place to be.

In about a minute the cruiser would be abeam. About then, one might expect the ordeal to begin.

'Layer – you there, 'Oops?'

Hooper looked to his left without moving his head.

'What's up, Pratt?'

'I been thinkin'.' Pratt sounded like a Londoner. 'I never did learn to play the 'arp. Teach you when you reports aboard, do they?'

'They'll give you a shovel, mate, where you're goin'. Now be a good boy'n shurrup, eh?'

Nick glanced aft, at the ensign drooping from the mainmast. Wet from the night's mist, in the almost windless air it hung straight down, limp as a dead bird hanging in a tree. The gamekeepers at Mullbergh hung vermin like that . . . But it would be visible and identifiable, he thought, from the cruiser, and it would be all the justification they'd need to open fire.

Hooper hissed suddenly, 'Sir – she listin', would you say?'

Nick raised his glasses and focused on her again. He couldn't see any list.

But she was very nearly abeam now. The range was about six or seven hundred yards – farther than he'd expected. And she was moving more slowly than he'd reckoned earlier. He told Hooper, 'Deflection *three* left.'

'Three left – aye aye, sir . . . Look there!'

'What ?'

'She – just sort o' leaned over, sir—'

'Hey!'

She'd lurched to port: a definite movement, which he'd seen quite clearly. He strained his eyesight now: the lenses of his binoculars were slightly fogged and he couldn't spare the time to clean them . . . 'Layer – am I dreaming, or is she down by the bow?'

Hooper laughed shortly. 'Don't reckon you're the dreamin' sort, sir.'

The cruiser's stern was rising as her bow dug lower in the sea, and she was listing so far to port now that one could see right into her bridge. It was empty. He thought, *They've abandoned her* . . . . But – left her engines going?

Perhaps they left a few hands aboard, and they'd left her bridge now because they'd realised she was about to sink? It was all theory – and not counting chickens: he thought suddenly, *there could still be a torpedo coming* . . .

They could have struggled this far with that intention; in such a condition wasn't it exactly what one would do?

She was going, though. Her screws were out of water, reflecting the light of sunrise as their blades turned slowly, lazily in the air.

Nick stood up. He told the gun's crew, 'All right. She's done for. Pratt give 'em a shout below, tell 'em all to come up and see this.'

The cruiser was standing on her nose, with nearly half her length – including bridge and foremast and the first of her four funnels – buried in the sea. A German ensign hung vertically downwards, banner-like, from her mainmast which was now parallel to the sea's surface. Nick heard cheering and whoops of joy as *Lanyard*'s ship's company came pouring up on deck. He put one hand out, leant against the gun, and at that moment the enemy cruiser seemed to lift a little in the water and then slip down into it.

She'd gone. Quietly, with no fuss at all. And *Lanyard* was alone again.

Through the pandemonium of sailors cheering, dancing, going mad, one had to take this in, take stock of an entirely new situation, the abrupt removal of what had seemed like certain doom.

He realised that since he'd stood up he'd been feeling wind on his face. He looked at the sea, and saw a flurry spreading across its surface, a sort of graining with white flecks in it. He looked at the ensign, and saw that stirring too.

Coming up so suddenly out of the dawn calm, one could

expect a blow. With three hundred miles of sea to cross, and *Lanyard* with only two boilers and a hole in her side.

One enemy removed itself, and another took its place.

'Sub!'

He looked down at the upper deck. He saw Worsfold, the engineer, peering up at him. Worsfold looked as if he'd spent the night working at a coal-face.

'You can take us all home now, Sub. But listen – no more 'n five knots, d'you hear?'

Chapter 12

The gig's oars swept to and fro in the lazy-looking ceremonial stroke in which Bates had trained his crew, and the waters of the Firth of Forth hissed and gurgled under the boat's stern as she gathered way towards the northern shore. It was a bright, sparkling summer day; a month had passed since the battle which people in Britain were calling 'Jutland' but which the Germans in natural perversity were referring to as the *Skagerrakschlacht*.

Hugh Everard, in his gig's sternsheets, looked back at *Nile*. She was showing no signs of rough treatment now. He'd brought her into Rosyth on the day after the battle, and since then taken her down to Portsmouth for dockyard repairs. Now this return to Rosyth was just a twenty-four hour call to replenish ammunition, stores and fuel on the way north to Scapa.

Jellicoe was being blamed for the escape of the High Seas Fleet. Beatty was being lauded as the intrepid young seadog who'd have scuppered Hipper, Scheer – done for Kaiser Willy himself, if *he'd* been in charge! Jellicoe, being the man he was, was declining to defend himself in public, while Beatty's stock soared without his having to say a word. He uttered no word on Jellicoe's behalf either; while Jellicoe had nothing but praise for all his subordinates, including Beatty.

In a minor capacity, Hugh was coming in for a share of the limelight; his action in turning out of the line to save *Warspite* had found glowing approval in all quarters. So one's star was rising once again . . . But for the next hour or two he intended to forget the Navy; he was on his way to see Sarah, at her father's house at Aberdour. He'd spoken to Buchanan this morning on the telephone, and the old man had told him that Sarah had returned from Mullbergh a few days ago.

She'd been at Aberdour when *Nile* had docked on the morning of 2 June, but he'd had no chance of attending to any private business or pleasure with such a maelstrom of work on hand. A few days later when he did try to contact her, he was told she'd left for Mullbergh.

He glanced astern again, across the Firth to the blueish haze over Edinburgh. Like many others in the Grand Fleet, he had mixed feelings now about that town. In the early days of June, there might even have been some satisfaction in turning the fleet's guns on it!

The Rosyth ships – including Beatty's *Lion*, badly damaged and full of wounded – had been boo'd by dockyard workers as they'd limped into their berths. Then – incredibly – wounded sailors on their way to hospital had been jeered at by civilians in the streets.

Bates had turned *his* guns on Edinburgh . . .

Hugh had sent him ashore to buy a few essentials – having almost no personal possessions left he'd hardly known where to start – but Able Seaman Bates got no further than the Caledonian Street station. Some lounging porters hooted at him; one of them shouted, 'Thank the Lord we've an army tae defend us!' A few minutes later, by which time Bates had laid him and his mate out cold and thrown a railway official through the window of the ticket office, considerably enlarging the window in the process, he was arrested. A magistrate fined him for assault and damage to property, and he'd then been handed over to the naval patrol and returned aboard *Nile*, where finally he'd been hauled up in front of Crick as a defaulter. There were several charges against him under the Naval Discipline Act, and the police sergeant who'd arrested him was brought on board as a witness.

Hugh heard all about it afterwards; it was still a pleasure to visualise the scene that morning on his ship's quarterdeck. Bates at attention with his cap off, brown monkey-eyes fixed on the commander while the charges were read out. Crick, taller than anyone else present, ramrod stiff behind a small table that had been placed beside 'X' turret, listening to Lieutenant Knox-Wilson's formal report of earlier proceedings. Knox-Wilson had been officer-of-the-day when Bates had been brought back by the patrol; he'd heard the charges read out there and then, and had no choice but to pass the case on to 'commander's report'. The regulating petty officer who'd been on duty then was here now at Crick's defaulters session: so was the master-at-arms, *Nile*'s chief of police.

The police sergeant described what had taken place at the Caledonian Street station. When he'd finished and snapped his notebook shut, Crick stared down his nose at Bates.

Bates's eyes didn't waver. He was ready for more punishment, well aware that the commander was not one of his admirers.

'What's your story, Bates?'

Bates told it, not wasting words, but not missing anything out either.

'Nothing else to say?'

'No, sir.'

Crick turned to the policeman.

'D'you wish to contradict anything this man has told me?'

'I couldn'ae, sir. I wasn'ae present, not when he started bashing 'em aboot.'

Crick's eyes returned to the defaulter. 'How much did they fine you, did you say?'

'Thirteen poun' twelve an' six, sir. They gimme time to pay though, sir.'

Crick asked the policeman, 'That's a great deal of money?'

'It were a great deal o' damage, sir.'

The commander nodded slowly, staring at him.

'Would you happen to know, sergeant, how many men we lost in the recent battle?'

'No, sir, I would not.'

'More than six thousand, sergeant.'

Crick's tone had hardened. The policeman looked down at his boots, and shook his head. Crick had turned back to Bates.

'I shall pay your fine myself.' He cleared his throat. 'No. On second thoughts, I believe the wardroom officers may wish to take a share in it. If you'd permit that, Bates?'

Bates blinked, twice. He nodded. Crick snapped, 'Case dismissed!'

Hugh returned his coxswain's salute as he stepped from the gig to the pier steps.

'Carry on, Cox'n. Be here at five, please. And you know I'll be needing you later, as well.'

'Aye aye, sir.'

Bates knew what for, too. He'd have his crew working on the gig now, back at the boom; for this evening's trip she'd be as 'tiddly' as any boat that ever crossed the Firth of Forth.

Hugh climbed the steps, and walked up the wooden pier.

Sarah was in his thoughts now.

She was – hardly the same person.

'So you're the conquering hero now, Hugh!'

'Oh, that's all rubbish . . .'

He felt as if he was talking to her through glass, a defensive barrier. He'd had things to tell her: and he knew – he'd assembled his thoughts, for about the thousandth time, during the short train journey out to Aberdour – precisely what he wanted to establish. He wanted an understanding: an indication would have been enough. More than that, in present circumstances, would have been too much to ask for. He wanted her to understand his own feelings for her, and accept them. Beyond that, time could be left to look after everything.

All right, so he'd be asking to have his cake and eat it too. But as much for her sake as for his own. And it made sense. One couldn't ignore this morning's front-page news – of the great offensive on the Somme, the long-heralded attack aimed at prising the Huns' strangle-hold off Verdun. Brother John had told Sarah months ago that when the balloon went up he'd be there; all this time his division had been training for it.

One couldn't ignore facts or discount probabilities. The war had been going on too long and the casualty lists had stretched too far for anyone to stay blind, or pretend blindness, about such things.

Sarah had greeted him effusively; that had been the first wrong sign. She'd been like a hostess receiving a visitor whom she might not have wanted to entertain. Buchanan had told him on the telephone that regrettably he wouldn't be at home himself he was off to London that afternoon but Sarah would be, and he, Buchanan, had been worried about leaving her alone. She'd be delighted to see him.

Less delighted, Hugh realised, than on edge. Twice she'd glanced anxiously at the clock.

'So sad about David.' He told her, 'I wrote to John, of course.'

He'd been called on down in Portsmouth by *Bantry*'s padre, a man called Pickering. Pickering and a number of wounded survivors in his care had been picked up soon after dawn on 1 June by a destroyer; they'd been on make-shift rafts, apparently. He'd spoken warmly of David's courage and steadiness below decks during the ship's last hours. Conditions must have been appalling . . . So much, Hugh had thought, for one's doubts of David.

Sarah preferred to talk about young Nick.

'Isn't it wonderful, what he did?' She added, 'And that was your doing, Hugh. If you hadn't arranged for him to be moved to that destroyer—'

'Yes, well. . . .'

She rattled on about Nick. Hugh found himself surrendering; it was impossible to switch the conversation to the personal level that he'd wanted. In any case, she was so different in her manner that it was like chatting to someone one hardly knew.

She said, 'I hope it won't change him too much.'

'Would you expect it to?'

There was a sort of gloss on her. Her natural prettiness had become what he'd have called a *London* Prettiness.

'Well, it's highly dramatic for him, isn't it. Recommended for – "accelerated promotion", is it?'

Hugh nodded. 'He's in for a DSC as well.'

She smiled, brightly. 'What are you in for?'

He shook his head. 'You needn't fear too great a change in him. He's now back up to his neck in hot water.'

'Oh, no!'

'He sent a man on leave. He'd no business to and he knew it, he did it surreptitiously, even got him a travel warrant and an advance of pay. The fellow wasn't entitled to leave or pay, and he and his wife left their home address and couldn't be traced so he has either to be allowed to stay on leave until he chooses to come back, or it's a matter of alerting police-stations all over the country to pick him up. Nick's not in great favour, I can tell you.'

Sarah had giggled. 'I remember. He was a bit worried, when he came to Mullbergh.'

'Indeed.'

'But compared to what he *did*—'

'He can thank his stars he has something on the credit side. But if he's going to let a bit of success go to his head—'

'Oh, Nick's not like that!'

He felt better suddenly; she'd looked and sounded like her old self, then. That vehemence: her love for Nick: this was Sarah!

He tried to take advantage of the moment . . .

'Are you – you yourself, Sarah – all right?'

'I hardly know what you mean.'

Her guard was up again. And she'd allowed herself another glance at the clock.

'I meant, are you happy. Because – Sarah, my dear, I've had a lot of time for thinking, lately. About you, and how I—'

'Hugh.'

He waited. She forced a smile. 'I do, to be truthful, have rather a dreadful headache. I think I'll go and lie down, when you've—'

'Oh, I'm so sorry!' He got up, quickly. 'If you'd said so before, I'd—'

'It's nothing in the least serious, just—'

'Time I moved, in any case.'

Whatever she said now, it was obvious she wanted him to leave. He opened the door for her, and followed her into the hall. Perhaps when he had time to think, he'd understand this . . .

'McEwan will send the motor round.' She spoke without looking at him. 'If you don't mind, Hugh, I think I *will* go straight up and lie down.'

'Of *course.*'

She'd rung for the butler; now Hugh watched her climb the curving staircase. McEwan came shuffling from the back regions, and she stopped on the first landing to give him instructions about the motor. Hugh waited, looking up at her; she raised a hand.

'All the very best of good luck, Hugh. I'm so sorry about my silly head. You *will* forgive me?'

That had been totally artificial ... The front door bell clanged. Sarah looked as if she'd been shot at: alarmed, flustered. McEwan, who'd begun to move towards the door of the servants' quarters, halted and turned about. Sarah was coming down the stairs: her cheeks were flushed, and she looked beautiful as well as upset.

McEwan opened the double doors to the storm porch and went through it to the outer door. As it swung back, Hugh saw an officer in the uniform of the Camerons. Sarah called out quickly – too quickly – 'Why, it's Alastair! Hugh, this is an old, old friend of my family's—'

'My *dear* Sarah.'

The Highlander advanced into the hall. Sarah told Hugh, 'Major Kinloch-Stuart. A *very* old – oh, you're a sort of cousin really, aren't you, Alastair?'

Kinloch-Stuart, Hugh thought, looked a bit surprised at that. Sarah added, 'My brother-in-law, Captain Everard.'

The two men shook hands. Kinloch-Stuart said, 'Captain of the celebrated HMS *Nile*, of course. May I say, sir, it's an honour.'

'McEwan, show Major Kinloch-Stuart into the drawing-room ... Alastair, would you excuse us, for a few moments?'

'Of course.'

'I'll come with you to the motor, Hugh.' Hugh and Cousin Alastair exchanged courteous goodbyes. Then he was walking out into the driveway with Sarah, knowing finally what all the clock-watching had been about, and the tension and the headache ... He felt surprise, and jealousy, and disappointment. He'd feel worse, he knew, presently, when it had sunk right in. But he'd no right to feel *anything*, he told himself. He'd assumed far too much, taken far too many things for granted.

Sarah murmured, 'I'm – sorry, Hugh, I'm so—'

'Why? Why should you?'

'It isn't – well, as it may seem, to be—'

'I've no idea why you should be upset. Or why an old friend shouldn't call on you.' Looking down at her, he met her worried, hazel eyes. He might have been looking into that photograph, the one Bates had rescued. He thought, *my God, but I've been an idiot!*

'Hugh – please understand – it is *not* as it might appear!'

He nodded, and smiled easily, seeing how desperate she was that he should believe her. He felt as if he'd been kicked in the stomach by a horse.

'It doesn't appear like anything at all. I promise you.' He could hear the motor chugging round from the stable-yard. He asked her, 'May I write to you, from up north?'

She nodded, seriously. 'Please. Soon. And – Hugh, don't stay up there too long?'

As it happened – no, he didn't expect he'd be up in Scapa very long.

Sarah had said – last time he was here, when they'd discussed Nick's future in the Navy – she said something like 'the Navy's your God, does it have to be his too?' And she'd been right, up to a point. In a way, the Navy was his God; and he was caught up in it all the more strongly, perhaps, for having been so to speak excommunicated, a decade ago. Perhaps one might profit from that now? Not only in the determination to make up for lost time, but from having been left with few illusions, no blind faith or blinkers.

Recent developments – Beatty's popularity and the criticism of Jellicoe, who was ten times the man Beatty could ever dream of becoming – was a perfect example of the need for such awareness. Jellicoe had given his whole life and his very considerable, exceptional talents to the Navy, and it was allowing him to be treated as a whipping-boy. Kicking him upstairs. Beatty was to take over as Commander-in-Chief, and

Jellicoe was to go to the Admiralty as First Sea Lord.

Hugh knew it privately, from old friends now at the Admiralty. He'd also heard a whisper – which it would probably never be safe or politic to allow past his own lips – that during the night of 31 May/1 June the Admiralty had intercepted and deciphered no fewer than seven German signals all of which had made it clear that Scheer was steering for Horns Reef, and they'd passed none of them to Jellicoe. They'd wirelessed two earlier intercepted messages to him, but these had conflicted with reports coming in at the same time from Jellicoe's own scouting cruisers. If the Admiralty had confided to their Commander-in-Chief the information they'd possessed themselves, the Grand Fleet would have been at Horns Reef at daylight and Scheer would have faced annihilation.

The car had stopped. Hugh Everard emerged with a start from his thoughts, realising he hadn't consciously seen a yard of the miles they'd covered. In the process, he'd managed not to think of Sarah.

He climbed out. 'Thank you, Hart. A very comfortable journey.'

Actually the man could have run over a cow, and Hugh wouldn't have noticed it. Half-a-crown changed hands.

'Thank ye, sir.' Hart touched his cap. 'An' guid luck tae ye all!'

Hugh wondered, *If you'd been on this shore a month ago, would you have wished us luck – or catcalled?*

The great chance had come, and it had been missed. The best one could say, perhaps, was that the High Seas Fleet would almost certainly not put out to sea again. An American commentator had summed it up neatly by observing that the Kaiser's fleet had assaulted its gaolers but was now back behind bars.

He watched the car drive away in its cloud of exhaust smoke and dust. Then he turned, strolled out along the railway pier. It wasn't much after four-thirty, but that looked like his gig leaving the boom already. Gathering way: but end-on, hard to see . . . He stopped, narrowing his eyes against the brightness on the water. And it was the gig, sure enough: he could see the slow rhythm of its oars.

Plenty of time . . .

The gig would be taking him this evening to dine aboard a flagship with an admiral who'd intimated that he'd like to celebrate Captain Everard's imminent promotion to rear-admiral. There'd been no confirmation yet about his new appointment, but there'd been a strong hint, privately, of a cruiser squadron. This, and other flag changes which would have to be announced first, was known at present by only a few men in the Admiralty, and Jellicoe, and Evan-Thomas, and the admiral with whom Hugh would be dining tonight. Before long, though, Jackie Fisher would read of it in *The Times*; and the old man could choke, if he cared to, on his eggs and bacon!

Halfway out along the pier; and the boat was halfway from ship to shore. This evening – he wasn't looking forward to it, but it was the sort of thing he'd have to learn to handle now – this evening the gig would display his pendant in her bows. The crew's drill would be immaculate, and the admiral, glaring down from his quarterdeck, would see nothing that could fail to please a seaman's eye.

If he doesn't have one, I'll lend him mine!

He suppressed both the thought and the smile that came with it. The order of the evening must be tact, diplomacy. There'd been too many rifts, cliques, factions; the whole Service had suffered from them in past years. The thing now was to forget personal views, likes and dislikes, and get on with the job in hand.

The gig's wake was a slim streak stretching back ruler-straight to *Nile*'s impressive silhouette. And she was an impressively happy ship these days. Experience of battle had given officers and men an appreciation of each others' qualities and a sense of inter-dependence that had perhaps been lacking earlier. At the cost of lives and ships, the Navy had a new edge to it, a sense of unity it hadn't had in years.

One had now to preserve that unity, and *use* it.

He waited at the top of the steps, and watched his boat curve in towards them.